"ARE YOU SAYING WHAT YOU'RE SAYING?

Elizabeth sighed. "Well, I hadn't exactly planned to make a declaration, but, no, there's been nobody in my life since you left."

Grant's fingers dug painfully into the muscles of his legs. He was beginning to tremble. She wasn't joking. The most passionate, responsive woman he'd ever known was telling him she'd lived like a nun for five endless, empty years, and all because of him. He wouldn't, he couldn't accept that. Half a decade ago he'd eased his conscience by telling himself his departure would be the best thing for Elizabeth as well as for him. Now, suddenly to learn that instead of giving her freedom he'd crippled her ... He shook with a sickening mixture of shock, guilt and rage.

For Richard and Joyce, and Jane, Linda and Sarah, with love.

LYNDA WARD
is also the author
of these titles in
SuperRomance

THE TOUCH OF PASSION
THE MUSIC OF PASSION
A SEA CHANGE

VOWS FOREVER

Lynda Ward

A SuperRomance from
HARLEQUIN
London · Toronto · New York · Sydney

All the characters in this book have no existence outside the imagination of the Author, and have no relation whatsoever to anyone bearing the same name or names. They are not even distantly inspired by any individual known or unknown to the Author, and all the incidents are pure invention.

The text of this publication or any part thereof may not be reproduced or transmitted in any form or by any means, electronic or mechanical, including photocopying, recording, storage in an information retrieval system, or otherwise, without the written permission of the publisher.

This book is sold subject to the condition that it shall not, by way of trade or otherwise, be lent, resold, hired out or otherwise circulated without the prior consent of the publisher in any form of binding or cover other than that in which it is published and without a similar condition including this condition being imposed on the subsequent purchaser.

First published in Great Britain in 1986 by Harlequin, 15–16 Brook's Mews, London W1A 1DR

© Lynda Ward 1985

ISBN 0 373 70162 4

Printed and bound in Great Britain by Cox & Wyman Ltd, Reading

CHAPTER ONE

ELIZABETH CONSIDERED ramming her Porsche into the rear of the truck ahead of her.

Only the conviction that her sleek, silver sports car would emerge second-best from such an encounter made her continue to lag fretfully behind the rust-pocked pickup that hiccuped tangy belches of unburned gasoline. At each new crest she prayed the highway snaking through the Ozark foothills would be visible far enough ahead to permit her to pass the balky truck. But every undulation seemed only to mask more bends, more knolls covered with dying grass and copper-leaved oak trees. Her frustration grew.

By the time the road at last straightened so that she could safely veer the Porsche into the left lane, she was frantic. Forgetting the automobile dealer's admonitions about carefully breaking in the new engine, she downshifted and rammed the accelerator to the floor. The car whined in protest as it shot forward. When she returned to her own lane, the pickup was already swiftly receding in her rearview mirror, a blob of darker color against the gray ribbon of paving. Easing back to the speed limit, she slumped against the seat. Only then did she realize her heart was still racing.

"Settle down," she ordered herself sternly, but the pounding in her chest persisted. As she always did at the first sign of tension, she began her progressive-relaxation breathing exercises, inhaling and exhaling to a slow, deliberate count until she could feel her heart rate subside. The technique, unobtrusive but effective, had saved her more than once during stress-filled boardroom confrontations. As well it should, she thought cynically; she had been taught by a master. The irony was so great she laughed aloud.

Knowing her apprehension would only feed on itself as she approached her destination, Elizabeth switched on the radio. Two days earlier, when she had first taken delivery of the Porsche in Chicago, the radio had been tuned to a classical station, which had still been faintly audible when she stopped a night later in St. Louis. Now, in northwestern Arkansas, only static blared from the speakers, scraping the nerves.

Grimacing, she began to cycle through the frequencies. Whistles and squeals separated the stations; farm reports gave way to violin-drenched country and western. A nasal soprano told her ramblin' man she was tired of waiting for him and planned to find someone new to keep her warm in her big lonely bed. Elizabeth turned off the radio. After she finished her business and settled once more in New York City, she'd have to see about having the car outfitted with a tape deck.

She had never been in this part of the country before, and the contrast to what she'd left behind was striking. Far to the north in Minnesota the first snow had already fallen, making her sister's drafty little house unbearably cold. Elizabeth had fled southward once she had fulfilled her family obligations, and in Chicago, where she had paused in her headlong flight, there had been a sting of ice in the winds that blew off Lake Michigan. But here in Arkansas, the tree-covered mountains were burnished by the Indian-summer sun. She never would have guessed it was early November.

The Porsche topped a low ridge, and suddenly Elizabeth could see stretching before her a wide, flat valley, alluvial plain of the shining river that gave the state its name. The valley floor was a patchwork of ocher and green. In the distance, on the water, a long barge heaped high with some kind of ore passed with lazy majesty beneath the raised center section of an old-fashioned arched iron bridge. A six-lane freeway slashed the terrain between Elizabeth and the river.

Gazing across the valley, she recalled her conversation with the teenager working at the last gas station where she'd stopped. While he had cared for the car, she'd gone to the rest room.

After washing her hands and sprinkling cold water over the back of her neck, she considered her teal-blue wool dress and knee-length suede boots. She'd selected her outfit carefully to impart a look of style and confidence, but now her clothes were too warm for the unexpectedly mild weather. Unless she wanted to rummage through her cases in the Porsche's forward luggage compartment, there was nothing she could do about the boots, but she did loosen a couple of buttons at her throat and push the dress's long sleeves up over her elbows. The effect was still good, if somewhat more casual than she had hoped for. At least she felt comfortable now. In a confrontation like the one ahead of her, she was going to need all her wits. Physical discomfort would be a distraction and, Elizabeth reminded herself as she fluffed her blond curls, her opponent was a man who never hesitated to take any advantage offered him.

By the time she stepped outside again into the balmy breeze, the boy had finished filling the gas tank and was scraping bugs off the windshield. He polished the glass with the kind of care usually reserved for antique crystal. Amused by his intensity, Elizabeth smiled as she asked for directions to her destination. He stroked the silky silver paint one last time before answering.

"Yes, ma'am—" he tugged at his billed cap "—I surely do know how to get to Ridleyville. My folks used to live there. From here, your best bet is to head south until you go under Highway 40, and then just keep bearing right until you end up at the old drawbridge—'s on the other side. That was the main route—" he rhymed the word with "out" "—through these parts before they put in the interstate, but hardly anyone goes that way anymore unless they have to. Too bad. Once upon a time it was a pretty nice little town."

For a moment his young face had darkened. Then he shrugged and chuckled. "Now don't forget, ma'am. You go *under* the freeway. If you get on one of the on-ramps by mistake, depending which way you head, you're liable to wind up in Little Rock or Fort Smith!"

Approaching the overpass, Elizabeth suddenly wondered if it might not be better for everyone if she did just head up the on-ramp and drive away—to Little Rock, to Fort Smith, to anywhere except Ridleyville. It wasn't too late to abandon this quixotic mission of hers. She could still go back to New York and turn everything over to one of those expensive but discreet lawyers the company retained to handle the personal affairs of its senior executives....

"No, dammit," she said harshly. "I will not be a coward. I owe myself this." Gunning the engine, she sped beneath the freeway.

RIDLEYVILLE, ARKANSAS—the town with a future, the battered sign declared optimistically. Population 2004. Elizabeth had no idea how many years the metal placard had stood in position at the end of the drawbridge, but someone had long since shot out the centers of the zeros, and coronas of rust surrounded the holes in the white enamel.

The road from the bridge was the town's main street, lined with storefronts in varying degrees of repair. None of the stores looked very new. Elizabeth slowed the Porsche to a crawl. With a sense of anticlimax, she realized she had no idea where she was supposed to go from here. She glanced around for clues.

The area looked almost deserted, empty except for a few nondescript cars and pickups, a handful of pedestrians. She passed a movie theater with a blank marquee, the doors boarded shut. Next to it was a Vietnamese restaurant. Farther down the street, two boys and a girl loitered beneath a ragged canvas awning, on which the words Dry Goods and Notions since 1906 were still faintly legible; neon tubing in the window declared the store to be a video arcade. When Elizabeth drove by, the trio broke off their conversation and stared at the Porsche. One of them whistled appreciatively. Elizabeth crept on, searching.

She stopped at an intersection where a single-lens traffic signal dangled from crossed wires, blinking red in all directions. Glancing down the side street, she noticed that Ridleyville's business district appeared to be only one street wide. Beyond the row of commercial buildings she could see houses and a red-brick school three stories high. When she spotted a tall steeple of ivy-covered stone looming in the distance, her hopes lifted. They plummeted again when she approached the bell tower and found that it topped a Catholic church. For a moment she debated stopping—

surely if there was a priest on the grounds he could help her—then farther down the road she noticed a service station.

Elizabeth passed the gas pumps and pulled up beside a man loading a tow truck. He ambled to her open window, wiping his hands on a rag as he gazed with open speculation. "You're not from these parts, are you?" he probed when she asked for instructions. "I can tell by the way you talk."

The remark startled Elizabeth. While living in Belgium she had grown used to being told she "sounded like an American"—as if, she realized now, all Americans spoke alike. The voice she had deliberately smoothed and refined when she had first entered the business world probably sounded as alien to the attendant as his own did to her. Even his so-called Southern accent varied from the ones she was used to hearing. The Arkansas dialect seemed to merge two regions, soft vowels blending with harsher midwestern consonants. A logical marriage, considering that geographically and culturally, Arkansas bordered on the Great Plains states.

While Elizabeth mused, not answering at once, the man asked, "You just passing through, or are you here on business or something?"

"You might say that."

He persisted. "That's quite a vee-hicle you've got there. I don't think I've ever seen one like it."

Elizabeth could feel herself getting harried, but she admitted she was at least partly to blame for the delay. If she preferred not to be noticed, she never should have succumbed to the temptation to purchase such a flamboyant automobile. Even in New York the Porsche would be distinctive; on a byroad in Arkansas it was unique. "I just bought it in Chicago a couple of days ago," she admitted.

The man frowned cryptically. "Oh. Up north." He turned toward the street and gestured with the rag. "To get where you're going, head on down that way two blocks past the Winn-Dixie market and then turn left. You can't miss it. It's kitty-corner from the Bailey place, a big white house with columns."

"Thank you very much," Elizabeth said, fighting a ballooning hollowness in her stomach. After all this time, all the travel, to be only blocks away...

The man grinned. "Happy to oblige." He glanced covetously at the Porsche once more. "Anytime you want your oil changed or something—"

"Thank you," she repeated, "but I'm sure I won't be here long enough for that." Returning his wave, she pulled out of the service station.

The "Bailey place" the man had mentioned was a turn-of-the-century mansion set back among gardens that, like the house, appeared to be going to seed. Diagonally across the street from it was a squat yellow-brick building of undistinguished architecture, where twin dogwoods flanking the entrance rained dry, curled leaves all over the lawn and the sign beside the walkway. Elizabeth stared at the cross on that sign. Here it was at last, the goal she'd been seeking since she'd embarked on her journey hundreds—or, depending on one's point of view, thousands—of miles earlier.

CHURCH OF THE GOOD SAMARITAN. Go and do likewise—Luke 10:37. Sunday school 9:00 A.M.; worship services 10:30 A.M. Sunday, 7:30 P.M. Wednesday. The Reverend Dr. Grantland J. O'Connor, pastor.

Elizabeth switched off the ignition and sank back in the seat, clutching her keys in her fist as she read the sign three times. Despite the physical evidence before her, she blinked in disbelief. Even now she couldn't accept it. She'd had days to assimilate the information she'd tracked down so laboriously, and still it didn't make sense. Nothing made sense anymore—it hadn't for five years.

The key ring in her hand jingled, and she realized she was trembling. The manifestation of insecurity surprised her. *Rule number one,* she thought, parroting lessons from the past: *Never give any outward sign that you are less than absolutely sure of what you are doing.*

She had taken that stricture to heart, learning to channel her nervousness inward, where it remained hidden from everyone but herself. The practice had served her well, particularly when dealing with European businessmen who expected an American—and a woman, at that—to be open and ingenuous to the point of gullibility. Elizabeth knew her carefully cultivated image of incisive self-confidence and impenetrable reserve unnerved a lot of people. But now she was unnerved, suddenly uncertain she had the strength to go through with the task she'd set for herself.

She would never accomplish anything huddled in her car. As she reached for the door handle, Elizabeth hesitated. She turned down the sun visor over the steering wheel to check her reflection in the mirror one last time. Despite the care with which she'd applied her makeup that morning, her complexion was pallid, high cheekbones standing out in stark relief beneath shadowed blue eyes. She had chewed the color from her lips, leaving them soft and tremulous. Grabbing her suede handbag, she renewed her lipstick and flicked a comb through her hair. Then, regirded, she strode up the leaf-covered path to the door of the church.

One side of the heavy double doors was unlocked, and once it closed with a bang behind her, Elizabeth found herself in a dim corridor. At the entrance the gloom was alleviated by colored light streaming through tall slits of pebbly amber and red glass. But all the windows along the outer wall were covered with velvet draperies. The enclosed air smelled musty. Opposite the entry, a long console table topped with a guest book separated two more sets of pecan-wood double doors; apparently they led into the sanctuary. On the right was an inconspicuous single door marked Crying Room. To the left, an arrow directed visitors to the church office. Elizabeth turned left.

As she approached the door, ajar at the far end of the hallway, she could hear the rapid, metallic tap-tap of a manual typewriter. A secretary was pounding on a vintage Royal, too absorbed in her work to notice the visitor right away. Behind her, French windows opening onto the grounds in the rear of the church were spread wide, making the room light and airy, a welcome contrast to the tenebrous corridor. A philodendron crept upward from a large unglazed pot. The big, ragged leaves trained along the top of the sill, reaching toward the inner door, where a small metal plate marked Pastor gleamed brazenly. Elizabeth couldn't look at it.

The woman at the desk appeared to be about sixty. Her hair, dyed black, was teased into an unflattering bouffant, but when she glanced up her smile was attractive, though apologetic. "I beg your pardon, ma'am, I didn't mean to keep you waiting. It's just that I was so busy cutting these stencils for this week's newsletter. May I help you?"

"I'd like to see Dr. O'Connor," Elizabeth said.

The woman's smile stiffened, and her enunciation became more precise. "I'm sorry, but from one to four in the afternoon is the time Reverend O'Connor has set aside for study and meditation. He's not to be disturbed. I'm Mrs.

Butley, the church secretary. Is there something I can do for you?"

Elizabeth gazed limpidly at the woman, her bland expression at odds with the wry chuckle she was trying to suppress. Many things seemed to have changed over the years, but obviously not his appreciation of a staunch sentinel to ward off unwelcome visitors.... She wondered if he also remembered the converse rule: never let yourself be put off by a secretary. Whether or not he did, Elizabeth did. Using a tone that had intimidated office dragons from New York to Brussels, Elizabeth said firmly, "Thank you, Mrs. Butley, but my business is with Dr. O'Connor. I've come a very long way to see him, so please tell him I'm here."

Mrs. Butley blinked. For the first time she really seemed to look at Elizabeth, noting the air of expensive chic that would have labeled her a stranger to the region even if her neutral accent hadn't. "But he—he— That is, I—"

"Now, please."

Mrs. Butley scrambled to her feet. "Of course, ma'am. Right away." She tapped lightly on the inner office door. There was no answer. After glancing inside, she looked back at Elizabeth with a puzzled frown. "I'm sorry, but the reverend seems to have stepped out a moment. I guess I was so busy I didn't even notice. Oh, well, perhaps he went to the parsonage for something. If you like, I'll go see if I can locate him."

"Thank you. I'd appreciate that." As Elizabeth watched, the older woman exited through the French windows and bustled along a flagstone path that crossed a field in the rear of the church. She passed a teeter-totter and a rusty swing set, the chains rattling in the breeze, as she headed for a two-story frame house about fifty yards away.

When Mrs. Butley stepped onto the screened-in back porch, Elizabeth's view was blocked by fingers of red ivy that clung to the supports and roof.

After a moment the secretary emerged from behind the vines and trotted around the far corner of the house, disappearing into a fenced area that from Elizabeth's perspective looked like some kind of garden. She turned away. Her blue eyes clouded as she stared sightlessly at the wall and commenced her breathing exercises once more.

"Ma'am..."

Mrs. Butley's timorous voice penetrated Elizabeth's concentration. Her vision cleared. Whirling on her boot heel, Elizabeth faced the other woman and the tall, casually dressed man who stood beside her.

She was unprepared for the magnitude of her response as she gazed at him. He should have been a stranger. His windblown dark-auburn hair was indifferently barbered, shorter than she remembered; his body was bigger. An extra ten pounds covered those seventy-four inches of muscle, nerve and sheer driving will. The weight suited him. No longer imperially slim, he looked solid, formidable— and the effect was devastating.

Elizabeth knew she ought to have the upper hand. She had taken every step possible to ensure herself a psychological edge in this confrontation, from the way she'd avoided giving her name to the secretary lest she spoil the shock of her unheralded appearance to her choice of wardrobe. His buff denims and tan chambray work shirt contrasted vividly with the understated elegance she recalled. She had rarely seen him less than perfectly groomed before; she'd never seen him wearing jeans. By all rules of power brokerage, the formality of her own dress ought to have rendered her more intimidating than him. But it didn't. The only thing that made him seem vulnerable at all was the look on his face.

Despite her plan to seize every advantage without hesitation, as she watched astonishment stagger him, his rugged features growing slack and defenseless just for an instant, she thought with compunction, *I should have warned him. It wasn't fair not to warn him.*

With an effort he disciplined his expression. He watched her warily. Realizing Mrs. Butley was observing them both, Elizabeth squared her shoulders and extended her hand. Her voice was steady. "Dr. O'Connor."

Something flickered in his eyes. "Ms...Swenson?" Elizabeth wondered if the secretary caught that subtle lift in his voice as he guessed her name. She nodded and braced herself for his touch, but before his fingers could brush against hers, he glanced down and noticed the grime on his nails. Jerking away, he exclaimed, "I beg your pardon!" and reached into the rear pocket of his jeans for a cotton handkerchief. As he cleaned his hands he said, "You'll have to excuse me, but I was helping my housekeeper's little brother dig for fishing worms, and—"

"I thought in the afternoon you were supposed to devote yourself to 'study and meditation,'" Elizabeth muttered.

"You don't necessarily have to read a book to study. On a day like today, just enjoying the beauty of nature can be a deeply rewarding spiritual experience."

Elizabeth gazed evenly at him. "I wouldn't know about that."

For a moment silence stretched between them. Then she said tonelessly, "We have to talk."

"Yes, of course." He grimaced at his hands. "I'm afraid I'm going to have to wash up first. If you'd care to wait in my office..." He turned to his secretary. "Mrs. Butley, do you think you could get Ms Swenson settled and then pour her a cup of coffee, with maybe some of your wonderful apricot-pecan bread?"

The older woman's sallow face pinked becomingly at his compliment. "I'd be delighted," she gushed as he loped away.

In the inner room, meticulously clean but cluttered and slightly worn-looking, the secretary clucked at the paper-strewn desk as she carried in a tray of refreshments. On a low table flanked by two aging petit-point armchairs, she moved aside an African violet. While she fussed, Elizabeth hovered restlessly. She stared at the bookshelves crammed with volumes of theology and philosophy—and more potted plants. Her eyes skated over a faded lithograph of *Jesus Knocking at the Door*, to rest, disbelieving, on a framed parchment that hung beside it. A small denominational college in Georgia declared that Grantland James O'Connor had been awarded the degree of Doctor of Divinity. Elizabeth's handbag slipped from her fingers, scattering the contents on the floor.

She blushed and dropped to her knees, fishing for a lipstick that had rolled under the coffee table. Mrs. Butley watched her agitation compassionately. Bending down to help, the woman scooped up Elizabeth's purse and handed it back to her. With gentle concern she assured her, "Honey, if something's troubling you, I know Reverend O'Connor will do whatever he can to help. Even in the short time since he's come here, it's obvious he's as understanding and conscientious a man as you're likely to find anywhere."

"Thank you. You're very kind," Elizabeth murmured.

Mrs. Butley looked uncertain.

Forcing a wan smile, Elizabeth said unconvincingly, "Really, I'll be all right."

With a puzzled nod the secretary went back to her own office.

As soon as the door closed, Elizabeth moved quickly. She shifted the armchairs and plopped into one so that her back was to the window. She laid her handbag in the center of the table next to the flowerpot and placed her saucer and cake plate beside it. By the time the man she was waiting for returned, she had already poured her coffee and was sipping it with deceptive placidness.

His gray eyes assessed the scene. She thought the corner of his hard mouth twitched as he pushed the door shut behind him, but he didn't speak until he sat down. Crossing his long legs so that the heavy muscles of his thighs strained against the brown denim, he said, "Hello, Liza."

"Hello, Grant," she whispered. He had to lean closer to hear her.

His glance skimmed over her, noting the way the soft blue wool of her dress defined her narrow waist, her small breasts. "I thought I remembered how lovely you were," he mused, "but now I find you're more beautiful than ever."

His deep voice betrayed his Savannah birth in the way it softened the rs, as it flowed across the syllables. His accent had always made Elizabeth think of honey and velvet. She shivered. To break the spell she countered, "I'm too thin."

"Well, perhaps a little," he agreed equably, "but I suppose that's to be expected if you still live on your nerves the way you used to.... I do like your hair short and curly that way. It's not so severe as the chignon you favored when we first met."

Elizabeth didn't want to talk about when they had first met. Through the door from the outer office filtered the machine-gun clatter of the old Royal. "Your Mrs. Butley must be a treasure. She's very pleasant, and she sounds like a wonder on that manual typewriter. How fast would she be on a good electronic one?"

Grant shrugged. "Who knows? I offered to buy her any new machine she wanted, but she turned me down. She said she was too old to change." He stared at Elizabeth. "More beautiful than ever," he murmured again. "Of course, I always knew you were a woman who would only improve with age. You must be...how old now, Liza? Twenty-eight?"

"Twenty-nine," she corrected, almost choking at the intensity of her reaction. Five years, she reminded herself. Five whole years, and still all he had to do was call her by that damned pet name.... She retorted, "And you've already hit 'the big four-o,' as they call it?"

A lock of ruddy-brown hair fell across his broad forehead as he shook his head. "No, I'm not quite forty yet, thank God. But soon. Sooner than I care to think about sometimes." Absently he smoothed back the hair with his hand, and for the first time Elizabeth noticed the tendrils of gray at his temples. She felt ashamed of her childish spite.

"Grant—" she began.

"Liza—" he said at the same time. Both of them fell silent, and then Grant said, "It's been a long time, Liza."

"Yes, I know." She set down her coffee cup, steeling herself to utter the words she had traveled hundreds, thousands of miles to say. "Yes, Grant, I know it's been a long time. That's why I had to see you. I want a divorce."

CHAPTER TWO

GRANT GAZED at Elizabeth. The light pouring in through the window behind her caught in the pale curls that haloed her small head. His eyes narrowed. "Did you think I was going to say no?" he asked quietly.

"I have no idea what you'll say or do, Grant."

He could hear the undertone of cynicism in her voice, the voice that had been so full of warmth and excitement when he'd met her, and suddenly he knew he was responsible for its being there. The realization surprised and distressed him. He'd assumed she'd got over him years earlier.

He glanced at the table between them, at her purse and plates lined up like a barricade across it. With an effort at lightness he noted, "You were really set to do battle, weren't you? All these little maneuvers calculated to rattle your poor unsuspecting opponent and give you the advantage in your confrontation. You've rearranged the furniture so that I have to stare into the sun while we talk. You speak in a murmur that makes me bend closer if I want to hear you. You spread out your personal effects in such a way that the table becomes your territory, with me the intruder.... About the only thing you didn't do was toss your coat across my chair so that I wouldn't have a place to sit down!"

"It's too warm for a coat," Elizabeth pointed out wryly.

With a grimace she picked up her handbag and dropped it onto the floor beside her chair. "I'm sure I must usually be a little more subtle than that." She sighed. "At any rate, people rarely notice what I'm doing. However, when one is up against the master strategist himself..."

A peculiar expression of pain washed across Grant's strong features, and Elizabeth hesitated, puzzled. "I'd think you'd be flattered to learn that even after all this time I still practice those techniques I learned from you," she said slowly. "Of course, from the very beginning you were a terrific teacher."

"Teacher." As soon as the word escaped her mouth, their eyes met, locked, an open channel between minds sharing the same memory....

In the perfumed shadows of her bed he had buried his face against the naked curve of her throat, gasping not only with the force of his own satisfaction but with the stunning realization that until that moment the vibrant, welcoming body beneath him, around him, had been virgin. When at last he was capable of coherent speech, he had lifted his head to stare down at her, all control gone, his expression for once bewildered and vulnerable. "Why me?" he asked hoarsely.

Her blue eyes were clouded, her damp skin flushed with wonder, pain and glory as she clung to him. Her answering smile was suddenly sirenic, womanwise. "I knew," she whispered triumphantly, a pink tongue flicking across kiss-stung lips that were salty with the tang of his sweat. "I knew you'd be my teacher...."

The hands lying open on his denim-clad thighs clenched into fists. "Why do you want a divorce?" he asked.

Elizabeth scowled. "What do you mean, 'why'? Our marriage exists only on paper. We haven't seen each other in years."

"That's just it." He reached for the coffeepot, and for a moment he was silent as he poured himself some of the steaming black liquid. To his amazement, not a drop spilled. Automatically he offered to refill her cup. She shook her head, watching with aching eyes as he resettled his long frame easily into the old armchair. His large sinewy hands folded around his china cup the way they used to swallow her breasts. Elizabeth shivered.

When he spoke again his voice sounded mellow with the deceptive silkiness his accent imparted, the silkiness his enemies had learned to fear. "Liza, at any time during the past half a decade you could have sued me for desertion. Yet you chose not to. So I'm naturally curious about your reason to suddenly seek a divorce now. Do you want to marry again?" His tone roughened. "Are you pregnant?"

Elizabeth drew a deep, raspy breath. "Would it be any business of yours if I were?"

Although Grant didn't move, all at once the strong planes of his face were sharp, pronounced, and his lounging posture radiated tension, as if he were coiled and ready to spring. His knuckles whitened around the coffee cup. "So long as I remain your husband, there might be some legal quibble about the paternity of—" He broke off, and his wrath subsided, softening to concern as he agreed, "No, of course it wouldn't be any of my business, unless you're in some kind of trouble. Is that why you're here, Liza? Do you need help?"

"No! I've managed just fine without your help for the past five years!" As soon as the harsh declaration had passed her lips, Elizabeth felt her own anger leaching away, only to be replaced by a leaden sensation of frustration and futility. Abandoning any pretense of composure, she leaned back in the chair, twisting her long neck to ease the knotted muscles. "No, Grant, I'm not pregnant, and I'm not planning on getting married again, at least not in the foreseeable future. It's just that I've been away for a very long time—ever since you left me, in fact. Now that I'm back from Europe, I want to straighten out some loose ends in my life, my family... you."

His expression was enigmatic. "So I'm a 'loose end,' am I? I suppose I ought to be thankful you don't call me worse." He lifted his hands briefly in a gesture of resignation. "Well, I'm sure you'll be able to wind things up with a minimum of fuss. God knows I gave you solid grounds for a divorce. No court in the country would deny your petition." Suddenly he frowned, distracted by a chance remark. "What were you doing in Europe?"

"Living there. As soon as the Avotel board of directors heard we'd separated, they asked me to take charge of the Brussels branch permanently."

Grant whistled. "Some promotion!"

"It did make quite a splash in corporate circles," Elizabeth agreed, her eyes alight with pride: "'Youngest woman executive ever to head international division,' and so forth. A few of the papers even forgot to qualify their praise by referring to me as a 'woman' executive. But surely you knew already? It made all the financial pages."

Grant glanced ironically around the cramped confines of his study; his eyes rested for a moment on the doctoral degree on the wall. "I haven't really kept up with business news since I left New York."

"The chairman told me that based on the work I'd done starting the Belgian office in the first place, establishing liaisons not only with the Common Market but with NATO headquarters, they'd wanted to offer me the position sooner. The only thing was, they knew I'd never accept a job that took me away from you...." Her soft mouth twitched sardonically. "Maybe I should be grateful you walked out."

"Maybe you should at that," he said quietly. Again they fell silent. Then Grant said, "Liza, if you want a divorce, I won't contest it in any way. Have your lawyer get in touch with mine, and they can work out whatever settlement seems equitable. I still own the co-op in Manhattan, but I've been leasing it out. If you want it, we may be able to arrange—"

"I don't need your condominium, Grant," Elizabeth cut in, the acid tone returning to her voice. "I don't need a settlement. In case you hadn't noticed, I've done very well for myself during the past five years. There's nothing of yours that I want."

"'Nothing'?"

Her blue eyes narrowed until they were slanted and catlike above her high cheekbones. "All right, Grant, I'll admit there is one thing—"

"Anything, Liza."

"'Anything'?" She leaned forward. "Very well, Grant, what I want is an explanation. I want to know what the hell the most predatory corporate shark on the East Coast is doing in a moribund town in Arkansas, playing at being a preacher!"

"I'M NOT PLAYING."

His tone was flat, uncompromising, as stern as the metallic glint in his eyes. Elizabeth remained skeptical. "No, Grant?"

"No. I will admit I never intended to become a parish minister. I've discovered that the scholastic life is very...restful...and since my ordination a couple of years ago I've been writing and doing historical research at the college near Atlanta where I earned my doctorate. But when the former pastor here had a stroke, the denomination's governing council needed someone to fill the pulpit temporarily. They contacted me because I was one of the few people available who could relocate at a moment's notice." He smiled faintly. "I told them I didn't know how good I'd be at the job, but I vowed to do the best God would allow."

That reference to the Deity sounded strange on his lips, Elizabeth thought, still baffled. She was vaguely aware that Grant had attended Sunday school as a child, but as an adult his spiritual life, like hers, had been marked not so much by disbelief as by the absence of any particular belief at all. The closest either of them had come to a show of faith had been to exchange presents on their one Christmas together.

"Are you telling me you abandoned your career and your life-style because of some midlife conversion?"

Quickly he shook his head. "It wasn't that simple. I—"

"Is that why you left me?" she rushed on bitterly. "That's rather contradictory, isn't it? Forgive me for not being more sympathetic, but I can't recall you ever showing any interest in organized religion. The one mystical force in your life was power—getting it, keeping it. Power was always the one thing you really craved, more than money, more than sex, the one game that truly aroused you." Her mouth twisted with confusion and hurt. "Grant, please don't toy with me. I can't accept it. I'm your wife, remember? I want to understand, but how can I? I know how single-minded you are when you want something, whether it's a company or a block of stock—or a woman. Can't you just tell me what it is you're really after?"

The gray eyes that regarded her were as impenetrable as a fog bank. Quietly he queried, "Would you believe me if I said I just want a little peace?"

Elizabeth stared at the man lounging in the chair opposite her. "Peace." What was that supposed to mean? He had never been peaceful, not even relaxed. In moments of repose his long lean frame had continued to radiate energy, rigidly leashed, a self-control that had awed and intimidated her. Even lovemaking had been a competition, a challenge of wills and bodies, a test to see which of them could make the other lose control, bring the other to climax first, most often. It was a contest she had found enormously exciting, one in which defeat had been as rapturous as victory. And except for the very first time they had made love, when the shock of her unexpected innocence had jarred loose his restraint, he had always vanquished her....

Jumping to her feet, Elizabeth crossed to the window, where she peered in the direction of the parsonage. Her husband's home. Her graceful hands clutched at the sill, and she leaned her forehead against the cool glass as she said thickly, "It was a mistake for me to come here. I was being noble. I had this idea a marriage was too important to end with a letter, but I didn't know how hard... I should have headed straight to New York City the instant I saw that my mother was all right."

With concern he studied her back, the fashionable blue dress clinging to her willowy, too-slender body, the crown of bright curls that mocked the despairing slump of her shoulders. He longed to take her in his arms, cradle her against him comfortingly, beg her understanding, but he knew he dared not. If he held her, he wasn't sure he'd find the strength to let her go.

Changing the subject, he asked, "Your mother's been ill?"

"Heart problems," Elizabeth murmured, still not looking at him. "Just before Halloween my sister Amelia sent word through the head office that our mother had had a severe angina attack. She insisted it was nothing critical, nothing to come home for, but she figured I'd want to know. That scared me. I mean, the fact that Amelia even bothered to contact me seemed to indicate the situation was worse than she claimed.... Anyway, I haven't taken more than a day or two off in all the years I've been in Europe, so I turned everything over to my second-in-command and caught the Concorde back to the States."

She fell silent, and after waiting for her to continue, Grant prompted, "Your mother's better now?"

Elizabeth smiled with relief. "Oh, yes. Apparently Amelia was telling the simple truth, after all. By the time I got to Minnesota, mom was already back at the dry cleaners where she's slaved for the past quarter of a century. You know, she still looks after Amelia's noisy brood while my sister works swing shift at the bakery."

"What about Amelia's husband? Isn't she married anymore?"

"Sure—for all the good it does her. Since he was a kid, my brother-in-law has never been fit for anything but making my sister pregnant." She shook her head in wonder. "True, my nieces and nephews are adorable—the baby's a little doll—and I suppose that's some compensation, but without some help from their father, they're such a burden on Amelia. Why she let him—"

"Maybe she loves him," Grant suggested quietly. After a moment he continued with conscious optimism, "I'm sure your family was glad to see you after such a long time."

"You'd think so, wouldn't you?" Elizabeth sighed. "But I felt unwelcome from the moment I arrived. They don't need me. I don't know why Amelia even bothered to call me in the first place."

"Maybe she loves you, too."

"And I love her," Elizabeth said helplessly. "When I saw her, I was as concerned about her as I was about mom. Amelia's not thirty-five yet, but she looks fifty—which I suppose is what comes of getting married at sixteen. But when I tried to show my concern, my sister just got angry. She seems to resent everything about me—my career, my clothes, the money I send them...."

After a second she continued. "Oh, Grant, I don't know what they want from me. I suggested that mom and Amelia and I go to Minneapolis for the weekend, my treat. I thought they might enjoy getting away, just the three of us. It would be a chance to catch up on old times while they relaxed. We could see a play at the Guthrie, maybe shop a little. I hinted—tactfully, I might add—that since Amelia's husband didn't seem to be doing anything else, it wouldn't hurt him to take care of the children for a couple of days."

Guessing what was coming, Grant tensed. "Amelia didn't like that, did she?"

Elizabeth turned to face Grant once more, her hands raised in an unconscious gesture of resignation. "She told me people with responsibilities didn't have time to go flitting off to the city. Besides, she didn't give a damn whether or not I was her sister, or how much money I had to throw around, but if I couldn't keep my own husband, I had no right to make snide remarks about hers."

"I'm sorry," Grant said, wincing. "I'm truly sorry it was my fault your visit wasn't successful."

She waved away his apology. "It wasn't your fault. I

should have guessed the visit was bound to be a disaster. Relations with my family have been strained for years. I love mom and Amelia, but we just don't have any common ground anymore. Maybe we never did."

Her voice trailed off; then she continued briskly, "Oh, well, I suppose you can say some good did come of this trip, though. As soon as I could escape, I headed south to Chicago and checked into the Park Hyatt. I needed to unwind. For a couple of days I just stayed in my room, sleeping, eating, thinking...enjoying American television, American plumbing. And eventually I realized I'm tired of being an expatriate. As much as I've enjoyed these years in Belgium, I know it's time for me to come home again, this time to stay."

Grant frowned. "Just like that?" he asked. "What about your job? You've built a remarkably successful career for yourself. Surely you don't mean to throw it all away?"

Elizabeth gazed at him in genuine puzzlement. "Why not, Grant? You did."

He uncrossed his long legs and stood up. Watching him, once again Elizabeth was struck by the subtle changes in her husband since they'd separated. The threads of silver in his auburn hair didn't signal any physical deterioration. There was tremendous strength in that tall, well-muscled body; the extra few pounds beneath the casual denim only emphasized the impression of latent power. His dress and grooming might not be quite so polished as they had once been, but she knew his mind was as sharp as ever. He was like a battle-scarred broadsword, no longer as shiny or perfectly honed as when it had been forged, but still true balanced and irresistibly deadly in the right hands.

When she met him he had been like a rapier, elegant and

lethal, every move—physical or mental—a poem of grace and cunning. In the world of late-twentieth-century high finance, he had been an eighteenth-century privateer, saluting his foes as he scuttled them. Facing him across a boardroom table for the first time, Elizabeth had been entranced by his business acumen, his confidence, his urbanity, his undeniable sexual magnetism. He had seemed the embodiment of everything she had ever fantasized in a man.

He still did.

When he crossed to her side by the window, she glanced away, not daring to look directly at him, disheartened by the realization that for her, his aura was as potent as ever. She found little comfort in the fact that he seemed oblivious to the effect he was having on her senses. "Liza," he said heavily, "you have to believe me when I tell you that abandoning my career—" he faltered "—abandoning *you* was the hardest thing I've ever done in my life. I did not make the decision lightly."

He did not touch her, but he was standing so close she could smell the subtle man-scent of him wafting across the narrow gap between them; she could feel the heat of his body. That heat had warmed and protected her from the very first day they'd met, wrapping around her in the night, weakening her defenses, lulling her inmost insecurities. Then suddenly it had been withdrawn, leaving her cold and bereft.

She swallowed with difficulty and forced her voice to remain steady. "How can I believe you when I still don't know why you left me? You never gave any explanations. For a year everything seemed perfect—until all at once you decided you just didn't want to be married anymore."

"Liza—" He reached for her.

She jerked away, stumbling against the petit-point armchair. She was losing control, breaking down—she, the unnerving Ms Swenson with her unshakable reserve and self-confidence. Her hands clutched at the frayed tapestry on the back of the chair. "Of course, the funny thing," she choked with a chuckle that sounded more like a sob, "the goddammed hilarious irony of it was that I had been the one who didn't want to get married. 'Why can't we just go on being lovers?' I asked you. 'Why must we risk our independence?' And you said, 'We won't be risking anything. Together we'll be stronger and more independent than ever. *For* ever.'" Her expression was bleak. "'Forever,' you promised, and then you were gone."

Just like my father, she thought. The unwelcome memories came flooding back.

Elizabeth stared through the window at the frame house covered with cold-reddened vines. Red had been the color of her childhood in Minnesota. Elizabeth knew most people envisioned her home state as the land of ten thousand sky-blue lakes, or of endless wheat-carpeted plains shimmering in the summer sun like living gold. But her Minnesota had been a desolate world of open-pit iron mines, huge ugly wounds in the earth. For a hundred years men had flayed the gentle, rolling hills, blasting and gouging away the rock to get at the powdery, high-grade hematite beneath, heedless of the havoc they wrought on the environment—or of the fact that the supply of ore was finite. Ecological awareness did evolve, but it came too late for some. By the time Elizabeth was born, the mine that had supported her drab little hometown for generations was almost played out.

Her earliest recollections were of toddling after her mother and big sister along red-dusted streets, carrying her father's lunch pail to the mine where he worked as a mechanic servicing ore carriers. Her father was big and fair, his coloring, like his ancestry, almost stereotypically Swedish. In his early twenties he had been as handsome as when he'd captained the high-school football team and "had to" marry the head cheerleader. Elizabeth thought she could recall arguments between her parents, usually about money, but mostly she remembered the way his laughter boomed throughout their tiny house when he paraded around with her, his little princess, on his shoulders.

Millie Swenson, Elizabeth's mother, was also of Scandinavian extraction, but her blond prettiness had faded early under the strain of caring for two young daughters and an undependable husband. Her lines had deepened when the sound of blasting stopped echoing through the town and a padlocked chain appeared across the mine entrance. After that there was less laughter in the house, and then there was none at all. Elizabeth's father had deserted them.

She shivered, and Grant said, "Liza, you'd better sit down. You're obviously upset."

Automatically she shook her head. "Of course I'm not upset." She didn't look at him. Her statement was patently untrue, and she knew he knew it, but the habit of trying to keep her hurt to herself was too deeply engrained. She had learned that at a very early age, after a series of well-aimed slaps taught her not to ask about her absent father. Her mother, who had left school without graduating when she became pregnant, went to work in a laundry, her backbreaking task to scrub out the ubiquitous crimson dirt that was all the town had to show for the mine that had once supported it. Millie had put her older daughter in charge of the younger—an unfortunate necessity, because Amelia, still only a child herself, had bitterly resented the responsibility. She used to vent her anger on her sister, taunting that their father hadn't loved his "princess" any better than he had the rest of them.

Poor Amelia, Elizabeth thought. Love was a rare commodity in their family. Elizabeth trained herself to live without it, but her sister was so desperate for affection that when she was only sixteen, she eloped with her boyfriend, a feckless youth no more mature than she was. The marriage seemed a recipe for disaster, two youngsters playing house, but astonishingly the union lasted, cemented by an unending string of babies and harsh economic necessity. Still, Elizabeth knew Amelia's life was a far cry from the cozy dreams of domesticity she had cherished as a girl.

Elizabeth's fantasies were different. She taught herself to read at a very early age, and the discovery, like the following school years, opened up a whole new world beyond the perimeter of her birthplace, an avenue of escape from borderline poverty. She began to long for travel, adventure, luxury. But when she tried to share her daydreams with her mother, Millie said scathingly, "I had dreams, too—until I met your father."

Oddly, although Millie blamed her absent husband for the many tribulations she faced, her sympathies were with her older daughter rather than Elizabeth. In Millie's opinion, Amelia's only fault was that she'd been indecorous enough to elope; marriage itself was inevitable. Men might be undependable, but they were a woman's lot. If she was lucky enough to land a good one, great; if not, well, it was up to her to make the best of a bad situation. Any girl who looked on work as more than a stopgap between childhood and wedding was "peculiar."

But to Elizabeth it seemed self-evident that the best way for a woman to live was independent of the consequences of a man's vacillating affections. And the best way to avoid becoming vulnerable was to make sure she had a good education and a better career.

Having decided on her goal, Elizabeth pursued it relentlessly. She earned straight As in high school. Recalling the name of her almost forgotten father, she applied to several companies that awarded grants to the children of miners. She won a full scholarship to an excellent university, where she studied business administration and graduated in four years with her master's degree. Her few recreational hours were spent at museums or plays or concerts.

During her final semester she typed papers for the head of the speech department, in exchange for coaching to remove the regional twang from her voice. By the time she burst onto the business world, she was cultured, accomplished and fiercely ambitious—and almost totally estranged from her mother and sister.

Elizabeth sighed. "How are your parents, Grant?" she asked to make conversation. "I was surprised to learn they'd moved to Mexico, now that your father's retired."

"They're well, thank you. They'll be pleased to hear you asked about them."

Elizabeth shrugged. "I liked your parents that one time we met in New York. I always regretted not getting a chance to know them better—although probably that's just as well, considering how things turned out...."

Again her words faded away, and she began to think about New York, the city where her career had taken off, the city where, at the age of twenty-three, she had met Grantland O'Connor across a bargaining table.

She had known him by reputation long before she actually faced him. Grant was a notorious corporate raider, a deceptively soft-spoken Southerner who had begun his career by ingeniously saving his family home, a moldering bungalow in the Savannah marshes, from foreclosure. While still in college he was known as a "boy wonder," but before he reached thirty that admiring nickname changed. He became the master of power play; proxy fights and hostile mergers were his specialty. Businessmen dreaded publicity about their companies in case it attracted his attention. Everyone knew that whatever Grantland O'Connor wanted, he got. On that day, what he wanted was Elizabeth.

She wanted him, too.

The feeling was unprecedented in her life. Despite the limited time Elizabeth had for social activities, over the years there had been boys attracted to her blossoming fairness, but she had shrugged them off. They had all seemed just what they were, boys, as callow and unreliable as her father. As she grew older, in college and then in her first jobs, men began to notice her, as well; still she wasn't interested. With the discipline that marked her every action, she put her intense sexual feelings on hold while she concentrated on succeeding.

But when she stared down the length of that mahogany table, past the parallel rows of note pads and water glasses arranged in front of each chair, and saw Grant, the attraction was instant and feverish.

He was a large man, tall, wide shouldered, with broad features and big hands. Yet the flesh stretched over his strong frame was lean, taut. If it hadn't been for the muscles, tensed and powerful even beneath the fabric of his finely cut suit, he would have looked almost gaunt. Instead, despite his formal manner, he radiated vitality, potency, the fiery glints in his dark hair a smoldering sign of the energy within him. Elizabeth wanted to tap that energy.

With difficulty she returned her attention to the meeting at hand. She was seated beside her employer, a man approaching retirement age who doggedly refused to admit he was past his prime. While he had never been overtly discourteous to Elizabeth, she knew he resented his company's being taken over by a new generation of executives—particularly women. He had insisted on heading the bargaining team, sort of a last hurrah, but Elizabeth could tell he was visibly flustered by the younger man sitting coolly across the table from him. His efforts at negotiation became less and less effective.

Elizabeth's job was to listen and observe, but when it occurred to her that in his agitation her boss was forgetting several telling points, she scribbled a suggestion on her note pad and surreptitiously pushed it in front of him. He scowled down at the lines she'd written. His jaw tightened. Sniffing audibly, he wadded the top sheet of paper into a ball and dropped it on the floor beside his chair. Elizabeth flushed. When she glanced across the table, she noticed Grantland O'Connor's gray eyes narrow as he studied her heated cheeks.

In the crush following the meeting, after her boss had reluctantly tendered a seat on his board of directors in exchange for Grant's promise not to attempt an unfriendly takeover for two years, Elizabeth was not overly surprised when Grant approached her, his manner unimpeachably circumspect as he introduced himself. But she was astonished when he uncurled his large hand and showed her the note her employer had rejected, smoothed out and obviously read. "The man's a fool," Grant murmured, his soft Southern accent making her shiver beneath her prim flannel suit. "If he'd taken the tack you suggested, he could have kept me off the board for at least another six months—plenty of time for him to line up support for his position. As it is, he's lost, and he knows it."

Elizabeth smiled hesitantly. As much as she admired his flair, she was uncertain she should be listening to flattery from the man who had just bested the company she worked for—no matter how attractive he was. She made a pretense of tucking a stray tendril of pale hair back into the tightly coiled topknot she wore to help her look older. Grant's fingers caught hers. His skin was warm and compelling against her own as he ordered softly, "Leave it, Liza."

Her lashes flew up, and with wide startled eyes she stared at him, her lips parting to protest the strangely intimate contraction of her name. Before she could speak, he silenced her resistance. During negotiations his manner had been correct, distant to the point of coolness. Now he drawled outrageously, "Don't fight me, honey, I like you all disheveled and fluffy. Have dinner with me?" Elizabeth could only nod numbly.

That night in her apartment they became lovers.

Grant was astonished by Elizabeth's virginity, but she was even more astounded when, in bed a couple of months later, he asked her to marry him. By that time they were all but living together, and when they weren't making love, he taught her about business and the uses of power. Under his tutelage her career was flourishing even more richly than before. Avotel, an industrial and communications conglomerate, had just lured her away from the employer Grant had defeated. But despite her happiness, despite the excitement and giddy wonder of being in love with this sophisticated, passionate man, marriage did not appeal to Elizabeth. She mistrusted its implications of role playing and, worse, dependence.

She tried to shrug off Grant's proposal, and his fingers tightened around her naked shoulders as he demanded, "Why not? Is there someone else you're interested in?"

"No, of course not," she murmured, stroking the deliciously lean body that by now seemed an extension of herself. She loved to watch his damp skin pucker into goose bumps beneath her caressing fingertips. "You know you're the only one I'll ever want, the only one who understands me."

His voice grew husky and coaxing as his mouth sought her breast. "Doesn't that prove to you we belong together? Darling, just think what it would mean, you and me together forever...."

"Together forever." The image those words evoked: a life of love, passion, with someone who shared the same ideals and pursued the same goals; relief from the constant draining fear of desertion that had nagged her since childhood. At last the image proved too alluring to resist. Against her better judgment Elizabeth succumbed. They were married by a judge during a long lunch hour, and Elizabeth moved her belongings into Grant's co-op overlooking Central Park. Together forever.

"Forever" lasted slightly more than a year.

Thirteen months after their wedding, Elizabeth arrived home, exhausted and dizzy with jetlag after a hectic, two-week stay in Brussels. She was establishing overseas divisional headquarters for Avotel, and while she loved the work, commuting back and forth across the Atlantic had left her little time lately to spend with her husband. She was eagerly anticipating just being with him, sleeping with him.

She found him packing.

Elizabeth stared at the clothes strewn around their bedroom, and she almost groaned with frustration. Grant was often called away unexpectedly on business—it was one of the prices paid for holding interests in so many companies—but damn! Just when it looked as if they'd have a chance to— Then she realized the trunks and suitcases he was methodically filling were far too large for a mere business trip. "What's going on?" she asked blankly.

He glanced up at her with eyes bleary and red rimmed, as if he hadn't slept in days. His auburn hair was unkempt, his strong features haggard and so pale she could actually see freckles, normally invisible, glaring liverishly against his skin. He needed a shave. "My God, Grant, what's wrong?" She dropped her attaché case and flew to him, clutching at him, pulling him into a comforting embrace. "Sweetheart, what's happened?" she repeated urgently. "Are you ill? Tell me!"

For long anguished moments he clung to her, his face buried in her bright hair. She could feel him tremble. Then slowly, reluctantly, he loosened the fingers digging into his forearms and gently pushed her away. She watched his mouth work mutely. He began throatily, "Elizabeth..."

She tensed. From the first day, he had never called her by her full name. To Grant and only Grant she had always been "Liza," his liquid accent softening the vowels, lengthening the syllables until they were sultry and sensual, a verbal caress.

"Elizabeth," he began again with a visible effort, "I don't suppose there's any way to make what I have to tell you painless, so I'll just try to make it brief. I've decided there have to be some changes in my life. I'm not sure what I'll do from here on out, except that I know I can't continue as I am. So I'm going to go back home, back to my folks' place in Savannah, where I can think. The one thing I am sure of is that I have to chuck it all."

Elizabeth gaped stupidly. "I don't understand," she whispered, licking her suddenly dry lips. "What do you mean, you 'have to chuck it all'?"

"Just exactly that," he replied, his voice more controlled than it had been a moment before. "I need to get away from the things that tie me to my old way of life. Everything must be left behind."

"Everything," he repeated for emphasis. "Everything, my darling—including you."

CHAPTER THREE

"LIZA, YOU'D BETTER sit down."

Grant's voice cut into Elizabeth's reverie. Her vision began to clear, and she squinted against the light pouring through the window. A small tow-haired boy in sneakers and dirt-stained corduroys clambered over the rusty swing set that rattled in the breeze. Elizabeth wondered if he was the housekeeper's son or little brother or whoever it was Grant had been helping to look for worms. Cute youngster; looked as if he were about five.

If Grant hadn't left her, by now the two of them might have had a child of their own. They had never discussed the possibility, though; indeed, the career plans Elizabeth had plotted as a teenager seemed to preclude a family. But now, as she approached thirty, her biological clock, or perhaps a simple craving for warmth and stability in her life, made the thought of children recur with increasing frequency. In the secret recesses of her mind she admitted that welling need was part of the reason she'd at last decided to clarify her marital status.

She swayed. Strong hands, more gentle than Grant's tone, caught her arms below the rolled-up sleeves of her dress. Confused by the seductive pressure of his skin, Elizabeth gazed at her husband as, for the first time in five years, he touched her.

Something deep inside her clenched hungrily, and her

mind shrank from that instant, fervid reaction. Didn't the yearning ever diminish? Was there never any relief from the persistent longing of one body for another? She had tried to forget him, the texture, scent and taste of his flesh. She had filled her waking hours with so much work that even her awed associates said uneasily she seemed to be driven, never guessing the exact nature of the demon. But there had been no way she could fill the void that ached, the dreams that tormented.

When she had first moved to Europe she tried to convince herself that sex with any reasonably presentable man would ease the craving. She had even dared to act accordingly—once. That disastrous evening was something she preferred not to remember. When her bewildered date had accused her of being a cold-blooded American bitch and a tease and slammed out of her apartment, Elizabeth, shaken, knew she'd had a lucky escape. After that, if pressed, she had claimed to be an advocate of the new celibacy. As the years passed, she got so she half believed it.

And now, and now to discover that all along her self-possession had been a sham, that she needed, wanted, Grant as much as ever.... She groaned aloud.

"You look as if you're about to collapse," he muttered with concern when he felt her tremble. Easing her into the armchair, he squatted beside her and set a fresh cup of coffee into her cold fingers.

"No, no, I'm all right." But the clatter of the saucer belied her words. Quickly lifting the cup to her lips, she made a pretense of drinking. "Really, I'm fine; just a little tired, that's all." She sounded distracted as she forced herself to count through the relaxation exercises Grant had taught her years before.

His mouth compressed into a tight line. He watched the

surreptitious but jerky rise of her chest, the momentary glazing of her blue eyes. Another trick she'd learned from him. Dear God, it was ominous, almost frightening to realize how pervasive his influence remained. He'd had no idea that after all these years... When the unnatural tension in her body eased, he said, "Not bad, Liza, but your breathing technique is getting sloppy."

Her lashes flew up, and bright color spattered her cheekbones. "I told you I was tired."

Grant patted her arm. His long fingers were rougher than she remembered, the tips slightly callused, catching at her smooth skin as they glided across it. "Of course you must be tired, if you flew into Little Rock today and then rented a car to drive here. I knew the instant I saw you."

His words disarmed Elizabeth. She had forgotten how sensitive to her physical state he had always been, how mindful of any fatigue or upset. She had loved his solicitude, yet she feared it, because it seemed too wonderful to last. Appalled by the force of her response to his casual caress, she shifted away. With great care she set down her cup and saucer. "I didn't fly to Arkansas. By the time I discovered where you were—"

"Why didn't you just ask my lawyer in New York? Along with the allowance he pays into your account each quarter, he's supposed to leave instructions on how to contact me in case you need me."

Elizabeth's nails dug into the arm of the chair. For a moment Grant thought she was going to lash out at him, but when she spoke her voice was even, too even. "I've never touched any of your money. Consequently I was unaware of your instructions. I had to locate you the hard way."

Grant rocked back on his heels. He stared at her, stupefied. "What do you mean?"

"Actually, the process was more time-consuming than difficult. I started by calling your parents' home in Savannah, and—"

"Dammit, Liza, I was talking about the allowance I've given you! Why haven't you taken it?"

With dignity she explained, lifting her chin, "After you walked out on me, I withdrew the money I had contributed to our joint account—not a penny more. Then I tore up my passbook. If you've continued making deposits, I wouldn't know about them."

She paused, letting the words sink in before she went on lightly, "As I was saying, the hardest part of my search was convincing the people I talked to that I was really your wife and had a right to know your whereabouts. The caretaker, or whoever it was who answered at your parents' home, told me they'd left the country, and he suggested that instead I try to contact you through your old alma mater. Of course I was surprised to hear you'd gone back to school, but you can imagine my utter amazement when—"

Grant jumped to his feet and turned away from Elizabeth. He didn't want her to see his expression. One stride carried him across the width of the cramped study, and he faced the wall where his doctoral diploma hung above the bookshelves. Blindly he stared at the parchment he had worked so hard to earn. Somewhere on one of those cluttered shelves was a slim volume, his doctoral dissertation: "Religious Symbolism and Iconography in the American Labor Movement, 1895-1920." It had taken him six months to write, studying and researching with the same monomaniac intensity he used to apply to the stock market. At the time, he had told himself that was important.

His shoulders hunched, stretching his shirt across the broad width, and his fists rammed into the pockets of his jeans. Elizabeth could see the tension that stiffened his spine, from the naked-looking skin at his nape, where a local barber had trimmed the hair too short, down to his flat buttocks. She tried not to recall how her fingers had cupped that taut flesh, those firm muscles when she had held him against her, inviting his arousal.

His candid display of nervousness surprised her. Grant had always been a master of body language, another of the numerous skills she'd admired and tried to emulate. In a boardroom, not even the flicker of an eyelid revealed his thoughts to his opponents. In a bedroom... Despite the tireless passion he'd shown her, she could only remember two other occasions when his body had proclaimed his feelings so openly: the day they met and made love for the first time, and the day he left her.

Grant swallowed thickly. "I'm sorry, Liza." She blinked at the guilt harshening the velvety slur of his voice. "I'm sorry. It never occurred to me that you'd refuse the money. I just assumed.... It—it bothers me a lot to think that at any time during the past five years, you might have needed my help and you wouldn't have known how to get in touch with me."

"But I didn't need your help."

He turned to face her once more. "You wouldn't have asked me even if you had needed it, would you?"

She shook her head. Her curls feathered across her cheeks, gold against ivory. Grant inhaled raspily. "I am sorry, Liza." He sighed. "I know I keep saying that, but I really do mean it. This is such a shock.... I didn't know I'd made you hate me."

"I don't hate you, Grant."

Elizabeth didn't elaborate on her statement, but she knew it was true. How could she hate him when the fault had been her own? She was the one who had mistaken lust and a certain mutuality of interest for lifelong devotion. She was the one who had foolishly allowed her desire for him to become so strong that she disregarded those lessons she had learned from her parents. And judging from the intensity of her physical response, she was the one who could let it all happen again if she didn't get away from him at once.

Reaching for her handbag, she stood suddenly. "Look," she said in clipped tones, "we seem to have strayed rather afield from the point. After five years, the circumstances surrounding the breakup of our marriage are no longer relevant. I came here today to tell you I intend to get a divorce. You say you have no objections. That's all there is to it. When I get to New York in a couple of weeks, I'll contact my attorney." She glanced toward the door leading to the outer office. All at once she remembered Mrs. Butley, typing innocently at her desk. Elizabeth and Grant had been closeted together for some time. She wondered if the church secretary had overheard any of their heated conversation, and if so, what interpretation she was putting on it.

Skirting the low coffee table, Elizabeth moved toward the door, but quickly Grant stepped in front of her, his large body almost touching hers. "Is this how it's supposed to end, Liza? 'So long and you'll be hearing from my lawyer'?"

"Under the circumstances, I think that's more than enough," she said, trying to ignore his nearness. With an effort she added reasonably, "Grant, everything germane has been covered. I can't see what would be gained by more maudlin reminiscences. You have work to do, and I want to get on with my trip—"

"'Trip'? Oh, that's right. You never did explain how you got here, if not by flying."

"It's no great mystery." Her fingers clutched her purse as she shrugged. "I bought a Porsche in Chicago and drove south. While I'm breaking the car in, I'm getting reacquainted with the country after being away so long." She paused, and her eyes warmed with the first genuine smile he had seen since they'd met again. "I'm having a wonderful time just driving wherever the spirit moves me. The Porsche is a joy to operate. But even though I'm not following any particular time schedule, I do need to start heading east. I want to be safely settled in New York before the first snow of the season hits."

Distracted, Grant said dubiously, "A 'Porsche'? A sports car with a high-performance engine is fine for cross-country touring, but it won't be the most suitable vehicle for stop-and-go Manhattan traffic, you know."

"Yes, I do know. I've already resigned myself to the necessity of frequent tune-ups. It's not overly practical, maybe, but I saw the car, and I wanted it. Surely you can sympathize with that."

Grant fell silent. After a moment he prodded, "Does this relaxed time schedule of yours have anything to do with the fact that you left Belgium so suddenly? Do you have a job waiting for you in New York, or did coming back to the United States mean you had to quit Avotel?"

Her smile broadened. "No, I didn't quit Avotel. I like my work, and in turn the firm appreciates my efforts. As soon as I told the chairman I'd decided to return to this country, the gears started moving. Quite simply, it seems he and the board don't want to risk losing me...."

Unlike you. The silent, accusing words formed in her mind. Elizabeth waited for her husband to comment, but when he didn't, she continued deliberately, "You needn't concern yourself about my career, Grant. I haven't been fired. I'm taking the rest of the year off as a long-overdue vacation. In the meantime my executive secretary has begun packing files, and a wall at the head office is being painted in preparation for the arrival of my two Brueghel engravings—"

She paused. When she spoke again, almost in spite of herself, her voice shimmered with excitement and triumph. "And at the general stockholders' meeting in January, I'm going to become the first woman ever to be named to Avotel's board of directors."

Grant's expression was unreadable. At last he murmured, "A directorship? *Brava*, my dear—if that's what you truly want out of life."

"Of course this promotion's what I want out of life—that and a divorce." She lifted her chin defiantly. "I don't need anything else."

Grant wondered whom she was trying to convince, him or herself. Quietly, he began, "Liza, everyone needs—"

In the outer office a commotion arose, and the door popped ajar. Mrs. Butley leaned her stiffly lacquered head into the room. "Forgive me for interrupting you, Reverend O'Connor, but Miss Bailey—"

Behind her another feminine voice trilled, "Don't blame Mrs. B. for the intrusion, Grantland! She tried to convince me you were busy, but I insisted." Elizabeth retreated in surprise as a woman of about twenty burst into the office, her arms weighted down by a wooden flat lined with rows of miniature clay flowerpots neatly filled with earth and sprigs of greenery. The secretary withdrew and closed the study door. Suddenly the air in the office was redolent and stuffy, the tang of potting soil mixing rather startlingly with the headier scent of Opium perfume.

Grant grimaced. "Really, Suzanne."

The intruder wasn't looking at him. She was staring with unabated curiosity at Elizabeth, her puppy-brown eyes flicking over the deceptively simple blue wool dress and suede boots. Elizabeth suspected she could guess the price of her ensemble within ten dollars.

"Suzanne," Grant said sternly, "Mrs. Butley has asked you before not to interrupt my meditation period."

The woman—or girl, for she seemed very young—tore her gaze away from Elizabeth to stare worshipfully at Grant again, and all at once Elizabeth knew Suzanne Bailey had a mad crush on the minister. Her voice would have betrayed her even if her expression hadn't. Tremulous with an odd mixture of bravado and uncertainty, she revealed her hopeless infatuation as she muttered, "I was only trying to help."

Poor kid, Elizabeth thought pityingly; then, recalling the splendiferous "Bailey place" across the street, she amended, *Poor little rich girl.*

Elizabeth could read Grant's expression accurately enough to know he, too, was aware of the girl's feelings. She watched him make note of Suzanne's short brown hair, freshly if unimaginatively coiffed; the petite but well-rounded figure that was amply displayed in tight designer jeans and a red silk shirt. The attractive and casually expensive costume was totally unsuited for the gardening she claimed she'd been doing, especially when worn with one of the world's priceyest perfumes.

Pointedly avuncular, Grant said, "Your advice and attention were very helpful while I was getting situated here at Good Samaritan, but now I must ask—"

Suzanne recovered enough to tease heavily, "Oh, Grantland, don't be pompous. Everyone in town knows most of the time you spend your so-called meditation period just reading. But as soon as I saw that gorgeous silver—" She caught herself, only to finish unconvincingly, "while I was gardening I decided to pot some herbs for the Women's League Christmas bazaar and bring them to your office."

Quietly Grant said, "Of course I'm sure everyone in the league will be grateful for your generous contribution. It's just that I understood all merchandise was to be stored at Mrs. Winters's home until the day of the sale."

Suzanne blushed. Elizabeth could see the color flooding the girl's creamy skin from her hairline deep into the vee of her half-unbuttoned shirt. In a tiny voice she stammered, "But you—your office is so much closer than Mrs. Winters's house, and—and I especially wanted you to see..."

Grant shook his head resignedly. Taking the wooden flat of pots from her arms, he sighed. "Yes, you may store your plants here, if it's more convenient for you."

When he set the flat on the low table beside the African violet, Elizabeth suddenly realized why the church office resembled a greenhouse. The new pots were obviously the latest in a series of floral offerings. As Grant bent to arrange the load, his gray eyes lifted, meeting hers ruefully, and his lips curled into a grin. Elizabeth smiled back. For a second they relished this unexpected moment of communication, almost like old times.

Suzanne noticed that exchange between the older couple, and her pretty, guileless features crinkled into a confused frown. Elizabeth's expression turned somber. She didn't want the girl to think she and Grant were laughing at her. When he straightened, his rugged features were blank. "Perhaps I'd better introduce you two. Elizabeth Swenson, Suzanne Bailey. Miss Bailey, Ms Swenson."

With mild humor Elizabeth observed that in Grant's soft

drawl, the title "Ms" was almost indistinguishable from the more common "Miss," although unlike many Southerners, he did not also pronounce "Mrs." as "Miz." She found it amusing that the most traditional region of the country had inadvertently blurred feminine honorifics long before it became fashionable elsewhere to do so. Elizabeth nodded. "Miss Bailey."

"Ms Swenson." Deferentially Suzanne returned the nod, although Elizabeth could tell the girl was still puzzled by her. Her brown eyes skimmed over Elizabeth's chic dress once more. "How do you do? You're not from around here, are you?"

I might as well be wearing a sign, Elizabeth thought. "No. As a matter of fact I—"

Suzanne brightened at once. "I thought so!" she gushed. "The minute I saw that sexy Porsche parked out front, I knew somebody new was in town. Nobody in Ridleyville could afford wheels like that! It looks like something I saw in one of my brother Bobby Lee's girlie maga—" She broke off, giggling. "Oh, my, that didn't sound quite right, did it? I'm sorry. I just meant it really is a fabulous car."

The girl was too ingenuous to be offensive. "Thank you. I think it's sort of fabulous myself. I'm enjoying it very much."

"Are you here for a visit, or just passing through?"

Elizabeth's good humor evaporated as she recalled the purpose of her trip. "I had to see Dr. O'Connor on business," she said. She glanced toward her husband. He was staring at her, his eyes curiously opaque, and when she met his gaze she suddenly felt breathless. Only with great reluctance did she return her attention to the girl. "It was nice meeting you, Miss Bailey, but now that Dr. O'Connor and I have cleared up everything, I guess I'd better be on my way.

It's going to be dark before I reach Little Rock." In her own ears her bright words sounded shrill and strained. "I do wish you luck on your bazaar." Squaring her shoulders, she stepped toward the door.

Behind her, Grant choked, "Liza—"

She shook her head fiercely. She would not look at him. "No, Grant. It's over. You'll be hearing from my— Goodbye." She fled into the outer office.

Mrs. Butley was no longer seated behind the typewriter. She had propped her ample hips on the edge of the desk and was smiling benignly at the small, flaxen-haired boy Elizabeth had noticed outside earlier. He sat grandly in her swivel chair, his sneakers sticking straight out in front of him. Short, grubby fingers balanced a mug of milky coffee precariously on one knee, while with his other hand he tried to cram a large slice of nut bread into his mouth. The secretary chided gently, "Now, now, Buddy, honey, not all at once. Nobody's going to take it away from you."

Elizabeth hoped to slip past unnoticed, but just at that moment the child looked up and called, "Hi, pretty lady."

Courtesy forced Elizabeth to halt. "Hi...Buddy, isn't it?" she replied with a reluctant smile.

Mrs. Butley slid off the edge of the desk. "Oh, hello, ma'am. Are you and Reverend O'Connor all finished, then?"

Aware of the two other pairs of eyes that watched her from the inner office, Elizabeth murmured, "Yes, we're finished."

Mrs. Butley surveyed her pallid features worriedly. "I do hope the reverend was able to help you with your problem."

"Everything's taken care of. Thank you for your concern." She tried again to escape, but a large hand curled with aching familiarity around her arm, restraining her.

"I'll walk you to your car," Grant said in an undertone.

"If you insist."

"I do insist." Grant was aware of the confusion on the faces of the other adults in the room, the covert glances at his fingers holding his wife's elbow, and he realized he was no more ready to offer explanations than Elizabeth was. To divert attention, he grinned at the boy behind the desk. "Hi, Buddy. I can see you've wheedled yourself into Mrs. Butley's good graces. Have any luck finding worms after I left?"

"No, thir," the child lisped, his mouth full of cake. "I quit. It wasn't no fun by myself."

"We'll try again later." Grant looked at his secretary, then at Suzanne, who stood just behind him, staring at him and Elizabeth with troubled brown eyes. Firmly he said, "If you two will excuse us for a moment..."

"Of course, reverend," Mrs. Butley replied.

Behind them Suzanne ventured uncertainly, "Grantland, I—"

Another voice drifted through the French windows, impatient yet musical. "Buddy! Buddy Waaaalker, where are you?"

The little boy jumped to his feet. "Here, Holly!" he squealed, jarring Elizabeth's eardrums, and a moment later a tall, rangy young woman about Suzanne's age came running along the flagstone path that led from the parsonage.

Her long, tawny pigtail streamed behind her as she approached the church. She wore a University of Arkansas sweat shirt emblazoned with the silhouette of a wild pig, the razorback, the school's mascot, and her polyester pants were smeared with flour, as if she'd absently wiped her fingers on her thigh. Elizabeth looked at her with surprise. Somehow she'd expected Grant's housekeeper to be older.

When she burst into the office, Holly Walker's hazel eyes focused at once on her little brother. Jamming the remainder of his nut bread into his mouth, he peered at his sister from beneath beetled brows. She glared and swept him into her arms. "So there you are, Raymond Buddy Walker! Am I going to have to paddle you to make you mind?"

Buddy giggled and kissed his sister crumbily on the cheek. "I love you, Holly."

With a resigned sigh his sister shook her head and hugged him. Chuckling, she implored Mrs. Butley, "Honestly, Doris, what am I supposed to do with this child? I *told* him—" She broke off when she noticed the other people in the room.

Her long, rather thin body grew rigid as her gaze flicked from Grant to Suzanne, but when she saw Elizabeth, she hesitated, frowning as if trying to place her. "Dr. O'Connor, Suzanne...ma'am."

Elizabeth felt Grant's fingers close around her arm. "Hello," she said, noting curiously that Holly was the only other person she had met so far who addressed Grant by his correct title of "Doctor" rather than the more common but inaccurate, "Reverend." She assumed Holly's careful speech had something to do with her having attended college.

Suzanne's greeting was grudging. "Hi, Holly."

"I beg your pardon, Dr. O'Connor," Holly said stiltedly after a moment. "I hope my brother didn't disturb you. He was supposed to play in the garden, but—"

"But there ain't nobody to play with!" Buddy protested pettishly, trying to squirm out of his sister's arms. Her grip tightened.

"You mean there 'isn't anybody,'" she corrected in low, stern tones, "but that doesn't matter. You know you're supposed to stay where I can see you, at least until Jimmy and Darrell get home from school. You mustn't bother people."

"Holly, he wasn't bothering anyone," Grant said. "In fact, I rather enjoy having him around. He livens up the place."

"Thank you, doctor, but that's not the point. Buddy has to learn to pay attention to me." The boy wriggled again, and this time she let him slide through her arms. "Oh, go play on the seesaw, squirt." She sighed, swatting his bottom easily.

"But Holly, you can't seesaw by *yourself*!"

"All right, the swing, then!" And with a shrill whoop Buddy scampered out into the breeze.

For a moment Holly was silent as she watched the boy mount the rickety swing set and begin to twist the chains, so that they scraped loudly and chillingly. Then, taking a deep breath, she looked at Grant again. "I really do apologize for Buddy, Dr. O'Connor. I know he's rambunctious, but it's only because he's so lonesome and bored. His big brothers are in school all day long, as you know, and his best friend's family just moved to Tulsa to find work. The other children his age have either started kindergarten this year or else, if their birthdays fall after the cutoff date the way Buddy's does, they're going to private nursery school."

Suzanne cut in sweetly, "Really, Holly, I'm surprised you don't put your brother in nursery school, too. I'm sure it'd quiet him down."

Elizabeth felt Grant tense, but before he could speak Holly answered her opponent. Her shoulders straightened in an unconscious gesture of pride. "My brother was in nursery school, Suzanne. He was doing very well—he even showed signs of starting to learn to read. But then we had to pull him out because we couldn't afford the fees anymore—after *your* brother saw fit to fire my father from his job at the pottery!"

The longer Elizabeth listened to the exchange between the two younger women, the more uncomfortable she became. She realized she was witnessing what appeared to be only the latest skirmish in a long-running battle, and she had no wish to be drawn into it. Surreptitiously she tugged at the hand still clenched around her arm. When Grant looked down at her, she whispered, "Please. I really must be going."

"Very well. If you'll excuse us..." he murmured to the others, and he led Elizabeth out into the dark, stuffy hallway.

The silence was oppressive as they traversed the corridor. Neither spoke; even the sound of their footsteps was absorbed by the carpeting and the thick draperies. Just inside the entrance Elizabeth hesitated. She knew this moment of farewell meant little, that it was only a redundant reenactment of their real parting five years earlier, but perversely she wanted to delay it as long as possible. Glancing around for something, anything, to say so long as it wasn't goodbye, she spotted the row of interior doors she had noticed when she first entered the building. With arch lightness she asked, "There's something I have to find out, Grant, or else it's going to bother me all day. I realize I don't know much about churches, but what on earth is a 'crying room'?"

Grant's brows rose. "Crying rooms are fairly common features of Southern churches, dating back to the days when most people brought their children with them to Sunday services. Essentially they're soundproof rooms with a big window looking out into the sanctuary. The service is piped in over the PA system. That way people with fussy babies can still hear what's going on without disturbing anyone else. Or, for that matter, the room provides a little privacy for any adults who may be moved to tears by the sermon...."

Aware she sounded asinine, Elizabeth persisted, "My goodness, does that happen often?"

"Well, not often during *my* sermons, honey," he drawled ironically.

Again they fell silent. Elizabeth gazed helplessly at Grant. Stripes of amber and red light from the narrow stained-glass windows fell across him, gilding his strong features, setting his auburn hair ablaze. The ache inside her throbbed so strongly she had to bite her lip to keep from gasping in pain. *Why did you leave me,* her mind cried one last time.

She knew the question would never again be asked aloud.

Staring down at her purse, she unfastened the catch and delved inside for her car keys. As she gripped the key ring, one end of her spotted scarf pulled out with it, and she tucked the colorful scrap of silk back carefully. She took a deep breath. When she looked up at her husband again, her face was an ivory mask, dignified and inanimate. Her lips scarcely moved as she said, "That's it, then."

Grant frowned. "I told you I'd walk you to your car."

She shook her head. "Thank you, but that's not necessary." She blinked, her polite composure threatened by the stinging behind her eyes. She could feel her throat constricting. "Grant," she whispered hoarsely, "while I don't pretend to understand what has brought you to this place, in this—this capacity, I do hope everything turns out the way y-you—" Her voice choked off completely. She spun away and shoved open the front door.

She didn't look back to see if he followed her. Her strides were firm, resolute as she moved toward the Porsche, glinting brightly in the sunlight. Dry foliage still rustled and skittered across the walk, and the warm breeze carried with it the sweet tang of burning oak leaves. She told herself it was the smoke in the air that made her eyes water.

"Liza, please wait."

When she reached the curb, his voice was right behind her, and she quickly hung her head so that ruffled wings of hair hid her face from him. Jamming the key into the door latch, she opened her handbag once more to fish around for her sunglasses. She saw his shadow fall across the smooth silver paint, but the image shimmered and wavered blearily.

"Please," he said again, and only after her eyes were safely camouflaged behind dark tinted lenses did she dare look at him. She knew her disguise had failed when rough yet gentle fingers reached up to trace the lines of dampness on her cheek.

"Oh, Liza." He sighed. "If only—" His words were drowned out by the dissonant roar of a powerful but ill-tuned engine, a car racing in their direction. Grant lifted his head, scowling. "What the hell?" he muttered as he stared past her shoulder.

Suddenly his face turned ashen. "My *God*!" he yelped, and his hands dug bruisingly into her arms. Before Elizabeth even realized what was happening, Grant lifted her bodily and heaved her away from the street, onto a pile of leaves on the church lawn. With a guttural cry he flung his long torso across hers just as an old Buick, battered and dotted with rust-red primer, jumped the curb and plowed into the back of her Porsche.

CHAPTER FOUR

ELIZABETH LAY SPRAWLED on the grass, crushed beneath Grant's sheltering body. Winded and stunned, she could still hear the crash, the ominous shattering of glass reverberating in her ears. Her head throbbed where it had struck the ground. A sharp twig poked painfully into the small of her back. Blinking, she tried to clear her vision so she could focus on the face, gray and distressed, that hovered just above hers. She told herself it was the fall and not the all-too-familiar intimacy of their bodies reclined and entwined that took her breath away.

Straining for air, she gasped, "I *knew* you'd put on weight, Grant!"

Instantly he levered himself away from her. His eyes searched her features. "Are you all right?"

"Y-yes," she said shakily, pushing herself into a sitting position. She fumbled for her sunglasses on the ground beside her. One of the lenses was a spiderweb of cracks. Dropping the glasses, she began to brush away the crumbled leaves that clung to her dress.

Almost at the same moment, the door of the Buick slammed, and the driver stumbled heavily onto the lawn. "Oh, God, I'm sorry," he groaned. "Ma'am, reverend, I didn't mean...oh, please, I'm so sorry!" Elizabeth could feel Grant stiffen in dismayed recognition, and she lifted her head to stare at the man approaching.

Except for a bright-red streak marking the soft folds of skin under his jaw, as if he'd hit his chin on the steering wheel, he appeared unharmed. He was of medium height, with a once-muscular body turning slack and paunchy. At first Elizabeth assumed he was middle-aged, but then she lowered her estimate. From the unsilvered darkness of his brown hair she judged he must be somewhere on the green side of forty-five. However old he was, he'd been drinking, and for a long time.

His intoxication was obvious from the lurch in his step, the repeated squint and lift of his veined eyelids as if he were fighting sleep. His plaid flannel shirt and heavy work pants reeked of stale beer.

"Reverend, please, I didn't mean to hurt anyone," he pleaded again. "I was just— The damned brakes must've give out or something."

"'Or something,'" Grant muttered impatiently, wondering how long a bender his parishioner had been on this time. "Don't worry. Nobody's hurt." He wished he could summon up a little of the charity and forbearance that were supposed to be hallmarks of his calling. The man was about as pathetic a case as Grant was ever liable to encounter in his ministry, a decent-enough guy beaten down repeatedly by personal and economic defeats. Who could say for certain that he himself wouldn't react in a similar manner, given those same circumstances?

Besides, Grant reminded himself grimly, there were far worse sins than drinking too much.

But when his eyes flicked over his wife's pale face and he saw the way she recoiled from the driver's helpfully outstretched hand, it was all Grant could do to restrain himself from slugging the man.

Bounding to his feet, Grant pulled Elizabeth with him.

She swayed slightly, and he slid his arm protectively around her waist to steady her. His eyes closed briefly at the contact. He had forgotten how very good it felt to hold her. "Are you sure you're all right?"

"Yes, of course," she murmured. Then she took her first look at the demolished Porsche, and Grant had to tighten his grip to keep her from falling again.

The front end of the vehicle appeared unharmed, the silver sheen almost mocking in its perfection. But at the rear, broken glass lay everywhere, shards of the sports car's back window, the Buick's headlights. The larger car had bounced as it hit the curb. Somehow the front wheels had lifted so they cleared the Porsche's sturdy bumper and landed with a downward impact, caving in the engine compartment completely. Even a cursory glance was enough to convince Elizabeth that the motor had probably been jarred loose from its block.

Hollowly she said, "Well, I guess that's one way to break in a new engine...."

Grant scowled. He was afraid Elizabeth's wry remark sprang less from resignation than from shock. Hugging her bracingly, he assured her, "Liza, everything will be fine." She smiled skeptically and pulled away.

All over the neighborhood doors slammed. People scurried out onto their front walks to see what had happened. Several ran toward the church, and from down the street an elderly man hollered, "Reverend O'Connor, are you and Clyde and the lady okay? Should I phone the ambulance?"

"No, thank you, Mr. Green—everyone's fine!" Grant yelled back. Behind him the church door banged.

The three women Elizabeth had met in the office raced toward the sidewalk and the growing throng. "Reverend, what happened?" Mrs. Butley cried, while Suzanne groaned at the destruction of the "fabulous" car. Holly stared frozen at the wreckage. Elizabeth was surprised when the young housekeeper separated from the crowd to approach the Buick's driver.

Her little brother scampered after her. "Wow! Wait'll I tell Jimmy and Darrell!" he crowed, gawking at the Porsche with saucer eyes.

"Better stay back, son," Clyde warned, and Buddy retreated to kick at the scattered leaf pile.

Holly's rangy body seemed oddly tense beneath her college sweat shirt. "You sure you're not hurt?" she said. The driver fingered his tender jaw and shrugged sullenly. In silence Holly gazed reproachfully at him until he flushed and shifted his weight from one foot to the other. Then all at once she burst out, "Oh, daddy, how could you? You *promised*!"

Elizabeth gasped. Holly Walker's father?

It didn't seem possible—certainly there was no discernible resemblance between the boozy driver and the well-spoken young woman, or, for that matter, between him and the small blond boy who romped around the churchyard. Elizabeth heard Clyde plead, "But, baby girl, it wasn't my fault. The brakes—"

"Who cares about the brakes? What were you doing here in the first place—and in that condition? You told me you were going to drive over to Dardanelle to see about a job!"

Clyde Walker's expression darkened with offended dignity at his daughter's interruption. "Don't you speak to me like that, young lady," he declared thickly. "Just because you've been to college.... I may've had to put up with that kind of talk from your mother, but I will not..."

"Poor Holly," someone in the crowd muttered, "Clyde's really tied one on this time."

"Yeah. Whenever he's so far gone that he starts talking about Kayrene...."

"Pardon me," Grant murmured, breaking away to stride resolutely across the grass. When he reached Holly and her father, he laid his large hands on their shoulders in a conciliatory gesture, gentle but firm. "Now listen, both of you. There isn't any point in getting riled. We'll work things out. Right now, let's just all be thankful no one was hurt."

Clyde looked mollified, but Holly remained troubled. She stared in anguish at the mangled automobiles. "That beautiful car..." she wailed, gnawing her lip. When she looked at Grant again, she asked fearfully, "Dr. O'Connor, how are we supposed to pay for the damage? We don't have any insurance."

Listening, Elizabeth tensed as she began to consider the ramifications of the accident. Her lovely, expensive new Porsche, so fresh out of the showroom that the dealer's sticker hadn't even begun to fade, was a wreck, possibly totaled, and all because some red-neck drunk—

Grant countered, "Holly, I expect Ms Swenson has insurance. In fact, I can't imagine her driving a car around the block without first making sure she has complete coverage." He regarded Elizabeth challengingly. "Am I right?"

She didn't know what he wanted her to say. Grant's easy familiarity with the Walkers, his concern for their feelings even when Clyde was clearly in the wrong, were utterly uncharacteristic of the man she had married, the man whose courtesy had been as compassionless as it had been impeccable. This was the man who would have sued someone like Clyde Walker for the shirt off his back—not because he had any wish to make that tattered shirt part of his wardrobe, but because he had a legal right to it.

"You do have collision insurance, don't you, Liza?" Grant repeated leadingly, his gray eyes boring into hers.

Dammit, she thought, *how dare he be so magnanimous!* It wasn't *his* Porsche that had been destroyed, just as it wasn't his insurance premiums that would skyrocket once she filed a claim. But as her lips parted in a caustic retort, she became aware of increasingly inquisitive eyes turning in her direction. Now that the initial shock of the accident had passed, bystanders monitoring the exchange between her and Grant were becoming curious about the minister's out-of-town visitor with the flashy sports car.

Pacing her breathing, Elizabeth replied cautiously, "Of course I have insurance, Grant. It took effect as soon as I signed the registration papers."

The Walkers—in fact, the whole crowd—seemed to sag with relief. But Elizabeth's attention was trained on Grant. His hard mouth shaped the words "thank you" as he smiled winningly.

Winning, Elizabeth thought, suddenly furious not only with Grant but with herself. Of course that was it. She had forgotten that every word between them was a contest, a battle. And as usual, she seemed to be conceding victory. Unable to face his smirking triumph, she whirled away.

But as she moved, all at once she became conscious of the slide of teal-blue wool against her skin, the luxurious drape of the dress she'd bought in Europe—then contrasted the dress with the cheap, worn clothing the Walkers were wearing. She remembered the check she'd blithely written to pay for the Porsche, a check for probably twice as much money as Clyde had ever earned in his best year.

Slowly she looked back over her shoulder. Clustered around Grant were the pathetic, defensive man, the wan girl with suspiciously shimmering eyes...the little boy.... Perhaps this time Grant's object hadn't been to bend her to his will? Could it be that for once he'd acted out of simple charity?

Whatever his motive, suddenly Elizabeth was very glad he'd stopped her before she'd lashed out at Holly's family.

With affected composure she said, "Well, now I suppose it's just a matter of contacting the nearest Porsche agency and getting an estimate on the repairs...."

Someone in the crowd tittered. "Ma'am, I sincerely doubt there's a Porsche dealer in the entire state of Arkansas. You might have to go as far as Oklahoma City—"

"There's one in Fayetteville," Holly interjected surprisingly. "I remember seeing it not too far from the university."

Elizabeth turned to Grant. His broad shoulders lifted. "That's close to a hundred miles away," he murmured. "Assuming they stock the parts you need, they'll still have to be shipped."

"Then how am I supposed to get out of here?"

"You don't," Grant responded bluntly. "Not right away. For the moment, it looks as if you're stuck in Ridleyville."

Elizabeth stared at him and tried not to groan aloud. Stuck in Ridleyville. It sounded like the title of a country-and-western song.

It wasn't the people that bothered her. Everyone she'd met so far had been courteous and friendly and eager to help, the antithesis of their city cousins. Other forces were at work. She gazed uneasily at Grant. Deep inside her fermented an unsettling mixture of frustration and anger and something else she refused to allow herself to think about. She couldn't, she *wouldn't* let it happen again, not when she'd almost escaped him forever.

Reminding herself that she was a capable businesswoman renowned for her cool head—a traffic collision should be child's play compared to some of the crises she'd coped with during the past five years—Elizabeth surveyed the wreck and tried not to wince. The rusty Buick had climbed onto the rear of the Porsche as if the two cars were giant tortoises trying to mate. The grotesque image might have been almost amusing, except that with the engine compartment crushed, the pristine sports car was almost certain to be declared a total loss by the insurance company.

At Elizabeth's side, Suzanne said, "What a mess!"

"It is that," Elizabeth agreed. "Tell me, Miss Bailey, do we have to leave the cars like this until a police officer can take a look at the accident?"

Suzanne frowned. "Around here it'd be the deputy sheriff. And yes, because there's so much damage, you will have to make some kind of report—or at least I think you will. I remember when my brother Bobby Lee was a boy. He was a wild driver, always banging up cars. But it seems to me my daddy was usually able to take care of things without the law getting involved."

Elizabeth glanced sharply at the girl; then her gaze crossed the street to the big house with the white columns. She had already surmised that the Baileys were Ridleyville's "leading"—meaning wealthiest—family. She wondered how much hush money had been passed over the years to keep the Bailey son out of trouble. Perhaps she was being catty, she chided herself. Suzanne seemed to have spoken in all innocence.

Regardless of whether the Baileys' social status granted

them special privileges, Elizabeth realized someone must have reported the collision, because within moments a deputy appeared. Grant introduced Elizabeth to the young man, and after the officer greeted her, he listened somberly to her account of the accident and expressed his regrets. Then, muttering, "Oh, Lord, this'll cost Clyde his license for sure," he turned to the Walkers.

Feeling like an intruder, Elizabeth looked away. It occurred to her that school must have been dismissed for the day; children laden with notebooks and lunch boxes were beginning to appear on the tree-lined street. The instant they spotted the accident, they all darted toward the churchyard to investigate. There was more traffic. Although the collision had taken place at the curb, passing vehicles swerved into the opposing lane to avoid the wreck. When Grant and the deputy approached Elizabeth again, she asked, "Shouldn't we clear the cars off the roadway before someone else runs into them?"

"Good idea, ma'am," the deputy agreed. "Come on, Clyde, let's see what we can do."

"Is there any chance you can back your car off Ms Swenson's?" Grant suggested, and Holly's father, more sober now, climbed behind the wheel of the Buick. But when he tried to start it, the engine wouldn't turn over. "Oh, well, look's like we'll have to do this the hard way," Grant judged when Clyde hopped out.

At once several other men and teenage boys ringed the entangled cars. Grant, Clyde and the deputy grabbed the bumpers. Women and children stepped out of the way, shouting encouragement as the men strained to rock the Buick loose. Metal scraped and rattled. Elizabeth moved closer to supervise, trying not to be distracted by the play of muscles pressing against the fabric of Grant's shirt as he heaved forcefully. By the time it became obvious that manpower alone would not be sufficient to separate the two vehicles, his shirt was plastered against his torso and the musky scent of his overheated flesh was strong in her nostrils. Wiping his face with a handkerchief, he announced, "The cars are practically welded. We're going to need a winch or something."

Elizabeth said, "Earlier today when I stopped for directions at a service station a few blocks from here I noticed a tow truck."

The deputy nodded. "That'd be Mack Winters's place. I'll radio him for you."

The young man jogged across the lawn to his patrol car, and Elizabeth asked Grant pensively, "Since it looks as if it will be a while before an insurance adjuster can get to my car, do you suppose the station owner might let me store it on his lot?" Wearily she ran her fingers through her blond curls. Suddenly she felt very tired.

Grant's eyes were hooded as he watched the action draw her shoulders back, stretching her dress across her high breasts. Enigmatically he murmured, "Liza, I'm sure the owner would be delighted to let you do anything you want."

Elizabeth dropped her arms. She hoped his obscure remark had been a compliment. In the silence that hung between them, she could feel her nerves growing taut. Digging into her handbag for her car keys, she said with deliberate cheerfulness, "At least I can be thankful the luggage compartment wasn't damaged. My clothes should be all right. If nothing else, I can change out of this dirty dress. Once I've cleaned up, I can telephone that dealer in Fayetteville—"

"Just don't expect to be able to get anything settled today," Grant cut in darkly.

Elizabeth realized she'd been babbling. Her voice was more subdued as she agreed, "No, of course not. I know it's going to take time. And since I obviously won't be driving on to Little Rock tonight, could someone please direct me to the nearest hotel?"

An odd hush fell over the people clustered around her. Mrs. Butley explained, "Ma'am, I'm afraid Ridleyville doesn't have a hotel."

"A motel, then. Surely there's something available along the highway."

"Not anymore. There used to be one, but it shut down after the interstate rerouted traffic away from here."

Elizabeth felt hollow. She tried to assimilate the knowledge that, for the moment, at least, she was stranded in a strange town, without transportation, without a place to stay. The realization confused and infuriated her. This was the middle of the United States, dammit, but she felt as isolated as if she'd suddenly been dropped into an alien country—more so, in fact, since she'd never had any problems coping in Europe.

Gradually she became aware of Grant studying her intently, his gaze unfathomable beneath a drooping lock of auburn hair. She hated for him to see her vulnerable like this. When he left her, she had sworn she would never ever ask him for help. Now she knew she had no choice. She swallowed. Hoarsely she asked, "Any suggestions?"

Tenderness welled up in him as he watched her struggle. He could almost hear her pride creaking its resistance to even this small effort to bend. Before he could reply, Suzanne chirped, "Grantland, your friend is more than welcome to stay with Bobby Lee and me while she's waiting to take care of her car. We have plenty of room."

Astonished, Elizabeth stared at the petite girl in the red

silk blouse. "That's very generous of you, Miss Bailey," she said. She knew Suzanne's offer probably sprang less from generosity than from a desire to keep close watch over a suspected rival and that if she did choose to stay with the Baileys, she might be subjected to a lot of none-too-subtle probing. Still, what choice did she have? Elizabeth sighed. "If you're sure I won't be a burden, then thank you, I do appreciate—"

"Yes, thank you, Suzanne," Grant cut in, his tone polite but adamant. "It's very kind of you to offer to put yourself out that way, but it's really not necessary. Until her car can be repaired or replaced, Ms Swenson will stay at the parsonage with me."

The gasps, the shocked expressions on the faces in the crowd were so exaggerated they seemed almost comical. Elizabeth declared, "Come on, Grant, you can't just—"

"Why not? It's the obvious solution, and you know it!"

Mrs. Butley sputtered, "B-but, Reverend O'Connor—"

The elderly man from down the street stormed querulously, "Now see here, young man—"

Grant silenced them all with a wave of one of his large hands. Elizabeth's mouth clamped shut, and she stepped back, watching his eyes narrow as he assessed the reactions of his neighbors. She had seen that look before, that air of grim resolve. Usually it had been in a boardroom, toward the end of grueling negotiations, just before he went in for the kill.

A woman with a light cardigan tossed over her cotton shift stepped forward, her face pale but determined. She nodded cordially to Elizabeth, then looked at Grant again. "Reverend," she said, picking her words with care, "we all know you're a good man, and we realize that right now you're probably just thinking of giving aid to the wayfaring stranger, as we're directed to do. I know there's room at the parsonage for any number of guests, but being a man of the cloth and all, I guess you haven't stopped to consider how it would look or what people might say if this lady were to stay overnight with you, a bachelor—"

Grant's expression softened. Gently he interrupted her. "But that's just it," he said with a reassuring smile. The woman hesitated, puzzled, and he continued gravely, "Although I do appreciate your kind words, I can tell you and the others have misinterpreted the situation here. Ms Swenson isn't a stranger—just as I'm not a bachelor."

He paused, and Elizabeth could see the group stir as the import of his words began to sink in. When Grant was sure everyone's attention was riveted on him and the elegant woman at his side, he explained calmly, "I promise there's not a reason in the world for anyone to get upset if Ms Swenson stays with me. Liza is my wife."

ELIZABETH TRUDGED WEARILY up the steep, narrow staircase, dragging her wheeled suitcase behind her as she followed Holly. At the landing she leaned against the railing to catch her breath.

In the silence at the top of the stairs, Elizabeth could hear the breeze rustling the ropes of red ivy that clung to the eaves of the creaky frame house. Boyish shouts filtered through from outside, where Buddy Walker had been joined by his older brothers, Jimmy and Darrell. Inside the parsonage the only sound was the low rumble of adult voices in the parlor downstairs. Now that the accident had been cleared away and the deputy had left, Grant was having a heart-to-heart talk with Clyde. The words were indecipherable, but Grant's tone seemed to mix stern reproof with compassion.

Holly's eyes probed Elizabeth's face. "Are you certain you weren't hurt in the wreck? After all, you were standing pretty close to the curb when my dad—when it happened."

Elizabeth could hear the embarrassment, and worse, the shame, still roughening the housekeeper's voice. She hated the idea that Holly felt guilty for her father's actions. Earnestly she insisted, "I really wish you'd quit worrying. The accident wasn't your fault. Everything's going to be all right. *I'm* all right."

"But you don't look all right. You're very pale."

"I'm just tired," Elizabeth said. "It's been a... an extraordinary day."

For a moment Holly's brows quirked, giving her smooth features a cynical cast that made her look far older than her years. "'Extraordinary'? *That's* an understatement. Your husband's bombshell was the most extraordinary and exciting thing that's happened in this town since the last kiln fire at the Bailey Pottery!" She regarded Elizabeth candidly. "And Dr. O'Connor, who's not exactly ordinary himself, claims there's 'no reason in the world' for questions. Does he really believe that?"

Watching the younger woman's thin face settle back into a pleasant, inquisitive smile, Elizabeth thought again how hard it was to believe Holly was Clyde Walker's daughter. Bright and well-educated, she didn't seem to resemble him either physically or mentally; Elizabeth supposed Holly must take after her mother, the Kay-something Clyde had mentioned so heatedly. Glancing at the University of Arkansas sweat shirt, she wondered if Holly had graduated from the school. Whatever her background, surely she was equipped for something better than keeping house.

Elizabeth decided to pay Holly the courtesy of being frank. "Of course Grant doesn't believe you won't have questions. But by phrasing his remarks the way he did, he relieves himself of the burden of explanation, and he puts anyone else in the wrong who dares to ask for any. It's a basic ploy in power politics."

Holly pursed her lips. "Interesting," she muttered. With a shrug she reached for the strap on Elizabeth's suitcase and began to tow it down the dimly lit hall. Outside the first door she paused. "From the remarks you made to Dr. O'Connor at the church, I don't suppose you plan to share his room?"

The door was slightly ajar, and glancing sidelong through it, Elizabeth spotted a mahogany four-poster covered with a beautiful, intricately hand-crocheted bedspread, once white, now ecru with age. In New York their king-size bed had been draped with a masculine-looking, earth-tone coverlet selected by a decorator long before Elizabeth had ever moved in with Grant. The two of them had planned to redo their home together, but somehow there had never been time. Turning away, Elizabeth whispered thickly, "No, Holly, Grant and I won't be sharing."

Without further comment Holly led Elizabeth down the hall.

The guest room was immaculate but drab, its fussy, flowered wallpaper faded except for brighter squares where pictures had once hung. The dark furniture was old, yet not quite old enough to have come back into fashion, and it had obviously been of only moderate quality when new. The most attractive items in the room were the crocheted dresser set and the lace curtains in the window.

When Elizabeth mentioned them, Holly explained, "The last pastor's wife made those. The house is full of her things. Needlework was her hobby, but I think mostly she was trying to find inexpensive ways to pretty up the place. She and her husband were here for twenty years, and Doris Butley tells me that in all that time the deacons never once allocated money for a serious redecorating job. They claimed it was enough that the parsonage was kept in good repair."

"How frustrating it must have been for her."

Holly shrugged. "I don't expect it's ever very easy being the wife of a clergyman."

Suddenly Elizabeth became engrossed in the task of arranging her toilet articles on the dresser. Watching her, Holly said, "The bathroom's down the hall, and there are fresh towels laid out for you. If there's anything else you need, please just ask."

Elizabeth aligned her brushes and combs with unnecessary precision. "Thank you. I'm sure I'll be very comfortable." She knew she sounded stilted.

Holly regarded her uncertainly. "Well, if there's nothing else I can do for you right now, Dr. O'Connor has offered to drive my family and me back to our house. I think I should get my father and brothers settled for the evening. Usually I have a casserole or something prepared for Dr. O'Connor's dinner before I leave, but today, what with one thing and another..." She hesitated. "Dr. O'Connor said you all could manage to feed yourselves, but if you think I ought to come back later—"

"Holly," Elizabeth reminded her kindly, "Grant and I managed the whole time we lived together. I'm sure we'll survive one evening."

Holly's scowl relaxed. "You're right. I did forget. I reckon it's just going to take a little while to get used to thinking of Dr. O'Connor as a married man. I always assumed he was a widower." She turned to leave, but at the bedroom door she paused and looked back at Elizabeth. "You know," she said, "I really *ought* to have recognized you the minute I saw you in the church office!" Before Elizabeth could ask her what she meant, Holly disappeared into the hallway.

Elizabeth perched on the edge of the bed and slipped out of her long, high-heeled boots. When she heard a car door slam outside, she walked to the window and watched the five Walkers climb into a late-model compact car and drive away, Grant behind the wheel. She wondered if the inconspicuous domestic sedan came with the house. Like the parsonage, it seemed inadequate but modest, and completely unsuited to the man she used to know.

Gathering up a change of clothing from her suitcase, Elizabeth padded down the hallway to the bathroom. She showered quickly, relishing the cool spray as she washed away the grit from her fall. After she dried off, she dressed again in natural linen slacks and a soft shirt of unbleached Indian gauze, the semisheer fabric so richly embroidered across the front she didn't need a bra. She felt comfortable and refreshed for the first time all day.

Staring at her tired reflection in the damp mirror over the small sink, Elizabeth massaged the lines of fatigue under her eyes and decided she'd be wise to rest for the evening. Her telephone calls could wait until morning. In the meantime, she and Grant could scrounge up something to eat, and then perhaps they'd chat about something pleasantly impersonal until Elizabeth could reasonably excuse herself for bed. It all sounded very calm and undemanding; relaxing. In fact, Elizabeth admitted sardonically, it sounded exactly like the kind of quiet domestic evening the two of them had so rarely had an opportunity to share when they lived together.

Her fingertips stilled. Was that why their marriage had failed—because they'd never had time to be quiet together, or for that matter, just to *be* together? When she thought back over the fewer than eighteen months from the day they'd met and become lovers to the day Grant had walked out on her, she had to admit they'd spent very little time in each other's company. They'd both been too caught up in their respective careers, she perhaps even more than he. Always full of energy and tension, always flying off in opposite directions, as if they were electrons whose very similarities made it impossible for them to be together. Even when they were together long enough to make love, their passion was too short-lived to be fulfilling.

"Was that what he meant when he said he was looking for peace?" Elizabeth mused aloud. Just then she heard a telephone ring somewhere in the house.

She considered just letting it ring; after all, if the call was important, whoever it was would probably try again later, after Grant got back. But then, she remembered, a minister was rather like a doctor, on call at all times. The person on the other end of the line might be one of his parishioners in the midst of some spiritual crisis. She could at least take a message.

As she listened for the direction of the bell, Elizabeth thought sardonically that taking a message would be the most wifely act she'd performed for Grant in five years.

But when, after frantic moments of searching, Elizabeth located the telephone on a nightstand beside Grant's bed, to her surprise she discovered the call was for her.

"Oh, wonderful! I was hoping I'd reach you, Ms Swenson—or I suppose now I ought to call you Mrs. O'Connor...." Suzanne's determinedly bright voice lifted leadingly.

"How nice of you to call," Elizabeth answered smoothly. "What may I do for you?"

Suzanne floundered, obviously disconcerted by Elizabeth's refusal to follow her lead. "Well, I wondered—that is, I just wanted to make sure you've recovered from that awful accident and that you're settled comfortably."

"I'm fine, thank you. Holly has made me very comfortable."

"Oh, yes, Holly," Suzanne repeated, her tone affected and sober. "A nice girl, but so sad, with all those little brothers and that *father*...." When once again Elizabeth didn't reply, Suzanne continued, "Actually, Ms Swenson, Holly Walker is part of the reason I've called. I'm sure she's going to be too busy tonight caring for her own family to look after you and the reverend, so I wondered if you and Grantland—your husband, I mean—would like to join my brother and me for dinner?"

Elizabeth hesitated. The last thing she wanted to do was spend an evening parrying Suzanne's unsubtle probes, but she had no idea what Grant would want her to say. The Baileys, after all, were his friends. "It's very kind of you to invite us," she answered carefully, "and just as soon as Grant returns, I'll ask—"

"Don't say no!" Suzanne cried. All at once she sounded sincere, and very young. "It'll just be potluck, very casual. You wouldn't have to dress up or anything. Oh, please! You don't know what it would mean for me to have a chance to talk to someone *new* for a change...."

Almost before she realized it, Elizabeth had accepted Suzanne's invitation.

Setting down the receiver, Elizabeth shook her head wryly. She must be weak from fatigue. Her associates at Avotel would faint if they ever heard of Ms Swenson actually giving in to someone else's pleading. Better never let the board find out.

She turned away from the nightstand and for the first time allowed her eyes to survey her surroundings. Like the guest room, the master bedroom was small and indifferently furnished, nondescript except for the beautiful handwork left behind by the wife of Grant's predecessor.

Elizabeth stopped at the dresser to admire the long, narrow scarf that covered it. As she fingered the delicate stitchery, she thought how ironic it was that the woman who had crocheted the intricately patterned cloth had done so as a thrifty means of decorating. Her work was the equal of some of the fabulously expensive Flemish laces Elizabeth had seen in Bruges.

Sighing, she started to leave; then she noticed the small, gilt-framed picture propped up on the far end of the dresser. All at once she knew why Holly had said she looked familiar.

It was probably a wonder anyone could recognize her from that snapshot, Elizabeth admitted, biting her lip. Over the years the instant-print photograph had faded, its colors taking on a bluish tint. Despite the distortion, the thin girl in the severe gray business suit still looked like what she'd been, incredibly young, endearingly innocent, her immaturity only emphasized by the way she'd scraped her blond hair into a tight little knob of a topknot. Her pale face still glowed with love. As she gazed up into the hard, gaunt features of the auburn-haired man who held her possessively against him, the wide gold band on her left hand gleamed, shiny new.

Yes, they had been married on their lunch hour by a judge, with only his secretary and receptionist for witnesses. The ceremony lasted one minute and forty-five seconds.

Nobody thought to bring flowers. As soon as the official had scrawled his name on the bottom of the license, they had hurried out the door—Grant had a two-o'clock appointment and Elizabeth was expecting an overseas call—almost colliding with a wedding party of Puerto Ricans just coming in. The bride was carrying yellow roses, and the groomsmen all wore tuxedos to match. A dozen jubilant family members trailed after them.

As Elizabeth and her husband struggled to pass the people streaming into the judge's chambers, suddenly Grant noticed a young girl clutching a small instant camera in her gloved hands. Whipping a fifty-dollar bill from his wallet, he asked her something in rapid Spanish, and before Elizabeth realized what he was doing, he jerked her into his arms while the child snapped their wedding picture, the only photograph ever taken of the two of them together.

The photograph she had searched for frantically as she packed to leave for Europe; the photograph over which she'd wept hot, despairing tears when she thought it was lost.

The photograph Grant must have taken with him the day he walked out on her.

CHAPTER FIVE

"ARE YOU SURE you want to go through with this?" Grant asked as he and Elizabeth crossed the street in front of the church and entered the shadowed garden surrounding the big white house. "I thought you needed to rest."

She tried not to snag her linen slacks on one of the scraggly bushes covered in rose hips lining the front walk. "Suzanne insisted. Besides, I assumed it was what you'd want." She smiled uncomfortably. "I'm sorry, Grant. I guess I forgot I don't know you well enough anymore to make assumptions about what you want."

Grant stopped; his eyes narrowed. "Liza," he grated, "you never knew me."

Elizabeth searched the planes of his face, limned in the amber porchlight. "Apparently not," she agreed tonelessly.

After a moment she turned away. Her voice was stiff as she repeated, "I do apologize for accepting the invitation without consulting you first. It's just that I thought these people were your friends."

"They're my parishioners. Or rather, Suzanne is. Robert Bailey rarely puts in an appearance on Sunday mornings."

Recalling the bitter reference Holly Walker had made to her father's being fired by Suzanne's brother, Elizabeth asked, "He's some sort of local businessman, isn't he?"

"He runs the Bailey Pottery, which is about the only major employer left in Ridleyville. It's a family concern. I believe Suzanne may be part owner, but Bobby Lee manages it."

Elizabeth hesitated. Lightly she ventured, "I couldn't help noticing that she seems to have a mad crush on you."

"I know." Grant sighed. "I wish she didn't. But some women get crushes on clergymen the same way they get them on doctors or college professors or anyone in a so-called position of authority. It's an occupational hazard, and about all the man can do is pretend he hasn't noticed." He lifted his shoulders in a guarded shrug. "You needn't worry, Liza. Suzanne's very young and romantic, but I expect her infatuation will die a quick death, now that she knows about you."

He turned to mount the steps; Elizabeth forestalled him by touching his arm. She chose her words with care. "Grant, you and I both know our marriage is only a legal fiction. If you...have any interest in responding to Suzanne, or to anyone else, for that matter, please don't let my presence bother you. I promise I won't interfere."

Grant's expression was absolutely unreadable as he stared down at her. "That's very generous of you," he muttered. Pulling away, he sprinted up the wide steps and pressed the doorbell.

Chimes pealed and echoed hollowly deep in the house. As the guests loitered on the porch, waiting for someone to answer, Elizabeth's eyes scaled the white fluted pillars, tall and impressive, that flanked the entrance to the house. From a distance the columns had looked like marble, but up close they appeared to be made not of wood or stone but some kind of ceramic; the ornate molded cornice over the front door, too. Elizabeth wondered if Bailey Pottery had manufactured these pieces. The workmanship was good, but patches of white paint had flaked away, revealing a dark-brown underglaze. The signs of deterioration saddened her. "This must have been quite a showplace in its day."

"It reminds me a little of the way my folks' home used to look, when I was growing up."

"Before you poured all that money into it, you mean?"

He nodded. Wistfully he remembered that although he'd shown her photographs, Elizabeth had never actually seen the estate outside Savannah that had belonged to the O'Connors' since a carpetbagging Yankee-Irish forebear bought it for back taxes from an impoverished Confederate colonel. That had been during Reconstruction. Over the generations most of the surrounding lands had been sold off, but the house itself remained. After marrying Elizabeth, Grant had hoped to arrange time in their frantic schedules to take her to Georgia on a belated honeymoon. He hadn't guessed that when he did at last return, he would be alone and in despair, like the Prodigal Son.

Nowadays the house was quaintly charming, snug and comfortable behind its hedge of palmettos, a far cry from what it had been when he was a boy. A century in Savannah's marshy seaport climate had taken its toll; the structure had decayed to the point where the only alternatives were to spend a very large amount of money virtually rebuilding it, or else to raze it. His parents, less than sanguine about the dry rot, mildew and myriad pests infesting the house, had been perfectly willing to accept the offer of a real-estate developer who wanted to build an industrial complex on the property.

But to Grant it had been home, and he loved it still. Although only a college student at the time, he was already displaying an uncanny intuition about stocks and investment, so he had begged his mother and father to delay one year, just twelve short months, to see if he could raise the funds to save the house.

Wheels within wheels, he thought sadly, remembering how each event in his life seemed to have led inexorably to the next. Because he was a good son, his parents had given him the opportunity he asked for. Because he was Grant, he had succeeded. And because he was a success, he had taken the first steps down the damning path that had eventually led him away from everything he truly cared about....

Glibly he said, "You know, Liza, the irony is that after getting the old place fixed up exactly the way I thought my folks wanted it, they don't live there anymore. My mother says the damp aggravates her arthritis. I hope that's the reason. I'd hate to think she and dad stayed in Savannah an extra twenty years because I bullied them into it. In any case, now that the two of them have moved to Mexico, where they seem to be thriving, and there's talk of turning the old homestead into a sort of superior bed-and-breakfast inn."

"But if your parents don't want the house anymore," Elizabeth asked reasonably, "why don't you take it? Quite apart from you being the person who almost single-handedly kept it from being leveled by a bulldozer, it's your heritage."

Grant's smile grew mocking. "But what good's a heritage if there's no one to pass it on to?"

Elizabeth recoiled as if from a body blow. Stumbling back, she could feel the blood drain from her face. Painfully she choked, "Oh, Grant, that's not fair, and you know it!"

Baffled, he stared at her ashen features. Only after a moment did he realize the interpretation she must have put on his ill-chosen words, that she had mistakenly thought his bitter humor was directed at her. "Liza, please!" He reached for her. "For God's sake, you can't believe I'd—"

The front door opened.

A jovial voice boomed from the doorway. "Sorry, reverend, I didn't mean to keep you—well, well, *well!*"

Shaking off Grant's comforting hand, Elizabeth struggled to regain her composure as she turned to face the man who greeted them. Her lips curled upward into a polite smile, but her inward reaction was curiously mixed. Suzanne's brother? Although Grant had described Robert Bailey as Ridleyville's leading businessman, from Suzanne's passing references Elizabeth had somehow pictured an incipient "good ol' boy," a pampered youth who drove recklessly and gawked at "girlie" magazines. This man appeared to be at least ten years older than his sister, dressed with a theatrical sophistication that seemed out of place on a Southern veranda—and he had a body that could only be described as that of a "hunk."

In fact, Elizabeth decided as Grant performed introductions, Robert Bailey bore a distinct resemblance to a poster she'd seen in Minnesota thumbtacked to her eldest niece's door. Amelia's daughter had assured her that the macho movie star was currently the subject of every American woman's most torrid fantasies. Elizabeth just wished the similarity didn't appear to be deliberate.

Robert Bailey was an attractive man, one who would probably seem especially exotic and desirable in a town like Ridleyville, but Elizabeth found the spectacle of anyone in his thirties mimicking an actor rather depressing.

Suzanne's brother wasn't quite as tall as his hero, about five foot ten, but his muscular body was displayed to equal advantage in custom-cut sportswear. The shirt was unbuttoned halfway to his low-slung belt and tight slacks. Several gold chains dangled into his thatch of chest hair. When he held the door open so that Elizabeth and Grant could step into the brightly lit entryway, she noticed that his darkbrown hair and mustache were styled identically to those of the actor. Against his rugged, tanned skin the blue eyes that flicked back and forth between his guests were just as bright. Elizabeth wondered if he wore tinted contact lenses.

I suppose he's not bad—if you like copies, she decided cynically. She herself didn't.

While she studied him, Elizabeth greeted Robert Bailey with her usual firm, businesslike handshake. From his expression she could tell the gesture startled him; she wondered if Southern women didn't shake hands. When she tried to withdraw from his grip, he refused to release her. Instead his fingers curled around hers in a way that was entirely personal. He assessed her slim figure with a candid warmth she supposed was meant to be flattering. When his eyes were drawn to her embroidered gauze blouse, Elizabeth suddenly wished she'd put on a bra.

"Well, well, well," he repeated effusively, "so you're the mysterious Mrs. O'Connor who's got my baby sister in such a state! Now I think I understand why the reverend's been keeping you all to himself. In fact, I'm surprised he's willing to share you even for one evening."

Grant's lips tightened as he watched Elizabeth try to free her hand from her host's grasp. He didn't miss Bobby Lee's interest in her unfettered softness. Jealous fury pulsed through him, but he forced his voice to remain cool as he murmured, "It was good of you and Suzanne to invite us to dinner."

Bobby Lee glanced at Grant, and his grip loosened. "After that terrible accident, it was the least we could do. Besides, I guess I feel a little responsible. Poor Clyde's been getting worse and worse ever since I had to let him go from the pottery. I had hoped the shock of losing his job would jolt him out of this depression of his, but...." He shrugged. "Well, from what Suzanne told me, I guess we should all just be grateful nobody was hurt."

Elizabeth stepped back. "But there was never much chance of anyone being injured, Mr. Bailey. I wasn't even in my car when the collision occurred."

"Thank God for that!" he intoned piously. "But please, Mrs. O'Connor, call me Bobby Lee. Everyone does. And I believe my sister said your name is Liza, isn't it?"

"Elizabeth." Even now she couldn't bear the thought of anyone but Grant calling her by that nickname. Almost against her will she looked up at him, remembering the times he'd groaned the word against the curve of her breast, making it the most intimate of endearments. Grant's eyes glowed, and she knew he remembered, too.

With heavy gallantry Bobby Lee declared, "Elizabeth, then. What a pretty...." His voice trailed off when he saw they weren't listening to him. Turning away, he led them into a spacious sitting room.

Despite the disrepair evident from the outside, the interior of the Bailey home was attractive and well cared for, furnished in French provincial. The suite of fruitwood tables and bergere chairs were excellent reproductions, obviously old, with a settled air about them that Elizabeth found very appealing. A large red hound dog, graying at the muzzle, slept at the foot of the chair Bobby Lee headed for. One of the animal's droopy ears was ragged, perhaps torn in a long-ago fight, and as Bobby Lee seated himself, he reached down to scratch behind it.

Through an archway Elizabeth spotted a formal dining room, where a long, linen-draped table had been set with china and crystal and a centerpiece of huge gold and bronze chrysanthemums. The effect was quite pretty, if a bit ostentatious for a "casual" meal. She smiled wryly. It looked as if Suzanne had decided to try a little intimidation of her own. Elizabeth had the feeling she was underdressed.

"Where's your sister?" she asked Bobby Lee. "I must thank her again for asking us over."

"Suzanne's in the kitchen." He nodded toward the dining area, and Elizabeth assumed there was a connecting door, invisible from her angle. In the distance she could hear running water and the clatter of pan lids.

"I'll go see if I can find—" she began, but her host cut her off.

"I'll get her." Lifting his chin, he bellowed, "Sue, what's keeping you? We have visitors. Get your tail out here right now!"

Elizabeth jumped. She was startled not only by Bobby Lee's earsplitting shout, but by his imperious rudeness. Even at their most quarrelsome, she and her sister, Amelia, would never have dared order each other around that way. She glanced at Grant. With a faint grimace he shook his head. His gray eyes telegraphed the message, "It's none of our business."

"Suzanne's been in a tizzy ever since she met you this afternoon," Bobby Lee continued easily. "When I got home from the plant she had the whole place in an uproar, cleaning up, cooking."

"I'm sorry to hear that," Grant said. "She promised we wouldn't be any trouble."

"Good company's never any trouble, reverend. Besides, it's good for her to have something to do besides pot houseplants that nobody wants...." He paused, eyeing Grant obliquely. "Or," he drawled with grating bonhomie, "make eyes at the preacher."

From the archway came a strangled sound. The three in

the sitting room jerked around in time to see Suzanne bolt back to the kitchen, in her haste almost tripping over the long apron protecting her orange silk-jersey hostess gown. The girl's scarlet face clashed painfully with the dress.

"Oh, hell," Bobby Lee muttered, his own face darkening when the other two looked at him reprovingly. Grant's lips thinned as if he were controlling his temper. Elizabeth ran after Suzanne.

She found her bent over the sink, biting hard on her lip. Gently Elizabeth said, "Suzanne, nobody's laughing at you."

Suzanne shuddered. After a moment she sniffled, "Bobby Lee is. He loves to laugh at me. Ever since I was a little girl I've had to put up with his teasing."

Elizabeth's response was instantaneous. "You're not a little girl now. Tell him you refuse to put up with his teasing anymore."

Sighing, Suzanne wiped her hands on her apron and turned to face Elizabeth. "You don't know my big brother."

"No, I don't. But I have a big sister who used to like to boss me around."

"And she doesn't boss you around now that you're grown?"

"No." Elizabeth saw no point in admitting that she and Amelia got along as adults primarily because they avoided each other's company as much as possible.

Elizabeth remained unconvinced. "Maybe it's different for sisters." With her knuckles she dashed away the moisture that still clung to her puffy eyelids. Squaring her shoulders, she faced Elizabeth with an odd air of dignity. "Ms—or I guess I ought to say Mrs. O'Connor—I'm truly sorry for that crack my brother made about Grant—about your husband. I'm sure he meant it as a joke, but Bobby Lee's sense of humor can be kind of, well, tacky. Sometimes I think he's just jealous."

"'Jealous'? Of whom?"

"Of your husband. Bobby Lee is used to being king of the hill around here, but since the reverend showed up, half the girls in town have been trying to attract his attention, instead."

"I'll bet," Elizabeth muttered under her breath. Women had always found Grant attractive. Even in a town as insular as Ridleyville, they'd have no trouble distinguishing between Bobby Lee's shallow pseudosophistication and the depth and quality of a man like Grant.

"You needn't worry, Mrs. O'Connor. Grantland's never looked twice at anyone who's chased him, including me. Seeing you, I can understand why." She paused, but Elizabeth was silent. Suzanne's tone became almost accusing. "Naturally, none of us guessed he had a wife. One thing we don't hold with in these parts is breaking up other people's marriages."

Elizabeth refused to be drawn. To change the subject, she glanced around the kitchen. Several elaborately garnished platters of food stood ready on the counter, a savory contradiction to her hostess's earlier claim that the meal would be potluck—unless, of course, the Baileys regularly dined on wild rice and duckling in sour-cherry sauce. "Is there anything I can do to help you?" she asked.

"No, thank you." Suzanne consulted her wristwatch. "I'm just waiting for the soufflé to finish baking."

The girl's stilted courtesy reminded Elizabeth of a child who had been offended. To cajole her out of her pout, Elizabeth exclaimed, "'Soufflé'? I admire your courage! The last time I tried to make one, it came out of the oven looking like a deflated volleyball."

Suzanne stared; all at once she relaxed and giggled conspiratorially. "I'll tell you a secret, Mrs. O'Connor. That's the way mine look usually. A friend mixed the ingredients for this one, and she promised that if I'd just time it correctly, it'd work. I do hope she's right. No matter how hard I try, I just can't seem to get the hang of French cooking."

Elizabeth looked again at the dishes that appeared to compare favorably with anything she'd eaten on the continent. "Somebody around here has the hang of French cuisine."

"It's not me," Suzanne admitted. "The only way I know to cook is down-home. After I found out you used to live in Europe, I knew that wouldn't be good enough for you, so I called Mei at her restaurant and told her it was an emergency. She brought over the duck and most of the trimmings, and she helped me put things together. If dinner had been left up to me, you'd probably have had to settle for fried chicken and corn bread."

Listening to Suzanne's disarming confession, Elizabeth decided that despite the girl's affectations, she liked her. "But corn bread would have been a treat. I love it, and I haven't had any in years, not since I left the States."

Suzanne looked surprised. "I didn't think of that."

Elizabeth studied the food platters again. "Is your friend French?"

"Vietnamese," Suzanne said surprisingly. "She was a cook at one of the embassies in Saigon, until the city fell. When she and her family became refugees, they were brought to the relocation center near Fort Smith. Some of the local churches chipped in to help her open her own restaurant, where she specializes in Southeast Asian cuisine. But occasionally she caters or gives lessons in French cooking."

Elizabeth was impressed by this small success story; still, she was puzzled. "I wouldn't have thought there was much call for an Asian restaurant around here."

"Next to California, this state has the largest Vietnamese population in the country. Mei says sometimes the climate reminds them of home.... But whatever the reason, most of the refugees who settled in Arkansas have fitted in well here."

The timer rang, and for a moment Suzanne busied herself with a pair of bulky oven mitts, withdrawing from the hot stove a perfect golden cheese soufflé with a high, crusty dome. It smelled wonderful. As Suzanne set the sizzling casserole on a serving tray, she peered narrowly at Elizabeth and added, "You know, Mrs. O'Connor, contrary to what a lot of people seem to think, Arkansas is *not* made up of just hillbillies and red-necks!" Without waiting for a response, she picked up the tray and carried it into the dining room.

As Elizabeth helped Suzanne bring serving dishes into the dining room, she considered the spirited retort the girl had flung at her—and admitted she probably deserved it. From the moment she had arrived in Ridleyville, she had regarded both the town and its people with a condescension and prejudice supposedly endemic to Southerners themselves. Suzanne had been right to snap at her. If she hoped to benefit at all from her forced stay in Arkansas, she needed to empty her mind of preconceived notions and study the people impartially. If she did that, perhaps by the time her Porsche was repaired and she could be on her way, she would have gained some insight into the Southern character.

Maybe then she'd be able to figure out what had gone wrong with her marriage.

Once the food had been carried into the dining room, Bobby Lee suddenly held out his sister's chair with punctilious ceremony. The display might have impressed Elizabeth more, except that as far as she could tell, her host hadn't lifted a finger to help Suzanne prepare the meal or even set the silverware. When Grant glanced questioningly at Elizabeth, she shook her head and slipped into her own place. She tried not to chuckle. Then Bobby Lee asked, "Reverend, would you favor us by saying grace?" and Elizabeth's humor vanished.

She had forgotten he was a clergyman. In Grant's office she had read the plaques that proclaimed him a doctor of divinity, an ordained minister of the Gospel, and she hadn't grasped what those simple words meant. Grant had been Grant. True, he was dressed more casually than she remembered and his regional accent was more pronounced, but he still seemed the same sexy, dynamic, forceful character she'd loved and lost five years earlier. Now as Elizabeth watched him bow his auburn head in readiness to offer up a brief prayer of thanksgiving for the food they were about to receive—a commonplace ritual the two of them had never, repeat never, participated in while they were together—she realized a new element had been added to his life since he'd left her. An element that made her feel uncomfortable, that bewildered and frightened her. An element she suddenly resented.

"Amen."

When Grant and the others raised their heads again, he stared at Elizabeth fixedly, his face troubled. He could read confusion in her eyes, confusion and, oddly, fear. He recognized the expression. He'd seen a similar one on his own face, back in the difficult days when he'd first found his life, his very thought processes beginning to alter irrevocably. Abandoning a mind-set, with its familiar, comfortable ideals and goals, had seemed as ominous, as downright scary as leaving home to explore wild, uncharted territory.

Please, darling, don't be afraid, he begged silently. *I promise you there's nothing to be afraid of.*

Elizabeth glanced down at her plate, veiling her eyes. She didn't want Grant to guess what she was feeling. Even to an unbeliever like her, it sounded—what was the word Suzanne had used in the kitchen—it sounded tacky to admit she was jealous of her husband's religious faith.

To distract Grant, Elizabeth served herself a portion of the soufflé, which tasted as good as it smelled, then turned to her host. She had always enjoyed serious dinner conversation. The only problem was, she was finding it very hard to take Bobby Lee Bailey seriously.

He was an attractive man, but he radiated machismo, a characteristic she detested. It showed in his style of dress, almost a parody of West Coast chic, and it showed in his attitudes, which seemed firmly rooted in the South—the antebellum South. His remarks to Elizabeth sounded so deferential that at first she wondered if he was being sarcastic. When she asked a question about the Bailey Pottery, he responded, "Oh, come, now, my dear, I'm sure a lovely woman like yourself would much rather not be bored with talk about business."

Across the table, Suzanne giggled. "Honestly, Bobby Lee, you're talking like a fugitive from *Gone With the Wind*!"

Her brother glared at her. "Courtesy is never outdated, Sue," he said heavily. "You would do well to remember that." Suzanne sank back in her chair.

Elizabeth didn't know whether to grind her teeth or laugh. She was beginning to see why Suzanne seemed to have no clear idea of how or in what direction to guide her life. While they ate, Elizabeth learned that Bobby Lee had been his sister's guardian for seven years, since their father had died. Although her costly perfume and expensive if ill-chosen clothing indicated she lacked for nothing materially, her brother treated her as if she were still fourteen, as delicate and brainless as a moth. And worse, despite occasional flashes of spirit, for the most part Suzanne reacted as if he were right.

Elizabeth supposed it was her irritation at her host's attitude toward his sister that made her return to the subject he seemed anxious to avoid. Setting her fork down beside the apple-and-marzipan pastry, which was delicious but almost too rich to eat, she smiled winningly at her host. "You know, Mr. Bailey—I mean, Bobby Lee—I've never seen a real pottery before. Way back in college my roommate took a ceramics class, and once I watched her throw a vase on a wheel, but I can't imagine what a large-scale operation such as your factory would be like."

The hint was unmistakable, as Elizabeth had intended it to be, and Bobby Lee's bright-blue eyes became guarded. "Well, ma'am, I'm not sure what you're expecting, but there's really not much to see—some machinery, a couple of tunnel kilns, big piles of broken pots. I'm afraid the Bailey Pottery isn't the place it once was. Nowadays it's mostly just noisy and dirty."

At the foot of the table Suzanne shuddered. "'Dirty'? My Lord, that doesn't begin to describe it! You can't take a step anywhere without getting filthy. After all these years, everything in the building is covered with a film of clay that's slimy when it's wet and dusty and crumbly when it's dry."

"The only time our daddy ever took a switch to Sue was the day she managed to spill a bucket of slip all over the brand-new party dress he'd just bought for her seventh birthday. Ever since then, she's stayed away from the pottery."

"Come on, that's not entirely true. I've offered to help—"

Ignoring her, Bobby Lee continued, "But she is right. Liquid clay seems to find its way into everything, and once it hardens, there's no way to get it out." He glanced significantly at Elizabeth's delicate, embroidered gauze blouse. "It'd be a real tragedy to mess up something as pretty as that outfit you're wearing."

Elizabeth lowered her lashes, resisting the urge to flutter them. "I'm sure I could find a pair of old jeans somewhere," she said demurely.

After a moment Bobby Lee surrendered. "Very well, ma'am, if you're really all that interested in seeing the factory, then I'd be honored to show you around. Will tomorrow do?"

When Elizabeth raised her head again, her expression was coolly triumphant. "Thank you, tomorrow will be just fine. I'll have to make some calls first thing in the morning about my Porsche, but after that I'll be free." She reached for her fork, and as she lifted another bite of flaky puff pastry to her lips, her gaze collided with Grant's. He was staring at her as if he'd never seen her before.

"I DIDN'T KNOW you liked to flirt," Grant observed, at last breaking his silence as the two of them strode along the flagstone path to the parsonage.

Elizabeth glanced sharply at him, but except for the amber light filtering through the vines over the back porch, the night was dark, too dark to read his expression. "I don't flirt. I despise that kind of sexual game playing."

"That's not the way it looked tonight. From where I sat, you seemed to be coming on to Bobby Lee."

Elizabeth exclaimed impatiently, "Oh, for heaven's sake! You heard how the man was carrying on. Even Suzanne commented. I was just giving him back a little of his own medicine. You know I can't stand to be talked down to." They reached the porch, and the screen door creaked as he pushed it open, almost covering Elizabeth's last muttered remark. "Besides, I don't like the way Bobby Lee browbeats his sister."

Grant shrugged. "As a matter of fact, I don't particularly like the way he treats her, either. He seems to show more affection for that old dog of his. But it's not up to you or me to interfere. The only person who can make Suzanne stand up for herself is Suzanne." He fumbled for his house keys.

Elizabeth stepped back out of his way, and as she did, all at once she was dizzy with remembered images that echoed and receded from the present like reflections in opposing mirrors. How many times in the past had she stood beside Grant, waiting in the corridor of the co-op while he unlocked their door? How many evenings had ended like this, her hovering at his elbow, hungrily watching each movement of his tall, lithe body, eager to be alone with him, resentful of every second that delayed the moment when they would be private, undisturbed.... Suddenly Elizabeth realized that for the first time in five years she would be sleeping under the same roof as her husband.

"Is something wrong?" Grant asked. He was holding the door open, waiting for her to step inside.

"No, everything's fine," she said stiltedly, trying to

avoid his pointed scrutiny. She didn't want him to guess he still stirred her as deeply as ever.

Elizabeth bustled into the kitchen. After the yellow porchlight outside, the glow from the fluorescent tubing over the sink looked harsh, bluish white, and she blinked hard. When her eyes adjusted, she surveyed the area curiously. Like the rest of the parsonage, the room was scrupulously clean, but worn and drab. Both linoleum and counter tops were faded and so badly scratched that Elizabeth was amazed Holly had been able to raise even a faint shine on them. The olive-green refrigerator reminded her of the model that had graced her mother's kitchen in Minnesota decades earlier, when Elizabeth was a child. The freestanding stove, white and chipped, looked even older; a twist of coat-hanger wire held the oven door shut. Someone had tried to make the two appliances coordinate with the rest of the room by covering the cupboards with vinyl in green-and-white plaid, but over the years the edges of the plastic had come unstuck. Elizabeth shuddered. "How can Holly stand to work in surroundings like this?"

"Holly's only been housekeeping here a little while. Instead you ought to pity the former pastor's wife, who not only worked but lived in this house for twenty years."

Elizabeth nodded grimly. "Holly told me the deacons, or whoever it is who handles the purse strings at your church, refused to pay for redecorating."

"That could be. Sadly, a lot of people seem to feel the expression 'poor as church mice' was meant to apply to the clergy."

Elizabeth was puzzled. "That still doesn't explain why you don't do something about this mess. You're not an ordinary clergyman, dependent on whatever salary your congregation pays you. You could afford to refurbish the house top to bottom a dozen times over."

"That's true, but—"

"Then if you don't have to stay in this—this squalor, I don't see why you put up with it. In Manhattan, even though your life-style could hardly have been called sybaritic, you always insisted on comfort."

"A lot of things that were important to me in Manhattan just don't matter anymore," Grant said.

She stared at him uncomprehendingly. "But why? I still don't understand." A distasteful thought occurred to her. "Good grief, Grant, surely this isn't meant to be some form of penance or—or mortification of the flesh, is it?"

Without warning Grant exploded. He could feel hot blood rushing to his face as he rasped, "For God's sake, Liza, you act as if I wear hair shirts and live in a cave! For your information, hermits and self-flagellation went out of style centuries ago. So kindly just quit being an idiot, will you, and stop making snotty, sarcastic remarks about something that's very important to me!"

Elizabeth's eyes widened. Stricken, she stared up at him. His features looked flushed and strained, more than ever the face of a stranger. In all the time they'd been together, Grant had never once lost his temper, never once spoken to her in anger. He had always been under control, even when he'd left her.

With a strangled whimper Elizabeth fled from the kitchen up the stairs.

For a fraction of a second after she'd bolted, Grant stood immobile, aghast at what he'd just done, just said. He didn't know why his temper had erupted like that. Perhaps her supercilious attitude had sparked it, although she had sounded more confused than condescending. Or perhaps his fury was a defensive reaction to being found wanting by the one person whose opinion had ever truly mattered to him.... "Liza, wait, I'm sorry!" he yelled, and sprinted after her.

He caught up with her just outside her bedroom. Fingers clamping over her wrist, he whirled her around, her body trapped between his and the closed door. Her head jerked up, and she looked at him with eloquent wariness from teary eyes. He could see the shadow of her breasts heaving beneath the embroidered blouse, each movement synchronized to the ragged little sobs that forced their way through her compressed lips. She didn't speak.

As soon as he realized she wasn't going to run again, Grant loosened his grip on her wrist, but he didn't step away. He couldn't. He was disturbingly aware of how soft she felt pressed against him, how warm and beguiling. When her tongue flicked across her parched lips, Grant almost groaned. Hoarsely he whispered, "I'm sorry, Liza. Please forgive me. I shouldn't have shouted at you. I don't know why I reacted that way, except—except I guess that for a moment there it sounded as if you were making fun of my beliefs."

She took a long breath. "If I offended you, I'm sorry, too. I promise I wasn't making fun of anyone or anything, I was just trying to make a little *sense*. Grant, do you have any idea how absolutely crazy everything that's happened today seems to me? I know we haven't seen each other in five years, but even in that length of time people don't ordinarily change to the point of being unrecognizable. *Everything* seems to have changed about you. Your looks, your goals—" she indicated the dingy interior of the hallway "—even your standard of living."

Grant chuckled, a reassuring rumble of good humor deep

in his chest. "Liza, dear, I haven't really changed all that much. If it'll make you feel better, you ought to know I'm just as aware as anyone of how decrepit this house has become. In fact, I've set aside my salary—which you're right, I don't need—and some additional funds for renovation, but not for now. I'll give the money to the church after the congregation hires my replacement. That way the house can be fixed up to suit the needs of the new pastor and his or her family. I'm just the interim minister at Good Samaritan, filling the pulpit till a successor can be found, and I don't feel it would be appropriate to make sweeping changes for my own convenience when I'm only here temporarily."

"Oh," Elizabeth mumbled, "I guess I didn't understand." She was uncomfortably aware of how close together she and Grant were standing, the unintentional but real provocation of this whispered conversation at her bedroom door. She tried to sound objective. "Of course, I ought to have realized I was wrong about you. I've never understood anything about religion."

His expression sobered. "Liza, would you like to understand my religion? If you're interested—"

Uncomfortably she shook her head. "I don't think so, Grant. That is, not if you're talking about trying to... convert me. I'm content as I am."

He flashed her a reassuring smile. "I wasn't planning to get on my soapbox, Liza. Actually, I just thought you might be interested in what I..." His voice faded away in embarrassment. "Although why I flatter myself you should care about what I've been doing, after all this time..."

"Of course I'm curious about what you've been doing, Grant—and why. I may not be prepared to argue comparative theology, but, yes, I'd like to learn about you."

He stared down at her, and his gray eyes began to grow

luminescent, like heating steel. His hands traced upward along the sides of her body, gently grasping her arms beneath the full, gauzy sleeves of her blouse. His breath was warm on her cheeks. "Learn about me, Liza?" he queried softly. "You mean you want me to teach..." His voice blurred. Bending his head, for the first time in five long, lonely years he kissed her.

Half a decade faded at a touch. Elizabeth had been desolate too long to think of resisting him; need—and curiosity—were too overwhelming. Her lashes drooped as she opened her mouth to him with a sigh.

Despite all the changes in him, he still tasted the same, she discovered with heady wonder as his tongue stroked her lips, her teeth, before probing deeper into her. Burning sweet, like red wine.... His touch still intoxicated her. He leaned against her, pressing her harder against the door, and her hands, crushed between their clinging bodies, wriggled around to explore the muscles of his chest through the fabric of his shirt. Savoring their solid strength, she was aware that he felt a little different, more powerful, more satisfying to hold. When he shifted his grasp from her arms to her torso, allowing his thumbs to graze the lower curve of her unconfined breasts, she flung her freed hands around his neck and stroked her fingers over the short auburn hair at his nape. Giddily she arched against him, eager to feel his desire—

"Liza, this is a mistake."

Startled blue eyes flew open. Suddenly he was standing at arm's length, his face pale, moisture on his brow. "I'm sorry, Liza," he said huskily. "I had no right to touch you."

Flags of hot color darkened Elizabeth's cheekbones, there for him to see, before she quickly averted her gaze.

For a moment she stared at the faded runner bisecting the hallway. *It's so easy for him to break away,* she thought. She told herself she ought to be grateful he'd ended the embrace, but she wasn't sure whether she ought to be dismayed or resentful of his apparent self-possession. *Why isn't it as easy for me?*

Even as that depressing question formed in her mind, she knew the answer. She couldn't break away from Grant because, despite all her attempts to armor herself against him, even after five years he remained her Achilles' heel, the one man to whom she was vulnerable. The tragedy was that she didn't seem to have the same effect on him.

Awkwardly in an effort to cover her embarrassment and hurt, she said, "You know, Grant, when two people meet after a long separation, no matter what's taken place in the interim, it's not uncommon for them to revert to patterns of behavior they displayed when they knew each other before. It doesn't mean anything. I think psychologists call it 'imprinting,' or something like that."

Grant relaxed visibly. "Yes, that's it exactly. Nevertheless, I am sorry I—"

Her innate honesty and pride wouldn't allow him to assume blame for what had been a mutual act. "Please, Grant," Elizabeth whispered, "don't apologize. I liked you touching me. That was the first time in years that anyone's cared enough to give me a good-night kiss."

He stared in stony silence at her for several heartbeats. Then, nodding, he said gravely, "Good night, Liza." He turned on his heel and stalked down the hall to the master bedroom.

"Good night, Grant," Elizabeth breathed. She knew it was going to be a long one.

CHAPTER SIX

THE NEXT MORNING, when Elizabeth awoke from a sleep troubled by vague, tantalizingly erotic dreams, she found that Grant had already left for his office. She wondered if he always went to work so early, or if he was just being tactful. Whatever the case, she was grateful he wasn't there. She didn't know whether she would have had the strength to face him across a breakfast table.

Holly had already arrived at the parsonage, walking across town with her little brother Buddy in tow. The boy appeared in reasonably good spirits, content to watch "Sesame Street" while his sister vacuumed and dusted, but Holly's mood was as dreary as the sky. A weather front had moved in during the night, bringing with it a thin layer of clouds that filtered out the sun's light, if not its unseasonable warmth.

The muggy, oppressive atmosphere took away what little appetite Elizabeth had, and when Holly politely offered to cook a hot breakfast, Elizabeth declined; all she needed, she said, was coffee and juice to sip while she phoned the Porsche agency in Fayetteville. At the mention of the car, Holly looked so guilt-stricken that Elizabeth wished she could have avoided the subject somehow. The girl almost seemed to be more of a victim of her father's wrongdoing than Elizabeth was.

Except for delays, inevitable because of the distances involved, arrangements for her car went smoothly. The dealer promised to dispatch an insurance adjuster to Ridleyville that day or the next. Elizabeth was just setting down the receiver when Bobby Lee Bailey's vintage red Corvette swung onto the parsonage's gravel drive.

"You're looking especially lovely this morning," Bobby Lee observed gallantly as he greeted her at the front door.

"Thank you," Elizabeth said, smiling ironically at his flattery. She knew her tidy beige skirt, blouse and flat-heeled shoes, while adequate for touring a factory, could hardly be called "fashionable." Bobby Lee, on the other hand, wore dark slacks, sport coat and tie, a textbook example of management dressing. In Elizabeth's opinion stylish conservatism suited him much better than the macho getup he'd relaxed in the evening before, but she wasn't sure this outfit expressed the true Bobby Lee. "You look very nice yourself."

Bobby Lee beamed as he climbed behind the wheel of the Corvette. "Always delighted to please a lady." His mustache twitched as he grinned meaningfully and reached for Elizabeth's hand. She distracted him by asking a question about his car.

They tooled along the old highway, passing the outskirts of Ridleyville and winding through a grove of hickory and shortleaf pines, while Bobby Lee expounded on the comparative merits of Corvettes and Porsches. He had just told Elizabeth that if she wanted durability she should "buy American," when the trees parted and he steered his car onto a potholed asphalt side road that led to a gate in a high brick wall. A pair of tall pillars supported a rusted iron sign reading Bailey Pottery Works. Beyond the gate the pavement widened into a parking area lined with a dozen sedans and pickups, and on the other side of the cars stood a cluster of large, dingy buildings and sheds, perched on a bluff overlooking the Arkansas River.

The unsightly plant was a jarring intrusion on the landscape, Elizabeth thought as she slipped out of the Corvette, not waiting for Bobby Lee to assist her. Even under overcast skies, the vista of rolling hills and autumn-burnished foliage looked as beautiful as it had when she'd first seen it. Glancing upriver, Elizabeth spotted the arched bridge that had carried her and her sparkling new Porsche into town—had it really been just the day before? She was losing all sense of time.

Bobby Lee's office was in a separate building at the front of the facility, and he stepped inside long enough to greet his secretary and fetch two scuffed yellow hard hats. "Safety rules, I'm afraid," he told Elizabeth with a chuckle as he watched her cinch the adjustment strap to fit her head. Pointing toward the first shed, where Elizabeth could see high mounds of sand and raw clay, he asked, "Well, my dear, shall we start at the beginning?"

By the time they had finished their tour in the storage yard, a light drizzle filtered from leaden clouds, making the ground tacky as they walked across it. The rain was little more than a fog, just heavy enough to increase the humidity and dampen the thick layer of dust blanketing the long rows of yellow and red bricks and the ceramic chimney pipe stacked in the storage yard. Elizabeth was grateful for the hard hat. Bobby Lee eyed her once more. "Are you sure you wouldn't prefer to go back inside to my office until the rain stops? It never lasts long, but we certainly wouldn't want to spoil your dress."

Elizabeth hesitated, strangely thoughtful as she surveyed the storage yard yet again. In addition to the bricks and chimney flues, pallets of drain tile and flowerpots in graduated sizes stood in the open yard; at the far end she could see sewer pipe arranged in a pyramid. From the way trash and weeds had collected inside the huge cylinders, it looked as if the pipe had lain there a long time.

Elizabeth glanced at Bobby Lee, shifting restlessly beside her. "Of course we can go back inside, if you like. I think I've seen enough for now."

She'd seen a lot more than Bobby Lee suspected, she thought as she followed him back to his office. Although she'd coerced him into this tour on a whim, with little purpose beyond deliberately spiting him, her trained eyes hadn't been able to avoid disturbing observations. While he had conducted her around the grounds, explaining the operation with a superficiality that bordered on condescension, Elizabeth had noted production lines not in use, inventory not moving, an obviously once-prosperous plant apparently deteriorating from lack of maintenance. The employees she and Bobby Lee encountered were all surprised and curious to see her, but they seemed equally as startled by Bobby Lee's presence inside the factory. It was never a good sign when the boss absented himself from the workplace.

In Bobby Lee's office, he tossed their hard hats onto an old-fashioned, freestanding iron safe and leaned back in his swivel chair. He grinned amiably across the width of his desk. "Well, Elizabeth, I do hope this little excursion has been as entertaining as you imagined it'd be, although I'm sure I—"

"How long has that second tunnel kiln been shut down?" she asked, thinking of the massive brick oven, idle and cold, that stretched almost the length of one of the buildings. Its twin was still in use, manned by sweating workmen in smoke-stained jump suits. Above the roar of the gas jets, Bobby Lee had shouted an explanation of the operation to Elizabeth. He had told her that unlike the intermittent kilns she'd seen in ceramics classes, the kind that were heated and cooled for each firing, a tunnel kiln burned continuously, with thermostats set to increasingly hotter temperatures along its length. A conveyer belt crept through the middle, and greenware loaded onto cars at the cool end was completely fired by the time it emerged from the other.

"The kiln?" Elizabeth prompted, and Bobby Lee blinked.

His expression became guarded. "We haven't used that line in three years."

"That equipment obviously represents a tremendous investment. I'm surprised you can afford to leave it unproductive for so long. What led to the closure?"

"The kiln needed some repairs," Bobby Lee muttered. Elizabeth gazed steadily at him, the obvious question unvoiced. Bobby Lee fidgeted with his tie, and after a moment he added grudgingly, "Not long after I took over from my father, I—that is, the company—lost a major contract that had been one of our mainstays since the fifties. A wholesale nursery chain decided to quit packaging its plants in ceramic pots, switched to plastics from Taiwan. Couple that with some other losses and a drop in brick sales because of the decline in the housing market, and we can't afford to make capital improvements."

Quietly Elizabeth said, "I didn't think we were talking about improvements, just routine maintenance."

Bobby Lee shrugged. "Yeah, well, it hardly seems worth the effort to fix things up. Energy costs have been eating us alive." He glanced at a pair of large, framed photographs on the wall above his desk, similarly posed portraits of two men standing beneath the sign at the entrance to the plant.

Although the subjects both appeared about forty years old, their styles of dress separated them by at least a generation. Elizabeth's suspicions were confirmed when Bobby Lee said, "My illustrious forebears. From the time grampa discovered that mining clay was a lot easier than mining coal, he assumed the Bailey family would keep the business going on forever, getting bigger and better.

"For many years it looked as if he were right. When he handed the company over to my father, the plant employed a hundred men and those kilns burned around the clock. But by the time I got saddled with the pottery, the economy and everything else had changed." He frowned resentfully. "People blame me for cutting back, but they tend to forget that in dad's day, the bill for the gas came to maybe three thousand dollars a year. Nowadays, in order to operate at full capacity, I'd have to spend as much as a hundred grand a *month*."

Hearing the undertone of exasperation in his voice, Elizabeth decided she'd pushed him enough. All her instincts and experiences told her the Bailey Pottery was suffering from bad management as much as from the energy crisis, but the situation was, after all, none of her concern. Bobby Lee was her host, not an employee. To placate him she agreed, "Lots of businessmen are suffering that way. Besides inflation, rising energy costs are probably the single greatest obstacle facing American industry today."

He stared at her. "I didn't realize you were so knowledgeable on the subject."

"It's my job."

Squinting pensively, Bobby Lee fell silent. Elizabeth had the feeling he was really seeing her for the first time. His gaze moved over her deliberately, but for once there seemed to be no sexual innuendo in his scrutiny, and when he did speak, his voice lacked the heavy-handed charm Elizabeth found so tiresome. He sounded confused and almost wary. "You're one of those big-shot women executives we hear about these days, aren't you—the kind who are just as high-powered and cutthroat as men?"

"Well, I do enjoy my work," Elizabeth murmured mildly.

"Lucky you," Bobby Lee drawled. "I wish to God I—" He broke off abruptly. Another charged silence followed, during which Elizabeth could almost hear his mind buzzing. "Pardon me for asking," he blurted out, "but isn't it kind of odd for someone like you to be married to a clergyman? All the typical preacher's wives I've ever known were mousy little nonentities in black dresses. How'd you and the reverend get together in the first place?"

Elizabeth was startled by the rush of resentment, absolutely illogical under the circumstances, that she felt on behalf of her predecessor, the unknown woman who had painstakingly crocheted lace curtains and tried to "pretty up" a dreary kitchen with stick-on plastic. "I doubt there is such a thing as a 'typical preacher's wife,'" she pointed out tightly. "Besides, Grant wasn't in the clergy when I met him."

Bobby Lee's blue eyes glinted. "I *thought* there was something different about him! You materializing the way you did just confirms it. I knew the minute he showed up in town that he was no ordinary pulpit pounder. He's too damned sophisticated, for one thing. No matter how quiet he pretends to be, he's obviously too experienced, too well traveled. A man who's seen the world isn't about to waste his time in a hick town like this one unless..." Leaning forward in his chair, he asked, "Tell me, Elizabeth, just what—"

Elizabeth was spared having to respond when Bobby Lee's secretary appeared at the door. "Mr. Bailey, when you get a chance, I need the cash box. And Clyde Walker would like to see you."

"Oh, hell," Bobby Lee groaned, sinking back in his chair. He glanced at Elizabeth. "Do you mind if Clyde comes in?"

"No, of course not. Shall I leave?" When Bobby Lee shook his head, Elizabeth folded her hands in her lap and made herself unobtrusive. She watched with interest as the person responsible for her being stranded in Ridleyville entered the office.

He scarcely seemed the same man who'd crashed into her sports car; only the deep bruise under his chin remained from the accident. Wearing freshly pressed work clothes, his clean-shaven face pale beneath a billed cap, Clyde Walker looked younger, healthier; it occurred to Elizabeth that not so long ago he might have been quite attractive. And he was sober.

As he stepped into the office, he stumbled, but the falter in his gait was caused not by intoxication but by the shock of seeing her. Catching himself, he whipped the cap from his dark hair and mumbled, "Good morning, ma'am. I—I didn't realize—"

"Good morning, Mr. Walker. How's the jaw today?"

Clyde hesitated, as if uncertain of her sincerity. "Oh, ma'am, I'm fine." After a moment he relaxed and touched the bruise gingerly, admitting with a reluctant grin, "As hard as I whacked that steering wheel, for a while there last night I was afraid I might have loosened some teeth. But now they seem okay, praise be. Thank you for—"

"Clyde, is there something I can do for you?" Bobby Lee demanded repressively.

Clyde stiffened. "Begging your pardon, ma'am," he muttered. Turning to the man at the desk, with grim determination he declared, "Yes, there is something you can do for me, Bobby Lee. You can give me my old job back."

Bobby Lee said, "I'm afraid that's not possible."

His refusal didn't seem to faze Clyde. Stoutly he persisted. "Why isn't it possible? I'm one of the best glazers this company ever had. When you laid me off, you promised it was only temporary, until you got some new contracts."

"But we haven't got any new contracts yet. Unless some of our bids start getting accepted, before long I'm going to have to let even more people go."

Clyde's burst of bravado faded, and he began to twist his cap nervously, crushing the stiff mesh between thick fingers. "Bobby Lee," he mumbled, "how long have you known me?"

"Ever since I was a snot-nosed youngster chasing after that souped-up Model T with the glass-pack muffler you used to race around town. The biggest thrill of my childhood was the day you let me sit beside you and shift gears while you drove."

"I remember that." Clyde chuckled. "I thought your mama was going to have a conniption when we roared past her coming out of the beauty parlor." He shook his head sadly. "Damn, those were the days...." Bracing his shoulders, he pleaded, "Bobby Lee, you've known me all your life, and you know I wouldn't beg if I wasn't about at the end of my rope. You've got to help me. I've looked everywhere for work, but there's just nothing available around here."

"Then maybe you ought to consider moving to someplace where there is work. You could try Tulsa or possibly even out West. Lots of other people from around here have headed that way. California—that's where it's happening these days. Hell, I'd go in a minute myself if I weren't tied down here."

Clyde shook his head fiercely. "No. I've said it before, I'll say it again: Ridleyville's our home. Besides, I know what happens when people move to the city. They end up twice as bad off as they were before, crammed into nasty little apartments where they can't set foot outside for fear of getting mugged. At least here my kids are safe and have room to play— But, God, it's tough! I used to think I had the world by the tail, but after Kayrene.... My little girl had to give up the college scholarship she studied so hard to earn, my boys all look like urchins—" His voice cracked. "Bobby Lee, you've got to help me! I'll do anything— sweep floors, drive trucks—"

"Clyde," Bobby Lee interrupted harshly, "after the way you got drunk and crashed into Mrs. O'Connor's car yesterday, I doubt anyone is going to trust you to drive a truck!"

Clyde choked, dark blotches of humiliation freckling his face as he glanced sidelong at the woman in the corner. "For God's sake, Bobby Lee!"

Elizabeth bristled. The instant Holly's father had begun to speak, she had realized she had no business witnessing this interview. If only she could have found a discreet way to leave the room, she would have. Now to be dragged unwillingly into the conversation—

Angrily she interrupted, "Mr. Bailey, what happened to my car is between Mr. Walker and me. You have no right to interfere."

Bobby Lee looked startled. Raising his hands, he surrendered. "You're right, ma'am, I'm sorry." Turning to the other man, he repeated, "I'm sorry, Clyde. I shouldn't have mentioned the accident. I was way out of line."

For a moment the office reverberated with strained silence. Then, his shoulders slumping in defeat, Clyde sighed. "No, you weren't out of line, Bobby Lee. You were just saying what anyone else would've. Everyone in this town knows what I've been like since my wife left me."

"Maybe that's all the more reason you ought to reconsider leaving this town, so you can make a fresh start somewhere else." Bobby Lee reached into the inside pocket of his jacket and withdrew his wallet. Counting out several crisp green bills, he said, "Clyde, as much as I wish I could give you back your old job, I just can't. It's the economy. But if you need a little something to tide you over—"

"Goddammit, I don't want a handout!" Clyde snapped, his flush deepening.

Still Bobby Lee thrust the money at him. "Now, Clyde, don't be too proud to let a friend help out. As you said, we've known each other all—"

Elizabeth grabbed her handbag and fled the office. She'd seen enough.

DECLINING BOBBY LEE's offer of lunch, Elizabeth thanked him politely for the tour and forced herself to wave goodbye as he sped away. Then she trudged up the steps to the parsonage. She wondered how she was going to be able to face Holly Walker after watching the girl's father abase himself.

The house was quiet and empty. Searching for Holly, Elizabeth wandered into the kitchen. As soon as she opened the door savory steam billowed out, redolent of ham, onions and bay leaf. A kettle of thick bean soup simmered on the stove. Taped to a cupboard was a note from Holly, saying that she and her little brother had walked to the supermarket to do the weekly grocery shopping; they'd be gone an hour or so, but there was a pan of corn bread on the table and salad in the refrigerator. Elizabeth peered doubtfully at the food. It looked as delicious as it smelled, and her stomach was beginning to remind her forcefully that she'd eaten nothing all day. Now, contrarily, she found she had little appetite. She was still upset by the scene she'd been forced to witness in Bobby Lee's office.

Trying to settle her nerves, she returned to the parlor and passed time thumbing through the variety of news and cultural magazines she found stacked on the coffee table. She deduced that despite his new profession, over the years Grant's interests had remained as diverse and far-reaching as ever; only business journals were conspicuously absent. Mulling over the significance of that, she was interrupted by the shrill creak of the screen door on the back porch.

"Liza, are you here?" Grant called from the kitchen.

"I'm in the living room." She could hear his strong footsteps striding through the house, closer, closer. Staring at the magazine clutched in her lap, she realized she was almost afraid to look at him. At the sound of his voice she had become aware of another kind of emotion upsetting her, a tension that had nothing to do with the morning's events. She wondered if he was as aware of it as she was; she wondered if he would gaze down at her and remember that kiss on the landing, or if he'd been able to dismiss it as easily as they'd both claimed they could. . . .

"Hello, Liza," Grant murmured deeply. "I'm sorry I missed you this morning, but I had to attend a prayer breakfast and then pay a hospital visit to one of my parishioners who's just had surgery. She was feeling depressed, so we talked for quite a long while." In the hollow silence of the empty house, his words sounded peculiarly intimate. "I gather you've been out to the pottery already. What did you think of it?"

Slowly Elizabeth raised her head. Today Grant seemed more as she remembered him from years past, his long, muscular body clothed in a well-tailored suit of good fabric, conservative cut. Her eyes inched upward, along the powerful legs in dark gabardine. His large hands were hooked casually in hip pockets, spreading his jacket open to expose a waist still trim despite the extra pounds he carried. His white oxford-cloth shirt—

Elizabeth gaped.

Grant was wearing a clerical collar.

Her look of dismay caught him off guard. He had been aware of—and rather enjoying—her intent appraisal of his body, and he couldn't imagine why she suddenly seemed so upset. Had he dribbled scrambled eggs over himself at the breakfast? "Liza?" he queried worriedly. Shaking her head, she averted her eyes.

All at once Grant felt himself grow cold. Her troubled stare had been trained on his neck. He almost growled with frustration. He'd forgotten the stiff white band around his throat; it was an emblem of his calling he wore only when it served as useful identification, such as during visits to hospitals or jails. Otherwise he avoided it, not because he wasn't proud to have the right to wear it, but because he disliked the air of saccharine piety most people instantly affected when confronted by a "man of the cloth." The collar tended to separate him from the very people he hoped to serve. He hated the idea that Elizabeth felt uncomfortable with him, too.

"If the collar bothers you that much I can always take it off," he suggested mildly.

Her eyes were wide and unnaturally bright as she looked

up at him. "Oh, no, Grant, of course it doesn't bother me! Forgive me if I seemed rude. It's—I'm just not used to seeing you in one of those...shirts."

In the face of her confusion, he relaxed. She wasn't being scornful. Touching Elizabeth's cheek gently, suppressing his instinctive reaction to the slide of her silky skin beneath his fingertips, Grant said, "It's not a whole shirt, Liza; just a neckpiece. And since I don't have any more calls to make today, I think I'll go change. It's too hot to be wearing a suit."

By the time Grant came downstairs again, dressed in casual slacks and a sport shirt, Elizabeth had laid out plates and silverware on the kitchen table. She'd set the electric coffee maker, the parsonage's one new appliance, to brew, while she ladled soup into shallow bowls. "You didn't have to do that, Liza. I meant to serve lunch. I told Holly not to worry about setting the table because I didn't know whether you'd be eating here or with the Baileys."

Seating herself, Elizabeth made a face. "Bobby Lee did invite me to a restaurant, but I declined. I just wanted to get away from him."

Across the table, Grant scowled. "What do you mean? Did something happen?"

"In a way." As she spread butter on a square of Holly's golden corn bread, Elizabeth began to recount the confrontation between Clyde and Bobby Lee. Grant listened carefully, his expression growing increasingly somber, until she concluded indignantly, "It was painful and embarrassing for everyone, and my presence just made it worse! I'm surprised Bobby Lee could be so insensitive toward someone who was once his good friend."

"Times change, relationships change," Grant observed. "In any case, Robert Bailey is not a man noted for his sensitivity. He's too used to being the big wheel in this town to give much thought to other people's feelings—not his sister's, certainly not his employees'." He looked at her. "And you, Liza," he asked quietly, "what about your feelings?"

She supposed that despite all their years apart, there must still be some weak channel of communication open between the two of them, because she had no trouble understanding the obscure question. Grimacing with distaste, Elizabeth admitted candidly, "I felt like a voyeur. I felt I'd been exposed to a lot of raw, naked emotion that was none of my business and that I'd just as soon not know about."

"But you have to take emotion into consideration when people's lives are involved. Otherwise, the consequences can be tragic. Believe me, I know."

Elizabeth frowned. Was he talking about the way she'd withdrawn into her shell after he'd left her? For a moment she thought he was going to continue, and she waited. He only smiled ruefully and jabbed his fork into his salad.

They ate without further conversation for several minutes, the only sound in the kitchen the quiet gurgle of the coffee maker. When the light clicked off, indicating the brewing cycle had finished, Elizabeth murmured, "I'll get that," but as she pushed back her chair, Grant leaned across the table and lightly caught her wrist to stay her.

"Let me take care of it."

Elizabeth settled back and watched Grant move efficiently around the kitchen, taking down cups and saucers from the cupboard, filling the cream pitcher. When he set a steaming cup in front of her, she smiled her thanks. "You ought to give Bobby Lee a few lessons. He seems to expect his sister to wait on him hand and foot."

"The last of the red-hot chauvinists," Grant agreed with

a grin as he resumed his seat. Again a friendly silence fell over the table, an interval of tranquility so soothing that Elizabeth could almost feel her stress and frustration leaching away into the quiet. Sighing, she wondered wistfully why moments like this were so rare. So short-lived.

Grant drained his cup and replaced it with a clatter in the saucer. He cleared his throat, and Elizabeth glanced quizzically at him, perplexed by his uncharacteristic diffidence. "Yes, Grant?"

He seemed to debate how to frame his question. At last he asked carefully, "Liza, earlier when you said you 'just had to get away from' Bobby Lee, were you implying that he made a pass at you or something?"

Elizabeth blinked. "No, nothing of the sort. Except for patronizing me almost beyond endurance, he was, as they say, a perfect gentleman. Why do you ask?"

Leaning back in his chair, his long legs stretched casually in front of him, his thumbs hooked into his pockets, Grant shrugged. "Just wondering. Last night at dinner I got the impression he was rather attracted to you."

"That was last night at dinner," Elizabeth drawled. "This morning, the instant he learned I'm one of those dreaded harpies known as 'career women,' he beat a hasty retreat." She recalled the heavy-handed deference Bobby Lee had displayed as he'd guided her through the factory, favoring her with fulsome compliments, taking her arm to guide her around even the smallest obstacles. She much preferred the cautious respect that had followed their interview in the pottery office.

"I suppose that if I hadn't scared him off, Bobby Lee might have worked up to a full-fledged proposition eventually. He seems to be the kind of man who thinks such behavior is expected of him."

"Despite the slight technicality of your still being legally married to me, you mean?" Grant pressed. Now he knew why he'd disliked Bobby Lee on sight.

"Really, Grant, I hardly think anyone who's seen us together these past couple of days would believe our marriage was much of a deterrent to...cultivating other interests." She hesitated, her soft mouth curving sardonically. Then she added, "But frankly, I'm glad I did inadvertently ward him off before things got too sticky. These past five years, I've learned men like that can be incredibly thickheaded when it comes to accepting that a woman's just not interested."

Grant's hands, which had been resting comfortably on his legs, balled spasmodically. She was joking; she had to be. "Are you saying what I think you're saying?"

Elizabeth sighed. "Well, I hadn't exactly planned to make a declaration, but, no, there's been nobody in my life since you left." Again she remembered the humiliating night in Brussels when she had tried—and failed—to make herself respond to another man; the night she had at last comprehended the severity of the wound Grant had inflicted on her. The night she had realized she would probably never be able to respond to another man again.

Grant's fingers dug painfully into the muscles of his legs. He was beginning to tremble. She wasn't joking. The most passionate, responsive woman he'd ever known was telling him she'd lived like a nun for five endless empty years, and all because of him. He wouldn't, he couldn't accept that. Half a decade ago he'd eased his conscience by telling himself his departure would be the best thing for Elizabeth as well as for him. Now, suddenly to learn that instead of giving her freedom he'd crippled her... Shaking with a sickening mixture of shock, guilt and rage, he said, "I don't believe I hurt you that badly. It's just not possible."

She drew back as if he'd struck her. Her mouth worked mutely as she tried to regain control. *Breathe slowly, Elizabeth, slowly and deeply. One, two. One, two. One—* When her heart refused to slow its ragged gait, she knew the technique was useless against the man who had taught it to her. "Is that how you excuse what you did to me, Grant?" She choked painfully. "You tell yourself it was all right to desert me because I wasn't in love with you?"

"You weren't in love with me," Grant insisted. His own control was slipping, and he could feel the specter of resentment long buried rising up to haunt him. "You were in love with my image, Liza—this fantasy vision you created of someone omnipotent and all-knowing. I was supposed to be the invincible corporate businessman who handily defeated all my foes, while at the same time serving as your mentor *and* your dashing, tirelessly passionate lover. God, sometimes I felt like a refugee from an old pirate movie!" His eyes narrowed. "In fact, didn't you call me that once or twice in the heat of passion—your 'buccaneer'?"

Elizabeth's bright head drooped. She whispered, "You bastard. That isn't fair, and you know it. Your image, your reputation existed long before I ever met you. In fact, you actively cultivated them!"

"Of course I did," Grant countered impatiently. "It was all part of the game. You ought to know that. Having a reputation for possessing power is almost as useful as power itself. I—"

He broke off. In his words, in his arrogant tone, he could hear disturbing echoes of the man he once had been; whom he had prayed never to be again. Gazing remorsefully at Elizabeth's bent head, he recalled what she'd said the night before about people falling into old patterns of behavior. It was a trap he had to avoid at all costs.

Gently he murmured, "I'm sorry, Liza. I shouldn't have barked at you. Please forgive me." He watched her raise her chin again, warily brushing curls away from her face as she glanced sidelong at him from pink-rimmed eyes. Dear Lord, he had made her cry. He wished he could kiss the tears away.

When Elizabeth continued to stare silently at him, he sighed. "Please, Liza, I am sorry for the way I spoke just now. I had no right." His jaw tightened. "But I can't apologize for what I said. You were in love with your image of me. From the first day we met, you never wanted me to be an ordinary man with doubts and insecurities. You wanted someone who could take control and never let you down, either in business or in bed. I just tried to give you what you wanted. The fact remains, Liza, you were my wife, but you never had any idea what I was really like inside."

Stung, she listened in disbelief. Damn him! How dared he blame her for the breakup of their marriage, when it had been he who'd ended it, he who'd packed his bags and walked away without a word, leaving Elizabeth as shattered and desolate as her mother had been when her father—

Scraping her chair on the scuffed linoleum, Elizabeth rose to her feet and glared down at the auburn-haired man seated across the table from her. She could feel herself quivering with suppressed emotion as she struggled to keep her voice steady. "You're wrong, Grant. I always knew that in one important respect you were just like any other man. I always knew you'd leave me eventually. I just never expected God to be my rival!"

Whirling away from him, she stalked out of the kitchen.

CHAPTER SEVEN

THE INSTANT Elizabeth flounced into the hallway, she regretted her melodramatic exit line. She had sounded like a bombastic idiot; even worse, she had sounded...irreverent. No matter what her own feelings, or lack of them, she'd always tried to be respectful of other people's beliefs. She had no right to use Grant's religion as a weapon against him. Shaking her head ruefully, she retraced her steps to apologize.

At the kitchen door she hesitated. Holly Walker was just lumbering in from the back porch, a heavy, water-dotted grocery sack balanced precariously in each arm. Behind her toddled Buddy with a loaf of bread clutched against his small chest. From the way he was squashing the plastic wrapper, Elizabeth thought the bread would be fit for nothing but crumbs.

"Thanks, Dr. O'Connor." Holly sighed breathlessly as Grant relieved her of her load and dropped the bags with a thud on the table. She swung her honey-colored pigtail over her shoulder and flexed her arms tiredly. "For a moment there I was afraid the bags were going to get wet and split. There's one more sack in the shopping basket outside. As soon as I bring it in, I'll have to push the cart back over to the Winn-Dixie. The manager let me borrow it long enough to bring the groceries here, but I promised I'd return it immediately."

"I'll take care of the cart," Grant said sternly. "You should have waited until you could borrow my car to do the shopping. There was no need for you and Buddy to walk in the rain."

"But I didn't want to trouble you."

"For heaven's sake, Holly, just because you're working for me, it doesn't mean..."

Elizabeth left again without saying anything. She made her way to the den. There was something poignant about listening to Grant make domestic arrangements, arrangements that excluded her.

Seated on a couch, she stared without interest at the television. An old situation comedy was playing. After a while Buddy came into the room and climbed onto the sofa beside her; soon he was giggling over the antics of the comedienne on the screen. During a commercial he said, "I like that show. It's funny."

"I used to like it when I was little, too," Elizabeth agreed with a smile, but she was concerned. Buddy was obviously a bright, inquisitive boy, but she wondered what he did for amusement while his sister worked. Sitting around the parsonage all day didn't seem like much of a life for a child. Carefully she asked, "Do you watch lots of television?"

"Not lots," he told her. "Holly won't let me. She makes me play outside part of the time, and sometimes she reads to me or draws pictures." He picked up a battered drawing pad from the end table and handed it to Elizabeth.

Flipping through the sheets, Elizabeth stared in surprise. She found charmingly penciled juvenile scenes that alternated with detailed representations of the church, the parsonage. The last page in the notebook was filled with a stark, near-photographic rendering of the two wrecked cars as they had lain tangled together after the collision the day before. "Buddy, these are very good," she said.

"My big sister is the best drawer in the whole state," he declared proudly, and began to tell Elizabeth some of the stories that went along with the pictures.

By the time Holly found them later, the boy lay snuggled against Elizabeth, asleep, his curly head resting on her lap.

"Oh, there you are, Mrs. O'Connor!" Holly said, and Elizabeth quickly shushed her, pointing to the napping child. Holly glanced down in surprise at her little brother. Her expression softened. "Poor kid, he must be worn out," she murmured, then raised her eyes to Elizabeth's. "Before he left, Dr. O'Connor mentioned you were back from the pottery, but when I didn't see you, I thought maybe you'd gone over to the church with him."

"Oh, no. I'd just be in the way there." Deliberately changing the subject, Elizabeth picked up the drawing pad. "Your little brother was showing me some pictures he said you made for him. They're excellent."

Holly's eyes were hooded. "Thank you. They're just quick sketches I do to help keep him entertained. He gets bored hanging around here all day while I work."

Elizabeth stroked the pale, soft curls of the sleeping child. Buddy really was a beautiful little boy. She wouldn't mind having one just like him. Quietly she assured Holly, "You do very well with him, you know."

The girl's thin shoulders shrugged jerkily. "I try."

"I had no idea you were such a talented artist, Holly. Was that your major in college?"

"Yes. I won a scholarship in a statewide competition. But I had to drop out of school in the middle of my junior year."

Remembering how she had struggled to win her own college scholarships, Elizabeth tried to imagine the pain and frustration the younger woman's simple, bleak statement must cover. She said sympathetically, "That must have been very hard for you."

"It was," Holly admitted. "I loved college. The work was fun, and for the first time I had a real social life, with dates and boyfriends."

"You didn't date in high school?"

"No. I was too busy studying, and besides, in those days all the local boys were chasing Suzanne—not that any of them ever expected to be good enough for a Bailey. They've all either moved away or married by now." Holly grimaced ironically. "I guess Suzanne and I were always a little jealous of each other. I headed the honor roll, and she became homecoming queen, but she wanted my grades, and I wanted her popularity." Holly sighed. "It's funny how things turn out, isn't it? In our graduating class, we were probably the two girls everyone expected to succeed—and now both of us sit around like characters in a Tennessee Williams play, living at home, with no jobs to speak of, no gentlemen callers...."

"Someone told me you quit college in order to help your family. I'm sorry you had to make a decision like that. I hope you didn't leave anyone behind who was...important to you."

Holly shook her head. "It wouldn't have mattered if I had," she said dismissively, her gaze lingering on her sleeping brother. "When the choice was between my personal interests or helping my dad keep the family together after mama lit out, there really wasn't much of a choice."

She spoke calmly, but the betraying catch in her voice told Elizabeth the situation had not been as uncomplicated as Holly pretended. "My biggest regret," she admitted reluctantly, "is that I wasn't able to find a job that pays better than keeping house. Dr. O'Connor is very generous, especially by Ridleyville standards, but since my father's been out of work..."

Elizabeth, aware she was risking a rebuff by probing into matters that didn't concern her, said frankly, "Holly, if money's the main concern, I don't understand why you remain in a place where your options are so limited. In a city, even lacking a college degree someone with your talent should have no trouble landing a job in paste-up or layout, at least, maybe for an ad agency. I'm sure you could support yourself and still send money home to your family."

"But money's not the main concern. The main concern is keeping the family together here in Ridleyville."

Thinking of the dying town, picturing its dismal streets, Elizabeth frowned. "I don't understand."

Holly slipped into a chair opposite the couch. "Yes, I guess that's true," she said without rancor. "I reckon maybe you have to be born here to understand. But Walkers have lived here for a century, ever since my father's great-grandfather first came to this part of the state right after the Civil War."

"He was a Confederate veteran?" Elizabeth asked. Such an ancestor struck her as rather exotic. Her own Swedish forebears hadn't emigrated to the United States until the 1890s.

Holly grinned, the first sign of genuine amusement she'd displayed since Elizabeth had met her; the smile made her look years younger. "Actually," she explained dryly, "my great-great-grandfather was a horse thief—and not a very good one, either, because he got caught. He was sixteen, and he was sentenced to dig coal. Mine owners and other businessmen could rent convict laborers in those days to take the place of the slaves they didn't have anymore. You'd think someone who survived two years in a labor camp would want to turn tail and run as far away as possible once he was released, but instead he stayed in the area. He married a woman from Indian territory—Oklahoma—and homesteaded a little farm. He'd fallen in love with the hills, the river—"

"The country around here is very beautiful," Elizabeth acknowledged.

"That's what great-great-grampa thought. That's what the people in this family still think. We may live in town instead of on a farm, but no Walker ever stays away for long—at least not the ones who were born here."

For a moment the girl was silent, and the cheerful smile lighting her young face faded. Elizabeth sensed she was remembering her absent mother, the woman who had "lit out" one day, leaving behind four bewildered children and a devastated husband. Recalling how she had felt when her own father had vanished from her life, Elizabeth's heart ached for Holly, for Buddy, for Clyde and the two older boys. She glanced down at the youngster napping beside her and tried to imagine what could possibly have happened to make Kayrene Walker desert her home, her babies. It was one question she knew she couldn't ask.

Holly said drearily, "Even when I went away to Fayetteville to school, I always knew I'd be coming back here. I wasn't sure whether I was going to try to be a free-lance artist, or if I'd get a teaching credential, instead. It didn't matter a whole lot, as long as I contributed something. But nowadays I keep wondering what kind of contribution I'm supposed to make washing dishes."

As Elizabeth listened to Holly, she was bothered by an odd qualm. She couldn't recall ever wondering how she might have made a contribution to her hometown in Minnesota.

By the time Jimmy and Darrell, Holly's other brothers, joined her and Buddy after school was dismissed, the drizzle had stopped and streaks of blue sky were opening among the leaden clouds. Holly told Elizabeth she'd left a chicken casserole in the refrigerator, to be baked whenever Elizabeth and Grant wanted their dinner.

The four Walkers set out on foot for their own home, with the three boys squealing and running circles around their sister. Buddy, revived by his nap, picked up a small dead oak branch and began to sprinkle the others with water that had beaded on the leaves. Holly watched their antics indulgently. From the back porch of the parsonage Elizabeth observed the loving care with which the young housekeeper shepherded the unruly trio, and she was struck by the deep bond Holly shared with her brothers, a depth of family feeling Elizabeth could only guess at.

She wondered if perhaps she ought to ring up Amelia, just to see how her sister and mother were doing.

Before Elizabeth could place her call, a claims adjuster from the insurance company telephoned to take her statement. Hoping to explain the circumstances of the accident without laying any more blame on Clyde than absolutely necessary, Elizabeth said nothing about his drinking. She assumed the report filed by the sheriff's deputy would probably mention Clyde's intoxication at the time of the collision, but if it didn't, she preferred not to bring up the subject herself.

When the adjuster finished recording Elizabeth's version of the incident, he made an appointment to meet her at Mack Winters's service station at ten the following morning, Wednesday, to look at the Porsche. Because of the value of the vehicle, he said, the insurance company preferred to have repairs performed by an authorized service center, and the adjuster promised Elizabeth they would have the car in the garage in Fayetteville by Friday. He did not, however, want to estimate how long the repairs would take.

Elizabeth was just hanging the receiver in its cradle on the wall phone when she heard heavy footsteps along the flagstone walk from the church. The screen door banged shut, and suddenly Grant was beside her, the aura she'd first sensed across a boardroom suffocating in the cramped kitchen. Grant's nostrils flared. Obviously he felt something, too.

Yet as strong as their mutual attraction was the memory of their last argument. The razorlike words still dangled between them. They regarded each other gingerly, waiting. It occurred to Elizabeth that she hadn't yet apologized, as she had intended. Forcing her lips into an uncertain smile, she began shyly. "Hello, Grant. Did you have a good afternoon?"

He seemed as flustered as she was. "It was so-so. A lot of paperwork, mostly."

"Is there much paperwork involved in running a church? I had no idea."

"There are always letters to answer, bills to pay." He shrugged, apparently unwilling to elaborate. "How was your day?"

She made a fluttering motion with her fingers. "It was very quiet—although I did find out steps are underway to fix my car."

"Good."

Helplessly she listened to his monosyllabic replies. They didn't even seem able to talk to each other anymore. She wondered why that bothered her. After all, she'd searched for Grant only because she wanted to end their marriage in a civilized way—or so she had thought. If that was the case, why was she hesitating now? They'd agreed on the terms of their divorce within twenty minutes of meeting again. With those arrangements behind them, surely the sensible thing for Elizabeth to do was to leave.

Taking a deep breath, she said, "I've decided that when the towing service picks up my car to haul it to the Porsche dealer, I'm going to hitch a ride. If I stay at a hotel in Fayetteville, I'll be able to supervise the repairs, and once everything's fixed, I can resume my trip immediately, without waiting for the car to be delivered back here."

"That's funny. I came to ask if you would consider remaining here with me at least until your car's fixed, maybe. longer."

Elizabeth wasn't sure she'd heard right. "What?"

"I want you to stay here with me," he repeated patiently. "I think we ought to try to get to know each other better."

Her eyes widened in disbelief. "I don't understand. Are you—are you talking about... getting together again?"

"Liza, please." He caught her arm when she looked as if she'd turn away. "I wasn't asking for a reconciliation. I wouldn't. I haven't the right."

She glanced from his face to the hand touching her forearm, then back again. She couldn't decipher his expression. "If that's not what you meant," she said reasonably, suppressing a peculiar twinge of disappointment, "what were you talking about? Why should we pursue our relationship if we know it's just going to break up?"

"But it's because we're going to break up that we need to know each other better. I realize that sounds paradoxical, but I've been mulling it over all afternoon." He released her and shoved his fists into his pockets, stretching the fabric of his slacks taut across his thighs. With long, nervy strides he began to pace the kitchen; his heels clattered on the linoleum as Liza retreated from his path. Watching each step anxiously, she waited for him to speak.

All at once he halted and looked gravely at her. "When I returned to my office after lunch, I did a lot of thinking about that quarrel we had. I was shocked by all the unresolved conflicts that had surfaced, conflicts on both sides. Until that moment I hadn't realized just how much anger still survived after all these years...."

He pulled his hands from his pockets and held them palms upward in a gesture of penitence. "Liza, I apologize for that crack I made about your being in love with my image. As you said, that was unfair, especially since if I'm honest with myself I have to admit I was guilty of the same thing."

Elizabeth's mouth suddenly felt parched. "I wasn't aware I had an 'image,'" she said, licking her dry lips. "At least, not then." The protective shell of the unnerving Ms Swenson had solidified only after Grant had left her.

Grant queried, "You mean it never occurred to you how mannered your worshipful-disciple posture was? For someone who was supposed to be an adoring student, you were downright aggressive in your determination to learn from me!"

"But you never said anything," Elizabeth pointed out with a frown.

"No, I didn't say anything, because frankly, most of the time I thoroughly enjoyed being your mentor." His eyes slid over her deliberately, the gray irises growing luminous with remembered passion. "Liza, you have no idea what a tremendous ego trip it was to watch you eagerly absorbing everything I taught you. You were a brilliant pupil. Talk about turn-ons.... But every now and then I wondered what was going to happen once you'd decided you'd wrung the last bit of useful knowledge out of me."

Elizabeth listened in bewilderment. How could he have envisioned their relationship as so—so parasitic? He made her sound like some kind of vampire. She knew she had loved him, and she had always thought, that to some extent at least, he had loved her. Hurt and affronted, she demanded, "Grant, are you saying you left me because you didn't want to wait around to find out whether I was going to leave you?"

"I think I'm saying our breakup was inevitable. You must admit our relationship wasn't exactly...healthy."

Elizabeth blinked guiltily. After five years of regarding herself as the injured party, it was difficult to admit she could also have been at fault. "I'm...sorry," she said slowly. "I never realized..."

"It's hard to see things clearly when you're proceeding from a lot of false assumptions—which is something we both seem to have done," Grant conceded. "That's why I think we owe it to ourselves to get to know each other better now. If we do, maybe then we'll be able to understand and come to terms with what happened five years ago." He paused before going on with an effort. "Maybe then we'll be able to avoid making the same mistakes in the future."

Elizabeth felt breathless. "When we marry someone else, you mean?"

"It's always a possibility," he said tonelessly.

All at once her knees were too wobbly to support her. Reaching for the edge of the table, Elizabeth sank into a chair, weak with betrayal. She reminded herself that only the evening before she'd blithely promised not to interfere in Grant's private life. "You—you have someone in mind?" she whispered huskily, staring at her hands.

His voice, usually softly slurred, sounded brusque, clipped, as he said, "Actually, Liza, I was thinking of you. You're still a young woman. You may decide you want to have children."

Children. How could she tell him she already knew she wanted children? With Grant speaking so calmly of their final separation, what good did it do her to dream of a small, sturdy boy like Buddy Walker; perhaps a little girl with coppery curls.... The images faded and blurred. Elizabeth raised her head to gaze at Grant, at the rugged, implacable features, the silver strands prematurely frosting the auburn hair at the temples. A determined man with principles uniquely his own; a man who would not allow himself to be swayed from whatever course he'd set.

"You've left me no choice, have you, Grant? If I want children, I guess I'm going to have to find someone else to be their father." She smiled whimsically. "Heaven knows I'd never cut it as a preacher's wife!"

Recognizing her attempt to lighten the mood, Grant said wryly, "Well, my dear, that's one job you'll never have to take on, because, just for the record, I'm a scholar, not a preacher. As I think I've explained before, I'm just filling in at Good Samaritan until a regular pastor can be found. My time is usually spent writing and doing historical research." He paused. "In fact, if you come listen to my sermon tomorrow night, you'll find out exactly how much of a preacher I'm not!"

When Elizabeth didn't respond at once, he touched her cheek and said seriously, "Please, Liza? You knew all about my work when we were living together. It would mean a great deal to me to have a chance to show you the kinds of things I do now."

Elizabeth knew she was more curious than ever about the forces that drove Grant, but still she hesitated. She tried not to press her face into the curve of his palm like a kitten cuddling for warmth. "Grant, I'd love to learn more about what you're doing, but won't it cause problems for you? I'm sure your parishioners are already bewildered by my sudden appearance, after they'd assumed you were a bachelor. If I start tagging along with you everywhere, what are they going to think?"

Grant pulled away and slid his hands into his pockets again. "They'll think we've been separated and are trying to work things out," he said calmly. "The more romantic ones will assume we've embarked on a second honeymoon and you can't bear to be apart from me even for a few hours. Whatever they think, they'll wish us well."

"And what happens after my car's fixed and I go away again?" Elizabeth persisted.

"They'll probably decide the honeymoon was a dud! Most people believe clergymen are eunuchs, anyway," Grant snapped in exasperation. "Liza, why should it matter to you what anyone in Ridleyville thinks? You're not staying. Let me worry about it!"

"But I'm only concerned about you!"

At that plaintive cry, Grant caught himself. "Right," he muttered roughly, his volatile temper subsiding as quickly as it had risen. "Oh, damn, I'm sorry I yelled."

Elizabeth looked away. "It's funny, but I don't remember us barking at each other before."

"We didn't. I'm not sure we were ever together long enough to get under each other's skin that way."

Elizabeth shivered at his choice of words. "No, not that

way, at any rate," she agreed, thinking of all the other ways their skin, their bodies had joined. Their eyes met again, and for a moment they shared erotic memories. Then she sighed. "Oh, Grant, we had so much at the beginning. What happened to us?"

There didn't seem to be any answer.

After a moment he pulled out the chair opposite her and sat down, looking at her thoughtfully. Slowly he said, "You know, Liza, if you really are uncomfortable with the idea of what people might think about your staying here, I've thought of a way to explain your presence in town. Who knows? Considering your business acumen, you might even accomplish something constructive while you're at it."

She glanced up cautiously. "What did you have in mind?"

"I was thinking that you might take a closer look at the Bailey Pottery, with Suzanne's and Bobby Lee's permission, of course. The company is obviously tottering on the brink of bankruptcy, and if it goes under, I'm afraid it will take what's left of Ridleyville with it. You've already seen what's happening to families like the Walkers as production is cut back. With your expertise, perhaps you could come up with suggestions to make the business viable again."

"I know nothing about industrial ceramics, though."

"You knew nothing about electronics when you went to work for Avotel, but as I recall, your first project there was to survey the sound-equipment branch and decide whether the corporation should keep it."

"And we recommended dumping it," she reminded him dryly. "*We* recommended—I was part of a team, remember? Not to mention the fact that we had two months to complete the study before we reported back to the board. I'm not sure what you think I could do in a few days, on my own—or were you planning to help me?"

Grant shook his head. "I'm afraid I won't have the time. One of the deacons told me this afternoon that the pastoral-search committee is finally ready to interview candidates. Since this is the first time in twenty years that Good Samaritan has convened such a committee, they want my recommendations."

"That's too bad. I could use your recommendations myself, if you seriously believe one person with management skills can save the Bailey Pottery."

Grant admitted, "I don't know about saving it—maybe the business is too far gone to save—but a little expert advice certainly won't harm anything."

Elizabeth deliberated for several moments. Then, pushing back her chair, she nodded. "All right. I'll see what I can do—but only with the Baileys' cooperation, of course."

"Of course. We could hardly take steps without it."

She paused, gazing across the table at him with puzzled eyes. "When you were a businessman, Grant, your experience and expertise outweighed just about everyone's, including mine—and no matter how cloistered a life you've lived the past five years, you can't convince me you've forgotten all you used to know about commerce and finance." She licked her lips meditatively. "So if you're truly concerned about the future of the pottery and, by extension, the town, then...well...I don't understand why you haven't tackled the problem yourself."

He looked up, a sad, almost wistful smile playing across his rugged features; it was an expression Elizabeth had never seen on his face before. He said softly, "Why don't

I... get back down to business? My dear, I don't have the courage."

WELL, *there's one way I've contributed to Ridleyville's economy,* Elizabeth thought sardonically as she watched Mack Winters's tow truck ease into the street, dragging her silver Porsche behind. Strips of loose chrome rattled alarmingly as the automobile bounced over the curb and onto the pavement. Hazard lights clamped to the twisted bumper began to blink in tandem. Elizabeth shivered. Her fingers clenched, and she heard the waxy crackle of the charge-card slip she still held in her hand. As she tucked it into her purse, she glanced once again at the amount scribbled on the bottom and tried not to wince. At least Mr. Winters had been delighted. Even with the discount he'd given her—"You being the reverend's wife and all"—the fee for towing her sports car to Fayetteville probably equaled several days' receipts at his service station.

Waving goodbye to the youth who was to watch the station in the owner's absence, Elizabeth slung her purse strap over her shoulder and turned to walk back toward the parsonage. Grant, ensconced in his office, polishing up his midweek sermon, had offered to loan her his compact sedan, but she had refused, saying she wanted some exercise. The stroll along Ridleyville's main street was pleasant and relaxing, exactly what she needed after the stress of the past couple of days.

Last night there had been no repeat of the first evening's passion. While they had eaten Holly's chicken casserole, by tacit consent Grant and Elizabeth had avoided further discussion of either business or religion, instead chatting about a number of impersonal subjects.

Elizabeth described some of the sights she'd seen in

Belgium, from the Wellington Museum at Waterloo to the diamond market in Antwerp. Grant in turn regaled her with anecdotes about the intrinsic difficulties of going back to school at thirty-five. "There I was, nervously clutching my shiny new notebook, when this *kid* walked in, barely old enough to shave, and I suddenly realized he was supposed to be my *instructor*!"

Both of them had laughed and joked, sharing camaraderie unlike anything Elizabeth could remember from the intense early days of their relationship. When she had excused herself for the night, she'd had the feeling she was bidding good-night to a friend.

Friend. Alone in her room, perched cross-legged on the crocheted bedspread, her hair still damp from her bath and feathering against her cheeks, Elizabeth had tried to make notes of what she'd seen at the Bailey Pottery that morning; she wanted everything written down while it was still fresh in her mind. Instead her pen kept stopping in midsentence while she thought of the pleasant, undemanding evening she'd just spent with her husband.

Friends. She'd like to be friends with Grant. She'd like to be able to smile with him, weep with him, share her innermost secrets without fear he would misunderstand or condemn. During the year when their marriage had been real and not just a legal technicality, she remembered them talking a lot. Yet she wasn't sure either of them had ever listened very much. Perhaps things would have been different if they had. But they were both passionate, intensely self-absorbed people, and she supposed they'd been too busy being lovers to take time to be friends.

A crisp breeze cut into Elizabeth's reverie as she continued walking, making her grateful for the light cardigan she wore. Although a rain-laden weather front had moved on during the night, leaving the sky a bright, freshly washed cerulean, now the air was noticeably cooler than it had been the day before. It had an invigorating edge that Elizabeth suspected signaled the end of Indian summer. Trees seemed to be dropping their multicolored leaves at a faster rate, and Elizabeth noticed a backyard garden where pumpkins glowed like globes of flame against their faded, drooping vines. She inhaled deeply. Somewhere nearby a neighbor was baking an apple pie, rich with cinnamon. The warm aroma floated lusciously through the neighborhood, reminding Elizabeth that she hadn't eaten lunch yet.

She ought to head back to the parsonage, in case Holly had something prepared and waiting, but she was in no hurry. She was enjoying her walk. Fall was her favorite season. She had always loved the colors, the smells, the light, clean feel of the air as it lost its summer mugginess. With the harvest came the sense of tasks accomplished and laid aside. To someone who had never allowed herself sufficient time to relax, to be still, autumn promised repose.

As she strolled along the sidewalk, an old pickup pulled up beside her, and a woman who looked vaguely familiar leaned out. "Good afternoon, Mrs. O'Connor. Can we give you a lift?"

"No, thank you," Elizabeth replied automatically, trying to place her. After a moment she recognized the woman as one of Grant's neighbors who had rushed to their aid after the accident. With more conviction she repeated, "No, thank you. I appreciate your offer, but I'm just out taking a little walk."

"Lovely day for it," the woman agreed cordially, drawing her head back inside the window. "In that case, I guess we'll see you at church tonight. Bye now."

"Bye," Elizabeth called after the truck as it trundled away. She went on, thinking about the incident, touched by the warmth and amiability displayed not only by that woman but by everyone she'd met so far in Ridleyville. Suzanne's dinner invitation the night Elizabeth arrived was only one example; someone else had already asked if she'd like to join a Bible-study group, and still another person had dropped by the parsonage to present her with a jar of brandied peaches, pineapple and cherries called Friendship Fruit.

Yes, they were all truly nice people, welcoming and unfailingly courteous despite their obvious curiosity about her and Grant's marital status. Some were going to feel as if she'd deliberately rebuffed them when she left town again.

Her disquiet grew deeper that night when she and Grant strode together along the flagstone walk to his office. In her entire life Elizabeth had attended church perhaps a dozen times, including weddings and her high-school graduation service, and she waited restlessly while Grant frowned over his notes. Voices, the noise of shuffling feet drifted in from the front corridor. Through the interior walls filtered the muffled chords of an organ pumping out something meditative that sounded like a Chopin nocturne. Elizabeth stared at the books, the diplomas, the potted African violet on the circular table. She wondered who kept Suzanne's plants watered.

Her eyes returning to Grant, she studied him appreciatively. He was dressed the way she'd always preferred him, in his dark suit, a plain white shirt and striped tie replacing the clerical collar she had found so threatening. Except for his too-short hair, he looked reassuringly familiar, more like the man who used to quell unruly corporate directors with a single glance from his steely eyes. She was astonished then she heard the neatly typewritten pages rustle nervously as he thumbed through them.

Elizabeth caught her breath, and Grant looked up in time to see the troubled expression flitting across her face. He smiled sheepishly. "Don't worry, Liza, it's a touch of stage fright, that's all. I'll be fine in a minute."

"I—I just don't think I've ever seen you acting overly agitated before, not even when you were getting ready to face down two thousand angry stockholders at an annual meeting."

"Facing an auditorium full of angry stockholders was never half as intimidating as trying to preach a sermon!"

"Then why do you do it?"

He folded the sheaf of papers and slipped them inside his jacket. He checked his wristwatch and straightened his tie. Then he looked at Elizabeth and said calmly, "I do it, Liza, because I couldn't face myself if I didn't."

She shook her head in confusion. "I still don't understand what you mean. What is it you find in religion that you didn't find in your old life?"

Grant's eyes lit up. "Do you realize this is the first time you've asked me that? I didn't think you cared."

"Of course I care," she responded roughly. "No matter how we ultimately resolve things, I'll always care about you."

He drew a ragged breath. "Bless you for telling me that, Liza. You'll never know what it means to me." They stared at each other in silence. In the sanctuary the organ suddenly grew louder, as if to signal. Shaking his head like a man coming out of a trance, Grant said reluctantly, "Look, why don't you ask me again, sometime when I have about a year to explain? Right now the service is ready to begin."

CHAPTER EIGHT

"EVERYONE WAS SO THRILLED to meet you last night!" Doris Butley gushed, her stiffly lacquered hair refusing to move with her.

"And I was delighted to meet them," Elizabeth replied as she sipped coffee in the church office. Grant was away making pastoral calls, and at midmorning the secretary had trotted over to the parsonage to invite Elizabeth to join her for her break. Mrs. Butley joked that if she didn't want to gain another five pounds, she needed someone to help finish the last of the apricot-pecan bread. Elizabeth thought it more likely the woman hoped to hear her impressions of the evening church service. "Everyone was very warm, very cordial," Elizabeth said sincerely. "I just felt a little awkward being the center of attention, that's all."

The night before, when Grant had left Elizabeth in the narthex, the church vestibule, explaining that he had to enter the front of the sanctuary from a side door near the pulpit, she realized his nervousness had been contagious. She didn't know how to act; on a one-to-one basis she had socialized with his parishioners easily enough. Yet she had no idea what the congregation en masse would expect of her. Suddenly she understood what he meant about feeling intimidated.

After Grant disappeared around a corner, she glanced through the open double doors into the auditorium, cravenly hoping the service would be poorly attended. More than half the seats were filled. Elizabeth sighed and braced herself. Ducking inside the sanctuary, she slipped surreptitiously into a back pew.

She sat stiffly on the hard, wooden seat, looking straight ahead as she waited for Grant to appear. Someone a few feet away dropped a mimeographed leaflet marked Order of Worship, and it fluttered to the floor in front of her. Automatically Elizabeth leaned down to pick it up. As she handed the paper back to the woman, she found herself gazing into the warm brown eyes of Suzanne Bailey.

"Mrs. O'Connor, how nice to see you again!" Suzanne exclaimed in a stage whisper, scooting closer. "I've been hoping we'd have a chance to talk. My, that's a pretty dress!" All around them people in adjoining pews turned to stare, their friendly smiles failing to disguise sharp curiosity. Elizabeth raised a hand in greeting, grinning weakly, but at that moment the organist struck a resounding chord, and Grant appeared in the front of the sanctuary. Heads swiveled forward again. Elizabeth sank back into her corner, limp with relief.

"Our call to worship tonight is Psalm 100," Grant announced, and throughout the congregation people reached for their Bibles. At Elizabeth's side, Suzanne opened to the designated verse as Grant began to read: " 'Make a joyful noise to the Lord, all the lands. Serve the Lord with gladness. Come into His presence with singing.' " The words rang out, clear and sonorous, their poetry increased by the obvious deep conviction in his voice. Elizabeth felt moved in spite of herself.

Then, on an unspoken signal, Bibles were returned to the pew racks and hymnals were taken out. Elizabeth glanced curiously at the mimeographed agenda. A song came next. She watched Suzanne leaf to the page number indicated, but before the girl reached it, from the pulpit Grant's deep tones said solemnly, "Before we sing our first hymn, we need to take a moment to welcome any newcomers. Are there guests or visitors here this evening who'd like to stand up and introduce themselves?" Elizabeth froze.

Suzanne giggled as once again people twisted in their seats to gawk. In the expectant hush Elizabeth blushed and retreated farther into the pew; she couldn't remember ever being so nervous in her life. Over the heads of the congregation, her apprehensive gaze met Grant's pleadingly. He nodded.

"Yes, ladies and gentlemen—" once again he assumed control of the audience "—I imagine by now most of you already know that there is indeed one very special guest in our midst tonight. She's obviously feeling a little bashful right now, but I hope your welcome will convince her there's nothing to be afraid of. Liza, won't you please stand up?"

Still she hesitated. Her eyes were locked with Grant's, and she sat immobile until she could feel Suzanne tug at her arm. Then, chiding herself for behaving like a child, Elizabeth rose, a strained smile pasted to her lips. The answering smiles on the faces around her looked genuine, as genuine as the warmth and, astonishingly, pride in Grant's voice when he said, "Friends, this evening I'm deeply honored to introduce to you my wife, Elizabeth Swenson O'Connor." The congregation began to clap....

"I certainly wasn't expecting applause," Elizabeth told Mrs. Butley ruefully.

"But that's just how we do it at Good Samaritan," the secretary said. "There was no need for you to feel shy. We always begin by welcoming any newcomers. It's friendlier.

Didn't you do it that way at the church that sponsored Reverend O'Connor's ordination?''

Elizabeth shifted uncomfortably. She could feel heat rising in her cheeks. "I, uh, that is, we—"

"You two were already separated then," Mrs. Butley supplied acutely. "I wondered about that. I knew he hadn't been ordained very long." Her expression was benign as she added gently, "Don't be embarrassed, honey. People understand about these things. Everybody just hopes and prays that the two of you are able to work out your problems."

"Thank you," Elizabeth murmured. "You're very kind."

After a pause Mrs. Butley added cheerfully, "Is that nut bread all right? Help yourself to as much as you want. I had a bumper crop of apricots this summer, and my grandsons gathered bushels of native pecans from along the roadside, but now we're all getting rather tired of eating them. I've been looking forward to baking persimmon cookies and the like—I have a tree in my backyard that's just loaded with fruit—but you can't harvest them until after the first heavy frost. Maybe now that the weather finally seems about to—"

She broke off abruptly, declaring, "Lordy, will you listen to me run off at the mouth that way! You don't want to hear about my persimmon tree. Tell me what you think of Ridleyville. Have you ever been in Arkansas before?"

"I've never been in the South before, period."

"And is it what you expected?"

Elizabeth considered. "Well, yes and no. I'd seen enough old movies to know the countryside would be beautiful, with all the woods and rolling hills, but I don't think I was prepared for the serenity, the sort of lush tranquility that overlays everything."

She hesitated, uncertain how to phrase what she wanted to say without sounding derogatory. "One thing that did surprise me," she admitted carefully, "was the people themselves, the variety of them, living and working together. Around town and at the service last night I've met Mexicans, Cubans, Chinese, Vietnamese. I guess I always envisioned a much more homogeneous society, certainly a more...stratified one."

"'Stratified'?" Mrs. Butley asked darkly. "Are you sure you don't mean 'segregated'? I know the reputation Arkansas has. On television they still show newsreels from the fifties of National Guardsmen escorting black children to school in Little Rock. And while I can't pretend this state has always been a shining example of social harmony—how many places are, if you're honest about it—the fact is, people here have moved with the times and are better off for it."

"Doris, you misunderstood me. What I was trying—and failing, obviously—to say was that to a Northerner like me, the name 'Arkansas' usually conjures up visions of hillbilly farmers in log cabins who plow with mules and make their own moonshine."

A look of humor returned to the secretary's worn face as she relaxed visibly. Refilling her coffee cup, she chuckled. "Now you sound like Kayrene Walker. I don't think she ever did quite forgive us for not being the simple rustics she'd always imagined."

The reference to Holly's absent mother caught Elizabeth by surprise. "She wasn't from around here?"

"My goodness, no. She was a city girl—Baltimore, or some place like that. I never did figure out exactly how she came to Ridleyville, but one day twenty or so years ago she showed up in her long patchwork skirt and her granny glasses, with her liberal-arts degree tucked under her arm. She was the first hippie we'd ever seen, and people looked at her as if she'd come from Mars—especially when she announced she intended to 'return to basics,' and rented a ramshackle little house a ways outside of town with no electricity or running water. For a while she scratched around trying to grow organic vegetables, but mostly living off the allowance checks someone sent her from back East. People got used to her. She was silly but harmless, and everyone pretty much left her alone...." Doris paused. "All except Clyde Walker, that is. He fell in love with her."

"And she loved him?"

"Everyone loved Clyde. God knows he was a handsome devil in those days, a real heartbreaker, carefree and always helling around. Younger kids like Bobby Lee Bailey used to tag around after him wherever he went. Kayrene may have thought he was a fellow free spirit, but when she got pregnant, she discovered just how responsible Clyde really was. He declared flatly that no child of his was going to be a bastard or live in a hovel, and he dragged her off to the justice of the peace.

"He got a job at the pottery—which was a good thing, because the allowance checks stopped coming—Holly was born and the three of them settled down to an ordinary, dull routine like anyone else. Kayrene hated it. She'd got tired of the simple life, and then she said she was sick of vegetating in a place where there wasn't anything to do but go to movies and get fat. Naturally Clyde would never consider living anywhere else—"

"I gather Walkers are funny that way," Elizabeth noted.

Doris nodded. "Oh, yes. Only Kayrene couldn't understand that. Over the years as the boys were born and money got tighter, her frustration just seemed to get worse, although I will admit she stuck it out for a very long time. She was the one who encouraged Holly to work so hard to earn that scholarship—only now I'm not so sure that was a good thing...."

"But what made her finally decide to leave?"

"Who knows. Maybe it was the sight of her daughter going away to college, reminding Kayrene of how she'd never done anything worthwhile with her own education. Or maybe the last straw came when the movie theater closed down. Some people say she met another man, although nobody knows who. I'm not so sure about that myself—in a town the size of Ridleyville, it's pretty hard to carry on an extramarital affair without someone finding out—but the fact remains that finally last winter she dug up enough cash from somewhere to buy a plane ticket back East, and she announced she was going away to 'find herself.' Then she just took off."

Elizabeth thought of the family Kayrene had left behind, the husband and children who still suffered because of her defection; she thought of her own father. "It's beyond me how anyone could be so—so selfish," she murmured painfully.

"I don't think it's a question of just being selfish. Not that I'm trying to excuse what Kayrene did, but when you get to be my age you learn that life is never as simple as it sounds. Heaven knows, although my husband and I were very fortunate in our life and our children, even in the best marriages there are moments when you feel like chucking it all."

"Chucking it all." Elizabeth trembled. That was the same idiom Grant had used when he had told her he was going away. "But doesn't it *hurt* to leave?" she cried.

Doris regarded her sympathetically. "I imagine it does. In fact, after what I've seen working in this church, I know it does."

Elizabeth took a deep breath. Yes, she knew it, also. For five years she had tried to pretend otherwise, but the memory of Grant's anguish that awful day was seared too deeply into her brain. Whatever his reasons for leaving, he had suffered when he'd gone away.

She wondered if her father had suffered, too.

After the secretary's coffee break was over, Elizabeth thanked her for the snack and headed back to the parsonage. Along the path she passed Buddy, perched disconsolately on the gym set, his face glum as he kicked his short legs in a futile effort to make the swing move. Elizabeth stopped. Soon the child was arching wildly back and forth, his crows of delight blending with the alarming creak of the rusty chains in a dissonant duet that echoed through the quiet neighborhood. "Higher, higher!" he cried, and Elizabeth pushed until her arms were tired.

"That's enough, Buddy." She laughed. "You're wearing me out. I have to go. You ought to be able to keep the swing moving yourself now."

"Will you play with me later?"

"We'll see." Waving, she continued along the flagstone walk.

At the back porch, Holly stepped out from behind the thicket of red vines and held open the screen door as Elizabeth mounted the wooden steps. "Thank you for taking the time to play with Buddy," she said gravely, a dejected catch in her voice.

Elizabeth glanced sharply at her as they went into the kitchen. Beneath her college sweat shirt the girl's thin body slumped, and her hazel eyes looked suspiciously pink.

When she felt Elizabeth staring at her, Holly scurried to the sink and began to dismember a head of lettuce.

"What's wrong?" Elizabeth demanded, looking at the razorback emblem between Holly's shoulder blades. For a moment the only sound in the kitchen was that of water gushing from the tap; then, as she turned off the faucet, her shoulders began to tremble. With a sob Holly tore away from the sink and flung herself into one of the kitchen chairs.

"What's wrong?" she wailed. "Dear God, what's *not* wrong?" She buried her face in her hands and began to cry.

Elizabeth didn't attempt to comfort her. The girl's lament was too painful, her grief too profound for conventional consolation. Moans interspersed with harsh gasps that seemed to be ripped from her. Elizabeth listened compassionately. She had cried like that once. She had been unpacking her clothes in her new flat in Brussels, in an apartment-hotel on the Rue Louise, and as she shook out her winter coat before hanging it in the wardrobe, a leather glove, size extra-large, had fallen out of the pocket, a strand of silver Christmas tinsel looped around the long, empty fingers....

Elizabeth stepped over to the counter, picked up a paring knife and methodically sliced tomatoes. By the time she finished assembling the salad, the girl's sobs had diminished into blubbery sniffles. As Elizabeth stretched plastic wrap across the top of the bowl and slipped the salad into the refrigerator, behind her she heard Holly say sheepishly, "I'm sorry, Mrs. O'Connor. You shouldn't have had to do that."

"No big deal." Turning to face Holly, she asked quietly, "Do you want to talk about it?"

Holly mopped at her eyes with the sleeve of her sweat

shirt. "There's not a whole lot to tell," she said dispiritedly, looking and sounding incredibly young. "Yesterday in the mail daddy got a notice from the mortgage company saying that if he doesn't bring the payments up to date by the end of the month, they'll start foreclosure proceedings. He told me if we lose the house, we may have to farm the boys out to some relatives in Missouri and Tennessee."

"Good Lord, is it really as bad as that?" Elizabeth exclaimed, horrified.

Holly's chin lifted a fraction of an inch and fell again. "It sure is."

"But there must be family or friends or even some kind of government aid—"

"Daddy's unemployment ran out months ago," the girl declared baldly, "and my father would literally rather die than ask for welfare. In fact, sometimes I wonder if that's not the reason he gets dr—" She caught herself before she could utter the damning words, and Elizabeth pretended not to notice the slip. Hastily Holly finished, "As for family and friends, of course they'd like to help out, but the best they could offer would be to take the boys into their homes. Things are tough all over."

"Things are tough all over." Elizabeth had heard that platitude too often to question its validity. It was her sister Amelia's favorite response to any remarks Elizabeth made that might be construed, however obliquely, as complaints about her own lot in life.

When Elizabeth mentioned to her brother-in-law, during one of their few serious conversations, that gasoline in Europe still cost three times as much as it did in the United States, Amelia had cut in with peevish sarcasm, "Yeah, things are tough all over, aren't they?" When Elizabeth asked her eldest niece to fill her in on the latest popular

American television shows, which were six months out of date by the time they aired overseas, Amelia had said it again. Her envy and resentment seemed to grow each time she glanced at Elizabeth's clothes or compared her careful, chic grooming to Amelia's own worn dumpiness. Ever since Elizabeth had started her first job after college, she'd regularly sent money home to Minnesota, but somehow those generous checks, meant to show her mother and sister that Elizabeth still considered herself part of the family, only widened the chasm between them.

"You're lucky to have relatives who care enough to help out at all," Elizabeth murmured.

Holly shrugged. "I reckon. Unfortunately good intentions don't have much value as collateral." Absently she began to pick at her long pigtail as she stared, unseeing, at the kitchen clock. "Daddy's so depressed these days he hardly remembers to get out of bed, so I've been trying to think of someone with the kind of money we'd need to get us out of the fix we're in, but I don't know anyone except maybe the Baileys." She laughed mirthlessly. "Suzanne's too busy pretending she's still homecoming queen to pay attention to other people's worries, and of course it's all Bobby Lee's fault we're in this mess in the first place!"

The words popped from Elizabeth's lips almost before her mind had time to form them. "I have the money."

Holly's eyes grew wide with astonishment, and a crimson flush crept upward over the girl's throat and cheeks, staining them the color of her sweat shirt. "I wasn't hinting."

"I didn't think you were."

"But why should you want to help us, especially when it was my father who wrecked your car?"

Elizabeth pondered her reply for several moments. How could she explain her quixotic offer when she wasn't certain she knew the reasons herself? Was she acting out of simple charity, concern for a fellow human being in distress, or was the answer more complex? Had she made the gesture because she knew Holly would accept it graciously, as Elizabeth's sister and mother never did, or was her generosity instead somehow tied to her feelings for Grant? Certainly it would please him if she found a way to help the Walkers. Did she want to please Grant? Maybe her actions were connected to her growing awareness of him, her fatalistic admission that, despite bewildering changes in him over the years, she loved him. In all probability, she had never stopped loving him.

"Mrs. O'Connor, if you're serious, then God knows I won't turn down a loan. Even if my father's too proud to accept a handout, I'm not. Still, I really don't understand why you'd offer one. You hardly know us."

Elizabeth gazed down at the lanky girl and thought of her loving concern for her brothers, her father; the sacrifices she'd made without hesitation to keep her family together. Somewhere in the corridors of the past Elizabeth heard a masculine voice hoarse with need echoing pleadingly, "Together. Together forever...." Another life, certainly another context, yet even after five years the strong appeal of that dream of unity, of belonging, had remained seductive enough to send Elizabeth on a quest halfway around the world. Now she honestly doubted she herself would ever find the phantom she pursued, but perhaps she could help another woman, younger and less cynical, achieve her own dreams.

Gently Elizabeth said, "The answer's simple, Holly. I just don't like the idea of a family being torn apart."

IN THE EVENING Grant closed the windows, shutting out the music that drifted across the field from the church, where the choir practiced. He lit the gas wall furnace in the hallway for the first time that season. The sheet-metal panels on the stove clanged and popped alarmingly as they expanded with the heat, and as the warm air circulated throughout the parsonage the atmosphere became pungent with the odor of burning dust. In the parlor Elizabeth's nose began to tickle warningly.

"Sorry about the musty smell," Grant commented with a grimace as he returned to the parlor. "But it shouldn't last long." He settled into a chair across from the couch where Elizabeth sat with her bare feet tucked comfortably beneath her. She was trying to tell him about her conversation with Holly, and instead of listening with proper pastoral concern, all he could think about was how he hungered to be on that couch beside her, on her....

"The thing that worried me most—" She broke off to sneeze. Quickly she fished inside her purse, lying on the end table beside her, and buried her face in her handkerchief.

"Bless you," Grant murmured automatically. His eyes narrowed as he watched her slender body bend and arch. The light from the table lamp burnished her cheekbones and glinted through her pale curls like platinum whenever she moved. She had taken off the cardigan she'd been wearing over her gauze top, and when she stretched sideways to return her handkerchief to the purse, the sleek curve of her breast was silhouetted through the embroidered fabric. He could feel his palms grow clammy. With herculean self-discipline he forced his attention back to what Elizabeth was saying.

"So you're going to give the Walkers a loan? That's remarkably generous of you."

Elizabeth smiled ironically. "Oh, no, it's not. Avotel pays me more than I have time to spend. By making the offer, I'm not giving up anything all that important to me."

Remembering how in the early days of their relationship she had rejected several excellent salary offers because she didn't think the job descriptions sounded challenging enough, Grant asked intuitively, "Money has never been all that important to you, has it Liza—I mean, except as an indication that your work is valued?"

"Everyone likes to think her work has value," Elizabeth said with a shrug. "'By their works ye shall judge them.' Isn't that something biblical, or did I misquote?" Without waiting for Grant to respond to her quip, she continued, "In fact, I suspect that a lot of Clyde Walker's problems have less to do with needing money than with feeling literally worthless."

Grant nodded. "Many people who are chronically unemployed reach that point. If their job skills have no value, they decide, that must mean they personally have no value, either. Of course, in Clyde's case his self-esteem had already been badly shattered when his wife walked out on..." He couldn't go on, and he felt himself flush. Jumping to his feet, he began to pace the room, skirting the coffee table to stop directly in front of her. "Liza..."

Elizabeth had to crane her neck to peer up at him. She scooted backward, deeper into the lumpy cushions of the sofa. With an impassivity she didn't feel she reminded him, "I survived, Grant. You didn't make me feel worthless. I wouldn't let you."

"Thank God for that!" He wondered if she had any idea how fervent his prayer really was.

Unable to resist his need to be close to her, he flopped down onto the sofa, his weight making the springs sag toward him. Elizabeth tucked her legs tighter beneath her to avoid brushing her knees against his thigh. Reminding herself sternly that she and Grant were discussing something important, she continued, "The thing that concerned me most about my talk with Holly was the way she kept referring to her father's depression. I could tell she was worried. I hope he doesn't do something desperate."

"Such as?" The house was silent except for the whisper of the heater, and in the quiet his voice sounded honey dark, honey smooth.

"I don't know!" Elizabeth retorted, exasperated with herself for responding to his nearness. "All I know is that Clyde Walker needs a job, and I intend to do what I can do help him get one. I would have liked to have been able to tell Holly that, but obviously I can't say anything until we've talked to the Baileys and got their approval."

"If you like, I can call Bobby Lee and make an appointment. Tomorrow's Friday. Will that be all right?"

"Of course. The sooner the better. But I'll want Suzanne to be there, too."

Grant's mouth twisted cynically. "You know, Liza, Suzanne may be part owner, but she has nothing to do with the running of the pottery. She lets Bobby Lee handle everything."

Remembering the dinner-table conversation several nights before, Elizabeth said grimly, "Yes, I do know. Still, she may be able to help me dig up the kind of information I'll need as quickly as possible, without disturbing her brother or interfering with the day-to-day operation of the plant."

"Do you have any idea how long your troubleshooting will require?" He paused. Then with the masochism of one deliberately probing a sore tooth, he persisted, "Or do you plan to leave as soon as your car is ready, whether your study's finished or not?"

Elizabeth's fingers, which had been resting lightly on her calf, suddenly clenched; through the linen fabric of her slacks her nails dug painfully into the muscle. "Although I do need to get settled in New York before the first of the year, I—I suppose I can stay here a few days longer. Maybe until Thanksgiving."

Grant reached over and took her cold hand in his warm one, lifting her fingers away from the fabric. Elizabeth tried to jerk away, but instead of releasing her, he forced his thumb into the tunnel formed by her tight fist. Deliberately he began to massage the sensitive pad of her palm with slow, seductive movements. One by one her knuckles relaxed. When he felt her tension ease, he whispered, his accent suddenly very pronounced, "I'd love to have you stay for Thanksgiving, Liza. No matter where I am, it's the one holiday that always makes me want to be down home again, with all that glorious Southern cooking—turkey with corn-bread dressing, giblet gravy, candied yams, pecan pie...."

"Sounds fattening." Elizabeth tittered uneasily.

His hand slid upward to stroke the fragile bones of her wrist; he could span it with his thumb and forefinger. "It wouldn't hurt you to gain a few pounds, you know," he murmured. Lifting her palm to his lips, with the tip of his tongue he began to map the upward course of the veins that showed blue-violet through her translucent skin.

Elizabeth shivered. His mouth was grazing along the inside of her arm, deliberately tantalizing. She tried to pull away, but the fingers that braceleted her wrist would not part. "Grant, please stop. We don't want this."

His russet-colored brows arched as he lifted his head.

"Don't we?" he mocked mildly. "I've wanted this since the moment you barged into my office the other afternoon." Pushing aside her wide sleeve, he returned his attention to her arm as he murmured, "Every night I've been slowly going crazy, knowing you were sleeping just down the hall from me."

"Grant," Elizabeth pleaded hoarsely. His tongue flicked over the inner fold of her elbow as if it were the most intimate and erogenous part of her body, each moist stroke generating sparks of sensation that arced along her spine, her extremities. She could feel herself begin to tighten responsively, while every other muscle seemed to relax; against her will she was growing languid, receptive.... With reluctant effort she attempted once more to free her arm, and this time when she jerked back, she caught him off balance and he fell against her. The two of them teetered precariously on the edge of the sofa.

Instinctively Elizabeth clung to him to keep from falling; Grant's grip tightened around her as he nudged her safely back into the center of the cushions. She was startled by the familiar security of his arms, the comforting weight of that long hard body sprawled over hers. He wanted her. His arousal was so unmistakable that Elizabeth gasped, uncertain whether she was dismayed or delighted by his urgency. Instantly Grant's mouth covered hers, the taste of her own skin still salty sweet on his tongue.

Doubt faded. Her eyelids dropped shut. As his hands slipped beneath her blouse to cup her unconfined breasts, she sighed lusciously. She could feel him quiver with excitement when his fingertips discovered her already-erect nipples, the puckered crests swollen and aching with her need of him. "Oh, God, Liza, let me see you," he groaned against her lips. "For five years I've dreamed—" Lifting himself away, he caught the blouse by the hem and jerked it over her head. He stared in wonder at her naked torso, her small breasts that were still high and firm as a girl's above the jut of her rib cage. Against her alabaster-white skin the rosy tips glowed their invitation.

"You still want me," he marveled, gulping thickly. "After all this time, I was so afraid—"

"Hush," she whispered. She fumbled with his shirt buttons, straining the threads in her haste to be near him. When the lapels flapped open, she slid her arms under the shirt and drew him down to her again, chest against breast. Arching against him, she curled her legs around his so that through the fabric of his trousers she could tease his muscular calves with the instep of one bare foot. She wriggled awkwardly beneath him, trying to find a more comfortable position on the lumpy couch as she pulled him deeper into the cradle of her thighs. "Hush," she said again. "Don't talk. Everything will be all right if we just don't talk."

Grant was too engrossed in the wonder of relearning her to hear the lingering uncertainty in her voice. Each movement of the tender body beneath him was driving him closer to the brink, that moment of sweet madness when he would cast off all his lately learned restraint and resume his primal identity, that of a man with his mate. He was going to make it perfect for her; he was going to make everything perfect for her from now on. They belonged together—and he would ensnare her in the web of their mutual need and bind her so close that nothing, no doubt or blame or question, however sharp, would ever cut them apart again.

Propping himself on his elbow to gaze lovingly at her features, Grant felt his arm slip off the edge of the narrow cushion, and he fell heavily against her, punching the air from her lungs. Her eyes flew open, murky with desire.

Kissing her lightly, Grant drawled, "Excuse me, darling, I didn't mean to squash you." He added, "You know, there's no need for us to try to make it on the couch like a couple of teenagers. There are any number of perfectly good beds upstairs."

The easy words, intended to reassure, jarred. Elizabeth grew very still. She blinked up into his face, her vision clearing; her mind clearing. She realized they were lying together half-naked, more than halfway to the point of no return. All the inhibitions and insecurity of five years of celibacy collapsed on her, crushing her desire as Grant's weight crushed her into the cushions. She loved him, she accepted that now, but she was neither emotionally nor physically prepared to risk being his lover.

She whispered, "Grant, please get up."

He felt her rejection before she spoke. He sensed her retreat before she twisted away from his seeking lips. His frustration was sickening. Cursing himself for opening his big mouth—she had *said* everything would be all right if they just didn't talk—he choked, "Liza, don't do this to me."

"But this isn't what I came here for!"

Disappointment was followed by bitter anger, and for one ghastly moment Grant knew he was out of control. "No, Liza?" he jeered. "Are you trying to tell me there was another reason you went to so much trouble to find me before getting that precious divorce of yours? Why else should you drive all the way to Arkansas?"

Elizabeth pushed at his shoulders. "Dammit," she shouted, *"I don't know!"*

The vehemence of her protest shocked him out of his rage. He stared down at her. His face changed color rapidly: white, then red. "Oh, Liza, I'm sorry," he groaned, and bounded to his feet. He picked up her discarded blouse and dropped it across her heaving bosom.

Elizabeth didn't react at once. Frowning quizzically at her, he had the odd feeling she was more startled by her reaction than he was. "I don't know why I came to see you," she repeated in hollow wonder. "I thought I did."

Grant's tension eased. "The unshakable Ms Swenson isn't sure about something? From you that's quite an admission."

She sat upright and slipped the blouse over her head, giving Grant one last heart-stopping glance of her beautiful breasts. Her expression was disgruntled as she brushed her curls away from her face. She repeated, "I thought I knew what I was doing. It seemed so simple. But now everything is different—you, most of all."

"You, too, Liza," Grant pointed out gently. "You're softer than you used to be."

She decided to take refuge in humor. "'Softer?' Really? I've always assumed I was rather bony."

"I wasn't talking about physically."

She lifted her gaze to his. Their eyes met. Then Elizabeth and Grant both quickly looked away. In those hastily averted glances was the tacit agreement that the attraction between them was too swamping—and too dangerous—to pursue yet.

Grant took a deep breath. Following Elizabeth's lead, he said wryly, "You know, honey, it's a good thing you called a halt, or else for a moment there I might have forgotten I don't make hostile mergers anymore."

She laughed aloud. The atmosphere lightened. "Well, now," Grant continued, "shall I call Bobby Lee and see what he says about your idea to do a workup on the Bailey Pottery?"

CHAPTER NINE

WHAT BOBBY LEE SAID was no.

In the Bailey living room he lounged on one of a pair of French provincial armchairs while he considered Elizabeth's proposition. His legs were crossed, a half-empty glass of bourbon neat balanced in his hand. The red hound lay curled at his feet, and every now and then Bobby Lee bent to scratch behind the dog's ragged ear.

Everything about him spelled the Southern gentleman at leisure, except his absurdly actorish outfit of low-slung jeans and designer shirt unbuttoned to the waist. Elizabeth, seated across the room with Grant standing behind her, noticed with relief that at least this time Bobby Lee had left off the gold chains. He really was a very handsome man, she thought objectively as she surveyed his dark good looks.

Perhaps aping others was a way of life for the Baileys, Elizabeth decided, glancing at Suzanne, who hovered over the cocktail table, fussing with bowls of chips and dip. The instant Elizabeth and Grant had entered the house, Elizabeth had noticed the blue-green wool dress, strikingly similar to the one Elizabeth herself had worn when she had first arrived in Ridleyville; Suzanne's looked new. While she supposed she ought to be flattered that Suzanne was trying to copy her, Elizabeth would have preferred the girl to have chosen a color and style more becoming to her petite figure and complexion. Parenthetically, Elizabeth also wished Suzanne would learn to be less heavy-handed with her perfume. The heavy scent of Opium clashed queasily with the aroma of guacamole and clam dip.

After serving Grant and Elizabeth the coffee they had requested instead of cocktails, Suzanne bustled around the living room, until Bobby Lee snapped impatiently, "For God's sake, Sue, quit fidgeting and sit down!"

Suzanne jerked up her head. "Don't talk to me like that. I'm not a child."

Bobby Lee looked startled. "Now, sis," he muttered placatingly, rubbing his mustache in a nervous gesture. When she shrugged and took her chair, he returned his attention to Elizabeth. The silence reverberated with unanswered questions.

As Elizabeth waited for him to respond to her proposal, she grew increasingly tense, uncomfortably aware of how equivocal her suggestion must have sounded; how presumptuous, if not downright insulting. Bobby Lee hadn't asked for help from either her or Grant. If the man had any pride at all, he'd probably interpret their offer as an accusation of incompetence— All at once Grant's hands slid over the back of her chair to rest on her shoulders in a gesture that was strangely intimate, strangely reassuring. His thumbs began to massage the back of her neck. Elizabeth relaxed.

Bobby Lee frowned and gulped down the remainder of his drink. The liquor roughened his voice as he asked indignantly, "Now let me get this right, Elizabeth. You and the reverend here are proposing to start telling me how to run my own business?"

"No, of course not," she answered calmly, straightening in her chair. Her host's obvious agitation only reminded her how important it was to maintain an appearance of control at all times, or at least during business negotiations, she amended. During the past few days she'd begun to suspect her self-possession was more a hindrance than a help in her private life. When she felt Grant's hands leave her shoulders, she leaned forward and ticked off points on her fingers. "I'm afraid you misunderstood my offer, Bobby Lee. First of all, Grant would not be involved in this project. I'd appreciate his assistance, but his ministry takes up all his time. Second, I would not be *telling* you how to do anything. I'd merely be conducting an evaluation in the hope that afterward I might be able to make a few suggestions to streamline your operation, perhaps ways to cut down on energy costs, or a new marketing strategy."

From above Elizabeth's head she heard Grant interpose deeply, "Bobby Lee, Liza's being too modest. You may not be aware that at the corporate level she has made this sort of study several times before—quite successfully, I might add."

Elizabeth was touched by the obvious pride in his statement, and she twisted in her seat to look up at him. Grant's smile was confidential and encouraging.

Petulantly Bobby Lee admitted, "I realized your wife was in business, reverend, but I didn't know she was some kind of female corporate whiz kid."

"Well, now you do know," Grant murmured.

Flattered and embarrassed, Elizabeth reached for the potato chips, and as she did, her eyes collided with Suzanne's as she sat hunched on the sofa. The younger woman was gazing at Elizabeth with an expression that bordered on awe.

"You really work with big corporations and things?"

"Yes," Elizabeth muttered uncomfortably. "Ever since I was about your age."

Bobby Lee stared at his glass and grimaced when he noticed it was already empty. His handsome face darkened. Sinking back in his chair, he conceded, "This is all very interesting, but I can't see what it's got to do with us. We're not discussing some *Fortune 500* company here, you know. We're talking about a half-assed little family operation in a backwater town in Arkansas."

"An operation that's vital to the survival of that town," Elizabeth reminded him.

Bobby Lee scowled, his lowering expression an odd mixture of irritation and confusion. "Why should that matter to you? You aren't from around here."

His gaze skated from Elizabeth upward to Grant, then back down again. Setting aside his glass, he wiped his damp palms on his knees and continued. "Reverend, ma'am, although naturally I do appreciate your concern—it's very commendable, I'm sure—I have to tell you you'd only be wasting your time doing fancy productivity studies at the Bailey Pottery. The company's been on the skids for years, and now it's too far gone to rescue. Times have changed. Technology and markets have changed. Nobody knows better than I do that it's only a matter of time until we go under completely—and frankly, I wonder if that wouldn't be a relief for everyone!"

"'Everyone'?" Grant queried softly. "It might be a relief to you to get out from under the burden of running a less-than-thriving company, but would losing their jobs be a relief to the men and women you still employ? Would losing their last hope be a relief to people like Clyde Walker and..."

Elizabeth looked away, unwilling to be drawn into an

argument about ethics. She didn't want to debate the relative duties of labor and management. Suzanne, however, appeared to be listening intently.

Bobby Lee exclaimed, "Dammit, man, climb down from your pulpit for a moment, will you? It's not *my* responsibility to save this stinking town!"

From the couch Suzanne offered quietly, "Maybe it is."

Conversation stopped. Three faces turned toward Suzanne, two mildly surprised, one annoyed. "Keep out of it, Sue," her brother warned.

She shook her head, her short brown hair fluffing limply around her head. "No, Bobby Lee. I won't keep out of it. I think Grantland's right. The pottery has been part of Ridleyville for three generations. People's lives revolve around it, and I don't mean only us Baileys. I know no business lasts forever, but you can't just let the pottery fail without at least making an effort to save it."

Bobby Lee snorted. "That's fancy talk coming from a girl who sets foot in the factory about once every five years."

Suzanne rose shakily to her feet. Her small face was flushed, and she was trembling with emotion. As Elizabeth watched, she wondered if Suzanne had ever seriously contradicted her brother in anything before. Her voice was about two pitches higher than normal. "Of course I don't go out to the pottery very often. First daddy, then you have always made it clear I don't belong out there. You tease me because I don't seem to do anything but putter around with potted plants, but for as long as I can remember, you've told me I'm supposed to stay home and keep house and concentrate on looking pretty until such time as a knight on a white charger sweeps me away to keep *his* house."

"Damn right you are," Bobby Lee growled. "Girls who don't have to work belong at home. You ought to be grateful to do a little housework in exchange for not having to get a job."

Suzanne glanced sidelong at Grant and Elizabeth and smiled wistfully. "Maybe I'd be more grateful if the nearest thing to a white knight who's ever showed up in this town wasn't already married—*and* married to a woman who's obviously done a whole lot more with her life than just sit around looking beautiful!" When Suzanne turned to Bobby Lee again, her sweet expression soured. She gulped and stroked the blue dress nervously. "I'm tired of waiting on you, Bobby Lee. I'm bored with gardening, which I never was much good at, anyway, and there's no point shopping for fancy clothes when there's nowhere to wear them. Since I graduated from high school, the only really enjoyable thing I remember doing was working with other church people to help Mei Nguyen set up her restaurant. I liked being useful. Now I want to do something useful again—like helping Mrs. O'Connor with her study of the pottery."

"There isn't going to be any study," Bobby Lee bit out.

Suzanne retorted, "Are you so sure about that? In case you've forgotten—maybe we've both forgotten—half of that business belongs to me, and I think the survey sounds like an excellent idea!"

"Hallelujah," Grant breathed, so softly that only Elizabeth could hear him.

She tried not to grin triumphantly as she murmured, "I was hoping you'd help me, Suzanne."

Bobby Lee turned on Elizabeth, his blue eyes derisive. "If you're smart, you won't get your hopes up too much. My sister would be about as much help to you as my old hound dog here would. Hell, she doesn't know a thing about business."

"But I can learn!" Suzanne cried indignantly. Once again her cheeks were flushed. This time it was not apprehension but sheer blazing temper that made her face burn from nose to hairline. "Dammit, Bobby Lee, don't treat me like a half-wit! I may have wasted my time in school, but I'm not stupid. I can learn to run the pottery just as well as you do." She paused for air, her bosom heaving jerkily as she glared at Bobby Lee. After a moment the tip of her tongue darted across her lips. Slyly she added, "In fact, brother dear, I bet I can learn to run the pottery better than you do. Considering the way the company's gone downhill under your management, I could hardly do worse!"

Just for a moment Elizabeth thought Bobby Lee was going to strike his sister. His fists clenched, and through his open shirt the muscles of his chest were suddenly visible, corded under the tanned skin. The dog at his feet whimpered uneasily. Behind her, Elizabeth sensed Grant's alertness, as if he were bracing himself to leap to Suzanne's rescue. Tension hung like smoke in the air. Elizabeth couldn't breathe.

Then all at once Bobby Lee relaxed. Sinking back in his chair, he shrugged and laughed. "What is this, Sue? Are you planning to stage a coup so you can kick me out of the pottery and take over the place yourself?"

She shook her head. "I just want to be part of things, Bobby Lee," she insisted, a catch in her voice. "I just want to feel there's something worthwhile for me to do around here."

Her brother shrugged. "But that's the problem, isn't it, honey?" he murmured. "There really isn't anything worthwhile around here...." With a raspy sigh he conceded, "Oh, hell, Sue, if you and Mrs. O'Connor want to conduct your fancy study, why should I stop you? It's not *my* time you'll be wasting!" He glanced across the room at Elizabeth. "Go ahead and start as soon as you want. Right now, if you're in that much of a hurry. But if you do begin tonight, I sincerely hope you don't expect me to work with you. I, for one, intend to enjoy my weekend."

"Monday will be fine," Elizabeth said. "And Suzanne and I will do our best not to interfere with the operation of the pottery. Since you were already kind enough to show me around the plant, I think she and I can begin by taking a look at your books for the past couple of years. In the end, money is the real measure of any business's success."

"The old bottom line," Bobby Lee agreed grimly, levering himself out of his chair. He picked up his empty whiskey glass. "Does anyone else want me to freshen his drink?"

"I DIDN'T MEAN to start a revolution tonight," Elizabeth said. She reached into the green-and-white kitchen cabinet for cups and saucers. When she closed the cupboard door, one corner of the plastic contact paper curled tackily under her fingers, and she tried to smooth it back into place. She abandoned her effort when the glue, which refused to adhere to wood, stuck to her nails.

Grant's mouth twitched as he watched her. Taking the cups from her, he filled them with fresh coffee. "I don't think you started anything, Liza. Suzanne has obviously been chafing under her brother's domination for a long time. You were just the catalyst who gave her the courage to speak her mind." He chuckled. "Meeting a woman like you must have been a real revelation for both of them. I don't know who was more startled."

"I do hope you're right." Elizabeth sighed. "I'd hate to think I'd caused trouble between a sister and brother. Most families seem to have enough problems getting along without outsiders interfering."

Grant could hear the sadness in her words. His tone gentled. "You're thinking of your own sister, aren't you?"

Elizabeth nodded glumly. "It upsets me more than I can say that Amelia and I are so alienated. I keep wondering what she wants, what more I'm supposed to do to make her stop resenting me, short of abandoning my career and moving back to Minnesota."

"Perhaps there is nothing more you can do. Some of the effort has to come from her side, too, you know."

"Yes, I do know. But I keep thinking if only... Since there doesn't seem to be anything on my agenda for this weekend, maybe tomorrow I'll call Amelia—I want to check on how my mother's doing, anyway—and I'll see if perhaps the two of us can talk awhile."

"It can't hurt," Grant agreed. "If you telephone in the morning, afterward you and I can spend the rest of the day together. Go for a drive or something, perhaps over to Fort Smith. It's an interesting city with a lot of history. I've been there a couple of times on business, hospital calls and such, but I've been hoping for an opportunity to go as a tourist. We could poke around the old courthouse and the pioneer museum. I understand they have a flourishing center for contemporary art, too."

"It sounds like fun," Elizabeth said, looking puzzled, "but can you do that—I mean, leave town like that? I thought ministers were supposed to be on call all the time, in case of crises."

"Even a clergyman gets a day off now and then," Grant said dryly. "There's an answering machine in the church office, and if there's a real emergency, the congregation at Good Samaritan knows to contact Ridleyville's other Protestant pastor. He and I fill in for each other."

"Oh. I didn't realize everything was so well organized. It sounds very businesslike."

"In many ways a church is a business, the minister just another employee," Grant bantered. "And it's a rare employee who doesn't insist on having at least one free day a week! Saturday happens to be mine. Believe me, I usually need it."

Elizabeth tipped her head quizzically. "That's funny. I don't remember you—or me, either—taking much time off from work when we were married—I mean, when we were living together in New York."

"Maybe that was our mistake."

Elizabeth frowned uncertainly. "Let me think about that a minute." She ducked her head to sip her coffee.

As Grant waited, he stared at her lustrous curls. Even in the unflattering kitchen light her hair was soft and radiant with the special glow that had always been uniquely hers. He had never been able to decide exactly what the color was—something airy and delicious, richer than melted sugar, more like spun honey. Whenever he looked at her, he hungered.

He loved to look at her. Her paradoxical mixture of physical delicacy and mental strength had entranced him from the beginning. He could still remember spotting her for the first time across a conference table, at the end that would have been considered "below the salt"—assuming a corporate shark like Grant had used such condiments when devouring his competitors.

Deep in discussion, he had been distracted by a little drama unfolding a few feet away: a thin feminine arm in gray flannel scribbled a message on a slip of paper and pushed it toward the man Grant was negotiating with. Grant's adversary, a pompous, incompetent ass, had stared at the note, sniffed loudly, then wadded the paper into a tight ball and dropped it onto the floor as if it were trash. Grant had scowled. In his opinion it was a serious tactical error for any employer to deliberately insult a subordinate, and he had peered past the man's bulky form to see who had been so scorned.

He had found himself staring at a slight girl, incredibly young, her beauty undiminished by her anonymous suit and the unflattering topknot into which she had scraped her Scandinavian-pale hair. She looked fragile, almost ethereal. Her shoulders were hunched, her cheeks tinted with embarrassment, but as he watched, her jaw tightened resolutely and the flush subsided. When she swiveled her head in Grant's direction and their gazes met, he was astounded by the strength, the determination he read in those wide, intelligent eyes.

Grant urged huskily, "Come with me to Fort Smith tomorrow, Liza. You told me you had no other plans, and I'm sure by now you must be getting cabin fever here at the parsonage. I think you'd enjoy seeing more of Arkansas. I know I'd like very, very much to share my free day with you." For a long moment she didn't move. "Please, Liza?" he pressed.

Slowly she lifted her lashes and looked at him over the rim of her cup. "You really want us to go sight-seeing?"

"I want us to spend the day together," Grant said candidly. "The sight-seeing is just a fringe benefit."

Still she hesitated. "I'm not sure it's wise—"

"You're afraid I'll try to seduce you again?"

Elizabeth frowned at his mischievous tone. Sternly she

said, "Grant, we'd be fools to pretend we aren't attracted to each other."

"That's very true," he conceded lightly. "But I promise I won't jump on you if you won't jump on me." His eyes narrowed. "Believe me, Liza," he said deeply, "I'll be the perfect host. You have nothing to fear from me. I'll never ask you for more than you're willing to give." Silently he added, *Darling, you needn't be afraid I'll try to seduce you, because of all the things I'll ever want from you, seduction is probably at the bottom of the list.*

Having promised to be the perfect host, the following afternoon Grant set out to live up to his promise. As the two of them strolled through the National Historic Site in Fort Smith, he was companionable, solicitous and entertaining, determinedly nonthreatening.

He was also so aroused by her nearness that he wondered how he was able to walk.

On the hour-long drive into Fort Smith they'd passed numerous billboards that beckoned luridly, See the courtroom and gallows of Hanging Judge Parker! Yet when they stood in the restored rooms where the nineteenth-century jurist had administered justice over thousands of miles of outlaw-ridden frontier, Elizabeth was surprised at how sedate the room looked. Whitewashed walls and neat rows of spindle-backed chairs, a simple dark desk with an American flag hanging beside it—these formed an unlikely backdrop for the man whose fearsome reputation remained undiminished almost a century after his death.

"History hasn't served Isaac Parker very fairly," Grant told Elizabeth. "In twenty-one years on the bench he tried more than thirteen thousand people, many of them murderers and cutthroats, and out of those thousands, seventy-nine went to the gallows. The tabloids of the day, which weren't all that different from tabloids nowadays, called him the 'hanging judge.' Tragically, the nickname stuck. What most people never know or don't care about is that he fought for years to improve prison conditions, he served on hospital and school boards, he sentenced youngsters who came before him to learn a useful trade and then wrote letters of recommendation to their prospective employers—"

Grant broke off when he realized Elizabeth was staring curiously at him. "Sorry, Liza," he muttered sheepishly. "I guess I was showing off some of the stuff I learned when I went back to school."

"That's all right," she said with a smile. "Actually, I was fascinated."

"Oh, yeah?" Grant drawled, cocking his head to one side and regarding her with an exaggerated leer. "In that case..." He caught her hand in his and led her out of the courtroom. His deep voice took on the singsong chant of a professional tour guide as he intoned, "If you'll look at the displays along this corridor..." Somehow his hand never released hers.

A chilly breeze rustled blood-tinted oak leaves, piercing Elizabeth's thin sweater as she and Grant stood on top of a low hill overlooking the Arkansas River. Thick grass not yet bronzed and flattened by winter spread in a lush carpet around the slate-roofed courthouse behind them. The growth spilled over the lip of the bluff almost down to the muddy bank, where a quarter mile of gray water the color of the overcast sky separated the bank from its twin on the Oklahoma side. Near their feet lay a worn-looking boulder of native granite a century and a half old, roughly the size and shape of the metal washtubs leaning against the walls of some of the older farmhouses she and Grant had passed during the drive from Ridleyville. On the inland side of the rock thick block letters were incised, United States. The side of the boulder that faced west, toward the river and the frontier that had once lain beyond it, was marked Cherokee Nation.

"From the Civil War clear into the twentieth century, this is where the westward expansion began, for the white man, at least," Grant said slowly. "For the Indians, this border marked the end of the Trail of Tears, in a way the end of everything." He glanced at the modern steel-and-concrete bridge that arched over the water just downstream from them; then he looked away, squinting into the distance as if he were looking into the past.

"Fort Smith was a jumping-off point for wagon trains heading west. Down at the river's edge somewhere along here, you can still find an iron ring driven into bedrock, where they mounted one end of the rope cable the ferry was tied to. There used to be another on the opposite bank, a few hundred yards upriver. In the days before the bridge was built, wagons, animals, people had to be hauled across the water on rafts, using pulleys and poles."

"I'd certainly hate to be on a raft if the cable broke or the river flooded," Elizabeth said, her gaze following Grant's toward Oklahoma. The country on the far side of the river didn't look frightening, and yet she tried to imagine how ominous those rolling, wooded hills would have seemed to pioneers for whom they were uncharted territory, alien and savage. She shivered.

Instantly Grant turned to her. "Are you cold?" he asked, frowning with concern. "The weather's changing so fast, I should have told you to bring a coat. I didn't think." Before Elizabeth could stop him, he slipped off his jacket and draped it around her.

Warmed by his body, scented with the tang of his aftershave, the jacket enveloped her like an embrace. The body of the coat fluttered capelike around her slender torso, while the long sleeves, dangling almost to her knees, slid over her shoulders like a caressing hand. Automatically Elizabeth caught at the zippered lapels, clutching them at her throat. When she fumbled with the slide fastener, Grant's fingers curled over hers. He slipped a fabric loop around a button at the neck, his knuckles lying heavily against her collarbone. "There, is that better?" he murmured. His hands didn't fall away.

"It's heaven," she whispered, closing her eyes a moment to relish the sheer sensual pleasure of the jacket's warmth— Grant's warmth. The wind was growing stronger, but in the shelter of the oversized coat she felt very protected, very secure. Her shivers subsided. When she glanced up to smile her gratitude, though, she noticed that the breeze gusting from lead-colored clouds was lifting and mussing tendrils of Grant's auburn hair, battering them against his stern brow. A gust plastered his flannel shirt against the brawny muscles of his chest and arms. The air dashing her cheeks suddenly seemed chillier. In the distance she heard a rumble of thunder. Elizabeth protested with concern, "Grant, I can't take your coat from you. You'll catch cold."

"I never catch cold."

"Don't be silly. Everyone catches cold. Besides, I think it's going to rain again. Here, you'd better take it back."

Awkwardly she tried to unhook the button Grant had fastened. His hands tightened over hers. "Keep the jacket, Liza. Just this once, allow me to do something chivalrous."

Baffled, she stared up at him. His eyes were the same turbid gray as the clouds overhead. When he saw her confusion, he reassured her. "Please, Liza, I want you to have the coat. If it does start raining, we'll share, but until then I'll be fine, I promise." He inched closer. His fingers unfolded and splayed gently around her throat, lacing through her silky curls to cradle her head as he urged her nearer. The front of his shirt brushed against her breast. She trembled. "Relax." He sighed, his breath sultry and inviting against her lips. "If you're really worried, you can keep me warm." His mouth came down on hers.

In that instant Elizabeth knew this kiss was different. Unlike the embraces they'd shared in the past few days, this was not a nostalgic recreation of former passions or a coercive demand for present ones, but something unprecedented; something quite new. Soft as the brush of a moth's wing, the pressure of skin on hypersensitive skin was tantalizing, tentative yet full of promise. Grant drew back. He knew his restraint perplexed her. He watched with satisfaction as Elizabeth's pupils constricted while she waited for his next move. Almost reflexively her tongue darted across her parted lips. He lowered his head again. This time when his mouth touched hers, the sheen of sweet moisture on her lips invited him closer, deeper.

He declined the invitation.

When he continued to glide his lips over hers without pressing more intimately into her mouth, Elizabeth tried to take the initiative, but the fingers laced through her hair stayed her movement as he pulled away again. Blinking with frustration, she protested, "Grant, don't tease me!"

"I'm not teasing you." His voice sounded ragged.

"Then why—"

Gruffly he said, "Darling, don't you know when you're being courted?"

This time Elizabeth drew back. Grant's hands dropped away, and she retreated a step, swathing his jacket more tightly around her to fight off the icy chill that pierced her the instant they separated. "'Courted'?" she echoed blankly, as puzzled by the old-fashioned word as she was by his unexpected endearment. "I don't understand what you mean."

"I mean 'court,' as in 'courtship'—you know, Liza, all that stuff we skipped six years ago, the time when a man and woman get to know one another better before they commit themselves to each other." He paused. "Or recommit, as the case may be."

Gulping, Elizabeth said hoarsely, "A few days ago you told me you didn't have the right to ask for a reconciliation."

"Maybe I was wrong."

Somehow that tentative statement touched Elizabeth more deeply than an outright declaration of love. The old Grant had never used the word "maybe." For that matter, neither had the old Elizabeth.

Grant continued. "Something's going on between us that I didn't expect. For years I pretended you were part of the old life I had to abandon in favor of, well, in favor of a new and better one, but the instant I saw you again, I knew I'd been lying to myself. You are as much a part of me now as you were before. Still, after the way I deserted you, regardless of how noble my motives were supposed to have been, I felt I was in no position to ask you to come back if you were happier without me."

"But I'm not happier—is that what you're saying?" she queried. "And because of my supposed unhappiness, you're willing to ask me to share this new, better life of yours?"

"Would it be so awful?"

Elizabeth swiveled away to stare at the brick courthouse

where Isaac Parker had once held sway. Recalling what Grant had told her about the man, she thought ironically that no matter how many good qualities the judge might have possessed, anyone who could sentence seventy-nine men to death must also have had a strong streak of ruthlessness in him, an unflinching determination to do what he felt was right regardless of the cost to himself or others. The same kind of determination Grant had displayed, in much less drastic fashion, of course, when he walked out on her.

Facing Grant again, she said earnestly, "You know, you keep talking about this wonderful new life of yours, but I happen to be satisfied with my old one. It's not nearly as negative as you seem to think. I like my job, I like my goals—I even like myself."

"That's wonderful, Liza," he inserted quickly. "I'm glad for you."

"If you're glad for me, then you must see I can't cast aside everything I've worked for because you want me to be something I'm not."

With one stride Grant crossed the gap between them. Wrapping his arms around her, he caressed the fine bones of her shoulders through the stiff fabric of his jacket. He could feel her shivering again, and he wondered if she trembled with cold or with apprehension, fear of the demands she thought he would make on her. "But, darling, I'm not asking you to *be* anything," he insisted. "I respect your beliefs and your talents too much ever to expect you to give them up for me, and frankly, I wouldn't want you to think of marriage to me as a poor alternative to your career. That's not what I'm asking.

"All I'm asking is that for a while, at least, you forget about those things that separate us and concentrate on all the things we have in common—like the fact that we do care about each other."

"But, Grant—"

"Hush, Liza." Again he bent his mouth to hers, and this time they didn't part until the crackle of lightning and splattering raindrops forced them to race across the broad lawn to the shelter of the courthouse, the jacket flapping like a canopy over both their heads.

CHAPTER TEN

BEING COURTED was a unique and very appealing experience, Elizabeth decided. She had had no idea what she was missing six years before.

From the time they left the historical park until Sunday night when she smiled at Grant across his parishioners' dinner table, their hours together were deliciously sweet, reposeful, demanding nothing but the willingness to relax and get to know each other better. At Fort Smith's art museum, they saw a display of exquisite wooden birds carved by a local artist; when Elizabeth fell in love with a goldfinch so delicate and lifelike that it seemed about to take flight, Grant bought it for her. She tried to protest that the gift was too expensive, but Grant brushed his lips across hers and murmured, "Please, darling, let me spoil you a little." Bemused by his gentleness, she could only nod her acceptance.

Saturday evening they dined in a restaurant in a beautifully restored Victorian hotel that was located, rather surprisingly, in the dingy center of the Fort Smith train yard. Conversation was light, as crisp as the wine accompanying their meal, and they were halfway through the entrée before Grant grinned wickedly and told Elizabeth that for decades, until the Second World War, the building had housed the city's most notorious brothel.

Elizabeth studied her surroundings curiously, this time

paying more attention to the tasseled velvet curtains and gilt-edged mirrors that, on second glance, seemed a little florid even by Victorian standards. When she looked at Grant again, her eyes sparkled. "In that case, should a man of your calling be here, even half a century after the fact?"

"Good question." He reached across the table and caught her hand in his. "While it's highly unlikely I'll run into any of my parishioners here," he pointed out, grinning meaningfully, "if anyone should happen to recognize me, I guess we'll have to think up some explanation." His thumbnail traced along the lifeline in her palm, the slow, scraping movement sending shivers up her arm. Elizabeth's fingers curled. Huskily Grant said, "We'll just tell them that like any good pastor, I've been out searching for my stray lamb—and now that I've found her, I fully intend to bring her back into the fold...."

Sunday night, while they ate dinner with Mack and Vera Winters, Elizabeth remembered that remark and smiled at Grant. At church that morning she had accepted the invitation from Mrs. Winters, head of the Women's League at Good Samaritan and wife of the service-station owner.

Vera's request was only the first of several. Elizabeth had forgotten how rapidly news spread through a small town, but before the worship service and during the fellowship hour that followed, members of Grant's congregation continually approached her to wish her luck on the productivity study. Elizabeth was struck by the optimism and encouragement of everyone who greeted her. Even people like Mack and Vera, who had no direct link to the Bailey firm, spoke as if she were doing them an enormous service.

"All this wonderful Southern cooking is going to be the death of me!" Elizabeth sighed, replete, when she realized

Vera had intercepted the smile she had flashed across the table at Grant. Dinner had been a feast of chicken-fried steak and garden vegetables, followed by a lattice-topped cherry pie oozing juice. Elizabeth was astonished at how much she'd eaten. Brushing a crumb of flaky pastry from the silk scarf she wore as an ascot with her blue dress, she said, "I'm sure I've gained five pounds in the past week."

"You can use it, honey," Vera insisted with a good-natured familiarity Elizabeth was beginning to recognize. Apparently it was considered acceptable for "pillars of the church" to delve into the private lives of their ministers and their families. Elizabeth's natural instinct was to retreat from the probing, but for Grant's sake she knew she had to endure it. Fortunately Mrs. Winters's amiable manner and twenty years' seniority took most of the edge off her personal remarks.

Vera declared, "I know being thin is fashionable among you girls—my daughters-in-law drive me crazy with their constant dieting—but I can't say I believe it's healthy. I think you already look a lot better than when you first came to town—prettier and more relaxed, with sort of a glow about you. Don't you agree, reverend?"

Grant's gaze locked with Elizabeth's, as stirring as a caress. "I think Liza always looks beautiful."

At the head of the table Mack Winters chuckled. "You know, Vera," he reminded his wife significantly, "there could be a whole lot of reasons besides your cooking for that glow in Mrs. O'Connor's cheeks! Anyone with half an eye can see these young people have decided to make a fresh start of things. Right, reverend?"

Grant's expression became hooded. "Well, we're trying," he muttered.

"You ought to do more than try," Vera chided with

stern piety. "A man in your position has to set a good example. 'Whom God has joined together,' you know..." Her eyes scanned Elizabeth's slim figure appraisingly. "Instead of wasting your time and money on fancy cars, you two ought to be raising a family. Like I keep telling my sons and their wives, nothing straightens out a couple's priorities quicker than a few babies. There's not some reason, is there, that you haven't—"

Elizabeth could feel her face growing hot. The conversation was getting entirely out of hand. She stared pleadingly at Grant, and he cut in smoothly, "Mrs. Winters, we don't have children because we've never been blessed with any. The answer is as simple—or as complex—as that." Pushing back the sleeve of his gray suit, he glanced at his wristwatch. "As much as I hate to call an end to a lovely and enjoyable evening..."

In the entryway Mack held Elizabeth's coat for her, and as she slipped her arms into the sleeves he whispered conspiratorially, "Now don't you worry about what Vera said. She's itching to be a grandmother, and she's convinced there's a conspiracy among the younger generation to keep her from becoming one! You and the reverend just concentrate on working out your problems, y' hear?"

"I hear," Elizabeth said softly. "Thank you. You're very kind." Impulsively she squeezed his leathery hand—and as she did so she wondered how long it had been since she'd made a spontaneous gesture of friendship toward anyone. She couldn't remember.

The walk bisecting the Winters's front yard passed beneath a spindly mimosa tree, twisted and skeletal-looking in the starry darkness. The tree was naked of leaves, but the dim light from the Winters's front porch outlined long, dessicated seedpods that dangled like sleeping bats from the thin branches. With each gust of wind the pods rattled snakily, and a few more dropped onto the still-damp lawn or the concrete sidewalk. Elizabeth's boots crunched the pods as she and Grant walked toward his car, parked at the curb. Halfway down the walk they halted and turned to wave one last time to their hosts. "Thank you again!" Elizabeth called to Vera and Mack, who stood just outside their open door. "It was a wonderful dinner."

"Yes, wonderful," Grant repeated.

"We were proud to have you," Vera assured them.

Her husband added, "See you in church next week."

"Of course. Good night."

Grant saw Vera grab Mack's elbow, and as they stepped inside, he heard her hiss, "Hurry up, it's almost time for 'Masterpiece Theater'!"

Grant started to turn away. All at once he halted, cocking his head. His nose twitched. Scowling, he yelled toward the closing door, "Mack, wait a minute!"

Mack stepped out onto the porch again. "Something the matter, reverend?"

"Do you smell smoke?"

The older man sniffed the air noisily. "Yes, I do," he agreed, puzzled. "But it's probably just someone using his fireplace."

Grant shook his head. "I don't think so. It's not burning wood I smell. There seems to be a chemical odor...."

Mack trotted down onto the lawn, Vera in his wake. Elizabeth watched, confused, as both men peered searchingly into the dark. Inhaling deeply, she, too, could detect the pungent, unpleasant aroma of ash floating heavily on the breeze.

All at once Mack choked, "Oh, my Lord, will you look at that." He extended a shaking finger into the wind, in the direction of the wood marking the southernmost perimeter of Ridleyville. Following his gaze, Elizabeth could see in the distance the tops of hickory trees and pines silhouetted against a lurid orange glow rising from somewhere beyond them. Rolling clouds of smoke obscured the stars near the horizon, and as she and the others watched, a tongue of flame shot into the sky.

Behind them Elizabeth heard doors slam along the street, and cries of alarm emanated from all over the neighborhood. Elizabeth clutched at Grant's arm, her eyes wide and anxious. Vera was clinging to her husband, too. "Is it a forest fire?" Elizabeth asked.

Grant jerked his head in grim denial. "No, darling," he said stonily. "I almost wish it was. That's no forest fire—that's the Bailey Pottery."

GRANT BANGED a heavy pipe wrench on the corroded fitting and cursed. The valve on the emergency pump, which was supposed to draw water from the river at the base of the bluff to feed the pottery's sprinkler system, was rusted shut.

"Hell!" he swore viciously. "Didn't Bailey maintain *anything* around here?"

Behind him, the factory was totally involved in the fire: kiln building, storage sheds, the front office burning out of control. Flames crackled and roared. The noxious stench of overheated chemicals made breathing difficult. Ash from the billowing smoke laid a grimy blanket over equipment in the yard and the townspeople who had flocked to the site to fight the blaze.

Each minute more vehicles squealed to a halt along the road outside the gate. In the ghastly yellow light from the fire, dozens of spectators were visible perched along the perimeter fence, seated on the stacks of sewer pipe. Grant heard the priest from Ridleyville's Catholic church shouting for parents to keep their children out of the way. Farm workers armed with shovels and hoes dug trenches around the edge of the fire, trying to prevent it from spreading, while others stood by with empty buckets. Without water they were helpless.

With straining muscles Grant and the deputy sheriff heaved one last time on the pipe wrench. The fitting would not budge. Shaking and ready to sob with frustration, Grant threw down the wrench. "Where's the fire department, for God's sake?"

The young man rubbed a palm across his sweating face and blinked blearily. "They're on their way, reverend." He coughed. "I radioed for emergency assistance the minute I got the call. The nearest station with a pumper truck is twenty miles away. If we can't contain the blaze and it spreads to the woods, Little Rock will dispatch a plane with fire-retardant chemicals, but by the time they arrive there won't be anything left of the factory except a few timbers."

"But we can't just let the place burn!" Grant exclaimed.

"There's not much choice if we can't use the sprinklers here. The town water system doesn't come out this far. At least we were able to close off the lines from the butane tanks before there was an explosion."

"Yes, thank God for that. We should be grateful no one's been hurt." Grant turned to survey the crowd. The people who had tried to fight the fire had fallen back, disheartened and defeated, to stare glumly as the pottery went up in flames. Grant wondered how many of them realized their whole town was dying with it.

Elizabeth appeared, lugging a plastic jug and a bag of

paper cups. When she handed water to Grant and the deputy, both men gulped thirstily, soothing their scorched throats. Grant rasped, "Thanks, Liza, that tastes wonderful! But I want you to stay back out of the way while there's any danger."

"Don't worry about me. I'm perfectly safe. Suzanne and I are just helping Vera. She already has her Women's League providing food and drinks, and I heard..."

Grant glanced past Elizabeth. He spotted a number of his parishioners in the crowd, Suzanne Bailey among them. Her face was grave as she bustled through the throng, carrying sandwiches to the volunteer fire fighters, but whenever one of them spoke to her, she paused to smile reassuringly. Several people hugged her.

On the far side of the yard two teenagers in Boy Scout caps waited resolutely, armed with first-aid kits. Grant recognized them as Doris Butley's grandsons. Surveying the crowd again, he frowned. One face that should have been there was missing.

"Where's Robert Bailey?" he demanded.

Elizabeth shrugged. "Suzanne said her brother had gone out for the evening, a date or something, but she didn't know where or what time he'd get back. When the plant foreman picked her up, she tacked a message to the front door telling Bobby Lee to come out here the instant he gets home."

"Assuming he isn't already shacked up for the night," Grant muttered waspishly. Catching himself, he continued, "Well, if Bobby Lee doesn't show up, Suzanne will just have to take charge. Poor kid, that'll be one heck of a way to begin her business training—"

His words were broken off by the screech of tires as a big four-wheel-drive pickup roared through the factory gate and braked abruptly. Elizabeth didn't recognize the driver, but the passenger door flew open, and Holly Walker tumbled out of the high cab. For a moment she gaped in horror at the blazing buildings; she jerked her head back and forth as she searched the crowd. When she spotted Elizabeth and Grant, she galloped toward them, her tawny pigtail streaming behind her.

"Mrs. O'Connor, Dr. O'Connor!" Holly gasped breathlessly, almost knocking the water jug from Elizabeth's hands as she clutched at her arm. "Do you know where my father is?"

Elizabeth stared at the girl's pinched, white face; felt the tremor in her bruising fingertips. All at once she was filled with a sickening sense of dread. "I haven't seen Clyde since this morning," she said carefully. She glanced at Grant.

He shook his head. "No, not since church. Why do you ask, Holly?"

Her hazel eyes flicked toward the deputy sheriff, who was listening intently. With a visible effort she squared her shoulders and swallowed thickly. She blurted out, "Daddy's been acting funny all weekend. He bought a bottle of champagne at the supermarket, and he doesn't even drink wine! He told me to put it in the refrigerator to chill, because soon our problems were all going to be over. He said—" she faltered, her voice quavering "—he said he was f-finally going to get the back pay he figured Bobby Lee owed—owed..." Her words died in a tremulous squeak.

Elizabeth looked at Grant, then at the factory beyond him. The masonry walls of the largest structure, the building that housed the kilns, still stood, but the roof had collapsed, and flames were visible through the row of shattered windows. The storage sheds were cubes of charred timber. One wall of the plant office had fallen outward. Worms of fire slithered along the ceiling beams that angled to the ground like lodge poles, holding the smoldering roof in a tent shape over the area where Elizabeth had sat with Bobby Lee. In the yellow light his desk was clearly visible, a hard hat rocking on it like an overturned tortoise. Except for one tall, metal filing cabinet that had fallen against the desk, the office furniture was in place. The floor safe stood open, the heavy door oscillating in the draft....

"The safe. The cash box," Grant groaned. "Oh, my God, that stupid fool!" He sprinted toward the office.

Holly's eyes widened fearfully. "Daddy?" she whimpered, turning as if to pursue him. Elizabeth grabbed her elbow. Holly began to struggle hysterically.

"Yes, keep that girl out of the way!" the deputy barked at Elizabeth, and he ran after Grant. A dozen other men followed.

In the moment that followed, Elizabeth was too intent on her scuffle with Holly to pay more than minimal attention to what the men were doing. She could hear the creak of timbers as they cleared the debris impeding their search. Her heart jolted when she heard Grant's yelp of pain as he tried to lift away the red-hot metal filing cabinet with his bare hands.

When a chorus of male voices cried out in dismay, she knew they'd located Clyde Walker.

"YOU'LL LIVE," Joan Morgan, the woman who directed Ridleyville's four-bed clinic, pronounced solemnly as she snipped the gauze she'd been wrapping around Grant's blistered palms, securing the ends with tape. During the night's frantic activities, tendrils of graying brown hair had escaped from her neat bun. They fluffed around her face as she muttered, "Although I'm not sure you deserve to. Why didn't you let me take a look at your hands hours ago, instead of waiting until your wife here collared me and told me what you'd done to yourself?"

"You had more important things to attend to," Grant grumbled.

Dr. Morgan clucked. "Men! They're always lousy patients, and I might have known a minister would have a martyr complex."

While she treated his injuries, Grant gazed out the window, his mind barely registering the nacreous light that shimmered along the eastern horizon, signaling the end of a truly hellish night. The clinic was quiet now. In the sterile blue fluorescent light the waiting room and hall were empty of everything but the nose-tickling odor of denatured alcohol. Only the scuff marks of heavy boots on the shiny vinyl flooring indicated that earlier in the night the building had been packed with fire fighters, paramedics, townspeople.

Grant had an odd memory of Suzanne and Holly clinging to each other, differences forgotten as the taller girl sobbed on her friend's shoulder, while the petite brunette hugged her comfortingly. When the fire marshal and the deputy sheriff drew Suzanne aside to request information for their official reports, Doris Butley took charge of Holly. Grant told his secretary to forget about coming into the church office later in the morning. The Walkers needed her more than he did.

As dawn broke across the sky, Grant could feel fatigue at last setting in, and with it, irritation. He stared in disgust at the white bandages cocooning the ends of both his arms from wrist to fingertip. "Listen, doc, does the dressing have to be so bulky? I feel like I'm wearing two catcher's mitts!" When he tried to flex his bound fingers, he caught his breath in a hiss of surprise.

"Come on, rev, none of that," Dr. Morgan chided, shaking her head. "Aren't clergymen supposed to have more patience? In a moment I'll give you something for the pain, but first I want you to promise to be good and accept the fact that you can't use your hands for a couple of days. First- and second-degree burns may not be critical, but they do require time to heal. With luck, I ought to be able to remove most of the bandages by, say, Wednesday or Thursday."

"With luck," Grant muttered. "In the meantime, how am I supposed to manage if I can't even blow my nose?"

Joan Morgan glanced sidelong at Elizabeth, who was seated in the corner of the treatment room, sleepily thumbing through a six-month-old *Time* magazine. "You can ask your wife to wipe your nose for you—or in case of emergencies, there's always your sleeve."

Elizabeth looked up and blinked, stifling a yawn. Her gaze sharpened when she noticed Grant's disgruntled expression. "I'm sorry. Did I miss something?"

Joan smiled. "I was telling your husband that if he'll quit pretending he's Superman for a few days, he ought to recover from his injuries just fine."

"Thank you, doctor, I'm very glad." Elizabeth set down the magazine. Plaintively she murmured, "I wish the same could be said for everyone."

For a moment the trio was silent, staring as if they could see through walls into the room where Holly's father lay unconscious, fastened to life by long tubes like mooring lines. Dr. Morgan's colleague, a young man placed in Ridleyville as part of a rural-assistance program, kept watch for changes in Clyde's condition.

"Is there any hope he'll recover?" Grant asked gravely.

Joan looked at him. "Miracles are your department, not mine." As she prepared a hypodermic syringe she sighed. "Maybe he will pull through—who knows? He was damned lucky that metal filing cabinet fell across him the way it did, providing some protection from the fire. He does have some third-degree burns on his legs, but mostly he seems to be suffering from smoke inhalation. The question is whether the damage to his lungs is irreparable."

"What do you think?" Grant persisted.

The doctor seemed to choose her words with care. "All his life Clyde Walker has been a strong man physically, vigorous, his health generally excellent. It's only in the past year, since Kayrene left him, that he's let himself go, and I suspect that despite a year of drinking, his body has enough residual strength to pull him through this crisis." She hesitated, and her shoulders slumped in defeat. "But if you're asking me whether in my honest-to-God professional opinion Clyde is going to die, then I'll have to say yes—because I don't think he wants to live anymore."

Elizabeth's eyes stung. "Oh, no," she breathed sickly. "Those poor children! Does Holly know?"

"She knows," Joan said. "After her father was brought to the clinic, the first thing I did was tell Holly I'd like to contact the burn unit at the hospital in Fort Smith. Our facilities here are limited, and they could have dispatched an emergency helicopter that would have arrived in literally minutes to pick up Clyde. Holly refused. She said her father wouldn't want strangers caring for him. He was born in Ridleyville, she told me, and by God he's going to..."

Grant finished for her. "And he's going to die here." His eyelids drooped shut, and Elizabeth wondered if he was praying.

After a moment Joan shook herself. "Here, rev, it's time to roll up your sleeve—or no, better let your wife do it." Quickly Elizabeth stepped to Grant's side and folded back the torn, ash-covered sleeve that at dinnertime the evening before had been part of a good white dress shirt with French cuffs. As she uncovered Grant's biceps, Elizabeth shuddered at the circular holes dotting the grimy fabric, the blackened edges stiff where live cinders had burned through the material and fused the cotton and synthetic threads. On Grant's tanned skin were several angry red welts.

"There, now," the doctor said, swabbing the needle mark with alcohol. "Go home and sleep this off, and by tomorrow—tonight, rather—you ought to be feeling a lot better. I'll write a prescription for some painkillers in case you need them, but unless you're careless, discomfort should be minimal."

"Thank you, doctor," Grant said, automatically extending his hand to her. He dropped his arm sheepishly. "It's going to take some getting used to," he admitted with a lopsided grin.

"You'll be fine. Just don't try to do any push-ups on those palms of yours."

"Right." Grant turned to follow Elizabeth, but at the door he hesitated. "Dr. Morgan, I don't know if anyone has said anything about money yet—"

Joan stiffened. "That poor, sweet child tried to bring up the subject, but I told her to forget about it until her father's better."

Grant nodded. "That's good, because what I want you to do is send the bills to me. I'm sure the Walkers don't have any kind of insurance, and they certainly can't afford to pay for his treatment, so I'll handle that aspect of it. I want Clyde to have everything he needs, including any additional nurses you may wish to call in for round-the-clock care."

The doctor's expression was inscrutable. "And let me guess. You don't want Holly to know where the money's coming from, do you?" When Grant didn't answer, Joan took a deep breath and said, "Sure, reverend, you're the boss. I reckon I can dream up some bureaucratic-sounding gobbledygook about government funding to explain the situation to Holly. I don't suppose either of you would happen to know offhand whether Clyde Walker is a veteran?"

Grant shrugged and smiled blearily. Picking up the jacket of his gray suit, which was also ruined beyond repair, Elizabeth shook off soot and clay dust and draped the coat over his shoulders. She urged, "Come on, Superman, it's time to go. You're just about wiped out, and I'd like to get you home before that shot takes effect. I don't relish trying to carry you up the stairs." Murmuring a goodbye to the doctor, she guided Grant out of the clinic.

The compact sedan parked at the curb was locked. "I need the car keys," Elizabeth said, and Grant tried to reach into his pocket. His muffled gasp of pain made Elizabeth bite her lip. "Here, let me," she said quickly, sliding her hand into his hip pocket. When she probed for the keys, unavoidably her fingers pressed hard into the muscles of his taut buttock. Desire swept through Elizabeth, powerful and nostalgic. She could feel Grant tense, and she froze, waiting for him to make some teasing remark. He said nothing. With great care Elizabeth withdrew the key ring from his pocket. The keys jingled musically in her shaking hand as she fumbled with the lock.

The streets were quiet as Elizabeth drove the short

distance from the clinic to the parsonage. In the rising light, the houses and shops she passed looked the same as they had the day before, placid and peaceful, but inside many of those houses were workers just waking to personal disaster. As they faced unemployment, Elizabeth wondered how long it would be before those people realized their individual losses were only the first in a ripple of tragedies that might affect the whole community. She recalled what had happened to her own hometown when the iron mine shut down. Barring miracles, this dawning Monday could be the beginning of the end for Ridleyville.

She passed the Bailey place. There was no sign of Bobby Lee's red Corvette. Elizabeth hoped he'd enjoyed his night with his date, whoever she was. She didn't envy him the work awaiting him when he finally wandered home.

Wheeling the sedan into the gravel drive beside the parsonage, Elizabeth said with forced cheerfulness, "Here we are!" Grant didn't reply. She glanced sharply at him. He was blinking hard, his eyes alternately squinting and extending to an unnatural degree. His head nodded jerkily. Touching his forearm above the bandages, Elizabeth said, "Dear, you're getting dopey. Let me help you inside."

"I don't need help," Grant protested impatiently, but he couldn't open the passenger door. With a rueful grimace he allowed Elizabeth to lead him into the house and up the stairs.

On the landing Grant excused himself and went down the hall, while Elizabeth stepped into the master bedroom to turn back the sheets. As she folded the heavy, cream-colored crocheted spread neatly at the foot of the bed, out of the corner of her eye she noticed a beam of sunlight glinting on the gilt frame that surrounded her wedding picture. She smiled wistfully at the image of the gaunt man holding the shy young girl in the topknot. How much she'd changed since then; how much they'd both changed.

The Grant she knew now was not the man she'd married. Except that both men seemed driven by forces beyond her ken, there was little resemblance between that ruthless, hard-bitten corporate raider—her pirate, her buccaneer—and the empathetic, altruistic minister of the Gospel he had become. Despite the seductive attraction of the old Grant, she knew he was a better man now. Was it simply a matter of being older and wiser—or was there more to him? If they ever hoped to make a life together again, she would have to try to understand the forces that had led to his conversion.

She was fluffing the pillows on Grant's bed when she heard his yelp of outrage. Dashing down the hall, Elizabeth found him in the bathroom. His face was white with strain, and droplets of sweat beaded his forehead. He held his hands shakily before him, glaring at the gauze with dismay and distaste. "Grant, what's wrong?" she demanded.

He swung on her, his eyes hot and wild. "With my hands wrapped like a mummy's, I can't even unzip my fly!" he shouted.

Is that all? Elizabeth almost laughed. Grant's display of temper seemed so uncharacteristic, and so childish, that nervous laughter bubbled up inside her, threatening to spill over. Then she looked at him again, and her amusement subsided. He was a proud, self-reliant man, unused to coping with frustration in any form, and now he was almost prostrate from the cumulative effects of pain, exhaustion and Dr. Morgan's injection. He needed sympathy, not derision. Reaching for his buckle, Elizabeth said calmly, "Here, let me do it for you."

Grant jerked away. "Dammit, Liza, I won't be treated like a two-year-old who needs his mother."

"Then we'll have to find some kind of clothes you can manage." Ignoring his protests, she unfastened the belt and unhooked the waistband of his slacks. Her unruffled demeanor wavered slightly when she fumbled for the zipper tab and drew it down over the nylon briefs that hid little of his pressing masculinity.

"W-why don't you step the rest of the way out of these slacks? I'm afraid what's left of your suit is a total loss, fit only for the garbage," she said as she bent to ease the stained gray flannel over muscular thighs and sinewy calves. When with lowered eyes she reached for the waistband of the briefs, Grant stilled her hands with his forearms.

"I can take care of my shorts," he grated, a hard flush burning along his cheekbones. "You go look for my bathrobe. It should be hanging on the back of my bedroom door."

Elizabeth fled. When she returned with the white terry robe, she found Grant sitting down in the bathroom, his slacks and shorts a welter around his ankles as he struggled to kick off his shoes without first untying them. Despite his intent expression, his head bobbed drunkenly. The medication had almost overcome him. "My buccaneer," Elizabeth murmured under her breath.

Aloud she said briskly, "Here, let me do that." She tossed the robe onto Grant's lap. "You'll never get the rest of your clothes off at that rate." She knelt at his feet and untangled the knots in his shoelaces.

"Liza—" he began unsteadily, but she cut him off with an impatient gesture.

"Grant, please don't give me an argument now. I want to get you to bed before you pass out on me. In any case, I don't understand why you're so bashful all of a sudden. This is hardly the first time I've undressed you!"

"I know, Liza," he mumbled. "Believe me, I know. That's just the trouble...."

He still had a beautiful body, she admitted as she stripped the tattered shirt from his shoulders. When she draped the robe around him and gingerly poked his arms into the wide sleeves, careful not to put pressure on his wounded hands, she tried not to be aroused by the strong plates of bone and muscle that girded his broad chest beneath a mat of wiry hair. One or two gray strands had sprouted among the red, but other than that he seemed unchanged.

"Stand up, please," Elizabeth said, and Grant stumbled slightly as she urged him to his feet. The lapels of the robe flopped open, revealing the naked sweep of his body from his chest to his bare toes. His waist was still narrow, his stomach hard and flat, his loins... Oh, God, she loved to look at him. When they had first become lovers, she used to lie beside him for what seemed like hours, languid and sated with the glory of their intimacy, while she gazed in wonder at his bold masculinity. The mere sight of him was enough to rouse her body to renewed hunger. And usually, and usually—

"Hey, shouldn't I be carrying *you* to bed?" Grant asked fuzzily when Elizabeth led him down the hall, staggering under his weight as she slung his arm over her shoulder and guided him toward his room.

"That only happens in books," she joked, trying not to see the erotic images his words conjured up. "Besides, haven't you ever heard of role reversal?" They lumbered into the master bedroom. As soon as Grant's shins touched the edge of the mattress, he toppled forward across the turned-back bedclothes, causing the mahogany four-poster to creak alarmingly.

"Grant!" Elizabeth cried, afraid he'd fainted. When his

body shifted restlessly and he nuzzled his face into the pillow, she knew he was all right. Tugging the sheets from beneath him, she covered him lightly. He made a snuffling noise that might have been, "Thank you."

The morning sun beamed through the window with ironic cheerfulness, and Elizabeth tiptoed across the room to pull down the shade. As shadows fell over the big bed and the man lying prostrate on it, she realized she, too, felt exhausted to the point of stupefaction. She'd been awake all night herself. Her bed in the guest room suddenly seemed very inviting.

She headed for the door, but before she could reach it, Grant's voice reached out to her. "Liza," he called with an effort, "don't go."

She turned. He was propping himself up on his elbows, staring at her with sleep-fogged eyes. "Please, Liza," he repeated blearily, "don't go. Stay with me. Sleep with me. It'll be so much more—more comfort—" He collapsed against the pillow again, his voice fading.

Puzzled, she gazed at him, wondering what he had been about to say. Did he want her to share his bed because it would be more comfortable, or had he meant that in his uncharacteristic state of vulnerability her nearness would be comforting? Elizabeth pondered a moment and realized that lying beside Grant's long, lean body again would be both. He was very comfortable to sleep with. In her whole life she had never rested so well, with such refreshment, as that year when she had slept in his arms. And yes, when she woke to the reality of what had happened to people she had begun to regard as her friends—the loss of hope for their town, the probable loss of human life—she was going to need Grant's comfort, as well.

Elizabeth began to undress.

When she had stripped down to her champagne-colored silk slip and underwear, she rounded the four-poster and slipped beneath the covers on the far side of the bed. Grant lay on his side facing away from her, his broad back in the terry robe like a great white wall, a sheltering wall, warm and protective.

Elizabeth watched him tenderly for a moment, listening to the slow, even tenor of his breathing. She whispered, "You're a good man, Grantland James O'Connor—and I love you." Snuggling as close as she could without disturbing him, she pulled the sheet over her shoulders and fell asleep.

CHAPTER ELEVEN

SHE WAS IN his bed. He could feel her slight weight compressing the mattress beside him. *Dear God,* he prayed, afraid to open his eyes to test the evidence of his senses, *don't let it be a dream.*

She seemed to lie sleeping in the crook of his arm, her head on his shoulder, tendrils of hair tickling his chin. In his nostrils was the tantalizing fragrance of her favorite shampoo, a dry, herbal scent that had always reminded him of sunflowers on a hot summer day. He could feel her moist breath filtering through the terry cloth where her face was pressed against his side, and one of her hands had slipped beneath the lapel of his robe as if searching out his heartbeat.

He couldn't remember how many times during the past five years he'd awakened to elusive memories, a phantom in his arms; how many times he had stretched out trembling fingers to caress the curve of a breast or stroke a thatch of tight, dark-gold curls. Only to have them dissolve at his touch. Too often his body had stiffened with mocking fervor, eager as an adolescent's—then subsided again, reminding him of all he had given up, all he had wasted.

If once more he lifted his eyelids to discover that she was not flesh, vibrant and warm beside him, but only an especially vivid specter he didn't know if he could survive the loss.

Steeling himself, he opened his eyes.

She was there.

The room lay in shadow. Grant blinked, disoriented not only by Elizabeth's nearness, but by the odd angle of the light. Usually in the morning when he awoke, errant sunbeams managed to dart past the crackled canvas shade as it oscillated in the air currents. Now, although Grant could see slits of blue sky lining the windowsill like a picture mat, the sun didn't appear to strike that side of the house at all. Craning his neck to squint across the room at the alarm clock on his dresser, he saw with amazement that it was after four o'clock. For some reason they'd slept all day.

Grant lifted his hand to rub his eyes, and he saw the bandages. Memory returned with a rush. He groaned.

Instantly Elizabeth was awake. "What's the matter? Are you in pain?"

Grant almost groaned again when her body slithered against his as she rotated in his arms. He couldn't tell which felt silkier: that wisp of a slip or whatever it was she wore, or her naked skin. One of her knees slid across his thighs as she levered herself onto an elbow to peer earnestly into his face. Grant's response was immediate and unmistakable—and tormenting. To that first prayer he added a hasty codicil, that his robe might not fall open. He did not want to embarrass her.

"Are the burns bothering you?" she asked, leaning over him. Her mascara was gone, and her sky-colored eyes looked peculiarly soft and ingenuous as she searched his features for signs of distress. She seemed younger, more like the girl he'd bedded so long ago.... "Bedded," he thought curiously; such a sterile word, and yet he supposed it was an accurate description of what he had done to her then, when possession had been his only goal. Love, as in "lovemaking," had come later, and even then he hadn't known how to deal with that fragile emotion. He prayed he'd do better now.

When Elizabeth caught his chin in her fingertips to study his expression, her nails scratched across the stubble of whiskers that almost flamed in contrast to his dark-auburn hair. "Too bad you weren't really a pirate," she murmured, smiling. "You could have called yourself 'Redbeard.'"

Trying to ignore the welling ache in his loins, Grant quipped, "There was already a pirate named 'Redbeard'—Barbarossa—in the fifteenth century. He became Holy Roman Emperor."

"Obviously you in an earlier life," she rejoined easily. Her blue gaze clouded at his patent unease. "Grant, you don't have to be brave with me. Tell me if you're in pain, and I'll get something to help you. Dr. Morgan gave me a prescription. Do your hands hurt?"

"Not my...hands."

Elizabeth stared down at him. He watched her glance flit across his face. Faint lines appeared between her eyes as she puzzled over his tension. He watched her, and he knew the exact moment when she became aware of the intimacy of their posture, her body sprawled over his; when even through the thickness of the robe she felt the force of his arousal.

She froze, and scarlet banners unfurled in her cheeks. "Oh, Grant," she whispered in a stricken voice.

She started to wriggle away, but he flung his arms around her waist, pinning her against him. "Please don't leave me."

Her squirms stopped. Licking her lips, she didn't speak.

"I love you," he said. "I need you. Even if it's only for

this one time, I need to look at you and touch you and taste you. I need for you to do all those things to me."

"Oh, Grant," she whispered again, a thready sigh in the dim stillness of the bedroom. Then she said, "Let go of me."

His arms fell away at once. Apprehensively he watched as she pushed herself into an upright position on the mattress, rocking back on her heels. If she climbed out of the bed, he knew he was going to cry.

Elizabeth caught the lace-trimmed hem of her silk slip in crossed hands and with one powerful, arching movement, pulled it over her head.

Her bra and the scrap of fabric that had covered her most private parts quickly joined the slip in a silken heap on the floor. Tossing her head so that her sleep-tumbled curls fluffed into a sunny nimbus around her small face, she threw back her shoulders and swayed seductively, inviting Grant's inspection. When she saw his eyes heat radiantly as he looked at her, she smiled.

She was naked. He had thought he would never see her naked again. Reverently he whispered, "Lord, you're beautiful." He watched her berry-tipped breasts bounce perkily as she preened for him; like the rest of her, they were small, and yet, he remembered, they always seemed to fit precisely into his large hands, the responsive nipples pressing urgently against his palms. A slender waist flared to narrow, curving hips; delicate, inviting loins parted into coltish legs long in proportion to the rest of her fine-boned frame. If she hadn't become a businesswoman, she ought to have been a dancer. She had legs perfect for pirouetting across a stage—or encircling a man....

Lightly she toppled into his welcoming arms. His muscular body jerked beneath her. "You mentioned something about needing me?" she murmured, and her mouth closed over his.

Dry lips pressed together with tender abrasion, then parted; hesitated; joined again, more firmly, more moistly. She opened her mouth, and throughout her body she could feel every sensitive zone respond to the hot invasion of his tongue. Her puckered nipples rubbed almost painfully against the rough, napped fabric of his robe, while arrows of sensation, no less acute, pierced navel and womb. She wriggled helplessly.

Grant said, "I want your skin touching mine," and he fumbled for the sash. His bandages impeded him. "Dammit all to hell, how am I supposed to make love to you if I can't use my hands?"

"Let me," Elizabeth said. Straddling him, she tried to loosen the bulky knot in the fabric belt. Maddeningly she muttered, "I think this is stuck."

The sight of her parted thighs, the musky scent of her femininity were pushing him dangerously close to the brink. "Don't tease me, Liza," he cautioned. "You're driving me crazy, and I can't take it."

"I'm not teasing." The ends of the sash fell away, and she spread open his robe to gaze transfixed at him. His lean, potent body glistened, rigid with passion, every muscle taut, awaiting her; his skin felt hot and flushed. In her own cheeks an answering flame ignited and burned downward over her throat and breasts. "I love to look at you," she whispered, awed.

"Look at me later." Grant was shaking visibly, his eyes turbulent. "Liza, please, don't wait! Let me feel you against me now, before I—I— Oh, hell!"

He moaned with despair and release.

"I'M SORRY," Grant said simply when he returned from the bathroom. He stood beside the four-poster, his robe draped modestly around him as he gazed down at her. She lay in the center of the bed, the covers jammed high up under her armpits, tight as a winding sheet. As she gazed blindly at the ceiling, her glum expression and the blotchy redness at her throat told him her arousal had not yet subsided completely.

"I'm sorry," he said again. "Nothing like that has happened to me since I was a kid fumbling around in the back seat of a '59 Chevy." His mouth quirked wryly. "Unfortunately when a man gets to be my age, it takes a little longer to recover from...excess enthusiasm."

She glanced at him with suspiciously glazed eyes. "Please don't apologize. I-I'll be all right in a minute. It doesn't matter."

Harshly he said, "Yes, it does matter. I wanted it to be perfect for you!"

"And I wanted to make it perfect for you," she countered in a tiny voice. "Only I guess I've forgotten how, after all these years."

"Maybe we're both out of practice," he suggested tenderly.

Her eyes widened, and she lifted herself on one elbow to gaze at him. "You mean—oh, Grant," she whispered.

"Darling—" he smiled ruefully "—I promise we'll get it right next time, but for now, may I just hold you awhile? It's important to me to feel your body against mine."

"Oh, please!" She flung back the cover on his side of the bed.

He shrugged off the robe and let it slide to the floor, grunting when the sleeves slithered over his bandages. He climbed into bed and drew Elizabeth gently into his arms.

She clutched desperately at him, her ivory-smooth limbs entwining with his as if she could find some ease by knotting their bodies together. Her breasts pressed against his rib cage. When she nuzzled her face into the crisp hair on his chest, his hypersensitive skin tingled at the liquid glide of her lips, or was it her tears? "I want you so much," she whimpered.

"I know, love, I know," he soothed. Then he said huskily, "Let me make it better for you."

Her lashes tickled as she blinked. Raising her head, she stared at him, her puzzled eyes filling his universe. "What do you mean?"

With an attempt at levity Grant chided dryly, "Don't tell me you've forgotten after only five years!"

She grew very still. Amazingly, he sensed, she was trying not to blush. "But your hands..."

"Some games can be played without hands," Grant reminded her. "Soccer is one. This is another." With an unexpectedly swift movement he rolled over, pinning her beneath him while he propped himself on his elbows. His breath stroked her face seductively. Lowering his head, for one moment he kissed her, lips and teeth crushed together urgently until he felt her arms wind around him and she returned his passion with equal vigor. When he raised his head again, he saw that her eyes glowed with new understanding.

With a sigh Elizabeth shifted beneath him, relaxing against the pillows as she opened herself to his worshipful exploration. She tilted her chin back so that he could trail the tip of his tongue over the ridge of her jaw. She shivered with delight when he nipped painlessly at the delicate skin of her throat. When his mouth closed greedily, first over one breast and then the other, she arched against him, deepening the caress.

As he paused in his inexorable descent to taste her navel, she reached for him. Her hand stroked down his back, feathering the blush of fine reddish hairs, downy soft, that spiraled into the hollow at the base of his spine. "Yes, oh, yes," she heard him cry as if in agony when her fingers splayed across his hard buttocks and shifted his position on the bed. And then, with love and renewed ardor and an imagination spurred by five years of celibacy, he plunged her into a fire storm of white-hot sensation that, phoenix-like, consumed and revitalized in the same moment. She clung to him starvingly and drew him into the inferno.

Much later they lay wound together, Grant leaning against a mound of pillows, Elizabeth curled around him in languid contentment, her head resting on his thigh. Except for the glow of the small bedside lamp, the room, the house, the sky outside were totally dark. He stroked her hair absently with the back of his wrist. Elizabeth had almost dozed off when she heard him take a deep breath and chuckle. "What's so funny?" she queried drowsily.

"Me," he said. "I was just thinking how differently I used to imagine it would be if we ever made love again. I was going to sweep you off your feet and carry you to the nearest bedroom, where I planned to dazzle you with my prowess and unflagging energy. Instead I was the one who was practically carried here; I managed to make a prize fool of myself and disappoint you; and as if that wasn't bad enough, now I'm afraid my energy is pretty well flagged for tonight." He sighed. "I guess I must be getting old."

"Thirty-nine is not old," Elizabeth replied firmly. "It's more likely you've just overexerted yourself. Dr. Morgan told you to take it easy for a couple of days. 'No push-ups,' I think she said."

At her choice of words, healing laughter bubbled from Grant's chest to echo around the shadowy room. He relaxed. "My dear Miz Liza," he drawled, his accent exaggerated comically, "surely you are in a position to testify I haven't done a single push-up all day?" After a moment he added, "More's the pity."

Elizabeth giggled and snuggled closer. The ecstasy he had given her still made her sparkle. "I'm not complaining," she told him dreamily. "There are lots of ways to make love. The only thing that counts is being with the right person."

"Yes, darling, I know," Grant said tenderly, brushing a silky curl from her eyes. Her sweetness lingered like a benediction on his lips. "What we shared was wonderful," he assured her, "but I don't think you realize how badly I wanted to feel myself inside you, a part of you. I wanted to dive into you so deep I'd never find my way out."

The erotic image made her quiver. "I want that, too," she said. After a moment's hesitation she added seriously, "But, Grant, I think it was probably better that things worked out the way they did, at least this time. I didn't come to Arkansas expecting us to be lovers. I'm not... prepared."

His hand stilled. "You don't use the pill or anything?"

"No. Not for years." The springy hair on Grant's thigh tickled Elizabeth's mouth as she smiled. "And for some strange reason I doubt you keep a supply of condoms in your dresser drawer now, right?"

"The Board of Deacons would never approve," he agreed solemnly. He sank back against the heaped pillows. He felt boneless, torpid, and yet more conscious of his own vitality than he had been in years. In the warm, intimate silence of the bedroom he could almost hear the hiss of blood slipping through his arteries; he could count the slow, steady rhythm of his heartbeat. That beat faltered slightly when he ventured, "Liza, would it be so dreadful if you became pregnant?"

She tensed. Pushing herself upright, she sat cross-legged on the bed, unconscious of her distracting nakedness. Her riotous curls made an incongruous frame for her grave expression. "We can't talk about a family until we've worked out our own relationship."

Grant's smile was wry. "I thought that's what we were doing."

"Sex isn't enough," Elizabeth insisted. "We were great in bed before, but somehow everything still fell apart. If you're seriously asking for a reconciliation, then I have to know exactly what it is you want of me." She paused before adding heavily, "I have to know I won't come home someday and find you packing."

Grant stretched out a bandaged hand to stroke the curve of her cheek. Softly he promised, "I could never leave you again. It would kill me. It nearly killed me five years ago, but at the time I was already so full of self-loathing that I almost welcomed the pain."

"But why?" Elizabeth pleaded. "What happened to make you hate yourself? Surely after all this time you can tell me."

Grant shook his head. "Don't ask me that, Liza. Even with the knowledge of God's grace, some things are just too painful to talk about. All I can say is that while you were in Belgium that last time, something happened that made me see myself as the man I had become; something so—so unspeakable I could never tell anyone, not you, not my parents."

"Only your God?" she supplied acutely. "You mean, something happened that made you feel so guilty you could only make up for it by becoming a clergyman?"

"Not exactly," Grant said. "Put that way, faith sounds like some kind of barter—make me feel better, and I'll believe in You. True belief is more complex than that. My interest in the ministry came much later, sort of evolving from my study and research. At the time I left New York, I wasn't thinking about God. All I knew was I wasn't a good husband for you. It seemed better for me to suffer than to harm you by sticking around."

Elizabeth considered his words for several moments. "Not a good husband." What did that mean, that there'd been another woman? Even as she mulled over that unappetizing possibility, she discarded it; Grant's reaction was all out of proportion to a sin as mundane as adultery. Whatever he'd done, it had been something horrific; she couldn't imagine what. Yet she knew if he didn't volunteer the information, she'd never ask. She wasn't sure she wanted to find out, anyway.

"And when you decided to leave me, for my own good, as it were," Elizabeth said evenly, "it never occurred to you that I might suffer, too?"

"I didn't let myself think about that. I suppose I figured—or hoped—you'd get over me and find someone else."

"But I didn't."

"I know," he said, "and that bothers me deeply. To realize I've found peace, but only at your expense.... But at the same time I'd be lying if I pretended I wasn't glad you're here with me again, in this town, in this bed. I want you to stay with me from now on."

Unflexing her long legs, Elizabeth swung around so that

her feet touched the floor and she could reach the undergarments she'd discarded hours—or was it years—before. As she shimmied into her slip and panties, she said, "And that brings us back to the same old dilemma, doesn't it? Grant, I'm truly happy you've found peace in your life. I hope I'll be as content in my own. But for us to have a life *together*, it seems as if you expect me to give up my job with Avotel, possibly even my whole career. I can't do that. If I did, I wouldn't be me anymore. My love for my work is as much a part of me as my love for you."

"I don't want you to give up your career," Grant insisted. "I've told you before. I'm very proud of your success, and I—"

"Then help me, please!" Elizabeth cried. At Grant's frown, her tone softened. She said, "Couldn't we work something out? I have to go to New York. Is it asking too much for you to join me there? You keep telling me you're a scholar rather than a parish minister. As soon as you've completed this temporary assignment at Good Samaritan, is there any reason for you not to move into the co-op with me? You could do your research at Columbia or a dozen different universities or libraries. New York's the best city in the world for writers."

Grant's face was troubled. "I'm not sure, Liza. The idea... scares me a little."

"The idea of spending the rest of my life without you scares *me*," Elizabeth said quietly, "but if we're honest with each other, it may still turn out that way."

"I'm just... not sure."

Grant stretched out a beseeching hand to her. She caught it, and for a long moment they clung to each other in silent desperation. Then, glancing at the clock on the dresser, she told him, "I'm going downstairs to fix something for dinner. We haven't eaten in nearly twenty-four hours. I also think I'd better call the pharmacy about that prescription of yours. You look pale. Before I go, do you need help with your robe?" He shook his head, and Elizabeth started for the guest bedroom to get her own bathrobe.

As she stepped into the hallway, Grant called her name. She hesitated. He asked, "Darling, do we have to work out all our differences right this moment? Can't we just let things ride for a few days, maybe think of this as sort of a second honeymoon?"

She smiled poignantly. "Honeymoons are supposed to come at the beginning of a marriage, not the end—but, yes, I'd like that very much."

Later, when she drove to Ridleyville's combination variety-and-drugstore to pick up Grant's medication, she added some personal items to her purchases. From the way the young clerk giggled as she rang up the order on the cash register, Elizabeth knew that by the following evening, everyone in town would be aware that Reverend O'Connor and his errant wife were sleeping together again.

"I WILL NEVER GET USED to drinking lukewarm coffee," Grant grumbled, regarding the tepid brown liquid with disgust. Over the rim of his earthenware cup tilted a tube of candy-striped plastic, its gaiety incongruous on the drab breakfast table.

Elizabeth sighed. She knew Grant found his inability to use his hands intolerable—he had protested every button and snap she'd fastened for him as she helped him dress—and she tried not to be baited by his ill humor. "It was your decision to drink through a straw. If you'd prefer your coffee scalding hot as usual, I'm perfectly willing to hold the cup for you."

"Liza, I won't have you feeding me. Stop treating me like a baby!"

"Then stop acting like one!"

For a moment, they glared at each other, and then, almost simultaneously, they realized how ridiculous their behavior was. Grant relaxed and laughed. "Will you listen to us? We're bickering as if we've been married for years."

"We have been married for years."

He looked across the table, his gaze tenderly searching out the curves concealed by the ice-blue wrap she wore over her nightgown. They hadn't tried to make love again the evening before, but when he awoke this morning with Elizabeth in his arms, he felt more invigorated and fulfilled than if he'd spent the night tirelessly exploring the mysteries of her body. He felt renewed. He said, "When I'm with you, Liza, I feel like a bridegroom."

Her face glowed. Reaching across the table to lay her hand on his arm, she whispered huskily, "Then stay with me today. Stay with me and love me."

He sighed. "I wish I could." Shaking his head, he said, "Darling, because of that fire a lot of people are going to suffer, and for many of them the consequences could be far worse than my second-degree burns. Some of them will be my parishioners, some won't—but whoever they are, they may need aid and comfort. I have to be there for them."

She was deeply moved by his concern, but still she protested. "You're sure? I do wish you'd rest another day before you try to go back to work."

"I'm sure." Raising his arms like a boy on a bicycle shouting, "Look, ma, no hands," he said, "I'm much better, truly. My palms are a little stiff and itchy, but I know

I'll be able to manage around the office. Mrs. Butley can dial the telephone or take dictation as needed."

Elizabeth nodded. "Of course, you're right. Just promise me you won't overdo things and make yourself sick, okay?" She kissed him lightly and held the screen door open for him when he bounded down the back steps of the parsonage to stride along the flagstone path to the church.

Elizabeth was pouring herself a second cup of coffee when she heard the familiar squeak of the screen. "Back so soon?" she exclaimed worriedly, fearful Grant had returned because he felt ill again. "Oh, dear, you aren't—" She broke off in surprise when Holly and her brother Buddy stepped into the kitchen. Holly slumped with fatigue, and on one cheek was an ink smudge from the newspaper she carried under one arm.

"What on earth are you two doing here?" Elizabeth had assumed the girl would want to stay at her father's side until his condition stabilized.

Holly looked startled. "I—I thought you expected us," she stammered in confusion. "I know I d-didn't come in to work yesterday, but I figured—" Her eyes widened. As Elizabeth watched, blood suffused Holly's face, painting her features a deep scarlet. "Mrs. O'Connor," she gulped, "do you mean you don't want me to come here anymore? After what my father did, you don't feel it would be f-fitting for me to keep house for—"

"Good God, no!" Elizabeth cried, appalled. "Don't you even dare think such a thing, Holly Walker! No one blames you for what happened." She glanced down at the child clinging to his sister's leg, his small face bewildered and troubled beneath the shock of tow-pale hair. Elizabeth's tone gentled. "Besides, Holly, as I understand it, at the moment nobody knows exactly what did happen. Until we find out more, we shouldn't blame...other people, either."

Holly nodded. Patting her brother's shoulder reassuringly, she murmured, "I guess you're right. Dr. Morgan told me the same thing. So did Suzanne. But right now I don't know what to think. Everything seems unreal somehow; tentative, as if I'm waiting for the other shoe to drop."

"Would you prefer to be at the clinic?" Elizabeth asked. "Don't think you have to wait on Grant and me if you'd rather be with your father."

Holly smiled wanly. "Actually, Dr. Morgan ran me out of there. She told me I wasn't doing daddy or anyone else any good by hanging around all day, and that she'd call me the instant there was any change. In the meantime, she said, it would be better for the boys if I tried to maintain their regular schedule as much as possible. So I sent Jimmy and Darrell back to school, and Buddy and I came here."

At first Elizabeth thought the doctor's instructions sounded rather heartless, but then, studying the girl's drawn face and shadowed eyes with concern, she saw—as she was certain Joan Morgan must have seen—that if anyone needed to maintain a regular schedule, it was Holly. She seemed about at the breaking point. She looked as if she hadn't eaten or slept in days. If the dull routine of cooking and cleaning could free her mind, even for a moment, of the anguish over her father's condition, then it would be good for her.

Elizabeth stood up, pulling her blue wrap more tightly around her. Briskly she said, "Well, Holly, I'm sure the doctor knows best. So why don't you go ahead with whatever you think needs doing around here, while I get dressed? Is that today's newspaper?"

Holly looked disconcerted by the sudden change of topic. Blinking, she pulled the rolled paper from under her arm and handed it to Elizabeth. The sheets had been folded so that one of the interior pages faced out, and at the foot of the page a short article had been circled with a ballpoint pen. "Here, I almost forgot. Someone gave this to me. It's last night's edition of the Little Rock paper, and there's an article about the pottery. I guess yesterday must have been a slow one for news, because apparently the wire services picked up the story about the fire. It mentions daddy—they got his name wrong—and Dr. O'Connor, too. I thought you might want to see it."

"Of course," Elizabeth said in surprise. "Thank you." She began scanning the smeared columns as she climbed the stairs.

The story was sketchy—and not wholly accurate. In a suburb of Arkansas's capital, it stated, a fire of suspicious origin had razed the historic Bailey Pottery, in operation since 1919. Two townspeople sustained injuries: employee Claude Walker, whose condition was reported as critical, and local minister Dr. G. J. O'Connor, burned slightly while rescuing Walker. Third-generation owner Robert Bailey, devastated by the loss, said it was too soon to predict whether the factory would be rebuilt.

Elizabeth's mouth curved cynically. Bobby Lee hadn't been there to fight the fire, but he certainly seemed to have made himself available to the press.

After Elizabeth had showered and dressed in a simple beige skirt and blouse, ironically the outfit she'd worn the day Suzanne's brother had given her a tour of the factory, she began moving her clothes and personal effects from the guest room to the master bedroom. For the present, at least as long as she stayed in Ridleyville, she and Grant would be living as man and wife. She wouldn't, she couldn't allow herself to think the future might be different.

She had just carried in the exquisite carved goldfinch Grant had bought her in Fort Smith and placed it on the dresser next to their wedding picture, when the telephone rang. Hollering, "I'll get it, Holly!" Elizabeth grabbed up the receiver before it could ring a second time. If the call was from the clinic with bad news about Holly's father, she didn't want the girl hearing it over the telephone.

She didn't recognize the caller's voice. Over a crackly line that sounded like long distance, a woman asked diffidently, "Is this the residence of Dr. G. J. O'Connor?"

Elizabeth's brows lifted. "Yes, this is Dr. O'Connor's home. I'm afraid he isn't here right now. May I take a message?"

"Not home?" the woman whispered brokenly. "Oh, no!" With an effort the caller asked again, "Then could you please tell me where I can reach him? I'm sorry to be so insistent, but it's very important that I speak to him."

"Of course. I'll give you his office number." Elizabeth rattled off the digits, and almost before the last one had left her mouth, the woman cried, "Thank you!" and slammed down her receiver. A moment later, listening acutely, Elizabeth thought she could hear the sound of another telephone ringing in the distance, from the direction of the church.

The incident puzzled her, but she forgot it by the time she was sitting in the kitchen with Holly and Buddy later in the day. During her break the young housekeeper had mixed a batch of kitchen clay to amuse her brother, and now she was molding little figures to illustrate the stories she told him. Watching Holly's skilled fingers rapidly pinch and press the malleable flour and salt into a series of clever animal characters that delighted the child, Elizabeth thought once again how very talented Holly was. As talented as the artist who had carved her goldfinch, for example.

Elizabeth gasped. Holly and Buddy stared at her, but she flashed a vague, preoccupied smile and shook her head. She couldn't talk. She had to think; she had to think hard. She had an idea how the pottery—and Ridleyville—might be revived.

CHAPTER TWELVE

"I know it's risky," Elizabeth told Suzanne and Holly, "but it could work."

The two younger women stared at her curiously. They were seated at the kitchen table of the parsonage, where Elizabeth had invited them to join her for coffee. Surprised but pleased, Holly had left her little brother napping on the couch, and Suzanne had abandoned her garden, where she'd been trying to rake the last leaves of autumn.

Since the idea fermenting in Elizabeth's mind would depend in great part on the cooperation of these one-time rivals, she wanted to hear their reaction before she broached the subject to anyone else. "Cream or sugar?" As she slid the china sugar bowl across the table top to Suzanne, it occurred to Elizabeth that the fate of the pottery and its employees, maybe even the whole town, could hinge on what was said in this unprepossessing room. It seemed an unlikely place to hold a summit meeting, she admitted whimsically, but, then, she had noticed that in the South the kitchen seemed to be the nerve center of the home, or perhaps this was a characteristic of life in small towns everywhere.

When she was a girl in Minnesota, she and her mother and sister had almost never used the front door of their tiny house, instead circling around the carport to enter through the backyard directly into the kitchen. The so-called living room in front had been reserved for "state occasions," what Amelia had defined with surprising wit as "funerals and visiting school teachers." Here in Ridleyville, even at the Baileys' moldering mansion, the only one who seemed really at home in the elegant parlor was Bobby Lee's dog.

Suzanne stirred her coffee and said, "You're telling me the pottery ought to be changed completely?"

"I'm saying it's time to get out of the business of making sewer pipe and flowerpots. That was fine a generation ago, but now the market's too limited. An operation like yours can't afford to compete with foreign imports and plastics. Your size is against you. What you need to do is find a product that can be made in relatively small quantities, with moderate overhead, and still generate good profits."

"That sounds like every businessman's secret fantasy," Holly noted dubiously. Elizabeth could tell the housekeeper was puzzled by her presence at this discussion.

Mildly Elizabeth said, "Actually, it's not such a secret, and it doesn't have to be a fantasy, either. With the right product, the possibilities are endless."

"And do you have a product in mind?" Suzanne asked.

Cradling her cup in her hands, Elizabeth suggested, "How about something that would attract the tourist trade; specifically, a line of distinctive, medium-priced art ceramics. I don't mean gimmicky junk like ashtrays that say 'souvenir of Arkansas,' but good-quality figurines people would be proud to display."

Suzanne's brown eyes were thoughtful. "Like some of the things they sell in airport shops," she said tentatively. "Pretty trinkets for travelers who don't want their families to think they forgot to buy them something."

"Exactly," Elizabeth replied, delighted the girl was

considering the matter. "They could also be marketed in the better department stores. If you're lucky enough that your line catches on as collectibles, you might even try direct sales, through magazines and catalogs."

"But wouldn't it take an awfully long time for a venture like that to pay off?" Holly queried.

"There would be some lead time, of course, but with careful planning you might begin to show a modest profit inside of a year. After that—well, in one of the business journals I read about a California woman who went from making pots in her garage to running a multimillion-dollar company in fewer than four years. Of course, I realize her success story is unique, but it demonstrates that the potential is there, if people are willing to work for it."

"I don't know anyone in Ridleyville who wouldn't be willing to work to get this town back on its feet," Suzanne said.

Elizabeth nodded. "That's a tremendous asset in itself. A pool of workers already skilled in the ceramics field. And if the line was to become very popular, it might mean jobs for more people in areas like packaging and promotion. Anything is possible. Conceivably there could even be an increase in local tourism, when visitors come to the factory. With a showroom, perhaps a seconds shop—"

With a bitter chuckle Holly cut in, "All these ideas sound mighty fine, but in case you two have forgotten, thanks to my father there isn't a factory anymore!"

Elizabeth stared at the housekeeper. Her hands were clenched, the knuckles white, and blotches of guilty color glowed clownishly on her face. Elizabeth sighed. Although Holly had many valid reasons to be distressed, the girl's determination to blame herself for her father's misdeeds was growing tiresome.

Apparently Suzanne felt the same way, because she snapped, "Confound it, Holly, don't go getting all remorseful again! The fire marshal told my brother it was his own damned negligence that let the blaze spread the way it did. There was trash everywhere, and the emergency water supply was useless. The insurance company's already giving Bobby Lee hell about it, although our lawyer says they'll have to pay up in the end."

"I certainly hope they will," Elizabeth said, "because you'll need that money. If the pottery is typical of most older companies, it's probably seriously underinsured—few policies keep pace with inflation—though with luck, whatever you collect will be enough to start retooling and developing the initial pieces of your new line. Once you've done some test marketing, you can use the results to secure venture capital, but until you have something concrete to show a banker, you'll have to come up with the cash on your own."

Suzanne blinked. " 'Test marketing, venture capital.' It sounds like a foreign language—and a lot of work!"

"I never said it would be easy," Elizabeth murmured.

From across the table Holly asked, "And just where do I fit in with all these grandiose plans? You said you needed me, but I've never worked at the pottery, and apart from a college economics class I only took because it was required, I certainly don't know anything about business finance. So what do you want me to do?"

Elizabeth glanced sidelong at Suzanne. Although so far the girl had seemed suggestible to her ideas, for Elizabeth actually to name staff, particularly for so critical a position, might be another matter. Fervently willing Suzanne to go along with her, Elizabeth smiled and said, "Isn't it obvious, Holly? I want you to be in charge of design." She held her breath and waited for reactions.

Suzanne's came first. "I think that's a great idea!" she gushed. "We'd need someone, all right. The plant foreman told me once that the pottery hasn't used any new designs since Bobby Lee took over from daddy, and Holly's certainly the best artist this town has ever produced. Not that Ridleyville's produced too many artists, I admit, but anyone who could win a statewide scholarship competition—"

Holly's hazel eyes widened with disbelief. "Me—in charge?"

Elizabeth said, "The job—and I assure you, it would be a very demanding job—would give you a chance to use your talents in a meaningful way." She paused. "I seem to recall your telling me you wanted to make some kind of contribution to your town."

Still Holly seemed skeptical. Watching her, Elizabeth realized the girl was afraid to believe what they were telling her, afraid because she could bear no more disappointment in her young life. "And if I took this job, w-would it—" She gulped and stammered. "W-would it pay more than I earn working for Dr. O'Connor?"

Elizabeth turned to Suzanne once more. "Well?" she muttered significantly.

Suzanne looked startled. "You expect *me* to name a salary?"

"It's your company."

Suzanne bit her lip. "I guess it is at that." Shaking her head, she mumbled, "Gee, I hardly know how to..." As Elizabeth watched, her heart in her throat, Suzanne scowled; then all at once her expression cleared, and she declared forcefully, "Well, hell, Holly, chief of design would be like an executive position, wouldn't it? Of course you'd make a decent salary! I can't say exactly how much it would be, but I'm sure you and your brothers—and your father, too, God willing that he gets better," she added gruffly, "I'm sure you could all live on it."

Holly blinked hard. Then she burst into tears.

When she began to weep with relief and gratitude, Elizabeth turned away discreetly and excused herself to rummage through the cupboards while Suzanne comforted her friend. As she made a pretense of looking for some kind of snack to offer her guests, she listened with a pang to the whispers shared by the two young women. Despite the superficial differences and petty jealousies that had divided them in the past, Holly and Suzanne really were friends. They really did care enough to share confidences and offer consolation in times of distress. Elizabeth rather envied them. She was acquainted with hundreds, possibly thousands of people on two continents, many with tastes and interests similar to hers, many whose company she enjoyed, but of all that multitude there had been few if any she could truly call friends. She wondered why she'd never felt the lack before.

There must be something in her nature that distanced her even from the people supposedly closest to her: her family, her husband. Only in the past few days had she allowed herself to become emotionally intimate with Grant. If they parted now, which would be the greater loss: her lover or her friend?

When Elizabeth set a plate of cookies and crackers on the table, Holly and Suzanne looked up in unison. Grinning abashedly, Holly asked, "Okay, how do we start?"

Methodically, Elizabeth refilled coffee cups. Returning the glass carafe to the counter, she slid back into her chair and for a moment sat with her elbows on the table, her chin resting on steepled fingertips. She closed her eyes in thought.

"You look as if you're praying for strength," Holly commented.

Elizabeth's lashes flew up. "Maybe I am," she admitted humorously. Her expression darkened as she regarded the two girls. "You're going to have your work cut out for you, you know. Even an informal feasibility study is going to require a lot of facts and figures, a lot of research into markets. Probably the smartest move you could make would be to contract with someone already experienced in the art-ceramics field to advise you. I might be able to get some names—"

"But I thought you were going to be our adviser!" Suzanne cried, dismayed.

"No. I'm just a troubleshooter, a diagnostician, if you will. I can point out problem areas and make suggestions, but actually doing the work is not part of my job. You need to learn to handle difficult situations yourself, if for no other reason than that I won't always be here."

Suzanne's mouth rounded into a soft, surprised O, a shape mimicked by her sparrow-brown eyes. Her expression was so childlike, so innocent that as Elizabeth watched her she felt a stab of apprehension and guilt, as if she were flinging a half-fledged bird from a high window into the breeze, there either to take flight or to crash on the cruel rocks far below. Elizabeth shook herself resolutely. Suzanne was neither a child nor a bird. If it wasn't for her brother's absurd chauvinism, she would have tested her wings long ago.

Thinking of Bobby Lee, Elizabeth said, "This is a big job you're taking on, you know, and there's no reason for you to try to handle everything yourself. After all, your brother has a vested interest in the success of this project. I'm sure if you ask him—"

"No," Suzanne interrupted flatly. "I don't want anyone to mention this to Bobby Lee yet, not until I at least have some preliminary information to show him. You know how he loves to put me down. Right now I don't think he'd listen, anyway. During the day he's busy filing insurance claims and handling the paperwork so the guys from the pottery can qualify for unemployment right away, and whenever I try to talk to him, he barks at me. The rest of the time he just sits around, staring at the walls and petting that flea-bitten old hound of his. No, for a while Holly and I had better work on this on our own."

"Whatever you think best," Elizabeth murmured, a little surprised that Robert Bailey was reacting so strongly to the destruction of the pottery. For years he'd treated it with studied indifference. On the other hand, the business had been his livelihood, and few people could take such a loss lightly.

Elizabeth's thoughts were interrupted by the squeal of the teeter-totter alongside the walk. Children's voices grew louder. School was out for the afternoon, and Jimmy and Darrell Walker were coming to the parsonage to join their sister and Buddy.

The cookie plate was empty and three milky glasses had joined the coffee cups on the kitchen table by the time Grant returned from the church. Suzanne and the four Walkers had just stepped off the porch. Elizabeth had heard Suzanne offer quietly, "Holly, why don't you let me look after the boys while you go see your dad?" Holly's response was drowned out by treble voices suddenly piping a greeting to Grant as he passed them on the flagstone walk.

"Hi, boys," he called cordially. "Holly. Suzanne." He paused long enough for the boys to exclaim over his bandages before he went up the back steps. He walked into the kitchen as Elizabeth carried the litter of cups and glasses to the sink. "Hello, darling," he said deeply, his eyes following her graceful movements. He surveyed the scene with mild curiosity. "You've been having a party or something?"

"Just a little chat about the pottery." Her senses leaped at the sight of him. Abandoning the dishes, she crossed the room to him and slid her hands around his waist. "I missed you," she murmured, drawing him to her. Her body rubbed with insinuating slowness against his as she stood on tiptoe and pulled his mouth down to hers. Hungrily she kissed him. As she pressed closer, her tongue a darting challenge to his, she could feel his long legs shift for balance; gauze-wrapped hands held her clumsily. He began to kiss her back. By the time they parted, Elizabeth's breasts were tingling, and Grant's taut slacks betrayed his stirring arousal.

Falling back against the doorjamb with an exaggerated stagger, he declared breathlessly, "Wow, Liza, if I'd known your welcome was going to be so enthusiastic, I'd have come home hours ago!"

Studying his face again, she could see that despite the waggish smile, his rugged face was drawn, grooved with lines of strain. "Maybe you should have, anyway," she said quietly. "I think you've overdone things today. You look tired."

Yawning capaciously, Grant conceded, "It has been quite a day."

"Because of the fire, you mean?"

He shook his head. "Surprisingly, no. Several people did telephone to ask about my hands, but I think it will be a while before the congregation begins to feel repercussions from the destruction of the factory. Right now most of the people who lost their jobs are just bewildered. It'll be several weeks before they get desperate enough to seek help. For the most part I was busy with normal church business, letters, bills and the like. It's amazing how much can pile up in just a day or two. I also suddenly realized I hadn't given any thought at all to tomorrow night's sermon."

"Oh, and some woman telephoned long distance for you this morning," Elizabeth remembered. "I gave her your office number. Did she reach you?"

Grant's expression grew guarded. "She reached me," he said tersely. "She needed to discuss...a personal matter. As I was saying about the sermon..."

Hearing the way Grant skated over the subject of that distraught early-morning caller, Elizabeth wondered vaguely whether the sanctity of the confessional applied to Protestant clergy as well as to priests. Whatever the woman's problem had been, clearly he had no intention of talking about it. Knowing she'd never ask him to violate a confidence, Elizabeth put aside her curiosity with a shrug and began laying the table for dinner.

"It's my turn to do those dishes," Grant said later apologetically, as he watched Elizabeth quickly wash and dry the few plates they'd soiled.

"There aren't all that many, but if it will make you feel better, I promise to let you have kitchen duty for a week once your bandages are off. Until then, I'll settle for moral support." She stacked the dishes in the cupboard, then turned to study him with concern. "Actually, instead of sitting in the kitchen talking to me, I think you ought to be in bed right now. You look worn out."

He glanced at his wristwatch, and the corner of his mouth quirked. Heavy lids hooded the expression in his silvery eyes. "Liza," he said darkly, resonantly, "I'm not a child, nor am I an invalid. If I go to bed at seven-thirty, it will not be to sleep." He held out his hand to her.

Elizabeth shivered. Hesitating only momentarily, she quipped huskily, "Well, I don't think there was anything very interesting on television tonight, anyway." Slipping her arm through his, she rested her head against his shoulder, and they started up the narrow staircase.

Wrapped in her blue robe, she emerged from the bathroom just as Grant said, "Did I forget to tell you? One of my calls today was from denominational headquarters. They've found a couple of candidates interested in taking over the pulpit at Good Samaritan."

Elizabeth's ears perked up. If Grant was relieved of his duties in Ridleyville sooner than expected, perhaps he'd be more willing to return to New York with her. "What happens when someone's interested in a pastor's job?" she asked.

Grant didn't seem to notice her tension. Still fully dressed, he leaned indolently against a bedpost, his wrists crossed behind his head. With his legs stretched before him, his body was a long bow, tensile with restrained power. Elizabeth could see the muscles of his thighs delineated through his slacks. Just looking at him made her hunger dizzily, but she knew that for the moment his thoughts were preoccupied with answering her question.

Staring into space, he told her, "The procedure varies with each denomination. In some, the hierarchy—bishops, synods, or whatever—appoints pastors for the local churches, but in the one I belong to, everything is done at the congregational level. I pass on the word to the search committee, and it's up to them to check out each applicant's credentials and so on. Eventually the committee presents its final recommendation to the congregation, and the members vote to accept or reject the candidate."

Elizabeth felt her spirits sink. "It must take a long time to reach a decision."

Hearing her disappointment, Grant turned to look at her. "When people's spiritual well-being is at stake, everyone wants to make sure it's the right decision," he said. His expression was somber then. "For example, by the time someone takes over from me here in Ridleyville, not just the church but the whole town may be in crisis. Ministering under those conditions will be a challenge and an awesome responsibility."

"Unless by then the crisis is over," she argued.

Grant's frown deepened. Straightening, he demanded, "What do you mean?"

"Oh, just some ideas I've been bandying around with Suzanne and Holly." Quickly she outlined her discussion with the younger women.

Grant listened doubtfully. At last he said, "Darling, you know I have the utmost respect for your skills, but I'm not sure even you can carry this one off."

"I'm not sure, either. But when those two girls walked out of here this afternoon, they looked optimistic for the first time since I've known them. At least I've been able to do that much for them. At least I've given them a little hope."

"You've given them a lot more than that, Liza." Tenderly pulling her into his arms, Grant feathered his lips over hers. He whispered, "I don't think you realize it yet, but what you've given Holly and Suzanne and everyone else in this town is your heart."

Smiling wistfully, Elizabeth snuggled her face into the curve of his throat. His after-shave blended muskily with his own unique essence, sultry and inviting. She sighed. "For a long long time, I didn't have a heart to give anyone. You took it with you when you left."

Grant slid one hand between them, straining to conform his bandaged fingers to the delicate contours of her breast. Even through the double thickness of gauze and robe, the extrasensitive flesh on his palm could detect the hardening nipple, and behind it the rapid throbbing of her blood. "If I did take your heart," he said huskily, "it's back again, stronger than ever. I can feel it pounding." He bent his head, and his lips replaced his hand, licking at her softness, dampening the fabric of her wrap until it clung and formed an aureole of darker blue around the turgid peak of her breast.

Elizabeth arched against him, her face aglow. "Then wouldn't you like to be closer to it?" she invited, guiding his mouth to her other breast, where he repeated the caress. Her fingers loosened the buttons of his shirt and splayed across the warm brown skin, threading through wiry auburn curls to touch his nipples. When he shuddered against her, she stroked downward until she located his belt buckle and the straining zipper beneath it. "Come find your heart," she urged, trembling. "Come inside me, love. Come fill me. Come...."

Poised over her, he gazed hungrily at her as she lay naked beneath him on the old four-poster. She was so fair. Except for the rosy tint in her cheeks and her nipples, her creamy skin was only a tone darker than the crocheted coverlet. Tendrils of hair fluffed silkily in her face, and as Grant brushed them away, he caught one corner of the spread and draped it across her forehead. Her golden curls gleamed through the lace as if it were a wedding veil. Had she wanted a veil six years ago? He'd been in such a rush to chain her to him that he'd never thought to ask.

Almost against his will his gaze flickered across the room to the dresser and their wedding picture, that stunned-looking girl in the business suit and the arrogant, possessive man who clutched at her as if he feared she'd try to flee him. No wonder they'd made a false start.... Legally they'd been husband and wife for six years, but Grant realized he wanted this moment to be the real beginning of their marriage. "My bride," he whispered.

His warm breath tickled Elizabeth's face as she stared up at him. "My lover." She sighed. When she felt Grant's hesitation, she knew her response had not been the one he'd been hoping for. Opening her body to receive him, she cried, "Oh, please don't quibble over the words..." and she slid her hands down his back to his buttocks, urging him closer. With a groan he surged against her.

They clung together, rocking and thrusting, demanding and giving. Grant's energy blazed, filling her with his heat and strength and life, and she mirrored it back to him a hundredfold. When he was about to reach his climax, obliterating the shadows of the dark void that had haunted her for so long, she tightened her body deliberately, pushing him over the brink. As the force of the explosion hurtled him into a dimension beyond pleasure, almost beyond sensation, he heard her sob, "Yes—oh, yes—oh, *yes!*" He hoped it was a vow.

THE NEXT FEW DAYS flew by quickly—too quickly, Elizabeth thought. At night in Grant's bed time was suspended, each second too bathed in ecstasy for her to count the passing hours. During the days, though, one event succeeded another at a dizzying rate. Grant behaved as if they would be together from now on, but he said nothing about moving back to New York with her. Elizabeth didn't press him for a decision; she knew he knew what she wanted. Yet the last fall leaves were burned, and Christmas commercials appeared on television even though it was not yet Thanksgiving—and Elizabeth was reminded with poignant insistence that soon she would have to leave Arkansas, with Grant or without him.

Joan Morgan removed Grant's bandages, revealing broad palms that appeared normal except for the raw pinkness of freshly healed flesh and one or two leathery patches where deflated blisters hadn't peeled away. As he flexed his stiff fingers awkwardly, curling and stretching the long digits till the knuckles popped, he glanced across the treatment room at Elizabeth and smiled provocatively. She knew he was anticipating the moment when he could touch her without bandages getting in the way.

For the text of his Sunday sermon, Grant chose several Bible verses that sounded vaguely familiar even to Elizabeth, something about considering the birds of the air and the lilies of the field and remembering that if God provided for their needs, how much more likely He'd be to care for his people. As Grant read the moving passage in deep, sonorous tones, Elizabeth glanced around the congregation. Interpreting the expressions on the faces of people confronting unemployment and personal catastrophe, she was glad he was able to offer them encouragement.

Elizabeth knew, too, that Suzanne Bailey had embarked

on the feasibility study as zealously as if it were a holy mission—or a secret one; her conspiratorial silence bordered on the absurd. Telling her brother she was "just curious about how bad off they were," she carefully studied the few records that had survived the fire. In the meantime, Elizabeth called Avotel headquarters. The chairman's jocular inquiry about when Elizabeth was going to quit fooling around and get back to work subsided into polite but reserved good wishes when she told him she and Grant were attempting a reconciliation. It was only after Elizabeth assured her boss she would return to New York no matter what happened that he relaxed and gave her the information she needed.

The Porsche dealer in Fayetteville telephoned with the news that Elizabeth's insurance carrier had authorized him to replace her car rather than attempt to repair the wrecked one. Luckily he happened to have an almost identical model in stock. If Elizabeth would settle for British racing-green paint, all she would need to do would be come in and sign the papers; otherwise she'd have to wait until he could locate another silver sports coupe, and with the holiday season approaching... Elizabeth decided she could live with the wrong color.

By the time the dark-green car was parked behind Grant's sedan in the parsonage driveway, Suzanne had girded herself in a smart new gray business suit that patently belied her claim that she needed "to shop." Then she'd embarked on a mysterious trip to the state capital in Little Rock. Neither the townspeople nor Bobby Lee guessed his sister was visiting the farm of a retired industrialist, once a famous entrepreneur and now an elder statesman of the business world, or that Elizabeth had used her Avotel connections to arrange the meeting. Although she didn't expect the man to involve himself directly in Suzanne's project, Elizabeth felt sure he'd be able to offer sage counsel. When Suzanne returned later in the week, Elizabeth knew at once that fascinating vistas of work and daring and enterprise had been revealed to the girl. Whether her efforts ultimately salvaged the Bailey Pottery, Suzanne was having the time of her life.

Elizabeth wished the same could be said for Holly. She seemed close to collapse. While Suzanne flitted around the town and the state, her friend worked daily at the parsonage and divided her evenings between her little brothers and her father's bedside. Clyde lay comatose in the small hospital, his condition essentially unchanged; his burns had healed, but he displayed no signs of alertness.

One night when Elizabeth and Grant accompanied Holly to the clinic, he asked Joan Morgan privately whether the man could have suffered brain damage during the fire, perhaps from inhaling toxic chemical fumes. She shook her head sadly. "There's no evidence at all of that kind of injury. In fact, physically Clyde seems to be rallying. No, I'm afraid I still think the real problem is that he's lost his will to live." She glanced toward the cubicle where the man lay in his twilight sleep. Beside him on a straight wooden chair sat Holly, a textbook on ceramic design and several art-pottery catalogs lying forgotten in her lap. Her face looked pinched and bloodless as she gazed at her father.

Joan added pityingly, "Of course, if he ever does come out of the coma, it'll just be to face an arson trial."

Keeping her voice low so the girl couldn't overhear, Elizabeth whispered, "I didn't know criminal charges had been filed."

"They haven't, not yet," Grant explained in matching tones. "No one wants to take any action until it's known whether he's going to regain consciousness. But the fire marshal definitely concluded the blaze had been deliberately set in the pottery office, probably to cover a burglary, and since that's where they found Clyde..."

"My God," Elizabeth groaned, gazing helplessly at the wan girl. "That's all that poor child needs right now. She already looks as if she's on the verge of a nervous breakdown."

"She has too damn many troubles for a girl her age," Joan agreed. "Let's hope something happens soon to lighten them."

Grant glanced significantly at Elizabeth before murmuring to the doctor, "Well, I do believe there may be something in the works." His smile was encouraging.

He flashed that same bracing smile at Elizabeth several nights later when they sat together on the love seat in the Bailey parlor. Elizabeth didn't notice. She was too apprehensive about the forthcoming confrontation. Against her advice, Suzanne had asked all the pottery employees to her home to discuss the future of the business—informing Bobby Lee of the meeting only after the invitations had been issued. She didn't tell her brother about the proposal she intended to make.

Elizabeth had tried to discourage her from announcing her plans so publicly, but Suzanne had refused to be swayed from the scenario she'd devised. She appeared to have visions of dazzling everyone with her newly acquired expertise.

Her forays into the business community had opened a novel and challenging world to her, one that left her giddy with excitement, practically intoxicated by the idea of making a success of herself and at the same time "doing something useful" for her friends and her town. Nevertheless, Elizabeth was intuitive—and cynical—enough to realize there was an element of spite in Suzanne's ambitions. She was determined to show her authoritarian older brother she was an intelligent and capable woman whether he thought so or not.

Suzanne was in danger of forgetting that whatever happened to the pottery, she was going to have to work with Bobby Lee, not against him. He was, after all, joint owner with her, and in practical terms he'd been the business's sole proprietor for seven years. Surely the situation called for a little tact.

When Elizabeth shifted restlessly on the love seat, Grant muttered under his breath. "You're as jittery as a doting mama whose child is about to give her first piano recital."

"If this is what it feels like, I don't think I'll ever make my children take music lessons!" she vowed.

"No? Darn, I was looking forward to us clustering around the old Steinway for family singalongs." Taking her nervous fingers in his, he laid their joined hands reassuringly on his thigh.

Through the crisp gabardine of his suit trousers, his body heat penetrated her hand soothingly, warming her almost as much as the thought of their children. "I guess I am a bit nervous," Elizabeth admitted. Her gaze skittered over the large living room. The furniture had been pushed back against the wall, making room for rows of metal folding chairs, which had been borrowed from the church. Beyond the archway she could see the long dining table laden with refreshments catered by Suzanne's Vietnamese friend.

The importance of the occasion was emphasized by the way Suzanne and Bobby Lee stood together at the front door, cordially welcoming each person who entered. Suzanne was wearing her new business suit—Elizabeth suspected it would become the young woman's favorite outfit—and Bobby Lee had donned his "management" blazer again. When Elizabeth had shaken hands with him earlier, it had been obvious that he was confused and irritated. Yet no sign of his agitation showed on his handsome face.

Grant said quietly, "Relax, darling. Robert Bailey is no fool. The pottery is his bread and butter, just as it is for everyone else in this room. He may be angry with his sister over her methods, but actually the prospectus the girls have put together is a sound one, surprisingly so, considering their inexperience and the short time they've had to work on it. I can't see him turning the idea down just because he didn't think of it."

Elizabeth's fingers clenched beneath his. "I hope you're right." She sighed. She wished she could get over the feeling something cataclysmic was about to occur.

CHAPTER THIRTEEN

CHAIRS SCRAPED AND RATTLED as people filed into the parlor, greeting one another with subdued enthusiasm, nodding cordially to Grant and Elizabeth. They were the only "outsiders" present, although Suzanne had wanted Holly to attend. She thought her friend ought to discuss her proposed job as head designer and perhaps show some preliminary sketches. Instead, at the last moment Holly had sent her excuses to the parsonage. After talking to Dr. Morgan, she felt she should spend the day at the hospital with her father.

Grant had taken the message without comment. When he relayed it to Elizabeth, they both wondered aloud if Holly was really anticipating some change in Clyde's condition. It seemed more likely she simply felt too bashful to face a roomful of people left jobless by his rash actions.

Studying the crowd, Elizabeth could tell from the variety of dress displayed that Bobby Lee wasn't the only person uncertain of the purpose of the meeting, whether it was intended to be business or social. Some men wore overalls, others sport coats. The pottery's three women employees had put on, respectively, a silk dress with a hat, a skirt and blouse and a polyester pantsuit. As people waited for the meeting to begin they shuffled restlessly, coughing and murmuring. A few craned their necks to gawk at the

French provincial furnishings, the silver coffee service on the dining-room table.

Elizabeth tried to guess how many of Bobby Lee's employees had ever actually been inside his home before. Not very many, she'd wager. For generations Ridleyville residents had staffed the pottery, but perhaps for them the owner's home, the fabled "Bailey place" with its tall white columns, had seemed part of another world, remote as Shangri-la. She wondered if it lived up to the expectations of those seeing it for the first time.

When the last visitor had arrived, Suzanne motioned for her brother to take his easy chair, which was positioned facing the assembly. The red hound lay in his accustomed spot at his master's feet, ignoring the scores of boots and shoes that passed within inches of its graying muzzle. As Bobby Lee bent down to scratch the dog's ragged ear, Grant muttered to Elizabeth, "You have to give Bailey full credit for aplomb. To watch him, you'd think he'd organized this tea party himself."

"Bobby Lee should have been an actor," Elizabeth agreed. "He seems to have a real talent for role playing."

Apparently his employees assumed Bobby Lee was the instigator of the meeting. No sooner had he taken his seat, with Suzanne on a folding chair next to him, when a man in the audience rose awkwardly to his feet. Elizabeth recognized him as one of the workmen she'd seen feeding greenware into the tunnel kiln the day Bobby Lee gave her a tour of the factory. The man fumbled with his billed cap, swallowed and said hesitatingly, "Bobby Lee—Miss Bailey, ma'am—before we get started, I think I speak for all of us here when I say how much we appreciate your taking the trouble to invite us into your home so we can talk about the situation with the pottery and our jobs. Of course we're worried, and—and, well, it means a lot to us and to our wives and families that you care enough to let us know what's really going to happen, instead of leaving us to depend on the gossip that's been running wild the past week or so."

"You can say that again!" someone else called from the side of the room, and the audience burst into spontaneous applause.

When the man sat down and the clapping died away, Bobby Lee smiled soberly and said, "Thank you, Les. I know the fire has been a shock, not just to us Baileys but to everyone in this town. After all the years we've worked together, you have a right to hear the news firsthand—" his voice dropped significantly "—good or bad."

An uneasy murmur rippled through the room. "Then you've already decided if you're going to rebuild?" one of the women piped up.

Even across the width of the parlor Elizabeth could see the uncomfortable expression in Bobby Lee's vivid eyes. He squinted darkly at his sister, but she didn't see; her gaze was trained on the sheaf of papers she clutched in her lap. Her limp curls seemed to quiver. Bobby Lee scowled, and after a moment he returned his attention to the woman who'd addressed the question. Floundering, he said, "Well, you know, hard economic times like these demand hard choices. When you consider—"

Suzanne lifted her chin resolutely. "If I might be allowed to answer," she interrupted in a squeaky whisper. Swallowing hard, she tried again, more firmly. "I have something to say, if I may."

Bobby Lee glanced suspiciously at his sister. With a shrug he sank back into his chair. "The floor's all yours, Sue. I hope you know what you're up to."

Suzanne squared her shoulders and rose to her feet. Her puppy-brown eyes looked glazed as she scanned the faces looking back blankly at her; she seemed to be inhaling slowly and deliberately, almost as if she were counting her breaths. Her eyes cleared, and her bright young voice rang in the polite but reserved silence.

"Ladies and gentlemen—friends—I reckon right now you all are asking yourselves why I'm standing up here. You're wondering where on earth that scatterbrained Bailey girl finds the gall to talk to you about the pottery, when there's not a one of you who doesn't know ten times more about the business than I do. It's true I've never paid much attention to what went on at the plant out there by the river. There are reasons for that, but I don't intend to go into them right now. Instead I'm going to ask your patience for a few minutes while I try to explain what I've been doing the past couple of weeks...."

At the back of the room, as Elizabeth listened to Suzanne, she shivered with suppressed anxiety. Grant felt the tremor, and he turned to smile reassuringly. One slim hand was pressed against the base of her throat as if she were trying to prevent her heart from bobbing into her mouth. With fond irony he murmured, "It's not easy being a mentor, is it?"

Elizabeth blinked. "What, dear?"

"'Mentor,'" Grant repeated, stretching out the word caressingly. "Hasn't it occurred to you yet that you've come full circle? The business lessons I taught you all those years ago, you're now passing on to those girls."

Elizabeth cocked her head, bemused delight glowing in her face. "I never thought of it that way before. I guess—I guess if I'm even half the teacher you were, maybe things will work out all right, after all."

"We can only hope and pray."

Suzanne talked steadily for twenty minutes. At first her presentation was clearly that of a novice; she stumbled over words and her voice alternately faded and boomed. Coughs and the restive creaking of chairs punctuated her awkward pauses. But gradually the merely courteous indulgence of the men and women in the audience changed to rapt attention. When she mentioned the name of the retired industrialist she'd consulted, several people gasped.

Elizabeth saw Suzanne glance furtively at Bobby Lee. Blinking and dazed, he looked as if someone had just slugged him. Suzanne grinned. Turning to her audience again, her initial diffidence disappeared completely. She spoke confidently, and transfixed, people strained to hear her. They frowned knowingly when she described the competition that had been fast driving the old pottery toward bankruptcy. They nodded with approval and interest when she cited figures on tourism in the South and offered projections on how much of that lucrative trade a renascent Bailey Pottery could hope to attract.

As Elizabeth listened, she could recognize the major points of the plan she had sketched that day in the parsonage kitchen. But her protégée, who only a short while before had been described as "fit for nothing but potting plants and making eyes at the preacher," had taken that scanty outline and fleshed it out into an insightful, competent and surprisingly detailed report.

Squeezing Elizabeth's hand, Grant said simply, "Liza, I'm impressed." She felt like weeping with pride.

Regarding the audience frankly, Suzanne concluded on a cautionary note. "Maybe it's presumptuous of me even to ask for your patience and support. Assuming everything goes as scheduled and the product line generates enough sales to make the company viable, it could still easily be a year or more before we're in a position to promise anything approaching full employment. That's a long time for people to go without jobs. When you consider there's no guarantee the project will pay off at all, then I wouldn't blame any of you if you decide to look elsewhere for work. But the fact is, the Bailey Pottery has been part of Ridleyville for three generations, a good part. And now we need your help. Without you people and your skills and your loyalty there's no chance at all the business can be saved. You *are* the Bailey Pottery." She glanced around the room and gulped. "Any questions?"

Before anyone else could speak, her brother's voice reverberated into the charged silence. "I have a question, Sue. Exactly how do you plan to pay for this fancy scheme of yours?"

"I thought I'd made that clear. Later we can try to secure financing, but for the moment, to cover initial reconstruction and start-up costs, the insurance money we collect from the fire—"

Bobby Lee drawled mockingly, "'The money *we* collect'?"

Suzanne looked troubled. "Didn't you understand? Perhaps from the way I announced my plans, you think I mean to take over. I'm sorry. That's not the way I want it at all! You're my brother. We're in this together. And when we rebuild—"

"We're not going to rebuild," he grated, "and that's final." Bounding to his feet, he loomed intimidatingly over Suzanne until she backed away, sinking into her folding chair. Her confidence ebbed visibly; she looked alarmed and cowed. Across the width of the parlor, her pleading eyes sought out her mentor's, but in a roomful of people

Elizabeth could only will Suzanne not to submit to her brother's bullying. Suzanne didn't seem to hear that mental message. Staring down at her lap, she began to pleat her notes into paper fans. Despite her gray flannel business suit, to Elizabeth she suddenly looked like a sullen child, the child she'd been when they had first met.

"Oh, no," Elizabeth whispered in dismay. "Don't tell me that after all that work she's done, she's going to let him walk all over her the way he's been doing for years! If only I..."

The distress in her murmured tones touched Grant. She really cared what happened to that girl, to these people. No wonder he loved her so much. Edging closer on the love seat so that their thighs touched, he wound his long fingers through hers. "Liza, sweetheart, you trusted Suzanne to learn to handle the business without your help. Now try to trust her to learn to handle her brother—and herself—as well. Besides," he added bracingly, "the meeting isn't over yet."

Elizabeth nodded tensely. Grant's words were reassuring. Yet her anxiety didn't fade as she watched Bobby Lee shove his hands into his trouser pockets and face the audience squarely. His handsome face looked dark and determined. "Guys—ladies," he said, nodding deferentially to his three female employees, "I want to apologize for this family tiff you've been forced to witness just now. It never should have happened. I take the blame for not finding out ahead of time what my little sister had in mind when she invited you all here.

"When she told me she'd asked you over today, I assumed she meant it was going to be sort of a reception, a chance for us to say thank you for all the hard work you've done over the years, not just for me but for my daddy and granddaddy before. I thought it was a great idea. My objection was that she didn't plan something fancier, happier, a sit-down banquet or a barbecue where you could bring along your wives and families. This piddling open house struck me as kind of funereal, like a wake."

He shrugged grimly. "Well, maybe it is appropriate for us to be holding a wake today—because, believe me, the Bailey Pottery is dead. Nothing short of the Second Coming could resurrect it."

The joke fell flat. In the uncomfortable silence that followed, Grant saw one or two people glance over their shoulders at him for his reaction. Bobby Lee's challenging glare contributed to the disquiet. Grant sighed tiredly. Despite the other man's unctuous courtesy, Suzanne's brother had always resented Grant. He wished there were some way he could convince him they were not competitors.

Bobby Lee recovered quickly. "Now, folks," he continued, "I'm sorry if that last remark sounded sacrilegious—I meant no disrespect, reverend—but you're all my friends, and I'm just trying to be honest with you. Everyone's seen the end coming for a long time. True, we didn't expect it to happen so suddenly. Believe me, no one regrets the tragic circumstances of that fire more than I do. But the fact remains there's not a man or woman in this room who, even before the fire, hadn't already given serious thought to what he'd do when it came his turn to be laid off. Am I right?"

He paused again, and this time the muffled response indicated he'd hit a nerve. He nodded. "Yes, I thought people with your experience would be able to read the handwriting on the wall as accurately as I did. One of the saddest lessons of maturity is learning how to face facts."

His expression hardened. "That's a lesson my baby sister here has never had to learn."

Suzanne stirred in her seat. She lifted her head, and a faint blush tinted her cheekbones. "Bobby Lee," she murmured warningly.

Her brother smiled patronizingly, then turned to the audience. "Now I want to thank you all for your considerable patience in listening to Sue while she rambled on about her outlandish schemes to save the pottery. I was as amazed as you were to hear about the high falutin company she's been keeping lately. Talking to millionaires sounds very impressive, although I can't say I approve her sneaking around behind my back that way. We all know she's a sweet kid, though, if a tad spoiled, and she means well. Certainly her concern does her credit. It's just that sitting around the house with nothing much to do, girls do get crazy notions about—"

Suzanne jumped to her feet. Her brown eyes flashed indignantly. As Elizabeth watched, she realized with relief that the girl hadn't succumbed to her brother's bullying, after all. "Dammit, Bobby Lee, shut up! Don't you dare talk down to me that way, as if I were seven years old!"

Bobby Lee recoiled, paling at her vehemence. His gaze darted sidelong to the gaping crowd. "For God's sake, Sue," he hissed, "watch your language! We have *company*."

"*My* language? And yes, we have company—because *I* invited them! You didn't have a thing to do with these good people being here. You weren't going to lift a finger to help them or try to save the business."

"The business can't be saved."

"Well, I think it can, and I intend to do everything in my power to see the Bailey Pottery start producing again."

"Oh, yes? And what do you intend to use for money? You've never worked a day in your life. There's not a banker anywhere who'd be crazy enough to loan you a dime!"

Suzanne said doggedly, "I'll use my half of the insurance money. I'll put up my half of the house as collateral if I have to. Daddy left everything, including the factory and its proceeds, to be shared equally between the two of us—"

"The only stupid thing the old man did," her brother cut in acidly. "He could have handled his will differently. He ought to have known I'd take care of you in any case." He laughed harshly. "By God, if it weren't so outrageous it would be hilarious. I've been working in that pottery for years—scrounging for orders, coping with outdated equipment, *paying insurance premiums*—while you never gave a damn about anything but where your next party dress was coming from! And now you dare talk about how 'we' are going to divvy up the money—"

He whirled and poked an accusing finger over the heads of the crowd, directly at Elizabeth. Dozens of heads swiveled to stare at her. "This is all *your* fault, isn't it? My sister didn't have an idea in her head until you cruised into town like Jackie Onassis, with your European clothes and your fancy car and your rich friends. You're the one who started upsetting things. You put her up to this!"

"Yes, I did," Elizabeth replied imperturbably. "I'm very proud of Suzanne."

Bobby Lee's mustache twitched. "Well, lady, you'd better be prepared to back up your pride with hard cash, because unless Sue can afford to buy out my half of what's left of the pottery and everything else, she can just forget her pipe dreams about rebuilding. I intend to liquidate all my assets and move someplace civilized, like California. If the rest of these people here are smart, they'll follow suit." Running his hands through his carefully styled hair, he exclaimed, "God almighty, I do wish outsiders like you and the reverend would stay away, or at least mind your own business! This is not New York! If you knew anything at all about this town, this state, you'd realize you aren't doing us any favors by pretending the factory can be saved. It's just like everything else around here—*dead*."

Elizabeth saw several heads jerk up, but before anyone could protest, his tirade was over. He sank into his chair, his handsome face grooved with bitterness. The dog at his feet whimpered, and he patted it absently. Noticing the faces that stared at him in stunned silence, he waved a hand toward the archway and said wearily, "Look, folks, why don't you all forget the past few minutes and go help yourselves to that buffet in there? It looks delicious. I think Mei really outdid herself this time. If you like, we can put on some Willie Nelson records or something. Anyhow, let's just eat and relax and enjoy ourselves. Have that party I thought we were going to have in the first place."

He glanced at his sister. "Sue, coffee's fine for you ladies, but can't you find something a little stronger for these men to drink?"

Suzanne's expression was wary. "Of course, Bobby Lee. I think there may be a case of beer in the pantry. I'll go check. While I'm doing that, why don't you see about opening the bar?" Dropping her crumpled notes onto her chair, she disappeared through the dining room into the kitchen.

After she left, the people in the parlor hesitated, perplexed by their host's sudden change of mood. Then the woman in the silk dress rose slowly to her feet and motioned for the other two to follow. With stilted brightness she declared, "Come on, girls, I for one don't intend to miss out on any of Mei Nguyen's cooking! I hope there's some of that wonderful shrimp quiche of hers." Her friends trooped dutifully after her.

The parlor emptied as people crowded into the dining room. Muttering something about the stereo, Bobby Lee vanished in the opposite direction. A moment later, throughout the house could be heard guitars and a smoky, graveled voice that melodically implored mamas not to let their babies grow up to be cowboys.

Grant and Elizabeth were left alone on the love seat; neither seemed ready to get up. Elizabeth let out her breath in a long, dispirited sigh. "It was all for nothing, wasn't it? We lost."

"You can't win them all, you know," Grant observed unoriginally.

"You always won."

With the tip of his index finger he captured her chin and turned her face to his. "No, I didn't. I just knew how to make sure word of my failures never leaked out. Besides, how can you say you've accomplished nothing? Surely it's obvious that knowing you has changed Suzanne immeasurably for the better. A few weeks ago she had no idea she could stand up to her brother. Now, although she may still knuckle under a bit from time to time, she's never going to be the same browbeaten little wimp she was when you met her."

"But what about poor Holly? For her this plan was literally a matter of life and death. When she finds out there will be no new pottery, after all, certainly no job as head of design, won't her disappointment be so cruel that she'll be worse off than she was before?"

"Liza, I promise you we will find a way to help Holly

and her family. At worst, between the two of us we can afford to subsidize the Walkers until the youngest of the boys is grown. We'll worry about that later. Right now I want you to quit blaming yourself because you think you've failed. There's nothing wrong with honest failure. The sin is refusing to try at all."

Elizabeth blinked hard. "Oh, Grant, that's sweet of you." She sighed, moisture beading on her lashes.

"To hell with being sweet," and his mouth closed hotly over hers.

Elizabeth's lips had scarcely softened under Grant's when the sound of a sheepish cough made the two of them jerk apart. The middle-aged woman in the silk dress had returned from the dining room, a coffee cup and laden dessert plate in her hands, and she was threading her way through the maze of metal chairs toward the love seat. When she reached her destination she smiled benignly and said, "Pardon me for disturbing you, reverend, Mrs. O'Connor, but there was something I wanted to ask you, if I may."

"Of course," Grant said. He rose and repositioned one of the folding chairs so that it faced the short sofa. When all three were seated, he asked, "How may we help you?"

The woman set aside her plate. "First, I guess I'd better introduce myself. We've never met—I attend the Catholic church, myself. My name is Shirley Ryan, and until the pottery burned down I was the shipping clerk. I'd worked there since long before Bobby Lee took over the business from his father, and I was hoping to keep working there until time to retire. Unlike most of the people here today, I don't really need the money from my job, thank God. My husband raises turkeys for one of the big meat companies, and we have natural-gas wells on some of our farmland.

What I do need is the work, the stimulation. Even if Bobby Lee is a diehard male chauvinist, I enjoyed my job, and believe me, I'm going to miss it if the pottery isn't rebuilt.''

"Oh, I believe you," Elizabeth said. "I sympathize completely."

Shirley Ryan nodded. "From what I've heard about you, I thought you might, young lady. I gather you're the person responsible for that proposal of the Bailey girl's?"

"I made a few suggestions. Suzanne and Holly Walker did all the work."

"Little Holly was involved in this, too? That's interesting, especially since poor Clyde..." She clucked regretfully. "Well, both girls did a good job. At first hearing their ideas sound very promising. But, Mrs. O'Connor, you're an experienced businesswoman, so I'd like you to give me your honest opinion. Could this project succeed?"

Elizabeth didn't hesitate. "Yes. Given time and a tremendous amount of effort and—"

"And money. That's the biggest obstacle, isn't it?"

"Yes. Since Bobby Lee says he wants to liquidate his assets in the pottery, the only way his sister will be able to keep what's left of the business intact is to buy out his interest. After that, she'll still have to raise enough capital to retool. That's going to be...tricky."

Grant said, "Right now Suzanne could use what's known in corporate circles as a 'white knight,' another company that's willing to help by buying an interest in the ailing firm without taking over completely."

The other woman looked thoughtful. "What if all the employees chipped in?" she ventured.

Elizabeth froze. "I beg your pardon?"

"It was something I read about that happened in... Pennsylvania, I think it was. A big grocery chain was about to close down one of its supermarkets, so the workers made pledges of around five thousand dollars apiece, and with those pledges as collateral, they were able to secure a bank loan big enough to buy the store from the chain. That way they all had stock in the business and ran it themselves. Would an arrangement like that work for the pottery?"

Elizabeth clutched excitedly at her husband's arm. "Grant, a co-op! I don't know why that solution never occurred to me. Employee-owned cooperatives are springing up all over the eastern part of the country, not just grocery stores but clothing manufacturers, newspapers, bakeries—"

"And a lot of them are going bankrupt as quickly as conventional businesses," he cautioned. "The amount of work involved is phenomenal."

"But if people are working for themselves—"

At that moment Suzanne and Les, the man who'd thanked Bobby Lee at the beginning of the meeting, joined the trio by the love seat. Suzanne carried a small tray with two coffee cups and a selection of hors d'oeuvres. With forced brightness she said, "Since you two seem to be too busy talking up a storm over here in the corner to get yourselves any refreshments, I thought I'd bring some to you. Grantland, I brought you both coffee, but if you'd rather have beer—"

"Coffee is fine, thank you."

Elizabeth could see pain lurking behind Suzanne's guileless eyes as she continued, "So what's the topic of conversation you all find so engrossing?"

"We were wondering if you've given any thought to turning the pottery into an employee-owned corporation," Shirley Ryan said.

When Suzanne looked puzzled, Elizabeth sketched the basic principle in a few words. Les frowned. "I don't know that I care for the sound of that. Isn't it socialism?"

Shirley sniffed. "Oh, don't be asinine, Les. There's nothing political about this. We're just talking about a bunch of people working together to make sure they keep food on the table for their children."

After a moment his scowl faded, and he nodded judiciously. "That does make sense. If this town doesn't get its act together soon, there's not going to be anything left for anybody." He looked gravely at Suzanne. "Miss Bailey, ma'am, I meant to tell you earlier, I was real taken with what you had to say about reorganizing the pottery. I didn't know you cared so much. I'm sorry your brother doesn't see it your way. Still, he's been fighting a losing battle for years, and if he's tired and wants out, I reckon that's understandable enough. But I was thinking, I have a little money put by. I was saving for a new four-wheel-drive pickup, but if it would help you..."

Suzanne looked astounded. "Why, thank you, Les. That's very kind of you."

"The lease on our gas wells was renewed this summer," Mrs. Ryan told her. "The money's just sitting there in the bank. I'll bet I could talk my husband into investing in the pottery."

Behind her, Bobby Lee's secretary, who had wandered over unnoticed, offered, "Suzanne, I'd been planning to take out a home-improvement loan to convert my basement into a game room, but if you need some cash—"

"I have a few dollars socked away—"

"Some treasury bonds—"

With each new pledge, enthusiasm grew. As people stepped forward, spontaneously volunteering their savings, even mortgages on their houses, Elizabeth turned jubilantly to her husband. She was almost bouncing on the cushions. "Grant, will you just *listen* to what's happening!" she crowed. "It's like—it's like—"

"Hey, what's this conspiracy going on over here?" Bobby Lee boomed with unconvincing good humor as he intruded into the growing throng. His mouth smiled jovially, but his eyes looked wary. "It sounds almost like you're planning a revolution."

Suzanne turned gleefully to her brother. "But that's what we're doing, Bobby Lee," she giggled exuberantly. "I think that's exactly what we're doing!"

ELIZABETH KICKED OFF her high-heeled pumps and waltzed around the bedroom in her stocking feet, giddy with triumph. Her pale hair fluffed softly away from her face as she threw back her head and twirled like a child. Watching the way her spine arched provocatively, thrusting her soft breasts against the bodice of her dress, Grant shifted restlessly. With an indulgent chuckle he observed, "If I didn't know better, darling, I'd say you were drunk."

She caught hold of one of the tall mahogany bedposts and flashed a dizzy smile in Grant's direction. "I am drunk," she said precisely. "Drunk with excitement, with happiness. I didn't fail, after all, Grant. Suzanne and her friends are going to make it. I know they will, with enthusiasm like theirs. Those people are going to band together and buy out Bobby Lee's half of the pottery. They'll rebuild it better than ever. Then they're going to revitalize their town's failing economy."

Grant's tolerant smile was tempered by the caution in his voice. "Before you make too many long-range predictions, shouldn't you be sure their enthusiasm will be sustained?

Of course Suzanne and her friends are feeling very up right now. Formulating new plans, exchanging ideas, that sort of thing is always stimulating, but how will they feel in a year's time, when the newness has worn off and they've had a few setbacks?"

Elizabeth blinked hard and her eyes cleared. "Darn it, Grant." She sighed. "Why must you be such a pessimist? You told me yourself it was the trying that mattered. At least these people have the courage and gumption to make an effort. They aren't sitting around moaning, 'Woe is us, the iron mine'—I mean the pottery—'has shut down and there's nothing we can do about it'!"

Grant heard that inadvertent reference to Elizabeth's hometown in Minnesota, and he chose to ignore it. Instead he said gently, "Liza, dear, I wasn't being pessimistic, merely realistic. If you're honest, you must admit the odds against this project's success are almost overwhelming. A bunch of inexperienced people trying to market an untested product in an unstable economy. But by instilling in them the self-confidence to try, you've given them a wonderful gift, one that will help them no matter what ultimately happens to the pottery." He smiled tenderly. "Although I hope I've already made it clear to you, I am deeply moved and very, very proud of the work you've done here in Ridleyville—as you should be yourself."

"Really, Grant?" She stretched out a beseeching hand to him. "Even though you chose to drop out of business, still you approve of what I've done?"

"With all my heart, darling."

She padded closer and began to toy with the lapels of his dress shirt. "Then show me you approve," she demanded mischievously. His buttons parted. Slipping her fingers inside his shirt, she threaded her nails through the coarse hair on his chest to find the heartbeat that drummed. Her eyelids drooped shut as her senses concentrated on the lurching pulse that telegraphed its need along her own nerves to the very core of her being. She swayed against him, and her coy tone firmed. "I've worked so hard. I need you to take me to bed and reward me...."

With a strangled groan Grant dragged her against him. Already tearing at each other's clothes, they fell together heavily onto the mattress, causing the bedsprings to creak shrilly. They didn't rest till dawn.

A SLIVER OF SUNLIGHT darted past the edge of the canvas window shade and pricked Elizabeth in the face. She awoke with a start. Grant slept, his naked body curled spoonwise around hers, one hand cupped heavily over her breast. Elizabeth's body ached pleasantly in a dozen unexpected places as she stretched languorously. Grant's grip tightened. He grumbled wordlessly, his lips moist on her nape, his whiskers bristling against her bare shoulder.

Elizabeth lay still again, savoring the feel and scent of him. How she loved lying in his arms, in his bed. As passionate as their relationship had always been, she couldn't remember the two of them ever sharing a night like the one that had just passed. They'd come together repeatedly, tirelessly, taking everything, giving more. Facetiously she had demanded a reward from him, but the one he had bestowed on her had been genuine, munificent and unsurpassed. For her ever to repay in kind would require a king's ransom.

Or a soul's.

She stiffened. With great care she eased herself from Grant's arms. He stirred. When her feet touched the cold floor, she held her breath anxiously until the even tenor of his breathing told her he had subsided into deep sleep again. Sighing with relief, she took down her wrap from the door hook it shared with Grant's bulky white terry robe and poked her arms into the sleeves. The silky fabric felt chilly as it draped over her naked body.

She gazed longingly at the bed, at the cozy sheets and blankets perfumed with the sweet fragrance of their loving. She wondered what would happen if she joined him again. She didn't dare. If she turned back now, if she lost herself once more in the inviting, sensual warmth of Grant's embrace, she was terrified she might never be able to find herself again.

Resolutely she walked away. Plodding barefoot down the narrow hallway, she stepped into the guest room to fetch her suitcases.

CHAPTER FOURTEEN

"You're leaving."

Behind her, Grant's voice dropped into the silence of the bedroom like a stone into a well, the hollow sound rippling and echoing back on itself. Elizabeth's hands, smoothing and folding her lingerie, faltered. Carefully she closed the suitcase. She turned to face him.

Blinking away the remnants of sleep, he stared at her with leaden eyes. He was seated upright in the bed. The sheets had fallen away, revealing his naked torso, the broad, muscular chest with its sprinkling of wiry hair, the powerful shoulders. At the base of his neck was a pinkish bruise purpling around the edges, a passion bloom left by her lips. Elizabeth quivered. When she dressed, she had noticed a similar mark on one of her breasts.

Grant studied the skirt, blouse and flat-heeled shoes she had put on. Elizabeth recognized the same gaunt tension that had mocked his repose when they had first met, when the strain of maintaining his facade often made private relaxation impossible. Six years before she had naively interpreted his constant agitation as a sign of boundless vitality and confidence, and had expected him to act accordingly. She wondered how she could have been so blind—or so selfish.

His tone was flat as he accused again, "You're leaving."

Elizabeth said, "It's time."

He let out his breath raggedly. "But I thought you were going to stay until Thanksgiving."

Only the faint ruffle of the curls framing her face indicated she had moved her head from side to side. Wryly she reminded him, "Thanksgiving is next Thursday. What difference will the intervening few days make? Will you have decided by then to come back to New York with me?"

"Liza, I can't just drop everything and leave with you. People need me."

"I need you."

That simple, unadorned statement of fact tore at him. She needed him. He needed her. For the first time Grant realized how easy his new life had been so far, how untested his faith; up to that point he had never been asked to give up anything that really mattered. Now he began to comprehend the magnitude of the sacrifices that would be demanded of him. With an effort he told Elizabeth, "I have a job to do here."

"And I have a job waiting for me in New York. This business with Holly and Suzanne has made me realize how very much I miss that job." She smiled sadly. "Grant, I've been trying to understand your new life and goals, and although I may not agree with the beliefs that drive you, I can certainly appreciate the work you're doing. Work is one thing I've always understood. I admire your dedication. Of course I don't expect you to abandon your responsibilities to your parishioners. I just hope that in the end you'll decide your responsibilities to me are equally important."

"Liza—"

She persisted. "I've suggested what seems to me to be a reasonable compromise in our situation. I hope you'll agree. But I can't wait here in Arkansas while you make up your mind about our future. I need to settle in Manhattan as quickly as possible so I can concentrate on my new position at Avotel."

Her blue eyes skimmed the ugly, faded paper that had hung on the bedroom walls for twenty years. She hoped Grant's successor, whoever he or she was, would finally be given permission to redecorate the parsonage. "I have to go. Once Good Samaritan has hired a new pastor—or maybe I should say, once you finally decide to emerge from this self-imposed exile of yours—well, then, I guess you'll know where to find me." She turned away and resumed packing.

Grant gazed hungrily at the sleek curve of her back, delicate yet strong; at the narrow but very feminine hips. She was such a pleasure to look at. Her natural grace imparted an indefinable air of style even to the mundane outfit she wore. How could he bear to let her walk away? Swallowing painfully, he forced himself to ask, "How long do I have to come to a decision? How long will you wait before you begin divorce proceedings?"

Her eyes burned grittily as if hot sand had been rubbed into them. Hoarsely she said, "Forever. I'll wait forever. No matter what happens between the two of us, I—I know now I was wrong when I thought I'd be able to make a life with anyone else."

"Funny," Grant noted without humor as he flung back the bedclothes, "that's exactly the way I feel."

As he edged past her, she stood rigid with apprehension, afraid the slightest brush of his tall nude body would shatter her into a thousand razor-thin fragments, like a crystal goblet improperly tempered.

He did not touch her. He grabbed a change of clothing

from the dresser and disappeared into the bathroom for a quick shower. When he returned a few minutes later, dressed in jeans and a flannel shirt, his water-darkened hair combed back slickly, Elizabeth's overnight bag and the larger, wheeled suitcase stood in a neat row at her feet, her purse balanced on top of them. She was slipping on her sweater.

"You're not even going to stay for breakfast?" Grant asked.

Elizabeth shook her head. "I'll get something along the way, thank you. If I make a good start, I ought to be able to reach Memphis by early afternoon. From there I thought I'd head northeast, through Kentucky and West Virginia. I've never seen the Allegheny Mountains."

"That's beautiful country," Grant commented neutrally. "Just watch out, in case you run into snow." Damn, he sounded as pat and uninvolved as a travel agent. He wondered if he was supposed to tell her to have a nice day.

"Well..." Elizabeth murmured as she hoisted the strap of her shoulder purse. She glanced down at the luggage by her feet. Stooping to grab the handle of the smaller overnight bag, she asked, "Could you help me with the suitcase, please? It's rather heavy, and I'm not sure I can get it down the stairs."

Grant flinched; his eyes clouded with confusion at his own reaction. "I'm sorry, Liza. I'll do anything in the world for you, but for pity's sake, don't ask me to help you leave me!"

Elizabeth blinked. "All right, I'll manage by myself." Picking up the lighter pieces of her luggage, she trudged toward the staircase. Outside the parsonage in the driveway, while she arranged her bags on the spotless mats in the trunk of her new, dark-green Porsche, she thought she heard the phone ring.

When she returned to the master bedroom to fetch her largest suitcases, the one with wheels and a towing strap, Elizabeth found Grant seated on the edge of the bed beside the nightstand, speaking into the telephone. His shoulders were slumped, his face gray and lined. His hands clenched lividly. Gravely he said, "I understand. I'll come at once." His hand fumbled when he tried to set the receiver back into the cradle.

Elizabeth's heart lurched when she saw the expression in his eyes. "Clyde?" she whispered.

Grant nodded. "That was Joan Morgan. She said Clyde's vital signs have started to jump around, indicating he's reaching a crisis point. Either he's going to break out of the coma at last—or else, more likely, he's going to die. Poor Holly's been at her father's bedside all night. She needs somebody with her."

"I'll come, too," Elizabeth replied instantly.

"That's not necessary. If you want to get on with your trip—"

Elizabeth's nostrils flared. "My 'trip'? Dammit, Grant, do you think I'm made of stone? The Walkers are my friends, too!"

Grant scrubbed the heel of his hand over his jaw, scraping a wide, reddish streak along the angular bone. Abashedly he sighed. "I'm sorry, darling. I didn't mean that the way it sounded. I guess I'm not thinking clearly at the moment. This is—this is the first time in my ministry that I've had to deal directly with death."

"I understand."

"I hoped you would." A heartbeat later he asked, "Liza, do you mind leaving me for a couple of minutes? I need to be alone."

She assumed Grant wanted a moment's privacy for

prayers. "Of course," she murmured, turning to walk away. When she reached the bedroom door she was surprised to hear him pick up the telephone again.

THE CUBICLE where Clyde Walker lay, maintaining his tenuous hold on life, was too small to hold more than a couple of visitors comfortably, so the people who came to join Holly sat in the waiting area. Singly and in pairs they filed into Clyde's room to pay their respects to the grieving, ashen-faced girl who clutched so desperately at Grant's hand; then they returned to the lobby. Elizabeth sat quietly in a corner behind a potted palm tree. When she and Grant had first arrived, she had accompanied him into the sickroom. Holly had smiled a wan welcome to Elizabeth, but it was Grant she had clung to, Grant whom she had begged for solace and encouragement. When Grant had opened his Bible, Elizabeth discreetly took her leave. She didn't want to intrude on their devotions.

She was surprised by the number of people who came to the hospital, many of whom she recognized by face if not by name: members of Grant's church, former employees at the pottery, local residents Elizabeth had encountered during her walks around Ridleyville. Shirley Ryan waited silently on one of the vinyl couches, knitting. Mack and Vera Winters dropped by. Vera told Elizabeth she had to hurry back to Doris Butley's house, where she was helping the church secretary care for Holly's little brothers. Jimmy and Darrell Walker both seemed to understand what was happening, Vera said, dashing away tears, but little Buddy kept asking, "Is daddy going to run off like mama did?"

Vera Winters was not the only person crying. Whenever Joan Morgan, the other doctor or one of their nurses wandered through the lobby, each was collared by distraught friends of the Walkers. The answer was always the same: "No change." And every time that message was repeated, women wept and men snuffled noisily into capacious handkerchiefs. Then invariably someone would try to lighten the mood by telling an affectionate anecdote about the man Elizabeth had known so briefly and so disastrously. She marveled at the loving concern they displayed. Clyde was a "character," everyone insisted, a good husband and father who had only gone bad after his beloved wife had been enticed away from her family by some stranger. Even his alleged arson was shrugged aside. "Now that we have those new plans for the pottery," someone said sagely, "maybe it'll all turn out for the best." Throughout the waiting room, heads nodded in solemn agreement.

Early in the afternoon, Elizabeth's growling stomach reminded her with embarrassing urgency that she hadn't eaten since Suzanne's reception the day before, nor, as far as she could recall, had Grant. She was sure that by now he must be starving. Picking up her purse, she walked quietly down the hall to Clyde's room.

Grant and Holly were standing in the doorway. Holly hung on to the doorjamb and peered anxiously into the room. When Elizabeth glanced inside, she found Dr. Morgan and her colleague bent over their patient's still form. For one jolting moment she feared the worst. Then she looked again and saw the regular rise and fall of Clyde's chest beneath the shapeless hospital gown; his color seemed to be slightly improved. The two physicians conferred in excited murmurs. Elizabeth turned to the girl beside her. "Holly?" she ventured, afraid to tempt fate by putting her thoughts into words.

Clyde's daughter shook her head. "I don't know, Mrs. O'Connor," she whispered huskily, following the doctors' every movement. "I just don't know." Although Holly's words were uncertain, for the first time in her hazel eyes Elizabeth could see a flicker of hope.

She glanced at Grant. He leaned against the corridor wall, twisting his aching neck so forcefully that Elizabeth could hear vertebrae pop. He looked drained. Touching his arm gently, Elizabeth murmured, "Darling, you must be famished by now. Why don't we get something to eat?"

Grant regarded her warily. "That's not necessary."

"I think it is. It's not healthy for you to go so long without food. You're a big man, and you've been under a big strain."

"Thank you, but, no. I'll eat later. Right now I can't leave the clinic."

"Then I'll run back to the parsonage and make some sandwiches and—"

Grant's large hand clamped around her wrist. "Liza," he gritted, "don't go."

She stared in astonishment. "Why on earth not?"

Grant took a deep, shuddering breath. "Because, I'm afraid if you leave now, you won't come back."

Gazing at her husband, Elizabeth didn't know what to say. She had made her offer in all sincerity, but now as she studied his beloved features, raked with anguish, she wasn't sure he wasn't right. Alone in the creaking, decrepit house that seemed to spell out all the differences between Grant's present way of life and the one they had shared, perhaps she would have lost heart. Perhaps she would have admitted how unlikely was her dream of the two of them ever living together again in harmony. Perhaps, as he feared, she would have loaded her last suitcase into the trunk of her Porsche and fled without saying goodbye.

Elizabeth's mind grasped for words to explain her own

fears to him, but before she could formulate an answer, she heard the front door of the clinic bang open. Quick, light footsteps skittered across the uncarpeted floor, followed by heavier ones, and in the lobby voices called out greetings. Suzanne and Bobby Lee had arrived.

Suzanne rushed down the hallway and flung herself into Holly's arms. "I'm sorry I wasn't here sooner," she exclaimed, hugging her friend. "I came the moment I heard, but I've had the telephone tied up for literally hours, making plans for the pottery. It wasn't until Mei dropped by the house to pick up her serving dishes that we found out—Oh, Holly! Is there anything we can do to help?"

"Pray, I guess," Holly suggested tiredly. She nodded diffidently at Bobby Lee, who stood just behind his sister. "It was good of you to drop by, Mr. Bailey," she said with stilted courtesy, "especially under these circumstances."

To Elizabeth's surprise, she saw a flush of crimson rise in Bobby Lee's throat and creep upward over his handsome face. His Adam's apple bobbed as he cleared his throat. "Holly," he intoned solemnly, "your father was—is—a friend of mine, no matter what." He stepped through the doorway to gaze at the man the doctors were examining. "Poor Clyde," he murmured. "Things would have turned out so much better if only he'd taken my advice and moved to California...."

At the bedside, Joan Morgan looked up. Pocketing her stethoscope, she motioned for Holly to approach. The girl froze. Joan repeated the gesture and smiled reassuringly. "Come on, honey, don't be afraid. I want you to talk to your daddy. I want you to tell him he's slept long enough and it's time for him to wake up."

"W-wake up?" Holly stammered in disbelief. Her face began to glow. "You—you mean—"

"I think so," Joan said. She stepped away from the bed, squeezing the stunned-looking Bobby Lee against the sickroom wall.

Still Holly hesitated. She turned questioningly to Grant. "D-Dr. O'Connor?"

"You must trust," he said, his eyes riveted on Clyde. Elizabeth moved closer to him, stepping out of Holly's way. Grant's arms dragged her against him. Trapped in his embrace, she could feel him shaking.

Suzanne nudged her friend forward, past her brother and the physicians. "Go ahead, Holly. Speak to him. The doctor's right. If your father's going to listen to anyone, it'll be you."

Timorously Holly approached the hospital bed. Her hand slipped awkwardly between the bars on the raised sides to touch her father's cold fingers. "Daddy," she crooned, "it's—it's time to wake up."

As Elizabeth waited for Clyde's response, she couldn't talk, couldn't move; she almost couldn't breathe. She realized she was clutching at Grant with as much force as he held her, and she wondered absently if her fingernails were going to leave crescent-shaped bruises in his skin. Outside in the corridor she heard the scrape and shuffle of shoes inching nearer. No one spoke.

Holly jiggled her father's forearm, taking care not to disturb the intravenous tubes. "Please, daddy," she said more forcefully, "you've got to wake up. You've missed so much these past two weeks. The boys have things they want to tell you. Darrell got a B+ on his spelling test, and he's so proud. Mr. Winters is teaching Jimmy how to check the oil on customers' cars at his filling station. And Buddy—that silly little guy swears one of his front teeth is starting to g-get l-loo—" When still Clyde did not stir, Holly's voice was swallowed by a strangled sob.

The girl's pain was more than Elizabeth could bear. She tried to tear herself from Grant's arms, but his grip was too strong. Feeling her wriggle, he frowned down into her glaring eyes. "You told her to trust," she accused in a deadly whisper.

Grant blanched. "Liza—"

At Clyde's bedside Holly clenched her father's arm and pleaded, "Daddy, you've just got to wake up! The doctors say you can do it if you try. Oh, daddy, please try! We need you. I need you. I know you quit caring about anything after mama left, and I've done my best not to let things bother you—but, please, daddy, you can't leave, too. I'm not strong enough to handle everything by myself!"

Silence thickened. Tension grew, writhing like a living thing, until someone in the crowd sobbed with pent-up emotion. Elizabeth trembled.

Clyde Walker's eyes opened. He blinked blearily at his daughter, and his dry, bloodless lips twisted and worked mutely as if he were trying to remember how to use them. Haltingly he mumbled, "B-baby girl?"

"Praise the Lord," Grant murmured deeply. That reverent whisper was picked up and repeated by the crowd; out of the corner of her eye Elizabeth saw Shirley Ryan cross herself. For the first time she began to truly comprehend the depth and sincerity of her husband's new way of life, the tie that bound him to these people. She knew she ought to rejoice for him. Instead the knowledge only made her feel desolate.

As people tried to cram themselves into the small room to see Clyde, to welcome him with joyful tears back into the world of the living, they jostled the two doctors, the

Baileys, Grant and Elizabeth toward the bed until they had to cling to the rails to keep from falling on top of Clyde. As Joan Morgan checked Clyde's vital signs again, her colleague tried to stem the flow. "Ladies and gentlemen, please," he cried, holding up his hands like a traffic policeman, "you must stay back. You'll all have a chance to pay your respects, but you must give Mr. Walker room to breathe. Nurse!" he called, and a woman in a starchy white uniform appeared and began shepherding people away. When the doctor was able to close the door behind her, he cast a rueful glance in Joan's direction and declared, "Small-town friendliness may have its advantage, but now I understand why city hospitals are run like armed fortresses!"

Clyde spoke again, his voice weak and fuzzy with confusion. "What's the...the matter, Holly?" he asked, feebly squeezing his daughter's fingers. "Why are all these people here?"

Licking away a teardrop that clung to the corner of her mouth, Holly beamed. "Everybody's just glad to see you, daddy." She sniffed. "You gave us quite a scare."

"I—I can't remember...."

Holly peeked uncertainly at Joan. "You've been unconscious since the fire at the pottery, Mr. Walker." His eyes widened in alarm. Reassuringly Joan added, "Everything is going to be all right now, I promise. Your burns are healing nicely, and your memory will come back soon. Don't be concerned if you feel a little disoriented at first. It's only natural."

Clyde digested this in silence. Joan glanced at her colleague and muttered, "Now that everything's under control, do you think anyone would mind if we took a break? I'm dying for some coffee."

Grant said, "Yes, why don't you both unwind a little? We can call if we need you. You haven't relaxed in two weeks."

As the physicians left the room, Clyde tried to wave. His pasty countenance was troubled. He peered anxiously at Holly. "Two weeks," he muttered in dismay. His labored breathing chopped his words. "Oh, baby girl. I'm—so sorry. Did you—manage all right—you and your brothers?"

"Oh, yes, daddy," Holly said brightly, tossing back her tawny pigtail as she squared her shoulders. "Everyone has been wonderful and so helpful. Doris Butley and Vera Winters took turns looking after the boys whenever I visited you, and the doctors let me stay as long as I wanted. Dr. and Mrs. O'Connor were very patient about my job. And Suzanne—well, you wouldn't believe what she and I have been up to...." She smiled her thanks to her friends clustered around the bed.

Clyde's filmy gaze lit on each person in turn. "I can't thank you enough—reverend—ma'am—Miss Bailey...." Squinting past Suzanne to her brother, who huddled silently against the wall, Clyde faltered. "Bobby Lee," he said hollowly, each syllable an effort. "I—I wish I could...remember...."

The emotional impact of Clyde's recovery appeared to be almost more than Bobby Lee could bear. His movie-star face looked haggard. "Well, don't strain yourself, old buddy." He chuckled uncomfortably.

Clyde scowled. "'Old buddy,'" he mused. "I guess we have always been buddies, at that...ever since we were kids...." His voice grew stronger as he became increasingly agitated. "I'm beginning to... You said you had a special job for me. I was so happy. Money's short, and I thought you meant... I'd take on anything that was honest, Bobby

Lee, but—but I hope you understand why I couldn't...do what you wanted me to do."

"Quiet, Clyde," Bobby Lee groaned.

The metal stand beside the bed rattled and swayed when Clyde tried to raise himself on his elbows, jerking his IV tubes. Instantly Holly forced him back against the pillow to prevent him from pulling the needles out of his arm. Clyde struggled to lift his head. He cried, "God knows I need work, Bobby Lee—but so does everybody else around here. I couldn't do that to them. I just *couldn't* help you torch the pottery!"

THERE IS A DISCERNIBLE GAP between lightning and the thunder that follows, between the explosion of gunpowder and the impact of the bullet. There was no gap between Clyde's words and Holly's reaction. "You bastard!" she shrieked at Bobby Lee, her young features twisted into a mask of hate. She shoved aside the stunned Suzanne and lunged for him. Her nails were aimed for his vivid blue eyes. "It was you, it was you, *it was you*!"

Before she could reach the man quailing against the wall, Elizabeth threw herself between them. "Holly, no!" she shouted, fighting to control the girl's lanky, rage-driven body.

Holly was almost too strong for her. "He tried to murder my father!"

"No, no!" Bobby Lee shrank from her. "It was an accident, I swear—"

"Liar!" Holly lashed out at him, but at the last moment Bobby Lee ducked behind his sister, and Holly's flailing fingers caught the other girl by mistake. Suzanne yelped with pain as Holly's nails raked twin weals into the soft skin under her ear. At that startled cry, Holly froze.

Grant ordered sternly, "Settle down, Holly. This isn't the way!"

"Oh, no," she whispered, staring at her friend. "Suzanne, I didn't mean..."

Suzanne blinked, bewildered, and touched her neck gingerly. "It's—it's all right, I think," she mumbled. "But this doesn't make any sense—"

At that moment the door banged open, and Mack Winters burst in. "What's going on in here? What's all the yelling?" Behind him half a dozen other faces pressed into the room.

"Bobby Lee tried to kill my father!" Holly shouted. "He set fire to the pottery!"

People gasped. "What the hell—"

Joan Morgan barged through the throng. "Out, all of you," she commanded. When the crowd pressed forward, muttering ominously, the other physician, in the hallway, called for the nurse. Together they ushered people away from the door. Bobby Lee hung back.

"You, too, Bailey," Joan ordered contemptuously.

"If I go out there—" he gulped "—they'll lynch me."

"That's your problem. We have a patient in here. Reverend, please get him out of this room."

Staring assessingly at Bobby Lee, Grant sighed. He handed Holly over to his wife. "Here, Liza, you take her. I'll see about Bobby Lee." He watched Elizabeth and Suzanne catch Clyde's distraught daughter between them and with soothing murmurs guide her into the corridor. With much less gentleness Grant grabbed Bobby Lee's elbow. "Come on, Bailey. Let's see how suave you can be without all the gold chains."

Some of Bobby Lee's bravado had returned by the time he leaned back against the vinyl couch in the lobby and crossed his legs nonchalantly. His surprising composure reminded Elizabeth once again of the macho television star he seemed to idolize. Surveying the irate faces ringed around him, Bobby Lee asked coolly, "So what is this—a kangaroo court? You all have me tried and convicted?"

"We'd be more than happy to hear your side of the story," Grant said.

Bobby Lee regarded him steadily. "Why should I say anything? I have the right to remain silent."

"Perhaps legally," Grant conceded, "but don't you think you owe these people an explanation? You claim to be their friend."

Holly, bracketed between Elizabeth and Suzanne, spat with distaste, "You called my father 'old buddy.'"

Elizabeth patted her hand mollifyingly. On the girl's other side, Suzanne, who obviously still hoped there'd been some mistake, pleaded, "Bobby Lee, all you have to do is tell us where you were the night of the fire. You didn't get home till morning."

He studied his sister's small, stricken face in silence for several moments. "I was... with a lady," he said at last.

"Who was she?"

Heavily he chided, "Sue, dear, I thought I'd brought you up better than that. A gentleman never tells."

"So what's stopping *you*?" someone in the crowd retorted waspishly.

"Bobby Lee," Elizabeth said, "we've already notified the deputy sheriff, you know. Innocent or guilty, sooner or later you're going to have to make a statement to someone. If you have an alibi, you might as well let us in on it now."

Bobby Lee glared at her, his eyes arctic with loathing as they raked over her slim body. Elizabeth met his gaze calmly. After several tense seconds he seemed to deflate.

Slumping against the couch, he declared bitterly, "God, I hate pushy females. You're a fine-looking woman, Elizabeth, but you're a troublemaker, and that's a fact. Why the hell you couldn't have stayed in New York where you belong..." He looked reproachfully at Grant. "This is all your fault, you know, reverend. If you hadn't brought her here so she could butt that pretty nose of hers in where it didn't belong, upsetting my little sister with her notions of saving the pottery, none of this would have happened."

Before Grant could respond, Suzanne cut in, mystified, "But why should there be trouble about putting the family business back on its feet? Isn't that what everybody wanted? I don't understand the problem. Elizabeth and I were just going to look over the books and things and make suggestions."

Elizabeth brooded. *Of course,* she thought. Why hadn't she seen it before? The answer was obvious, but the shock and horror of finding Clyde half-dead in the ash and rubble had erased the possibility from her mind. She glanced up at Grant; his grim expression mirrored her own. Reluctantly Elizabeth turned again to Suzanne, whose innocent confidence in her brother tore at her. She hated to disillusion her.

Elizabeth said gently, "Suzanne, I suspect the very fact that we were going to look at the books *was* the problem. I've always had a hunch the Bailey Pottery suffered from more than a depressed economy. At a guess I'd venture your brother has been raiding the company's assets for years."

Suzanne gaped. Whirling on Bobby Lee, she demanded, "Is that true? Have you been embezzling from the pottery?"

"It's not embezzling when it's your own company," he countered doggedly.

The angry exhalation that whispered through the crowd was drowned out by Holly. "But why did you have to hurt my daddy? He didn't know what you were doing. He didn't even work for you anymore!"

For the first time Bobby Lee looked chagrined. Rubbing his jaw as if it itched, he shifted uncomfortably and said, "Holly, I never meant to hurt your father. Believe it or not, I was trying to do him a favor." Noting the skepticism on the faces staring back at him, he grimaced. "It was supposed to be so easy. My foreman told me a few weeks back the emergency water supply wasn't working right, and the last time one of the kilns burned, several years ago, the fire marshal suggested the whole place ought to be rebuilt. All I wanted was for Clyde to wait until I was well out of the way and then set fire to the papers in my office. As soon as I collected on the insurance, I was going to pay him enough to get him back on his feet again."

Grant probed cynically, "And it never occurred to you that if something went wrong, Clyde might be blamed for the arson? Wouldn't people grow suspicious if he suddenly came into money?"

Bobby Lee shrugged. "Who'd know about the money? My plan was for him to move someplace else and make a new start. Only the damn fool refused. He said no matter how much I kept pestering him, he wasn't going to leave Ridleyville, just as he wasn't going to help me set the fire. When I began to demonstrate how simple it would be to get a blaze going, he got all excited and tried to grab the matches out of my hand. Instead he... slipped and knocked over the filing cabinet. One of the drawers slid out and hit his head. Hard. He didn't move. I panicked. I thought I'd— I headed out of town and spent the night at a hotel in Fort Smith. When I figured it was all over, I came home."

Bobby Lee's confession was greeted by stupefied silence. Jerking his head back and forth to meet the ashen, disbelieving stares that taxed him, he cried, "For God's sake, I thought he was dead! You folks don't think I would have left him there if I'd known he was *alive*, do you?"

Elizabeth asked, "But if what you say is true, I don't understand why you elected Clyde to be your accomplice in the first place. Even in the short time I've been in Ridleyville, I've learned the man refuses to move."

"I figured if he helped me, then finally he'd *have* to leave town, and I wouldn't have to look at him anymore. It was worth a try. Goddammit, it was driving me crazy this past year, ever since his wife took off, watching him go downhill, drinking and moping around town with that long face of his—"

"But why should Clyde's marital problems be any concern of yours?"

Bobby Lee's eyes were faded and dull. "Because I'm the one who gave Kayrene the money to run away."

Holly stared incredulously. "No—*no*," she squealed, half rising from her chair. "I don't believe you. She'd never desert daddy for you!"

"She didn't leave your father for me," Bobby Lee said impatiently. "If it's any comfort, as far as I know Kayrene didn't leave your father 'for' anyone. She just left. She was fed up with life in this town—which God knows I can understand—and she needed cash to finance a trip back East." His eyes bored into Holly. "Listen, honey, I may be guilty of a lot of things, but your mother had made up her mind to light out long before she ever came to me. It was just a matter of her finding someone to bankroll her."

Holly shook her head. "But why should you give her money? What could she offer you in return?"

Bobby Lee's eyebrows rose sharply. "You're nearly twenty-one, girl," he drawled. "Use your imagination."

Holly whimpered and jerked in disbelief. At her side, Elizabeth caught her breath with a hiss. The cool, cruel bastard—she'd like to kill him! The odd thought occurred to her that in Ridleyville's stratified society, seducing another man's wife was a crime almost more heinous than attempted murder. All around her she could sense people in the lobby reacting with similar violence to Bobby Lee's flippant words. She began to understand how mobs erupted.

Before anyone could speak, Suzanne leaped to her feet. The anger and disillusion and resolve in her face told Elizabeth she would never be a girl again. Looming over her brother, she lashed out, "Robert Lee Bailey, how dare you? You're my own flesh and blood, damn you, but who do you think you are to speak to Holly that way, gloating like that? How dare you betray your friends and your hometown—not to mention me, your only kin?"

Bobby Lee eyed his sister strangely. A flush of sizzling color seeped under his tanned cheeks like lava; his mustache twitched; his shoulders hunched and lifted ominously. All at once he erupted. "Betrayal—what betrayal? I always took good care of you, Sue. You always had enough money. After daddy died I could have packed you off to boarding school, but instead I kept you underfoot, me working in that lousy factory so I could buy you party dresses. Did it ever occur to you that I wanted out, that I had plans that didn't include a baby sister or sweating away the rest of my life in clay and muck? I wanted to go west, to California, but, no I was saddled with the responsibility of the pottery; with you.

"From the time I could walk I had it drummed into me

that I was supposed to keep the pottery going, no matter what. I had to 'save Ridleyville'! Bull! Ridleyville isn't worth saving, and even if it was, why should it be up to me? This isn't home! It's just a benighted backwater. Nobody in his right mind stays here when he can be off somewhere else enjoying *real* life. If these so-called friends had any gumption or ambition..."

If mother and Amelia had any ambition... The all-too-familiar words echoed damningly in Elizabeth's mind. How many times had she thought them? Worse, armored with her unflinching conceit, how many times had she actually said them to the two women who shared her blood? Bobby Lee's tirade battered on her eardrums. Elizabeth lifted stricken eyes to Grant's. His stony gaze locked with hers. "Do we have to listen to this?" she mouthed mutely.

He glanced at the people standing transfixed around him; then he nodded toward the exit. Beyond the glass door Elizabeth could see the sheriff's patrol car pulling to a halt at the curb behind her green Porsche. The deputy sprinted up the walk.

"It's about time," Elizabeth muttered with relief. She grabbed her purse and leaped to her feet.

At the exit the deputy began politely, "Good afternoon, Mrs...." His voice faded in confusion as Elizabeth charged past him. Automatically he held the door open for her.

"Thank you," Elizabeth choked, not looking at him. "Goodbye."

In the lobby Grant hollered, "Liza, wait!"

She fled to her car and sped away.

CHAPTER FIFTEEN

IN HER DISTRESS as she raced back to the parsonage, Elizabeth lost her way and turned down the wrong street. She found herself in front of Good Samaritan instead of at the minister's house behind it. Staring around, she tried to remember the route to take to her destination. Her mind was blank. She knew she knew the facade of the yellow-brick church, the moldering mansion with its tall columns. Yet somehow her surroundings seemed as unfamiliar as they had the afternoon she drove across the arched iron bridge into town.

She remembered the way she had crept along the main street, gazing around her in distaste. A "benighted backwater," Bobby Lee had called his home, and that first day she might have agreed with him—just as she might have said the same thing about her birthplace in Minnesota. But Bailey was wrong about Ridleyville. Despite its economic difficulties, the community was vital, the inhabitants kind and courageous and resourceful. Was she equally wrong about her own hometown?

Her palms sweated. Rather than try to retrace her course, it might be simpler to leave her car where it was and walk across the field to the parsonage. Most of her luggage was already in the trunk of the Porsche; all she needed to fetch from Grant's house was her wheeled suitcase and the small box in which her wooden goldfinch had been carefully packed. Clenching the steering wheel, she jerked the sports car to the curb, scraping the shiny hubcaps.

As she strode up the walk to the heavy double doors of the church, Elizabeth was aware of the passing season. Indian summer was a memory; autumn evanesced, leaving winter. The day she had arrived in Ridleyville, the weather had been too warm for her woolen dress. Now as a sharp breeze cut through her sweater and fluttered her skirt, it was too cold. The twin dogwood trees flanking the walk were bare, their last curled leaves long since raked and burned. The lawn was a mottled brown. Only the cross-emblazoned sign was unchanged: Church of the Good Samaritan, she read again. The Reverend Dr. Grantland J. O'Connor, pastor.

That first day, she had been astonished and affronted by that sign, confirmation of the news that Grant, her dynamic lover, had indeed become a clergyman. Then it had seemed like an outrageous and rather tasteless joke.

Today, scanning the words once more, she realized how remarkably appropriate they were. Despite not being a churchgoer, Elizabeth was familiar with the parable of the Good Samaritan, the traveler who had gone out of his way to give aid and comfort to an injured stranger. In Grant's new life he was bringing similar aid and comfort to the people of Ridleyville. She had been naive and incredibly selfish to hope he'd give it up for her.

Elizabeth was beginning to think she'd been as imperceptive and self-centered about the other relationships in her life.

Intending to short-cut through Grant's study to reach the path to the parsonage, Elizabeth stepped inside the church. The air was as musty as ever. Red and amber light from the narrow, stained-glass windows dimly illuminated the vestibule, outlining the doors to the sanctuary and the console table that held the guest book. Realizing she'd never signed the church's register, on an impulse Elizabeth crossed the anteroom and flipped the book open. She wanted to leave behind some evidence that for a few brief days at least, she had shared in the life of this parish, this community.

She glanced at the names already inscribed on the creamy parchment:

Mrs. John H. Hunnicutt.
Mr. and Mrs. Gerald Baxter and daughters.

As usual, Elizabeth found the traditional, male-oriented forms of title vaguely annoying; they made her wonder if the women listed warranted names of their own. During the time she and Grant had lived together, she had refused to open any mail, usually of the junk variety, that came addressed to Mrs. Grantland O'Connor. In firm, defiant strokes, rendered especially impressive by the black ink and broad-nibbed fountain pen she habitually used—another power ploy she'd learned from Grant years before—she wrote at the bottom of the list, "Elizabeth Swenson."

Her hand faltered. Although she had always used her maiden name for business, now somehow the name looked bald and incomplete, even...lonely. Besides, the identification no longer seemed appropriate. She was not a single woman. If this trip had served any purpose, it was to convince her that regardless of whether she and Grant lived together, they were very much married and always would be. That simple, immutable fact was going to color their actions for the rest of their lives.

After a tiny hesitation Elizabeth slashed a hyphen behind her surname. "Elizabeth Swenson-O'Connor." Yes, that was it, she decided with satisfaction; she liked the look and the sound of it. When she took over her directorship at Avotel, that's how she'd have herself listed on corporate documents.

Blowing the thick ink dry, Elizabeth closed the guest book carefully and returned her fountain pen to her handbag. Then she burst into tears.

Her first reaction was amazement, quickly superseded by indignation, bitter resentment of her weakness. She hadn't cried, really cried, since that time in Belgium. She hated to cry. She hated the ugly, blubbery sounds she made, and she hated the way salty drops stung her eyes and melted her mascara. Most of all she hated how vulnerable she felt when all her fabled control deserted her and left her prey to her emotions.

If she let go, she could tell, the outburst was going to be long and noisy; she had been building up to it for a long time. The sobs that tried to force their way through her throat were saturated with pain, years of pain. She shook with the effort to suppress them.

Elizabeth sniffed loudly, the sound only partly muffled by the long, velvet drapes lining the corridor. Angrily she jerked open her handbag again and fished inside for something to blow her nose with. Despite the blessed release of crying, she refused to stand there like an urchin child. To her disgust, all she found in her purse was an empty tissue packet. Knowing that even if she ran, she couldn't possibly reach the parsonage before she'd be forced to use her sleeve, Elizabeth glanced around desperately for a rest room. All at once she spotted the unobtrusive door marked Crying Room. She bolted for it.

The soundproof compartment was compact but comfortable. When she closed the door, automatically locking it, and flipped on the light switch, a circulating fan hummed, preventing the air from becoming stuffy. A single, padded pew faced a glass wall level with the last row of seats in the sanctuary. Elizabeth noticed a built-in nursery table with shelves and an odd-looking circular well at one end; after a moment's puzzlement she identified it as an electric baby-bottle warmer. Sternly she refused to let herself think of the babies she and Grant would never have; it was the one subject guaranteed to make her lose control. Continuing her frantic search for tissues, to her immense relief she finally located a carton, in a cupboard beside a plastic bag of disposable diapers.

Delicately Elizabeth blotted her nose dry. Sinking weakly onto the pew, she fell apart.

She didn't know how long or how hard she cried, only that when the sobs at last subsided, her eyes burned and her head ached. She felt neither rested nor relieved. Catharsis, if that was indeed what she had just achieved, didn't seem all it was cracked up to be.

A dozen soggy tissues lay scattered on the pew and at her feet. Grimacing with distaste, she began to pick them up. As she dumped the sodden wads into the wastebasket, she was jerked from her torpor by the sound of someone trying the lock.

"Liza, let me in!" Grant's resonant tones, muted and dulled by the solid door, were barely audible.

Wondering how he'd found her, Elizabeth reached for the knob. She hesitated. What was the point? What could they possibly say to each other now that would not serve to reinforce the insurmountable differences between them? Facing him one last time would only make her departure that much more agonizing. "Go away, Grant!" she shouted against the crack in the doorjamb. "I love you, but it's never going to work. We live in two different worlds now!"

He tried the handle again. "For God's sake, Liza, don't be childish! I can unlock that door if I have to. Mrs. Butley has a spare key somewhere in her office. It's just a matter of locating it."

"Please go away!" Elizabeth repeated. "I don't want to see you anymore." This time he didn't answer. Her ear flattened against the wood, she waited apprehensively. She was startled by a sharp sound just behind her, the rattle of knuckles on glass. Whirling, she found Grant in the sanctuary, his face pressed against the crying-room window, staring in.

Mashed against the glass, his rugged features were distorted. His jutting chin, the tip of his nose and the ridge of his brow were flattened into irregular ovals, paler than the rest of his flushed skin, like patches of clown makeup, an effect reinforced by his wildly disarranged hair. Around his mouth a nebula of steam formed comically on the window, clouding and clearing with each puffy, gasping breath. Only his wide gray eyes spoiled the merry effect: they were opalescent with torment.

He spoke. The public-address system wasn't turned on, so that through the soundproof window Elizabeth couldn't hear him. When she shook her head in confusion, he repeated his words more forcefully. She couldn't read his lips.

One of his large hands crept upward, reaching. Choking, Elizabeth watched its starfish progress. Petitioning fingers pressed hard against the glass, seemed to will themselves to press through the glass to get to her. Elizabeth sighed. She couldn't resist that appeal. Slowly she lifted her own hand and laid it over his, stretching her shorter digits with difficulty to align the tips; when he saw what she was doing, he forced his hand flat until the two hands fit, palm to palm. Elizabeth smiled ironically. To her gullible vision it looked as if they touched, but her skin could feel the transparent fraction of an inch of hardened silica that still separated them, cold and invisible and unrelenting. Like a god. Like her own fears.

Grant's other hand moved; Elizabeth tried futilely to touch it. His mouth bloomed on the pane, warm and welcoming; she tasted only chilly flavorlessness. When she leaned her torso against the window, her nipples straining their invitation through the fabric of her blouse and sweater, the blunt fingertips spanning the turgid peaks touched only glass.

He pulled away in frustration. Pointing in the direction of the crying-room door, he mouthed the words "let me in," shaping each sound deliberately so that she couldn't fail to read the message on his lips. Elizabeth hesitated. As long as he stayed outside, as long as he could not truly touch her, she was safe. The glass box was her protection.

And her prison.

She unfastened the lock.

Instantly the door flew open, banging against the wall so hard that the little room reverberated with the sound of it, and Grant was with her, holding her, caressing her; no longer a sterile shadow, but vibrant and warm and real. He trembled violently. As they kissed, she could taste the tang of salt on his lips, smell the pungent muskiness of his damp flesh. When her arms wrapped around him and her hands splayed across his back, she could feel the muscles beneath her fingertips twitch with exertion. Suddenly she realized his shirt was plastered to him, drenched with sweat.

Perplexed, Elizabeth lifted her head. "What happened? You feel as if you've been running."

Grant's grip did not slacken. "I have," he said hoarsely. "I ran after you."

"All the way from the clinic?" Elizabeth gasped in wonder. "That must be at least a mile!"

"More," Grant huffed, "and I'm too old for that sort of thing! But you took the car, remember? If I'd been thinking straight, I would have borrowed someone else's, but I saw you run out the door, and oh, God, I was so afraid I wouldn't reach you before you picked up your luggage and..." He paused to regard her whimsically. "It was only by accident that I spotted your Porsche out front, when I cut across the Bailey's garden. Why did you come here to the church? I expected you to head for the parsonage."

Mumbling with embarrassment, Elizabeth admitted, "I got lost."

Grant gazed tenderly at her. He stroked her fair hair, feathering the curls through his fingers. His eyes flicked toward the glass window that overlooked the church sanctuary. His smile was gentle. "Maybe not as lost as you think, darling," he murmured enigmatically.

He sobered. "Why did you run away so suddenly? I thought you'd decided to delay your departure for a while, but at the hospital you just bolted. What happened? Liza, when I got here, I heard you crying."

Elizabeth's eyes widened. She glanced at the door standing ajar: two inches of solid pecan wood. "If you could hear me in the corridor, I must have really been bawling."

"It broke my heart to listen to you. I know how painful

it is for you to let yourself go. Please tell me what made you fall to pieces that way. Was it because you thought there was no hope for the two of us?"

Elizabeth nodded. Leaning her head against his chest so that she could hear the pounding of his heart, she conceded, "I suppose that was mostly it. I still don't see how you and I can reconcile our differences and build a life together. But there was something else, too. It was one of those moments of acute self-realization when the skies open up and the sun shines and all at once you see yourself as you truly are—"

"Sounds cataclysmic," Grant interjected.

"It was, almost as overwhelming as that moment years ago when you told me you were leaving...." Her arms tightened around him. "It happened while I was listening to Bobby Lee rant. He told his sister he had no responsibility to the people in Ridleyville because it's just a hick town not worth caring about. When I heard that, I suddenly realized he was saying almost exactly the same thing I've said myself about my hometown. In my own way I've been just as arrogant and self-indulgent as he—"

"Liza, surely you must realize there's no comparison between you and Robert Bailey! The man's an egocentric criminal."

"Most of our differences are only a matter of degree," Elizabeth insisted. "While I can't imagine deliberately harming other people, I *have* been so determined to be independent that I haven't been very concerned about others whose goals are different from mine. My own family, for example. When I think of the way Holly and Suzanne have struggled to help their relatives and their community, I feel guilty. I never felt any responsibility for my town. In fact, I was always contemptuous of the people who stayed there. I couldn't wait to get away from Minnesota—and worse, mom and Amelia. All those years in Europe, I never once took time off to visit them...I never called. I sent money instead of letters." She sighed dismally. "It's no wonder they hate me."

"I don't think they hate you, Liza," Grant reassured quickly. He was too perceptive to downplay those occasions when Elizabeth had, in fact, been narrow-minded where her family was concerned, but he could see there had been intolerance on both sides. "After all, you still love your mother and sister, even though they've never tried to understand why you wouldn't be content as a traditional housewife. Neither of them has made an effort to maintain what could be called a regular correspondence with you. However this estrangement started, all parties share the blame."

"That's very comforting, but I still feel guilty."

Grant nodded. "I can understand that. The question is, having recognized the situation, what do you propose to do about it? It's not too late for a reconciliation. You can let your guilt be a boulder blocking your way, or you can push it to one side and use it as a milestone, pointing your life in a new direction."

Reluctantly Elizabeth smiled. "Now I know you're a clergyman! That sounds suspiciously like an excerpt from one of your sermons."

His mouth quirked wryly, but his eyes were somber. "Sorry, I didn't intend to preach. I was trying to remind you you should be thankful your sin is one that can be rectified. Some of us aren't so fortunate."

"What do you mean?"

With great care he unwound her arms from his waist and set her away from him. Sliding his fists into the pockets of his jeans, he stared blindly through the glass wall. The planes of his face suddenly looked sallow and gaunt with distress. "Five years ago I killed a man."

Elizabeth gasped. His voice was pitched low, but the terse, unbelievable statement rang clangingly in her ears. She felt dizzy. Shaking her head, she sank onto the pew once more. "I don't believe you."

He gazed with compassion on her bleached, shocked face. He wondered if he was cruelly selfish to unburden his soul by telling her the ugly secret he had never confessed to anyone, except in prayer. He wondered if he was a fool. When his story was finished, would she still love him? He sat beside her on the padded bench and took her cold hand in his. He half expected her to try to yank away, but she didn't. For a long moment he looked into her eyes. She waited.

Toying with her fingers, Grant began. "Do you remember Pierson Chemicals?"

Elizabeth blinked; twin lines pinched the bridge of her nose as she delved into the back of her mind. "'Pierson Chemicals,'" she echoed hollowly, then, as if reciting by rote: "Small research firm in Florida, did some innovative work in the field of nonpetroleum-based plastics, acquired potentially valuable patents on a couple of processes using sugarcane. Went public in the late seventies but still couldn't raise the capital necessary to put those patents to use. Ripe for a takeover."

Marveling at her retentive powers, Grant said, "I took it over."

"You did? When? I never heard."

"You were commuting back and forth to Belgium on a regular basis. What little time we had together, we didn't waste talking business. Besides," he said, "by the time the deal was finalized, I was back in Savannah at my parents' home, searching for peace among the palmettos."

Elizabeth persisted. "I still don't understand. What does a takeover have to do with killing someone? You used to buy out small companies all the time. It was your job."

"Yeah, I was a real wheeler-dealer, wasn't I?" Grant muttered scornfully. "A shark, a corporate hit man. And to think I used to *relish* that reputation...." He let his breath out in a hiss. "When I learned about this shaky little company in Tallahassee that could make high-grade plastic out of a renewable crop like sugarcane, I knew I had to have it. I didn't give a damn about Pierson Chemicals itself. It was the patents I wanted. A Brazilian conglomerate was interested in another company of mine, and with those patents as leverage in the negotiations.... So I filed notice with the Securities and Exchange Commission that I intended to acquire a majority of Pierson Chemicals' stock, and I plunged in, waving my checkbook."

"You got the stock?" It was not really a question. Grant had always got everything he wanted.

"Oh, yes. It was ridiculously easy. Jack Pierson—the company's founder, chairman of the board, chief chemist and possibly night watchman, as well—was a brilliant research chemist, but he had no head for business at all. His forte was developing formulas, not marketing them. Profits were practically nil, and he hadn't paid his stockholders a dividend in years. They jumped at the chance to sell out."

As Elizabeth listened, Grant's fingers tightened crushingly around hers. She almost yelped. His pallor told her he was approaching the climax of his story. In deadly tones he said, "Shortly before you were to return from Belgium that last time, Jack Pierson showed up at the co-op. We'd never met face to face before. He turned out to be a man in his late fifties, kind of mousy, the stereotypical absent-minded professor. He was totally exhausted. He'd driven all the way from Florida, he told me, because he was afraid to fly.

"We sat down, I offered him a drink and he came to the point. He asked if it was true that after I acquired Pierson Chemicals I planned to strip it of its assets, the patents, and dissolve what was left. I said yes. It was, as I pointed out, 'just good business.' That's when he began to beg."

"Oh, Grant," Elizabeth whispered dolefully. He clung to her as if to a lifeline.

"I asked Pierson why he was so upset. Rather impatiently I assured him I'd see the usual golden parachute was provided for him. The man was so naive about business that he'd never even heard the term. I had to explain it was corporate slang for the payoff that cushions a top official's fall from power. That only seemed to make him more agitated. He told me Pierson Chemicals meant more to him than money. He'd built the company from scratch. It had become everything to him; his wife, his family, his friends. It was, he said as I pushed him out the door, the one thing in the world he had to live for."

Grant paused and gazed achingly at Elizabeth. "I didn't know he meant that literally."

She was almost afraid to ask. "What happened?"

Grant released Elizabeth's fingers and covered his face with his hands. She wondered if he was praying. His voice was muffled in his palms as he said laconically, "He headed back to Tallahassee that night. On the expressway outside Philadelphia, his car jumped the center divider and drove straight into the path of an oncoming truck."

"Oh, my God."

Grant lifted his head to look at her. "I didn't even hear about it for a couple of days. Apparently his trip had been a spur-of-the-moment decision, and nobody knew he'd come to see me. Even in New York, he'd shown up at the flat rather than my office. The Pennsylvania Highway Patrol said he must have fallen asleep at the wheel; but I knew better. I knew my greed for power and my ruthless determination to make a few more bucks that I wouldn't even have time to spend had driven an innocent man to suicide."

For several minutes the only sound in the little room was the hum of the circulating fan. Then Elizabeth asked, "Why didn't you tell me this five years ago?"

"I didn't dare. I kept thinking about what I had become, how far I'd drifted from the little boy who used to go with his mother every Sunday to that white-steepled colonial church on Oglethorpe Avenue. I felt guilty and disgusted with myself, but what really frightened me was the danger that I might turn you into the same kind of ruthless monster. For some unfathomable reason you wanted to be like me. You were so sweet and unspoiled when we met, despite your ambition, but you admired me because I was a cutthroat businessman. You were in love with my image as a corporate pirate. How could I make you understand I didn't want to be that kind of man anymore? If you had tried to talk me out of changing my life, where would I have found the strength to refuse you?"

Elizabeth looked bemused. "I never realized before that I was such a temptress."

"You could give Delilah a few lessons." Grant sighed.

She laid her hand on his thigh, savoring the feel of the heavy muscles. "My Samson," she teased fondly. Her expression sobered. "So after you left New York, you went home looking for your childhood faith?"

"I went home looking for peace," Grant corrected. "After the first storm of remorse subsided, I told myself I'd find serenity if I settled Pierson's affairs. Without him the company was worthless, but I made a generous offer for the shares his few loyal stockholders still owned, and I pensioned off the employees. Instead of dealing with the Brazilians, I arranged for the royalties from Piersons' patents to fund a research fellowship at the University of Florida."

"Did all that help you feel any better?" Elizabeth queried.

Grant grimaced. "To my surprise—and, frankly, indignation—I learned peace was something that can't be bought. I was tempted to say to hell with my reformation and go back to my old life. But I kept thinking of you. I felt you were better off without me, and I honestly never expected the two of us to meet again. If we did, I asked myself, how could I face you as I was? I decided to return to school and look for some answers. The search was not easy, but eventually I found them in faith."

Elizabeth nodded and said, "You know, sweetheart, despite the fact my beliefs are not the same as yours, I'm very happy you've found peace in your religion. I . . . I rejoice for you."

Grant's eyes grew luminous, taking on a silvery sheen. "Liza, you'll never know how much it means to me to hear you say that. It makes my own decision that much easier."

"What decision?"

"I've made up my mind that when a permanent pastor is installed here at Good Samaritan—and from the looks of it, that should be fairly soon—I'm going to move back to New York with you."

She caught her breath, afraid to believe what he was saying. "T-truly?" she stammered, her hand at her mouth.

"Truly, darling," he whispered. He brushed aside her fingers to trace the ripe curve of her lips. Elizabeth nipped softly, catching his finger between the moist folds of skin. Grant inhaled raggedly, and his eyes grew murky. With difficulty he pulled away and returned to what he was saying.

"Liza, this morning when you were packing, you made reference to my 'self-imposed exile,' and thinking about it, I know now you're right. I never really overcame the fear that gripped me five years ago, the fear that if I returned to my old milieu I'd revert to my former ways. All my so-called scholarly research has been an excuse to hide out in colleges and libraries, which is much easier than testing myself against the temptations of the business world."

Elizabeth's fingertips trailed up his arm. "But now you're ready to take the test?"

"With you at my side," he said thickly, "I know I can't fail. Besides, after seeing the way mere girls like Holly and Suzanne are willing to risk everything for the greater good of all, I know I have to take some risks, too. I have a lot of business skills that could be employed in a positive way. For a start, I think I'll see if I can arrange venture capital for the pottery. I doubt it's occurred to Suzanne yet, but now that her brother's confessed to arson, the insurance will be worthless. Once I've done that, I can continue writing if I want, but there must be lots of small businesses and charitable organizations that could use my skills and experience."

"I'll say," Elizabeth murmured, winding her fingers around his neck. She drew his face toward hers. "Just think," she whispered, "with Grantland O'Connor on the side of the angels, the corporate world will never be the—"

Someone pushed open the front door of the church.

The heavy wooden slab creaked as it swung sideways on its hinges; the noise carried clearly into the crying room. Startled, Elizabeth and Grant jerked apart. In the silence the sound was vaguely theatrical, like something from a horror movie. The squeak was followed by a muffled thud as the door's automatic closer pushed it back against the stop. Light, tentative footsteps ventured into the vestibule. A woman's voice called uncertainly, "Is anyone here?"

Grant stood up. "I'd better go see who it is."

"I'll come with you," Elizabeth said. She flashed a conspiratorial smile as she smoothed back a lock of auburn hair her fingers had just mussed. "Whoever she is, it's a good thing she didn't show up five minutes later. Your parishioners have been scandalized enough already."

Grant swooped down and planted a hard kiss on Elizabeth's lips. "*Definitely* a temptress." Together they walked out of the crying room.

The tall, rawboned woman's hazel eyes widened with surprise as the two emerged into the lobby. She seemed vaguely familiar, but studying her, Elizabeth couldn't imagine why. She was certain they'd never met. The woman appeared to be in her midforties. Her attractively styled dark-blond hair was streaked with gray, and the shirtwaist dress and jacket she wore looked travel-rumpled. When she stepped toward Grant, even in the dim light Elizabeth could see that her features were haggard with distress and, astonishingly, fear.

Chewing away the last of her lipstick, the woman asked tremulously, "Are you Dr. O'Connor?" The voice, too, seemed to be one Elizabeth had heard before. "Dr. G. J. O'Connor?" the woman amplified, and all at once Elizabeth realized she was the mysterious person who had telephoned the day news of the pottery fire had hit the national wire services.

Grant stepped forward, holding out his hand in welcome. "You're Mrs. Walker, aren't you? I can't tell you how very thankful I am that you decided to come, after all."

Elizabeth stared. Walker? Clyde's wife? Kayrene? All at once she knew why the woman seemed so familiar. Except for the difference of twenty-some years, her daughter looked just like her.

Grant's fingers closed warmly around Kayrene's. She said choppily, "As soon as you hung up this morning, I—I knew I had to come. I couldn't just sit there not knowing. But finding a flight from Baltimore to Little Rock...I had to borrow the money from my father...almost impossible to rent a car without a credit card...all the time wondering if I'd be too late.... Oh, please, Dr. O'Connor, tell me he's not—not—"

Grant said, "Clyde is conscious now, and he's going to recover completely."

"Oh, thank God!" She dropped her face into her hands and sobbed. Her thin shoulders shook as she wailed piteously, "I was so afraid I'd never get a chance to beg him to forgive...so sorry. How could I...such a selfish, stupid...my husband, my babies...so afraid...."

Elizabeth listened with compassion to the tragic moans that repeated gaspingly. From the rumors she had heard since arriving in Ridleyville, she had been prepared to hate Kayrene Walker, to despise her the way she had the golden-haired giant with the booming laugh who had deserted the young Elizabeth, Amelia and their mother. But looking at Kayrene, Elizabeth realized the woman was not some kind of unfeeling, narcissistic monster, only a very fallible human being, hurt and confused and pathetic. Maybe the same was true of her father, wherever he was.

When Kayrene's choking cries subsided to mournful whimpers, Grant asked softly, "Mrs. Walker, have you been to the hospital yet?"

She raised red-rimmed eyes. "I couldn't," she admitted hoarsely. "I drove within two blocks of the clinic, but all at once I knew I didn't have the courage to walk in by myself. That's why I came here, instead, praying I'd find you. You were so kind when we talked.... I've wronged Clyde and the children more than I'll ever be able to make up, and I need their forgiveness. I need *them*. But what if they don't need me anymore?"

"They need you," Grant said gravely. "I won't pretend it's going to be easy, but believe me, they need you. And if it will make it easier for you to face them, I'll be happy to go with you back to the hospital." He glanced at Elizabeth. "Do you mind, darling?"

"No, of course not," she said automatically.

Kayrene looked at Elizabeth. "Oh, I beg your pardon, I didn't mean to be rude! You must be Mrs. O'Connor, aren't you?" When Elizabeth smiled, Kayrene continued shyly, "I—I hope you won't mind me borrowing your man for a while?"

Elizabeth shrugged. "A minister's wife has to get used to other people making claims on her husband's time." Wanly Kayrene repeated her gratitude and headed toward the exit. Elizabeth turned to Grant. Delving into her handbag for her car keys, she told him, "You can use the Porsche, if you like."

"Thank you." He pocketed the key ring. "Thank you for everything." As the double doors closed behind Kayrene, Grant dipped his head to brush his lips over Elizabeth's. Suddenly he pulled her tight against him. "Oh, Lord, I love you!" he groaned.

Elizabeth whispered, "And I love you. I've always loved you."

They held each other in silence. Then reluctantly he released her. "Liza," he murmured, "I do have to go. I don't know when I'll be back. I'm afraid the reunion is going to be more than a little traumatic for all the Walkers, and I'll have to stay as long as I can be of service to them."

"Of course you will. I understand."

Grant looked at her for a long moment. "You really do understand, don't you, darling?" he breathed. "Thank God—thank God!" Resolutely he again turned toward the front door of the church. As he strode across the vestibule, he called over his shoulder, "I'll come home to the parsonage just as quickly as possible."

"I'll be waiting for you," Elizabeth promised.

**March's other absorbing
HARLEQUIN *SuperRomance* novel**

HOME AT LAST by Barbara Kaye

Leah Stone was a single mother... but still a wife. In the six years since her husband had vanished, she had accepted her strange role, though she had missed Jim every day of those six years.

When Leah met her husband again he was Jacob Surratt, a prominent Phoenix physician. He didn't know her at all.

Yet this fine man fell deeply in love with her, so that Leah was tempted to play a dangerous game. She urged Jacob to remember, while someone else worked to lock the past away for ever....

A contemporary love story for the woman of today

These two absorbing titles
will be published in April
by

HARLEQUIN
SuperRomance

SPANGLES by Irma Walker

When she was in the cage with her cats, lion trainer Tanya Rhodin had the upper hand. So why, when it came to Wade Broderick, did she feel so out of control?

The millionaire businessman had run away to the circus to fulfil a boyhood fantasy, but when the colour and pageantry of the travelling show faded for him, he would leave.

The circus was Tanya's whole world. She knew it would be folly to become involved with an outsider. But Wade made her aware of a hundred new feelings . . . and one of them was love.

SHELTERING BRIDGES by Bobby Hutchinson

An attractive coal-mining magnate, a beautiful valley homestead and the perfect teaching job—Alana Campbell's star was definitely on the rise!

Opening up young Bruce's silent world was the most rewarding experience of her life—and living with Bruce's father was the most exciting! But communicating with the gorgeous Rand Evans was almost as great a challenge as with his deaf son. The man was impossibly secretive, and Alana suspected his activities weren't strictly legal—or moral!

But she was bound to this strange yet familiar man. They were soulmates; she felt it in his touch and saw it in his eyes. . . .

These books are
already available
from

HARLEQUIN
SuperRomance

TOUCH THE SKY Debbi Bedford
SONG OF THE SEABIRD Christina Crockett
PERFUME AND LACE Christine Hella Cott
BELOVED STRANGER Meg Hudson
THE RISING ROAD Meg Hudson
A DREAM TO SHARE Deborah Joyce
SILVER HORIZONS Deborah Joyce
COME SPRING Barbara Kaye
WHEN ANGELS DANCE
   Vicki Lewis Thompson
MOONLIGHT ON SNOW Virginia Nielsen
THE WILD ROSE Ruth Alana Smith
THROUGH NIGHT AND DAY Irma Walker

If you experience difficulty in obtaining any of these titles, write to:

Harlequin SuperRomance, P.O. Box 236, Croydon, Surrey CR9 3RU

Readers in South Africa write to:

Harlequin S.A. Pty., Postbag X3010, Randburg 2125, S. Africa